J. M. Lawler was born in Murwillumbah, Australia. She spent much of her youth drawing and writing, and went on to study languages and political science at the Australian National University in Canberra. She moved to Sydney, rock-climbed in any spare moment she had, and ended up as a Police Officer and then Intelligence Analyst. J. M. Lawler lives in Adelaide with her two children. *The River and the Ravages* is her first book.

Contact J. M. Lawler:
On Twitter and Instagram @jm_lawler
www.jmlawler.com

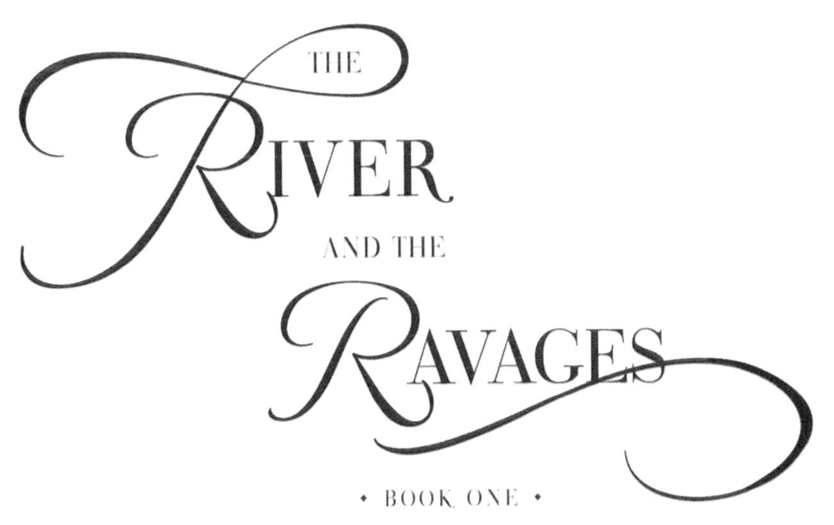

THE RIVER AND THE RAVAGES

• BOOK ONE •

J. M. LAWLER

LITTLE CROW

First published in Australia in 2017 by
Little Crow Publishing
Adelaide, Australia

www.littlecrowpublishing.com

This paperback edition 2017
1

ISBN: 978-0-6480714-0-2

Set in Adobe Caslon Pro

Printed and bound in Australia by
Lightning Source

For my sisters.
And for sisters everywhere.

Two roads diverged in a wood, and I -
I took the one less travelled by,
And that has made all the difference.

Robert Frost, 'The Road Not Taken'

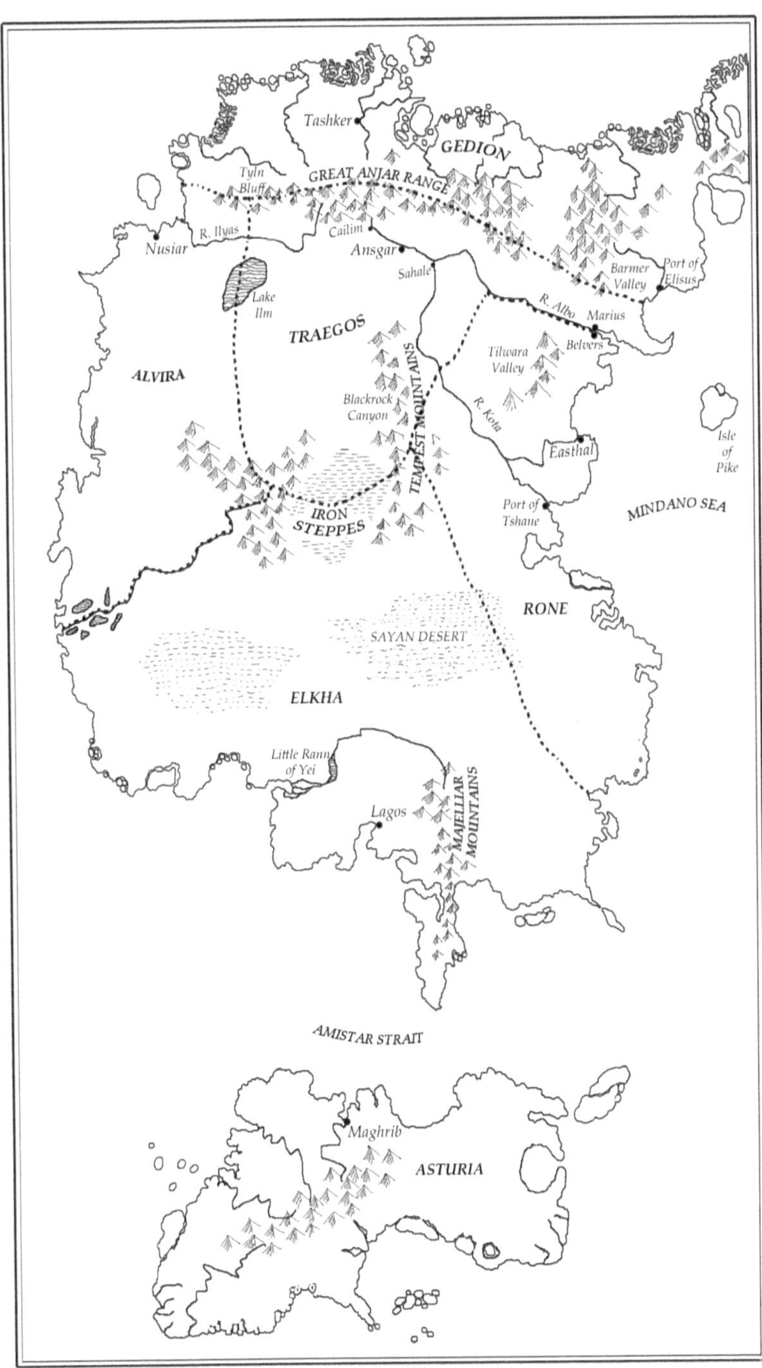

Tashker
GEDION
GREAT ANJAR RANGE
Tyln Bluff
Cailim
Nusiar
R. Ilyas
Ansgar
Sahale
Barmer Valley
Port of Elisus
R. Albo
Marius
Lake Ilm
TRAEGOS
Belvers
Tilwara Valley
ALVIRA
R. Koha
Blackrock Canyon
TEMPEST MOUNTAINS
Easthal
Isle of Pike
Port of Tshane
MINDANO SEA
IRON STEPPES
RONE
SAYAN DESERT
ELKHA
Little Rann of Yei
Lagos
MAIELLIAR MOUNTAINS
AMISTAR STRAIT
Maghrib
ASTURIA

1

The Quiet Goodbye
Traegos

Aaliya couldn't remember when her fascination with flying creatures began, but she suspected it was when she watched her mother catch large moths in jars and then release them near light. They'd scatter around all crazy with their freedom to go anywhere yet inexplicably drawn to the flame. The one her eyes were fixed on as she stood beside her mother's prostrate body darted erratically between the lit candles cluttering the enormous candelabra. It's wings of soft gold flying so close to it's own annihilation, yet seemingly finding comfort there. She felt an uncontrollable urge to reach out and grab it. Instead her eyes followed the moth until the candlelight became a blurry backdrop. Aaliya had never been great at curbing spontaneity, but she at least liked to believe she had always tried to behave in a way acceptable for her position. But without her mother, something inside her had shifted. And she too felt the need to dance close to the flame, even if her own papery wings became singed and charred.

    She lowered her face to her mother's, their noses gently

touching. It wasn't cold like she had expected. In fact, for a brief moment Aaliya thought there had been a glorious mistake and that her mother was still alive. And then she kissed her mother on the lips. There was no response. Only the sound of her lips gently pressing on still flesh. The sweet sound of connection, Aaliya was sure she'd never forget it. Her father had asked her not to do anything outlandish during the funeral rite. To kiss a woman on the lips while she is lying still and lifeless is considered unnatural. She did it proudly, and would cherish it forever.

Helena lay there in a simple white dress, overlaid with exquisite lace. The marble slab was draped in red velvet and gold tassels, and seemed to reflect a warm glow onto her skin. She still looked beautiful to Aaliya, even though her body had been racked by disease for many months. The doctor had on countless occasions performed bloodletting to encourage the disease to seep out. Day by day her body became weaker, and each day Aaliya was sure she had shed enough tears to overflow whole rivers. And now here she stood, her eyes dry and wretched and raw, unable to shed a drop. Was it shock that it was finally over? Maybe relief? She ran a finger over her mother's forehead, down the bridge of her nose and across her cheekbones. The bones jutting through on her face looked as though they could crumble under human touch.

The nave of the aedes loomed large and majestic. Massive stone columns rose up to the ribbed dome where geometric patterns fanned out from the centre like awakened flowers. The symbol of Traegos was omnipresent. This kingdom, indeed this city Ansgar, were all she had ever known. For years she had looked longingly at the mountain peaks in the distance to the north and south of the capital. Too many waking hours were spent fantasizing about travelling to remote parts of the realm. Her father had tried furiously over the years to force her to see that contributing (even simply through compliance) to his successful business empire was a sure path to a meaningful life and lasting happiness. She wanted to please him, she really did. She just didn't want to go about it his way.

The stained glass high on the western wall was aglow with colour, the sun hitting it and sending what seemed like a rainbow into the vast room. Light was all around, but right now Aaliya felt lost in some sort of abyss of darkness. She ran her hand down the front of her dress. It was one of the new ones from her father. It was black with a simple, loose drape and for a brief moment she started picking at an imaginary blemish in the fabric. She longed to be in a small stone bunker. Anything besides this grand pretence, this grating ostentation.

Aaliya raised her head and looked over her shoulder, her eyes resting on her father and sister standing nearby past the edge of the steps. The figures appeared as little more than dark shapes. She tried to focus on them for a moment, tried to understand even briefly what they were feeling, but she couldn't decipher their features. Their faces bare as lamps. All she noticed was Maddalena's hair, running thick and dark over her shoulders like spilt molasses.

There must have been at least one hundred people in the room, most of whom Aaliya didn't know. She wanted them all to leave but instead their steadfast gazes followed her every move.

Aaliya made her way down the steps and took her place beside Maddalena.

"Nice display, Aaliya," Maddalena said, "I almost shed

a tear."

"A tear might do you the world of good right now," Aaliya responded.

Thormund craned his head and looked in Aaliya's direction. She was old enough to be independent of his authority, but still felt like a child of six whenever he looked at her with those severe eyes. Aaliya wondered if he developed that look of menace to use in his business dealings, or if it had always been a part of his character. She suspected it was simply him.

The thurifers surrounded Helena's body, swinging their censers and sending clouds of incense high into the room. They walked around her several times, their long gowns of black silk swooshing like waves on a dark sea. One of the thurifers, wearing a veil with a strand of jewels wrapped around her forehead, stopped behind Helena's head. All movement was stilled in the room except for the gentle swinging of the censers. Using her finger dipped in a pot of white paste left near the marble slab, she painted the symbol of Traegos on Helena's forehead: bands of light bending away from the crescent of the moon. Through darkness comes light.

Twenty or so voices from the choir then released their haunting and unearthly sounds. The veiled woman moved to the darkened space at the edge of the room, followed by the other thurifers. The heavy scent of myrrh suddenly hit Aaliya and she breathed it in deeply. She wanted the smell of the occasion to linger inside her long after this event was over. But it was the singing that kept Aaliya rooted to the spot. Their melodies filled the enormous space like light shining in, and somehow the interminable darkness lifted. It was what she had been thirsting for, and for a brief while, allowed herself to become lost in those sounds.

Movement started to fill the room and the heavy oak doors were opened. The large area, still cloudy with incense, filled with hard sunlight and revealed the worn, ruined surfaces underfoot. The crowd commenced chattering and making their way like herded sheep to the light of the large doorway. Aaliya stood fixed to the same spot. She wasn't ready to go. She wanted all the people to leave so that she could be alone with her mother. Together. Alone.

Maddalena started walking with Thormund towards the exit where they stopped to talk to Helena's brother and other members of her family. They had come a great distance to attend the funeral, and Aaliya knew Simeon to be a good man, but she simply wasn't up for conversation.

The nave had almost been emptied when Maddalena and Thormund finally reached the doorway.

"You are coming, aren't you?" Maddalena said brusquely, turning to look back at Aaliya.

Aaliya shook her head. "I'm not ready."

Thormund left Maddalena's side and walked back towards Aaliya. "You can't bring her back. The Reiners need to move on," he said in a quiet, prosaic way. Thormund had a way of speaking softly but with an undeniable edge that was obvious to anyone near him.

Silence.

Thormund continued. "A new time is before us all now. I know you loved your mother, and her passing is a truly unfortunate event, but there is little time for self-indulgence. There is a lot that needs to be done."

My father, thought Aaliya, a man living in the future. Even this most sacred ritual of paying his last respects to his wife would have been like a sentimental wallow in the past. He was ready to move forward. Life, after all, was a contest. Every part of him was always planning the next step, outmanoeuvring any obstacle. Maybe that was the way to survive in the world? Identify the threats, real and imagined, and systematically knock them down and shit on the wreckage. Aaliya was aware he'd built a hand-paved path to the good life for her and Maddalena as he knew it to be. She certainly hadn't been encouraged by her father to believe there was any other path worth following. But she secretly knew there could be.

Aaliya made her way to a seat in the middle of the nave. She sat down and closed her eyes. She was finally alone. Her mother lay a distance away and Aaliya felt like she had made some progress. She wasn't by her mother's side anymore and the gesture felt monumental. But it hurt so much. Her heart being gripped by talons and slowly shredded. She started crying quite silently, and then something swept over her and she gasped between sobs. Tears spilled from her eyes and she clutched at her sleeve just to have something to hang onto. But she didn't dare open her eyes. It was there in the blackness she could see Helena most vividly and she didn't want to let her go.

"You coming, Aaliya?" Maddalena asked.

Aaliya realized she had been staring at her hands, noticing lines she's never seen before. She lifted her head and looked at Maddalena as she stood with the light from the doorway framing her. Maddalena was standing there as graceful and steadfast as an emotional warrior. Aaliya felt like she was dead inside, like all her organs had turned to ash. She wondered where Maddalena lodged her pain, how she numbed herself so neatly. Thormund, no doubt, admired this quality in his eldest daughter. When they stood together they looked unified and strong.

Aaliya started walking towards the doorway. Maddalena and Thormund followed behind her, as if to make sure she was leaving. Once she was out in the open, away from people, Aaliya stood there under the sky and looked up. The clouds above were thin and rippling, as though they were on the edge of unsettled weather. A band of black birds soared overhead. A lone bird launched from a high branch in a nearby juniper tree, flapping its immense wings in long strokes in an effort to catch up to the flock. Aaliya watched it, feeling as though she was watching her mother leaving. It wasn't so much that she believed her mother to be a bird. But that the bird was a harbinger. And that the moment was wondrously curious as to require acquiescence. When at last the bird caught up to the flock, Aaliya watched them dip out of sight somewhere over the river.

The world was an altered place. The man Aaliya loved was arriving tomorrow. He was coming to marry her sister.

2

Abundance

Aaliya woke up feeling groggy, unstable. It had been a restless sleep. Images of a creature, part man part beast, returned to her mind as she slowly opened her eyes. She lay looking up at the turquoise canopy draping the top of her bed. The creature, she recalled, had been making love to her, pressing its half man body into hers from behind. This hulking mass gripped her body like a rag doll. It's eyes burning red behind her. Deep, violent thrusts entered her body and made her gasp in pleasure. The monster snorted wildly as it feverishly devoured her energy, her life.

Aaliya shook her head and blinked. What was becoming of me? She slipped back under the covers, a feeble attempt at protection from her own thoughts. Her eyes moved slowly around the room. It was sparse and neat. She tried not to be too attached to things, but she couldn't deny it, there were things in her room she simply loved. The large rug at the foot of the bed featuring a pattern of twelve pointed stars outlined in blue; the pewter chest, on top of which sat her collection of silver and copper jewellery. And birds. Birds everywhere. Every feather she had ever found, every bone, every nest, was lovingly displayed on her sideboard. Amongst her found objects, she proudly placed items she had made over the years. Small leather hand-stitched finches, darts and arrows with feathery flights. Sometimes all it took was the light hitting one of her treasures at a certain angle for her to reach out and touch it with the same sense of wonder she felt when seeing the item for the first time. She especially loved the way night seemed to bring her belongings to life. She would walk past her sideboard holding a candle, just to see the shadows of her treasures move across the wall, her birds seemingly taking flight. Every object had a memory, a story. Where she had been, or what she had been doing the day the item was found or made. Her mother had once told her she was a strange spirit with the hair of an animal and mottled wings. Some days she felt like she could stay in there amongst her treasured possessions all day.

The steely predawn light coming through the window told her it was early. Aaliya lay, ruminating, for what seemed like an hour but was probably only fifteen minutes. She rolled herself onto her side and planted her feet onto the floor. She at last felt the need to move her body. To feel the day.

She got out of bed and circumspectly got into the same loose clothing and boots she had been wearing the day before the funeral. Aaliya applied kohl around her eyes and gathered up her heavy lengths of dark hair and wrapped it neatly into a bun. She changed her mind. Reaching up she pulled out the pins, letting her hair fall onto her shoulders. She grabbed a satchel off the floor and left the room.

Out in the corridor Aaliya gently shut the bedroom door behind her. The house was still and silent. She leapt down the staircase and entered the kitchen, where a squat older woman, all wide hips and soft body, was chopping up spinach. Upon seeing Aaliya, the woman placed her knife down on the chopping board.

"Good morning, Nella," Aaliya said, almost gasping for breath in the clutch of the maid's strong arms.

"Good mornin' to you, Aaliya. How are you doin'?"

Aaliya simply didn't know how to answer that. All she knew was that she was in a strange state between shocked and numb. She thought she would wake up and have no control over her emotions. Instead she felt quite rational, even accepting. She just knew she had to keep walking, keep making, keep riding. Just don't stop doing.

"I'm alright," she lied. "Truly I am."

Nella pulled her close again. "If there's anything I can do. Anything."

"Thank you," Aaliya whispered. She let her body soften, resting her head on Nella's meaty shoulder. "I'm going for a ride."

She pulled away from the maid's embrace, and opening up her satchel, placed a couple of apples in the bag.

"Just don't go too fast today, eh?"

Aaliya smiled and kissed Nella on the cheek. "Of course not."

She said goodbye and within seconds she was outside walking along the Vysarq. The Reiner house was located on one of the twelve main streets that made up the capital, all flowing into the Great Market which dominated the city square. Like many other houses situated along the main streets, it was red roofed and made of brick. The main street upon which her home was situated was quiet in the early morning, weak light softly illuminating the colours of the homes near her own. Aaliya turned onto Floran Road, the yeasty smell from the nearby brewery assaulting her senses.

She walked a small distance further and noticed the masts from the tall ships berthed at the quay. The sun was just starting to peak over the horizon. The sky was a pale blue covered with high, scattered clouds like tossed stones, all pinks and greys. She arrived at the stables to find herself alone. She took down her saddle from its usual place and walked towards her horse.

"Hello my beautiful man." Aaliya stroked the blaze of white on the horse's face and planted a kiss on his muzzle. "You ready for a little run this morning? I sure am." She reached into her satchel and placed an apple on the palm of her hand. The horse hungrily ate the sweet fruit on offer.

Aaliya set up the saddle and hoisted herself up in one fluid gesture. She motioned the horse out of the yard and onto the path that snaked along the River Albo. Aaliya lead the horse over the stone arched bridge. Ansgar Castle loomed ahead, appearing vast and unyielding. Once across the river, Aaliya provided little prompting to her horse. He knew exactly where to go. A path leading away from the castle drew them into a thicket of trees. Entering the royal forest always felt like an act of pure joy to Aaliya. Most of her fondest memories were from times she had spent exploring the rambling, bountiful landscape beyond the castle walls.

Aaliya gave Providence a strong kick and he leapt to a canter. The thud of hooves hitting the ground. The feeling of tearing up the air. No destination. Just movement and unrestraint. Aaliya propelled her horse to a full gallop, the wind roaring in her ears. Her hair flew like bird's wings around her face. She never tired of this exhilaration. But today felt different, like Providence and her were one being, racing through the forest as if primed for attack. She let out a war cry, and it seemed to echo throughout the valley.

Ansgar Castle gripped the craggy limestone earth like a giant's hand. Situated beside the River Albo, its massive scale cast a boundless shadow over the land and there were days when it's imposing presence seemed to alter weather systems. The colossal stone walls towered above the ground, men and women reduced to the stature of ants. The large and elaborate vaulted entrance was protected by a curtain of iron and oak. From the rectangular defensive tower one could see across the land beyond until the ground appeared as a stain on the horizon. And as far as the eye could see was a chalky landscape, rugged and unrelenting. Evergreen oaks, pines and nut trees squeezed into the few patches of ground where rocks and stones gave way. The long summer had been particularly harsh, the grass now lay parched and brittle as a stowaway's throat.

It was these woods, clustered between the castle and the river, that felt like a sanctuary to Aaliya. As a young girl, she went in there as often as she could and felt the wonder of the place. Anything was possible. In there she was an explorer, a traveller, a girl with a whole new world to discover. With her mother's blessing, Aaliya would grab a neat parcel of sausage, bread and olive paste from Nella and head into the forest to spend her days. Her friend, Jakob, would sneak out of the castle's kitchen to join her when he could. A right scolding from his mother would invariably follow her discovery. Which would delay his next jaunt with Aaliya by a maximum of two days and six hours. But no one was counting.

As Aaliya grew older she became less reliant on Nella's generosity, as she started to learn instead about the food that could be found in the forest. Nuts and seeds, berries and fungi were all plentiful. She just had to know where to look and what to look for. Aaliya felt pretty sure about nuts and seeds, albeit with a bit of trial and error. She wasn't so sure of berries and fungi. She collected samples and presented them to people she thought might have the answers.

Aaliya showed the samples to Nella and Jakob's mother but, to her surprise, it was her own mother who was able to help. Aaliya used to think that Helena was a queen. The way she would walk into a room with the grace of a lioness, her robes immaculate and her dark hair pulled back in exquisite knots and loops, she looked the vision of a stately woman. But Aaliya came to know a woman who was almost child-like in her love of discovery. They started going into the woods together almost every week, sometimes to find wild mushrooms and berries, sometimes just to walk. It was the happiest time in Aaliya's life. She was in the place where she felt most connected, with the person she deeply loved.

Abundance was everywhere with Helena's guidance. She showed Aaliya what was safe to eat. She taught Aaliya to read the sky. The drizzle that would follow low shapeless foggy clouds. The thunder that would follow tall, towering clouds. Helena encouraged Aaliya to respect what the sky was telling, but it was not in Aaliya's nature to follow this advice. She still chose to ride out when those high milky clouds rolled in just to feel the pounding rain against her body. But she nonetheless gained Helena's ability to smell both danger and opportunity, to feel it and see it.

Early one spring morning, Helena and Aaliya slipped into the woods, a heavy fog hanging over the canopy. The air was filled with the sour, earthy scent of growth and death.

Upon rocks, tree bark and the forest floor new forms of life had seemingly sprouted overnight. Orange fungi and green, velvety moss amassed on every surface. Every step Aaliya took seemed to sink her into the sodden ground. So utterly pure and quiet was the morning, each exhale seemed clamorous.

The woman walking beside Aaliya on that morning shouldn't have been there. Helena was the wife of an influential merchant and for her to be scrambling over rocks or walking over sodden ground was inappropriate, almost irresponsible. Even then, at her young age, Aaliya knew it was a big thing. She didn't know the extent of the risk however, and Helena never let on.

They found a small tree with waxy thin leaves and fruit dangling like small red eyeballs. Aaliya approached it and picked off a couple of the fruit, looking at them in the palm of her hand.

"We tried this one before," Helena said. "Do you remember?"

Aaliya pulled her parchment out of her leather satchel. She would often take cuttings back to her room and use charcoal to draw the shape of the leaves and the form of the fruit.

"Taste it," Helena suggested.

Aaliya put one of the fruit in her mouth. It tasted bland with a slight bitter edge around the skin. She didn't particularly enjoy the taste, and was surprised to watch her mother pull off many of the red fruit and place them in her mouth.

"Manzanita," she said, spitting out the seeds. "We have many of these trees around my home in Rone. I remember wandering out and eating these by the bucketful."

"They're not very tasty though," Aaliya said, screwing up her face as she chewed on the bitter flesh.

"They're better cooked. But you could travel from here to Alvira living off these little gems."

"Is that what grandfather did when he went exploring?" Aaliya asked.

Helena smiled. The thought of her father clearly brought warmth to her expression. Helena had told her many stories about her father's adventures. He considered himself to be a saunterer. Not so much an explorer of new lands but moreso a man who desired nothing more than to go walking. His travels captured Aaliya's imagination. Helena had told her about his journeys to rarely ventured parts of the realm: the central deserts of Elkha, the towering mountains of the Majelliar Ranges, the swampy neverworld of the Little Rann of Yei. Aaliya would sit gripped through her mother's accounts of his adventures, not wanting the tales to end.

"I'm sure he did," Helena said. "He mostly worked it out on his own, but he also learnt a lot from talking to people. He tried many things and I believe got sick on occasion. When he went off on his walks, he fully adapted to the world around him. He didn't fumble through the forest like what we're doing now. He learnt from everything around him. He walked through the forest like a fox," Helena imitated the full-body alertness of a predatory animal, "he listened to the birds," she turned her head to a distant sound, "he felt the wind and watched the clouds. People thought he was mad. Why does he not take a horse? Why walk those great distances? He had bountiful land and a thriving farm, yet it was the world beyond that called him. I don't even think it was the discovery of new places that he was so drawn to. I think it was more a need to be calm and alone. To be in unfamiliar places, allow himself to get a little lost perhaps. It was like he didn't have a particular home. He was at home everywhere."

"Did you ever go with him?"

"Once. When I was about ten years old, just a bit younger than you are now. I went with him to Marius, which probably doesn't sound like a significant journey considering our home was in the Tilwara Valley. But we went the long way, on foot to the River Kota then we sailed down the river to the Port of Tshane on a small boat, where we boarded a caravel and sailed up the coast to Belvers. What we see of the world, Aaliya, is a mere sliver of what's out there. Much of it is hidden from us. We can't see it with our eyes alone. We need to use all our senses." Helena threw a handful of fruit into her mouth and quietly chewed. "This fruit was plentiful along the banks of the River Kota."

"Can we go somewhere together?" Aaliya asked hopefully. "Can we go to Rone, or Alvira or somewhere new?" The thought walking in the woods, but on a much grander scale thrilled her. Her mind instantly filled with new places to discover, new things to touch and feel and learn. Even as a young girl, Aaliya knew she wanted to know more. A restless energy for experiences was coursing through her blood.

Helena placed her hand on Aaliya's shoulder and pulled her close. "Oh sweetheart, I'd love nothing more. For you and Maddalena to come with me to other parts of the realm. It's just…not possible…"

"I don't want father to be the king's friend. I just want to go and travel the way you did with your father."

"I only went once. And do you know why I only went once? Because it's not something young girls are meant to do. It puts wicked thoughts in your head," she said rustling Aaliya's hair. "My mother saw to it that I stayed close to home after that journey and never went out again."

"Maybe father will be alright with us going – "

"No, he won't."

The voice from behind startled them both. An acerbic tone that was both harsh but utterly familiar. They turned around to see Maddalena standing a short distance away, her long slender body draped in a pale blue dress with a black cloak around her shoulders. She had grown to be a striking young woman. Even though her dark hair was wrapped neatly into a braid, the moist air gave her a slightly dishevelled appearance. Her full mouth seemed stretched across her face in a weird, uncomfortable expression. Partly proud of her discovery, but unsure of her next move.

"Maddalena, we're looking for food…" Helena said, a look of confusion on her face.

"I know what you're doing. You told me weeks ago. Well I told father, and he's not happy."

"We're just picking fruit. Come and join us," Helena said, motioning towards her.

Maddalena held out her hand for Helena to stop. Aaliya never forgot that gesture. It was the first time she had seen Maddalena assert herself with the venerability of someone already a queen. It was as if the tables had turned and Helena was answerable to this young woman who was flesh-and-blood, yet a complete enigma.

"You're plotting to leave father," Maddalena said. "You two have been planning it for some time."

"What are you talking about?" Helena said, screwing up her face.

"I know you want to leave. You've probably never

wanted to be here. Well you don't deserve him. You just want to turn your back on father and have our name - "

It was too much to listen to. Aaliya quickly ran up to Maddalena and pushed her with all her force. The momentum of pushing into Maddalena's body was such that Aaliya went tumbling to the ground with her like a sack of flour. Aaliya started hurling punches at Maddalena's face, and Maddalena returned the violence striking Aaliya hard. Helena started yelling at them both to stop. She felt her mother's hands on her body attempting to drag her away, but Aaliya's arms kept flailing about like they had a will of their own. Maddalena was four years older than Aaliya so her blows had some power in them. Some felt to Aaliya as though they were cracking bone.

Soon there were more than Helena's desperate hands tugging at Aaliya's body. Two men, including one she knew to be her father's business partner, Viggo, had pulled her away. She was so furiously worked up she tried to break free from their grasp, but they held her tight.

Viggo eventually let Aaliya go, but she remained held by a short, stocky man. Aaliya looked hard at Viggo as he stood a short distance away from her. His eyes were like shovels of cold ash, his long grey hair pulled back into a severe tail. Viggo's attire always seemed to resemble that of preacher. A black cravat featured tightly around his neck, the stand-up collar of his dark embroidered shirt was tucked into his navy woollen pants. A silver beard wrapped around his face in a neat arc. There was something dark and otherworldly about the man, and Aaliya wished deeply he did not feature in her life. He was always there, but never for the purpose of good, in her mind. Like some sort of leech sucking the life out of her family.

"Madame," Viggo addressed Helena coolly, "this jaunt is over. Your husband has demanded you return home."

"I need to talk to my daughters alone. Now leave us be," Helena retorted.

"It's an order from your husband. You are required to return home."

"I am not going until I've talked to my - "

"Now!" Viggo shouted.

Helena looked from Viggo, to Aaliya and Maddalena, to Viggo again. Defiance was not something her mother was comfortable with, but Aaliya could see she was battling whether or not to take this fight on.

"Don't go," Aaliya said, hoping her words would be enough to give her the confidence she needed to stand up to Viggo, and ultimately, Thormund.

But there was some higher priority for Helena, some deep sense of responsibility Aaliya just didn't understand as a young girl. Being a mother, being a wife, being a woman of prominence.

Helena turned to her. "We'll do this again soon, Aaliya." She then started walking in the direction of the castle, Viggo and the stocky man following behind her.

Maddalena looked at Aaliya with a smirk that clearly exemplified a notion of victory. "She won't be doing this again."

"Why would you do this to her?"

"She humiliates him. And so do you. You two coming our here behind his back. People have noticed."

"I don't care that people have seen us," Aaliya replied.

"Ungrateful, that's what you are. Stupid and ungrateful. Our family has wealth and power - "

"You sound just like him."

Maddalena smiled sardonically. "Maybe I do. As for you…you'll forever be catching up to me."

"I don't want to catch up to you. That's what you don't understand. I don't want to be like you at all."

Aaliya returned to her home that day to a beating from her father. For the next three months, Aaliya spent many of her days lying still on the floor in the living room of their home, under her father's watchful gaze. Any movement when she was not given permission resulted in a caning across her legs. A heady mix of fury and hunger to please coursed through her veins.

One day, as the cold wind of late autumn briefly abated, Thormund grabbed hold of Aaliya and walked her the length of the Vysarq all the way to the maker's quarters and into a saddle making workshop.

Thormund never foresaw the consequence of leaving her in the workshop that brisk autumn morning when she was twelve years old. "Just get her making stuff," he had told the Master Saddle Maker, Olle. "Get her learning some self-control. And wipe those fanciful notions out of her head. Her damn mother has a lot to answer for." Thormund owned and collected rent from most of the workshops in the maker's quarter of the capital. He was their boss and as far as he was concerned, they could help instill some discipline in his daughter.

Aaliya sensed her father begrudgingly accepted the way saddle making came to shape her life. He mentioned at one point it seemed to keep her "out of trouble", but she knew he also held a deep respect for craftsmanship and entrepreneurship. Traegos had become a kingdom renowned for its objects of exquisite beauty and resourcefulness in manufacturing. Merchants travelled from distant lands to buy Traegos goods. It all came back to the contest.

While Aaliya immersed herself in saddle making over the years, she watched her sister grow into an ambitious young woman who rarely left their father's side, except to spend time with her lovers, of whom Aaliya suspected were numerous. Maddalena married and soon thereafter became a widow. She was determined to make an impact on political and business decisions, and to her credit, put in the hard work to acquire the knowledge and strategic insight to successfully do this. Maddalena was more statesmanlike than most of Thormund's cronies.

Aaliya continued to venture into the woods. Sometimes with her friend, Jakob, but mostly on her own. Helena didn't join her again. She often fell sick and then it reached a point where she could not even get out of bed. Years went by and she seemed to wither like a leaf in the sun, until she was a shadow of her former self. It was like she had just given up on life. Aaliya couldn't help but feel that it was partly her mother's insistence on being a rule follower that killed her. Aaliya knew she wasn't a stupid child as Maddalena had expressed. She knew what awaited her. She just didn't feel like waiting for it to happen.

3

Conflict and Consolation

Maddalena picked up her quill and began caressing her cheek with it. She always came to these council meetings with her pot of ink, a piece of parchment and her favourite quill. It was quite an extravagant writing tool, the soft feathers at the base tawny brown with striking black spots. Maddalena liked to think of writing as her secret weapon, the thing that set her apart. The other ignorant oafs in the room, her father the exception of course, probably thought she was there to take notes for her father like some dutiful secretary. But she did it only for her own learnings. A word here and a word there were all she needed to prompt her to think about the discussion that had taken place, and whom had made what assertions.

The stroking of her face with the quill eased her into such a restful state, her mind started drifting to thoughts of her lovers. She really shouldn't arrange to meet her boys straight after these council sessions. The very thought of them interfered terribly with her ability to concentrate on the proceedings. Her previous occasion in their company just a week ago had been full of such extraordinary ecstasy, she could only imagine the wickedness that lay ahead for her today.

She looked across the table. Viggo was looking at her like he could read her thoughts. His glare so unnerved her she hastily put the quill down on the table. That man is forever scrutinizing me, she thought, waiting for me to slip up. Maddalena was sure Viggo was quite vexed her father had included her in his confidence. The ego of these men both humoured and angered her. She was more worthy of being here than any of them.

The sight of Viggo staring at her had been a timely reminder to remain focused and careful. Thormund sat at the end opposite the king's vacant chair looking restrained and immaculate. Although situated in Ansgar Castle, the room belonged to Thormund Reiner. Maddalena smiled at the thought of her father having a quiet word with the king over the way the room was decorated. The one window rarely caught natural light, keeping the room in a perpetual stony darkness. It was sparsely furnished, and a certain dank mustiness that a room gets when it's closed and empty for too long, lingered. No paintings were hanging from the walls, no ornaments on display. The room was occupied solely by an ebony table and ten high backed chairs. The chairs were of a simple, pragmatic style featuring nothing garish. Fine craftsmanship was readily available and yet the room conjured a stark space that was a vision of order and consistency. The space wasn't so much a council chamber as a mirror of Thormund himself. It was a room that did not encourage distraction and demanded the full attention of all inhabitants. It worked most of the time.

Thormund was a man with a logician's fervour for organization. Tidiness was more than the state of one's surroundings. To him tidiness was what kept one in power.

It filtered through everything and was expected from all around him. Mess was what happened in those states that had gone over to the people. In his opinion it leads to utter chaos and it was never going to happen in Traegos while he had influence.

An extremely large man trudged through the doorway, the cloth contained in his black robes could have sufficiently covered five beds. A shiny bald head sat on his slumped shoulders and seemed to denote a lack of confidence. But he was no fool. Darius was the king's closest confidante and the expression of impotence he regularly wore on his face concealed a sharp intelligence. He murmured a greeting to the occupants of the room, scrapped a chair heavily along the stone floor and sat down with an audible groan.

"The king has taken ill and will not be present at session today," Darius said as he placed his parchment and quill on the table.

Maddalena saw her father roll his eyes. It was a poorly kept secret that the king rarely made it out of bed these days. Across the city the gossip was incessant about the king and whether or not he was still fit to rule. Everybody knew he spent most days lying in bed in a drunken stupor, weeping over the loss of his precious son. Maddalena was sure she would have married the prince had he not met an untimely death after being crushed by a falling wooden beam while he sat on his chair in the Great Hall.

Murmuring rose around the table and Darius silenced the group before ruffling the pages of parchment in front of him and continuing. "The first item for discussion today is the Charter of the Forest. The king would like a decree that any man caught felling trees in the royal forest be hung."

Muted voices proclaiming "hear, hear" could be heard

from two, perhaps three men. Thormund straightened himself and inched his chair further under the table.

"He can't hold onto it forever," Thormund said calmly. "We need wood and charcoal. Furnaces in this city are burning night and day melting iron into steel. Our steel goods are prized across the realm. Anything that halts production is a poorly thought out decision."

A tall thin man, Thormund sat with his back so straight his posture almost rendered him part of the furniture. His beard was immaculately trimmed and his white hair short and neat. Care and attention to the micro details were what set him apart. Although the backs of his hands were still smooth and soft (possibly from years of remaining in his study) the deep 'm' shaped furrows that cut into his forehead hinted at his stormy side. Even from across the room, one always got the sense there was some potent energy crackling through his stoic veneer.

"You're not kidding anyone, Reiner," quipped Councillor Erhardt, leaning forward on the table with his pointy elbows. "You just want the land cleared to put your bleaters on it. You'd have sheep occupying the alleyways off the Vysarq if you could."

Thormund slightly clenched his jaw. "Erhardt, we've been listening to your unproductive drivel in this room for a year now. The fact remains, if it weren't for my sheep and the industries I have in this city filling ships with manufactured goods, we wouldn't even be sitting in this room. We'd all be poor as mice fighting over the scraps tossed our way by Rone and Gedion."

"That's laughable," said Councillor Erhardt. "Your empire serves no one but yourself."

"Enough," Darius interjected. "Enough you two. The

royal forest around the castle will remain intact for the time being. A death sentence to any man found felling trees in the forest." He dipped his quill in his ink pot and scrawled notes on the parchment before him.

"It is excessive," Viggo suggested, his silky voice breaking the silence. "I have advised the king that reducing the royal forest by even a third and grazing animals there, sheep being the most profitable at the moment, will contribute approximately one million krones to Traegos' economy. Raw wool, additional manufacturing in the city, not to mention taxes charged on the export of woollen goods are all things one can expect from expanded wool production. And right now prices are high."

"Short term thinking, Viggo. Short term," said Councillor Erhardt, waving his hand dismissively. Erhardt's slightly beaky nose was always the first thing people noticed about him as it seemed to give him the countenance of a man on guard. An obstructive, disgruntled character, his long straggly hair hung down his face like a grey rag. Maddalena thought the king should have removed him a long time ago, but she was sure he insisted Erhardt remain as the conservative voice who saw only intractable obstacles everywhere. It was useful to have such a person on council when the king wanted to press home his agenda.

"Our military bases along the Albo are costly to maintain, are they not, Councillor?" Viggo asked.

"Councillor Erhardt may have a point."

Maddalena and everyone around the table looked in the direction of the voice that had just spoken. Ariaen Clausen would sit through these sessions and listen with some sort of monastical discipline, then finally open his mouth and say something that usually cut to the core of the matter. Maddalena was wary of him, and she suspected many men hated him. Mostly and not least his brother, the king.

Ariaen's mass of black hair was closely cropped. Great wide sideburns grabbed hold of his cheekbones and drew attention to his long, thin lips. "Our military bases are costly to maintain which is why the importance of long term planning must never be overlooked."

"What are you suggesting?"

"That we keep the interests of our society as a whole at the forefront of our decisions. Not just in the hands of those in power."

"Humph," Viggo scoffed, "and that's why you'll never be in power, Ariaen. Big on the rhetoric, light on substance. Even you don't know what that looks like."

Ariaen opened his mouth to say something.

"Councillors, I insist we move on," said Darius. "The king has made his position clear."

The council session pressed on. Without the king present, the discussion moved slowly. Viggo and Thormund argued their positions, Councillor Erhardt and Ariaen countered them. The remaining men in the room swung between the two parties. Darius did his best to maintain a sense of order but the strongly held differences seemed to stifle consensus. Maddalena thought about Gedion and Rone, and wondered if their council sessions were also marred by conflict.

It seemed like an hour passed before they finally arrived at the topic Maddalena was here to participate in, her marriage into the kingdom of Gedion.

"Tyln Bluff has been a part of Traegos for centuries," Maddalena heard Councillor Erhardt lament, bringing her to full alertness.

"It's worthless land," Thormund replied, almost sounding bored at discussing this deal again so close to the wedding. "Our goal has always been and always will be the Port of Elisus. Without it, Traegos is forever reliant on the River Albo. Rone and Gedion, meanwhile, go from strength-to-strength dominating the Mindano Sea."

Councillor Erhardt continued, "Should we not be seeking land in the Barmer Valley in exchange for Tyln Bluff? It's a ludicrous deal!"

"Do you really think Gedion would just hand over the Barmer Valley?" Thormund said, raising his voice. "We invaded that area ten years ago to try to win back our land there. We were not successful. It's now about stealth. It's about strategy. Tyln Bluff is a piece of worthless land, which is precisely why it's so valuable. It deflects attention away from what we really want. For us to try again to obtain the Barmer Valley would be anticipated by Gedion and therefore instantly opposed. We don't want a reactive enemy, and this way we have the suspension of conflict until a more advantageous time for us. In the meantime, wealth creation through trade routes for our goods, and blocking an alliance between Gedion and Rone are good outcomes from this deal."

"Rumours are, Seigneur Reiner, there is silver to be mined at Tyln Bluff," Ariaen said.

"It's a rumour we've heard for the past ten years," Thormund replied.

"This is true," Viggo said, placing his elbows on the table and interlacing his fingers. "It's been investigated without success. Seigneur Reiner is quite right. Traegos needs to keep its attention focused in the east."

Councillor Erhardt chuckled. "Well of course you say that, Viggo. You two are in business together!"

"And I am also the king's financial advisor," Viggo said coolly. "Let's not forget what has been gained. Madame Reiner is to marry the inheritor of the Isle of Pike. Do I need to once again outline the significance of this parcel of land in the Mindano Sea? Do I need to draw out shipping charts showing the frequency of ships hauling copper from the island back to the mainland? Do I need to put a map in front of you to show you how close the island is to Rone, and which is no doubt causing our friends in Easthal to be shitting water right now? Do I need to also point out on such a map just how close it is to the Port of Elisus, which, as Seigneur Reiner previously highlighted, is the goal for our kingdom? As I said before, our focus is to remain in the east. The king has given his blessing to this wedding. He believes it is a union that will unequivocally serve Traegos well. He has even kindly offered the castle's Ceremonial Room for the marriage to take place in."

"It's a gamble," muttered Councillor Erhardt, "a massive gamble."

Maddalena was sure she saw a glint in her father's eye inviting her to speak. "I understand you're not a gambler, Councillor. But some of us know with gambling that you play the games you can win," she said, coolly smiling at Erhardt as she spoke.

She hoped her expression didn't betray her longing. She didn't want to give so much as a hint to how much she wanted this marriage. Maddalena hadn't spent time in the company of the young man from Gedion she was about to marry, other than the brief cordial meeting they shared when he had visited Ansgar with his uncle two years earlier to establish a trade route for copper. She knew him to be a man of Gedion nobility; the circumstances surrounding the death of his nobleman father, still mysterious and shadowy. And she, or course, knew about the great geographical asset that was in his name. Of less importance (but of interest to her) was that she also knew him to have had an affair with her sister during that visit two years ago. Maddalena was sure Aaliya thought the affair had been undertaken in perfect secrecy. What a fool. Didn't her little sister know she could literally sniff that kind of thing out?

No, it wasn't out of spite she wanted to marry the man from Gedion (although there was something deliciously satisfying in that). Maddalena considered her skill in recognizing an opportunity to be now quite honed and polished. Gedion was quite simply, a prize. It was a kingdom growing in prosperity and power at a rate that loyal men and women of Traegos were failing to fully comprehend. And she was about to be a part of that advance towards greatness. Thormund understood it, of course. He saw the benefits for the business. And he knew having a trusted person in Gedion could prove to be very useful in the likelihood old animosities between the two kingdoms resurfaced.

But any prudent person knows you keep your most deeply desired longings to yourself. And what she didn't tell a soul was that she wanted her own power, to finally achieve separateness and forge her own path away from her father's watchful gaze. She had been working towards this moment ever since her last marriage came to an abrupt end. She knew it was only a matter of time before her father announced another potential suitor. The dull reality of matrimony was simply something she believed she could not avoid as the daughter of Thormund Reiner. As marriage clearly lay ahead on her path (and the thought of ending up a spinster adding a sense of urgency to the situation) she was determined, at the very least, to work out what would be best for her. In her effort to find out, visits to Thormund's library became daily occurrences. She made regular forays to the Grand Market seeking out gossipy tidbits. Mostly, however, she talked to Thormund at length about the state of kingdoms on their border and beyond. About the rise of the insurgency movement. About where power was rising and where it was collapsing. And from her endless reading and quest for information, she made it quite clear to him. Gedion, and only Gedion. And as close to royalty as possible.

Maddalena had told her mother six months ago about her plans to marry the nobleman from Gedion. Her mother was gravely ill at the time. Her room had a repugnant, lingering smell like she was dead already. "Don't do it, Maddalena," she had advised. "You'll end up like me." How could I possibly end up like her? Maddalena thought. I know exactly where I'm going and it's not following your sad and sorry footsteps to the grave. Maddalena felt she had been right all along to remain close to her father. The woman she had seen yesterday lying on a marble slab seemed a complete stranger. She felt pity, such wasted opportunities when she could only see forging ahead to greatness.

"Enough, Maddalena. Your contribution is not required here," Thormund said firmly.

Maddalena blinked, wondering if she had heard correctly. Erhardt made a portly grin, and for a brief moment Maddalena contemplated throwing her ink pot at his face. Why did her father humiliate her like that in front of the other councillors? Censuring her like she was a naughty child.

The room started to feel stifling to her. She always displayed ceaseless loyalty to her father while others came and went. Betrayal was all around like a persistent stench. Yet she was steadfast by his side. Providing insight into people and their motivations where his limited grasp of the human mind would not, and could not, go. How she longed to be a man sometimes. To swear and fuck and slash with impunity.

Darius announced the end of the session, and Maddalena was the first to get up and scrape her heavy wooden chair along the stone floor. She gathered up her writing implements and parchment and started to leave the room.

"Maddalena, I'd like to see you in the Solar," Thormund said.

She turned to face him. "I have some urgent business to attend to."

Thormund raised an eyebrow.

"I won't be long," she added, taking a more conciliatory tone.

She hurried from the room and left all thought of her father, her upcoming marriage, the whole shitty, thankless task of it all behind her.

Maddalena walked briskly down the corridor, her long dress flapping about her ankles. She cursed all the stairs in the place as she climbed up to the fourth floor. It was a floor that seldom saw people this time of day. A number of castle staff had their bedchambers on the fourth floor and had already left to start their day's work. She looked around as she stepped out of the stairwell and saw a person at the southern end of the corridor, where she was headed. Maddalena walked nonchalantly towards the person, a man with a neat black beard and a green cap on his head. She looked sideways at his face just as they were about to pass each other. He touched the rim of his cap and nodded his head before continuing down the corridor. She had seen him before but surmised he was no one to be concerned about.

Once he had passed she picked up her pace. She arrived at the last door on the left. She did her secret knock, not too loudly, just loud enough to be heard inside. There was no response. She pressed her ear to the door but couldn't hear anything from inside the room. She tried the door handle and the door clicked open. Momentarily she felt a sense of annoyance as she had told them numerous times to keep the door locked. She paused on the threshold, surveying the room. Where were they?

The room was dark, the late morning sun fanned out onto the ceiling from the top of the drawn curtains. The large canopy bed to her right was in a state of disarray, sheets pushed back and the red brocade bed cover hung haphazardly almost falling onto the floor. Straight ahead from the door, situated on a large woven rug, three leather-upholstered chairs sat vacant around a low round table. She closed the door behind her and made sure to lock it.

"Santo? Joshva?" Maddalena called. Still no response, she moved towards the table and placed her writing implements on top of it. The decanter of wine was half empty, and two tankards sat beside it with obvious signs of activity. She heard a slight shuffling sound and looked around the room, before focusing on the door to the linen cupboard. She approached the cupboard, biting her bottom lip as she walked. Oh, how she loved surprises!

Maddalena slowly turned the handle to the door and pushed it open. The dim light from the main room entered the confined space and draped the two naked bodies squeezed inside.

A man with a thin moustache was leaning back, his arms raised above his head and holding onto some shelves. A look of delight was on his face, his angular jaw rested open, his eyes closed. The other man had his back to her, and was kneeling at the crotch of the standing man.

"Is that you, Maddalena?" the standing man said, failing to open his eyes.

"Was I really that late? You boys couldn't wait?"

He opened his eyes. "We like to think of it as warming our bodies up for you, my Dearest."

"Well, Santo, I'm ready…and waiting," Maddalena licked her lips and moved to the side to observe as much of the scene as she could. "Actually, don't stop now. This is delicious." She lifted her dress and slipped her finger beneath her undergarments. "That's just beautiful, my boys. Ohhh…" she groaned as her finger fluttered and flicked.

Her two beautiful boys getting off in front of her was intoxicating. She heard Santo's breath become more erratic, mingling with her own rasps. He suddenly pulled out of Joshva's mouth, his large slick cock momentarily dangling free. Maddalena reached down and violently pulled off her undergarments. In one swift move, Santo grabbed her backside, lifted her and lowered her onto his hard-on. She slid straight onto it and released a deep, primal groan. Her juices had been flowing long before this moment. She had been almost dripping while she was in the meeting, anticipating the sweet sublimity of this muscle inside her. She moved her hips up and down, undulating in slow, long movements whilst cradled by Santo's strong arms. They kissed like savages, sucking tongues and licking every part of each other's mouths, teeth and gums.

With Maddalena straddling him, Santo clumsily made his way to the bed, bumping into the chair, which knocked the wine off the table. Santo swore loudly, Maddalena and Joshva laughed like drunkards. When they reached the bed, Maddalena fell back onto it with a thump.

"Oh my stallions, do me good," she said.

Santo flipped her over onto her stomach and pushed the dress towards her waist. Maddalena lifted herself up onto all fours and eased back onto his finger delighting in the sharp pressure of it. Pleasure vibrated through her body, hot and maddening. Joshva stood close to her face as Santo placed his hands on either side of her rump and started rocking into her.

"Closer," she said, breathlessly. Joshva shuffled closer and her tongue darted out finding the deep slit at the tip, which she probed into playfully before sliding her wet mouth over the length of his hard-on.

Maddalena closed her eyes and relaxed into the intoxicating sensation of the two cocks pressing into her. All this man to myself! She felt like a wild animal, a three-headed beast. Maddalena stayed with the thought as she relaxed into the wave of pleasure that swept through her body. The room seemed to be spinning and she could barely breathe. Groaning and sucking at all that man flesh. She looked up to see Joshva's chest heaving, his composed face twitch and furrow. He then whimpered, his penis jerking inside her mouth. Santo continued to cradle her rump, his laboured breath telling her he was close. A deep animal grunt and a deep press into her flesh, she felt him climax.

The three collapsed on the bed together, intertwined their bodies and for one long, tranquil hour they ran their hands over each other, occasionally chuckling, kissing each other's necks, earlobes, nipples.

Maddalena cradled her arms behind her head looking up at the fabric draped across the top of the expansive canopy bed. She noticed a flower in the red brocade. And although the print had numerous flowers, she became fixated on this one golden feature. The star shape in the middle of the flower was embroidered in white, and even in the dull light she could make out the stigma in the centre. It looked beautiful, delicate.

She felt warmth run through her body to her fingertips. Why couldn't the rest of her life be as simple and uncomplicated as time with her boys? They were an enormous relief for her. Did they realize how much she needed them? A flutter of panic swept over her. I can't let that happen, she thought.

She sat up suddenly feeling anxious and uncomfortable. "Get up."

They made no effort to move. It was as if they had seen it all before.

"Are you two just going to lie around all day?"

"Calm down, sweet pea," Santo said, "there's no rush."

Maddalena slapped him hard across the face. "Get up!"

Maddalena went to slap him again, but Santo grabbed her forearm in a vice like grip. "In a hitting mood are we?"

"Let me go." And then, before she could stop herself she blurted out, "my father is expecting me."

"Daddy is expecting you. Big important things to discuss, have we?"

"Yes, actually. Some of us have minds capable of thinking of things beyond what's between our legs."

Both men laughed and joked. "Why?" they sniggered,

both holding her firmly.

"Let me…*go!*" Maddalena struggled.

"I don't think our lady is really ready to go, do you, Santo?" Joshva asked, pushing Maddalena back down on the bed.

"Not at all, Joshva, not at all." Santo got up and walked around the other side of the bed where he grabbed Maddalena's arms and pinned them down.

And she wasn't. She wanted to feel oblivion again. Oh how she wanted it. Nothing else mattered.

Joshva spread her legs wide and pressed his tongue into her mound. Santo loosened his grip, and then let go altogether, running his hands down her body until his fingers found her nipples. He pinched and played with them as they rose up like hard berries.

Maddalena started getting breathless. It was all too beautiful. Santo, behind her, placed his head over her face and kissed her hungrily.

"I'm going to do you slowly, Lady Reiner," Joshva said.

"Queen," she said, throatily, "Say I'm your queen."

"Queen…Queen Maddalena…" Joshva said.

The pressure of only a small part of his hard-on felt like a delectable tease to Maddalena. An intense craving worked up inside her.

"Oh you've got to give me more. I'm begging you."

"You want more, Queen Maddalena?"

"Oh yes, please!"

But he didn't. Not at that point anyway. His short movements continued, prolonging her craving. Her itch became almost unbearable as a wave of pleasure starting forming in her body. Blood rising behind her eyes.

And then he went into her deeply. "Oh, let me die."

Her body shook, a great long spasm that had her moaning like a pigeon.

Joshva continued moving into her, groaning "my sweet queen". She reached up and ran her fingers through Santo's hair, his face still close to hers. He smiled at her, and she smiled back at him, momentarily surprised at such an act of tenderness.

At that time, in that room, Maddalena had all she needed. She wanted to linger there a while longer.

4

The Hive

The workshop was situated at the northern end of the Vysarq in an alleyway known as Rawhide Lane. It was an area of activity and craftsmanship, heat and sweat. If the chatter from the inhabitants ceased for one moment, only the dull, cushioned sounds of hand tools working leather would be heard. As a workshop district, Rawhide Lane was relatively free of the smoke and chemicals that plagued other areas. The smell that filled the air instead was somehow comforting, an earthy scent, a collision and clash of animal manliness and oily, feminine richness. Light came over the rooftops and lit up the cobblestones and the grey stone walls. Signs swung above door frames featuring vividly painted symbols instantly recognizable: saddles, buckles and fittings, harnesses and reins. The street outside the workshops was a daily scene of orderly clutter, not dissimilar to the world behind the walls. People milled about the tea traders on the street, before disappearing back into their workshops to create for the realm.

The saddlery workshop was flanked with animal hides and copious tools that climbed the walls like strange bugs. Olle referred to the workshop as The Hive. A tall, stocky man, Aaliya had come to learn that leathercraft had always been in Olle's blood. His closely cropped grey hair was so thick and wiry, barbers complained after each visit that Olle's hair blunted their shears. His complexion was much too sallow and pale, a hazard of working inside for much of his life. But there were benefits from what she could see. His face was hardly lined. His hands instead told his story. Years of lathering them in greasy lanolin had kept his hands as soft and supple as a child's belly. Each day he could come into the workshop and breathe in deeply until his lungs could take no more, and then exhale with a smile. Just like her beloved mentor and friend, Aaliya never tired of the animal smell that encased the space.

Olle was a man with a passion for self improvement. He didn't indulge in gossip or slander, and generally worked in a room separate from the other saddle makers. He wasn't, however, without the ability to share jokes and banter with the other men. In fact, the ease with which he conversed and his fidelity to his craft and to people, inspired many who came into contact with him.

Aaliya could recall the day her father brought her to the workshop like it was yesterday. She remembered the uncomfortable feeling of her father's grip around her arm, the pair of them standing near the door like lost deers. Olle had invited them both in but she didn't leave the doorway. She just stood there, wary and apprehensive. Olle had mentioned how he had finished making a saddle for her father a couple of months before the unexpected visit. It had been his finest work to date, he had said, featuring an inlaid padded seat, wide ears to support the rider's back, and intricate floral tooling across all the leatherwork. But she knew even then, she was looking at something special. The newly made saddle was situated on the bench, and Thormund walked over to it and instantly began running his hand along the dip in the seat, his fingers probing and caressing the floral work. He was clearly a man mesmerized. The beauty of the saddle seemed to deport Thormund to another place and time. When Thormund finally came around, Olle was given brief but firm instructions to teach Aaliya leathercraft for a small monthly dividend. Aaliya could tell Olle was far from comfortable with this instruction. He probably didn't have time for such a responsibility. She was wise enough to know that for someone in Olle's situation, looking after a twelve-year-old girl would only have been seen as trouble, not to mention burdensome. Expectations usually accompanied such transactions.

She started to turn up regularly, three or four times a week. She was never put out by the heady smell of the oils and fats in the leather or the swearing by the men as they shouted to each other from the different rooms. And it was only Olle she came to watch. On occasion he tried to engage her in conversation, but she rarely responded. She wasn't interested in words. Her eyes fixed on what his hands were doing.

One day, after she had been visiting for several weeks, Olle gestured with a swing of his head to the tool rack. "Could you get me the stitching awl?"

Aaliya knew the implement he needed. He was at the stage of threading the leather around the cantle and she had seen him doing this part on a previous saddle.

This time, she walked over to the tool rack and pulled the stitching awl off the hook and handed it to him.

"Thank you, Miss." Olle went about stitching the cantle into place with strips of rawhide. "What's your name?"

he asked.

"Aaliya."

"Mine's Olle."

She looked briefly into his eyes before focusing once again on what his hands were doing.

"You're a curious young thing, aren't you?"

Aaliya smiled, but remained silent.

She continued to visit the workshop. Some days, she virtually ran the length of the Vysarq to get there as soon as she could. Tasks in the beginning were simple. Olle had her sharpening his awls and knives on the whetstone, preparing his paste, cutting out the various saddle shapes. He talked to her about forming the perfect ground-seat, about balance and ensuring the rider feels close to their horse; the tactility of leather to be cut, moulded and pressed into something of lasting practical beauty; and of being a meticulous craftsman, working with one's hands and using one's mind.

He told her all about the different hides: deer hide, cow hide, rabbit hide, their colour and texture and the variations in thickness depending on what part of the animal it came from. "The hide is thickest along the length of the animal's back, and it gets thinner towards the belly. This hide over the back is butt leather, we need this for the high-wear parts of the saddle. Here, you can feel the difference, even with your eyes closed." He taught her the various tools he used: awls for pricking, marking and stitching; knives including the half moon, the trenchet, the paring knife; as well as needles and pincers and shears. And he talked her through the parts of the saddle, "I mainly get requests now for a higher cantle and pommel to prevent the rider from being unseated in battle."

Over time he guided her through some small projects:

a small satchel with a drawstring, followed by a pressed leather journal cover. She never once complained about the messiness of the environment or the hard physical work. In fact, sometimes she felt locked into a sort of internal battle with herself while she worked away. Wondering whether she could complete the task she had been set, but not willing to show it. Her determination seemed to impress the Master Saddle Maker. His two words "well done" were not thrown around lightly, and when she heard him utter those words it was as though her insides erupted into song.

The other saddle makers would nod their heads in what appeared to be a sense of disbelief whenever she arrived. For the first year, her presence seemed to be a source of amusement. They would laugh at the way she would come to the workshop in drab, basic tunics but would be wearing the most exquisite necklaces and earrings; the way she would shift strands of long hair out of her eyes and end up smearing black grime across her face. By the second year, the laughing stopped. Aaliya would watch Olle intently and then go away and capably achieve any task set her like she was born to do it.

She was captivated by making, and not just content to follow and be guided by her experienced mentor. She created and adapted saddles from her own thoughts and ideas. There were times Olle lamented the seemingly insane decision allowing a teenage girl into his workshop. Her impulsiveness and proclivity to not think things through enough caused Olle grief on several occasions, sometimes involving time consuming repairs to delicate pieces. "Slow down," he insisted, "you are capable, you know you are, but you need to slow down and listen." Despite the age gap between them and the vastly different worlds they occupied, the friendship unexpectedly developed into something warm and trusting.

The saddles Aaliya made with Olle became sought after by lords and knights in kingdoms beyond Traegos. She worked hard and relished the pain of it. Her hands were kept soft by the lanolin and she thought they were as beautiful as the saddles she was making.

As the years passed on, Aaliya began to open up about her family, mainly talking about her mother. Olle would occasionally ask about her about her sister, but she would just look away and respond that she didn't want to talk about her. One day Olle asked her about her father. He wanted to understand her father's reaction when he received the saddle made for him. He also wanted to know why a man of Thormund's status would leave his young daughter in the hands of another man, a complete stranger who worked in the grubby, greasy world of saddle making.

Aaliya had taken a long time to respond, as if trying to organize the puzzle pieces herself. When she finally spoke, she quietly said that the saddle had been the finest piece of workmanship her father had ever seen. Although she was far from certain, she surmised that the saddle was a turning point, a symbol that Thormund Reiner had arrived. To be able to afford an object of such exquisite beauty and ride amongst men of nobility was the destination, the goal he had been working towards his whole life. When Aaliya turned her thoughts to her father's decision to leave her in the workshop that day, she shrugged her shoulders and simply said, "I think it was because he loves beautiful things."

"So go and embroider a cushion," Olle replied, unconvinced.

"Well, okay, maybe he wanted me to learn something

more challenging."

"From an old man? You were twelve! It's unheard of for a young girl of your status to be without a minder, let along work in a grubby workshop."

"You don't know my father. Hard work is life's only pursuit in his mind. I think he truly did want me to learn a craft, something where I would need to demonstrate commitment and discipline. But it goes without saying, that the end product had to be something beautiful, something lasting."

"Think I'm beginning to like the man."

"You don't know him at all."

"No, I don't. But you have to understand, your father could have chosen anything for you; embroidery, tailoring, silver-smithing. But he chose saddle making. He's a merchant, Aaliya."

"I'm not following."

"It connects to his own soul. It's about travel, expansion, movement, growth."

"Hmm," she said, looking back down at her stitching.

"You don't understand, do you?"

She didn't look up from her handiwork. "I…I think I do."

"Believe me, you'll understand when you're older. You'll understand regrets, thwarted ambition, lost love, disappointment. And you'll come across things, seemingly inexplicable things, that represent your hopes and dreams, that go deep into the core of who you are, even if for a short period of time."

"Like sentimental things?"

"I guess you could say that. Sentimental attachment is certainly a part of it, but there's more to it. The essence of what I'm trying to say is that for a while the item shapes you. And then you need to let it go, willingly or otherwise."

They resumed their work, and for a while only the sound that could be heard in the room was of leather thread being pulled through a punched hole.

Olle said at last, "It was an act of love. Your father… bringing you here. You do know this, don't you?"

She looked up at him, astonished that someone as intelligent as Olle could conclude so decisively that what her father did was an "act of love." In her mind, any love that resulted from the gesture was pure coincidence and not at all part of his original intention. "I never thought of it like that," she replied.

When Aaliya walked into the workshop, just two days after her mother's funeral, Olle was sitting on a stool at the bench as though simply waiting for her arrival.

"Come here, girl," Olle said, standing up and holding out his arms.

Aaliya walked into his embrace, buried her face in his chest and slid her arms around his tall frame. She remained in that position for a while. Worn and tired, she felt like she should be crying. But again, the tears didn't flow. She felt as washed out as an overused rag. She didn't understand it, but there seemed to be some disconnect between her sadness and her body's ability to manifest it. What resulted was a feeling of being dead inside. Living and breathing, walking and talking, but somehow not whole. Like bleeding badly from a wound you can't see. You know something is not right but it takes the reaction of another person to pull you to your senses.

It would have been a full ten minutes before Aaliya raised her head off Olle's chest and pulled herself from his embrace.

"How are you going?" Olle asked quietly.

Aaliya raised her head. "I feel…I feel off-balance. Like I'm dancing on a stage that's being dismantled. I miss her so much. This might sound strange, but it's like I'm having to relearn how to be in the world. The script that was me was taken with her to the grave. And although there was no script, just her ability to know me and accept me as only she could, her death has left me feeling incomplete. Like I'm now existing part here, part in some other place. Does that make sense?"

Olle held her close again. "Absolutely, my girl. It will take time to heal. Give yourself time."

"Father wants me to let go and move on."

"You will need to move on, eventually. But if you can, look at death, sit with death for a while. Otherwise you will not learn how to live."

"What do you mean?"

"The permanency of death is terribly confronting. Many want to run from this notion of an ending, somehow repudiate it. But loss…loss is one of the few guarantees of life. You will experience loss and there's nothing you can do to stop that happening. All you can really do, armed with this knowledge, is be present. That's what I tell myself. Here is my leather punch, here is my workshop. Just be here, now." Olle opened his arms and looked around him. "This is my life, and it's a good one. Where I used to fear death and saw only what was no longer with me, I instead started to see what was in front of me."

"But it hurts so much, Olle. Have you ever experienced anything like this before?"

"Yes. Yes I have. At my age it is hard to not be touched by death."

"I miss her so much. I want her back."

"The hurt…I know. It's unlike anything, isn't it? Your journey will be your own, it will be different from mine. But you'll arrive at the same place, Aaliya. Like I said, just give yourself time."

Olle walked out of the room and returned a short time later with a partially covered saddletree. "Now, I don't know if you're up for it…" Olle placed the saddletree and extra leather on the bench. "I want to try and fit the jockeys today."

They worked together for a while, their usual routine, before Olle broke the silence. "I noticed two men riding into the grounds of the castle late yesterday. I was quite admiring their saddles, actually. Looked like they had been made in Maghrib. Lovely high ornamental seats."

Aaliya paused from hammering, an instant quickening of her heart. "They may have been Seigneur Justen Laus and his uncle Pieter Laus. Justen is here to marry Maddalena."

"He just rides in...with his uncle? For his wedding? No other family or minders?"

"It's been hastily put together."

"Where are they from?"

"Gedion."

"Northerners," Olle said with a tone of perplexity. "Endless winter. Those ridiculous fur hats. And every meal tastes like salted fish. Well…every meal is salted fish for that matter." Olle started punching holes in the leather, getting the piece ready for stitching. "Their firewater is good though. Finya I believe it's called."

"You've been up there?"

"Yes, about six years ago I made a trip to Gedion. They're a crafty lot. I don't know if it's the cold, which somehow binds them together and sets them apart, but they certainly viewed me with suspicion. Which was fair enough. Maybe I was there doing something worthy of being suspicious of."

"Really? You?"

"Kingdoms have very distinct values and beliefs, as I'm sure you know. There may not be lines on the ground for borders, but you'll always know when you're in a new land."

"I haven't travelled at all, Olle. It would be a stroke of luck for me to be given the opportunity to see other parts of the realm."

"It's not really about luck. If it's something you really want to do, you'll make it happen."

Aaliya smirked at the simplicity of the comment. Easier said than done.

Olle started lacing the leather together. "You see some strange things in other places. In the north they have this tradition in the early spring of placing the head of a wild boar in a barrel, which is hung between two trees. Men ride towards the barrel and before they veer off they throw a spear at it in the hope of knocking the head out. The one who does manage to knock the head out is the 'lumivere', the darkness lifter. The wild boar symbolizes the long, dark winter, which must be cast off so that spring may come. Men, women and children then sit around fires and roast black sausages. The men drink their fair share of Finya. Who knows what goes into those sausages. They taste pretty good though."

Aaliya's head was down, focused on her task.

Olle continued, "People are moving across borders

everywhere. No longer content to stay in one place. This kingdom used to be the only place for high-level craftsmanship. The epicenter of production for all things beautiful and necessary."

"So what's changed that?"

"Many things. Ship building in Rone, for one. Their ports are flourishing. Rone is attracting skilled workers from far and wide as merchants there are able to move goods more efficiently."

"What keeps you here?"

"I have good work here," he said, "and, some unfinished affairs."

A loud knock startled them both. They both turned in the direction of the door, which creaked open and a young woman wearing a white, tightly gathered dress entered the room. Catja had a petite frame and an impossibly long neck. She had a tendency to shape her eyebrows into almost a straight line, which combined with her deep set eyes, made her appear more serious than her character actually was. She was a young woman who wanted to live an extraordinary life and kept prodding Aaliya to try new things and new experiences. And although Aaliya was hungry for experiences too, she was also a content daydreamer happy in her thoughts or making and reading.

"Good morning, Olle. Aaliya, I thought I would find you here," Catja said, closing the door behind her.

"Good morning, Catja," replied Olle.

Aaliya hadn't been able to share her grief with Catja since the loss of her mother. It was like such discussions inconvenienced Catja; interrupted the flow of her sunny, optimistic demeanour. Olle was the only person who seemed to 'get' her. He could sit with discomfort or difficult emotions. In fact, it was like he valued these things and saw them instead as leading to even deeper connection. Catja was always advising Aaliya that she won't attract a man being morose or depressed. Aaliya didn't think of herself as morose, just a person with feelings that sometimes couldn't be hidden or compressed.

"What's going on?" Aaliya asked.

"You've got dance practice, my friend. Your sister's wedding is only days away and we've got much to perfect," said Catja with the authority of a teacher.

Aaliya released an audible groan. She was sure the gods were punishing her for being a recalcitrant child. When she danced, her arms and legs floundered around like limbs on different trees. She wholeheartedly loved music, but this appreciation had never manifested into an ability to move with a sense of bodily coordination.

Catja made her way for the door, and Aaliya, walking backwards, shoulders slumped, farewelled Olle.

5

The Dance Practice

From a distance, the group of women dancing in the late morning sun looked like a copse of strange trees. Thin bodies and long bending arms swayed and rocked. Their silhouettes appeared graceful, though somewhat peculiar. Not quite belonging to the world around them. It was Aaliya's favourite part of the Ansgar Castle grounds. The area was wide, open, and in the summer heat, appeared as a brassy haze. The ring of limestone outcrops and pine trees along the perimeter gave the place the feel of a natural arena.

Catja and Aaliya walked towards the dancers and crossed the grounds under the shade of an oversized oak tree. Instant relief. Aaliya wondered why they weren't practicing under the magnificent tree while it was so hot.

"You're late," Maddalena said as the two women approached. She continued with her moves, clapping and twirling.

"I'm sorry," Aaliya replied, trying to fall in with the steps she only vaguely knew. "Caught up with something else."

"Please tell me it was doing something exciting."

"It doesn't get much better than rigging leather over

a saddle tree."

The other ladies laughed.

"See," Maddalena said looking around her. "It's embarrassing."

The woman out the front of the gathering had a face like a dried pear, brown and fissured. Her grey hair was pulled back into a bun so tight her eyes looked as though they were being stretched by invisible fingers. She paused from clicking her castanet and gave Maddalena and Aaliya a stern look, before once again resuming the snapping of the instrument. It crossed Aaliya's mind that she may have stood a chance with dancing if only she had a teacher who wasn't so wooden and trite.

Aaliya leaned in towards Maddalena. "How are you feeling about the wedding?"

Maddalena opened her mouth wide as if to yawn. The very word 'wedding' seemed to create an instant drowsiness over her. "I'm looking forward to seeing the gifts I shall receive. I have asked for gold, and I do hope I receive plenty."

"You have an interesting way of looking at something that is about to change your life forever."

"Oh, don't get all philosophical on me. I know what it's about. And looking forward to being given gold is as worthy a feeling as any for an otherwise dull affair. You'll understand that one day."

It was the first conversation they had had since their mother's funeral. The realization of what was taking place in a couple of day's time finally hit Aaliya. A ripple of tension ran along her shoulders. Her arms became as stiff as wooden blocks. The knot that had been there in her stomache all those months as her mother withered seemed to tighten and constrict. She had pushed thoughts of Justen down so low she was sure they were literally gathering dust. Mother is dying, that's all you can focus on she had repeatedly told herself. It's all you're allowed to focus on. Be there for mother. Mother. Mother. And now, with her gone, Justen entered her head fully formed. That thought that had been pushed down so low now reared like a monolith behind her eyes. And she couldn't unsee him. He was there whether her eyes were closed or open. She felt disgusted at herself. How could she replace thoughts of her mother so quickly? What a shameful thing to do! Did you really love her as much as you thought you did? It was merely an affair, she admonished herself, and it was two years ago. It belongs to a time forgotten. But why was something that was supposedly little more than a temporary tryst causing such havoc in her mind all of a sudden? Why was she sweating like an ox at the thought of seeing him again, maybe today, maybe tomorrow? He was marrying her sister. She had convinced herself that if she didn't acknowledge her feelings for Justen while her mother was dying, that they would just fade into some imaginary backdrop. She had never been more wrong about anything in her life.

The instructor came over to Aaliya, grabbed her wrist and lifted up her arm in a motion of frustration. Aaliya made a weak attempt at adjusting, before falling back into lackadaisical movements.

As if sensing Aaliya's turmoil, Maddalena blurted out, "Mother would be disappointed. Again. She said something about friendship being important in a marriage."

It took a moment for Aaliya to realize that her sister was talking to her. "She said the same thing to me. Sounds like good advice."

"But then I wouldn't have Justen, would I? And there's

a sweet victory right there."

Aaliya sensed her sister's eyes on her, possibly trying to determine her reaction. Aaliya became suddenly aware of the soundlessness of the other women. Even the instructor wasn't telling the women to be quiet anymore. Maddalena's moves seemed to become more fluid and natural like she had just got an annoying pebble out of her shoe. Aaliya looked to the instructor and did her best to do the same, but kept faltering.

The lesson dragged on. The sun was high and hot. The slight breeze which had kept much of the morning pleasant, had disappeared.

Then something caught the instructor's eye. She craned her neck like a bird. Her moves became suddenly accentuated, the clicking of the castanet took on a new vigour. It was like she was doing a private recital for the king.

Aaliya looked behind her. Everyone turned around. Two men were approaching on horseback. As they came closer Aaliya recognized them: Justen and Pieter. Her first thought was that they had changed little over the past couple of years. With every step their horses made towards the gathering, Aaliya felt her knees get weaker. This was not good timing to see Justen. Aaliya could barely hide her discomfort. She felt messy, unpredictable. She knew this moment was coming when they would see each other again. There had to be a better scenario: sitting across from each other at dinner, a chance meeting while out riding, anything so long as she had just a bit more time to recover from the event she had just experienced. But practicing an activity for which she had the skill level of a turtle, all the while standing beside someone who had the perceptiveness of a hound, was about the worst possible scenario imaginable.

"Come now, ladies," the instructor said. "Sharpen your moves. Aaliya! Where is your head? Left arm across your body, be graceful, my girl. Like a swan!"

Even though the instructor clearly wasn't appreciating her effort, Aaliya silently congratulated herself on being able to do anything remotely coordinated.

Pieter and Justen pulled up their horses close to the small group. The two horses were black and so dense with muscle they looked as though they could cross whole seas. Justen adjusted himself in his saddle and for a moment looked as though he was contemplating dismounting. His eyes swept across the faces in front of him. When his eyes found Aaliya's, he instantly smiled. He still had those dimples set into his cheeks that she was so fond of years ago, that handsome clownish appearance. She was sure he relished this playful aspect of himself. She smiled back and self-consciously ran her hand along her hair which was bunched up in a messy braid. She resisted looking down at what she was wearing, but knew it to be one of her functional tunics she normally wore when visiting the workshop. They lingered there a moment longer than they should have. His eyes then moved across to Maddalena, still standing beside Aaliya. He tucked long pieces of hair behind his ears, nodded his head and smiled again. He then closed his eyes for the briefest of moments, as though giving himself an opportunity to realign himself.

Two years ago when they had first met, Justen's looks struck Aaliya as somewhat otherworldly. His skin was pale, almost translucent, and in stark contrast to the bronzed look she was familiar with. His dark hair was sticking out in every direction like something he had tried to tame but had given up on. A beard wrapped around the bottom of his oval face and even that had a certain dishevelment. But he seemed so utterly comfortable with himself. No pretention, no insecurities.

They had sat across from each other during a dinner in the Great Hall. Justen had been visiting Traegos with his uncle to establish a trade route for copper, which had been found in the cold, black hills of Gedion. Winter was bearing down on the inhabitants of Ansgar with a great fury at the time and the company of Justen simply seemed to render the bleakness to light. It was never meant to be a serious thing. They initially thought they had limited time to be together. Aaliya had seen her father wrap up deals in days with less confident merchants. The two visitors from Gedion, however, had the same dogged determination as Thormund and the negotiations stretched into weeks. The two lovers threw themselves into their passion. For Aaliya, it was a new world she knew nothing about but let herself be guided by her hunger to explore.

When it looked like the deal had finally been struck, a storm rolled over the land like a great curse. The sky heaved with rain for another couple of weeks and the land turned to mud. The mountain pass back to Gedion became impassable. Their reckless, feverish lovemaking of the early days turned into a slow burn where every touch, every gesture was slowed down and savoured. In Justen's arms Aaliya found a place that felt like home. She believed that everything was right and good in the world.

Although they had the luxury of additional weeks, it still came to an end too quickly for both of them. Aaliya watched Justen leave from the window of her bedroom. He looked back, his eyes darting all over the front of her home to find hers. When their eyes did meet on that winter morning, a sad but beholden look passed between them. Aaliya felt loved and valued, and Justen had enriched her life immensely.

"Good afternoon, ladies," Pieter said, bringing Aaliya back out of her thoughts.

The group of women chorused their reply.

Catja, ever bold, stepped forward slightly to greet the two men. "Are you both enjoying Ansgar?" she asked.

"We're enjoying it immensely," Pieter replied. "You've picked a fine spot to rehearse your dancing. I've never seen such a beautiful vista before." Pieter was all decked out in his finest Gedion livery: a green satin jacket and knee length riding boots, and on his head a wool hat with a red ostrich feather. His pale face was moist and flushed, his large aquiline nose as red as a cherry. Aaliya imagined Pieter to be a man who would normally take great care with his grooming rituals. Riding during the hot afternoon, however, seemed to turn his normally taut, balmed moustache into a shaggy, brown nest. And there in the middle of his face, as if lost in the sheer expanse of his long, unblemished forehead, were his small blue eyes.

Aaliya's eyes turned back to Justen. She wanted him to look at her again. To give her a sign that he was feeling it too, this aching to be touched, for their lips to meet. Just when she thought she could not bear his averted eyes any longer, he looked her way. A warm smile crossed his face. They lingered in that place of obliviousness probably a bit too long again, but for Aaliya, she could have happily built a home there. It was a wonderful place to lose herself.

"Seigneur Laus, how will you be spending your time until your wedding?" Catja asked mischievously.

Aaliya rolled her eyes. Unbelievable, she thought.

"I do believe I'll be meeting with the king and Seigneur Reiner this evening. I'm sure they will have some suggestions of sport to partake it," Justen said.

"Sport?" Catja said. "Traegos is famous for its sport."

Giggles burst from the women. Even Aaliya couldn't hide a smile. The instructor, however, maintained stern composure.

Catja continued, "Archery perhaps? Horse-riding along the river? I have heard the forests hold particular appeal for those from Gedion."

Aaliya coughed and nervously rubbed the side of her forehead. As she had seen her do many times before, Catja was skilfully piecing the puzzle together with the selective information she had. Aaliya momentarily considered ending this speculation now. Throwing up her hands and shouting, "I surrender. Yes, Justen's the one I had an affair with two years ago." But it was only a momentary consideration. Aaliya simply wasn't ready to have this revealed to her sister.

"*All* of Ansgar is worth exploring," Aaliya said, "as I'm sure you found on your ride this afternoon." She cringed slightly at the awkwardness of her own words.

"Indeed we did," Justen replied.

Maddalena stepped forward, a gesture of confidence after standing behind others for too long. "I would be honoured to join you to do some *exploring*," she said with particular enunciation of her final word.

Pieter piped up. "Madame, that would be wonderful. I look forward to talking to your father and arranging this for - "

"Right now, Seigneur Laus. Right now." Maddalena stepped closer to Justen. "Do help me up please."

Justen reached down from his saddle to grab hold of

Maddalena's arm and hoisted her up onto the back of his horse.

"I've grown weary of this session. Goodbye ladies," Maddalena said with a smile.

Maddalena wrapped her arms around Justen's waist and the three on horseback cantered away.

"Right. I think we're finished here today," the instructor announced, wearily concluding there was no hope of anyone concentrating now.

Aaliya was grateful. She couldn't take anymore prancing around in the sun after watching Maddalena ride off like the victor winning the prize. She started making her way back towards the bridge with her friend.

Catja hooked her arm into Aaliya's. "He's the one, isn't he?"

"What?" She briefly considered denying it, then thought, what was the point of lying. "Yes. Yes he is."

"Ouch. That's got to hurt."

"You have no idea."

"Does Maddalena know?"

"No." Aaliya shook her head. "You can't tell her, Catja."

"What's there to tell? You had an affair a couple of years ago and fell in love. You probably still love him, but he's about to marry someone else and you'll both be going your separate ways. That's the story, isn't it?"

"Yes. No. I don't know."

Catja tugged on Aaliya's arm and they stopped walking. "What are you thinking?" Catja asked.

"Nothing." Aaliya tried to appear calm and unfazed.

Catja looked at her with an expression of disbelief. "Nothing?" she repeated.

It was useless. Aaliya had kept it to herself, but now

just wanted to let it out. "I still want him."

"And?"

"And what?"

"And your next move is…?"

"I don't know, Catja. My mind's a muddle. I went to my mother's funeral two days ago. Justen turns up. He's about to marry my sister."

"Mmm. Tricky."

"That's putting it mildly."

"You could just let it all go. Keep to yourself over the next couple of days. Lay low. Before you know it, it's wedding day, they do their thing then they take off back to his homeland where you don't see them again for a long time."

"Yeah. I could do that."

"But that's not what you're going to do, is it?"

Aaliya didn't know the answer to that. No plan had formed in her head.

"I remember walking across these grounds with you," Catja continued, "the day you told me about your first passionate affair. I couldn't get enough of your recollections of making love in the forest or this man having his way with you in the back shed of your home. I know you've kissed other boys before, and we've shared some great stories about fooling around with the young men around here. But that day I could see something in you had changed. You had fallen in love. There was this buzz around you."

Aaliya nodded, agreeing.

"It's still around you."

"It's crazy, Catja," Aaliya said, shaking her head.

"Crazy. Love does that to a person."

They kept walking, Aaliya's mind wandering to her previous affair with Justen.

"Can I make a suggestion?" Catja said at last.

Aaliya nodded.

"If you're feeling the need to let your hair down, there's a dance on at the Willowmead Inn tomorrow night."

"I can't go there. My father would kill me if he found out."

"Come by my place around ten o'clock if you're interested."

"I won't be up for it," Aaliya said.

"We'll see," Catja said, smiling.

"In seven days he'll be married."

"Yes. In seven days."

Outrageous and risky as it was, Aaliya still wanted Justen. She wanted his hands on her, wanted his lips covering her. She wanted him, body and soul. And Aaliya thought that maybe, even if it was for just a brief moment, that might be enough to satisfy the hunger inside her.

It would only be a short time. A brief fling. No harm need come from it if done in secret. The wedding was very close.

Only seven days.

6

Perfect Creations

Maddalena dipped her finger into the bowl of water on the bedside table. Scalding. She could never get her baths to be this hot, but this would be how she would have them every time if she could. She imagined sinking in warm blood and felt instantly relaxed. She propped her foot up onto the bed and reached for the jar of cream on the table. The concoction was thin and oily, and smelled of myrrh and calamus. It smelled of sex. But she drew that connection a little more readily than other people. The cream was prepared especially for her by the apothecary. She smeared it along the length of her leg below her knee. Pulling the razor out of the bowl of water, she ran the blade slowly up her leg.

"Do you ever take your eyes off my cunt?" she asked, wiping the excess cream onto a small towel and dropping the razor back into the bowl.

Santo didn't avert his eyes from her naked sex. "Well, not when your cunt is so close to my face." He propped himself up further with his elbow, his head cradled in his hand.

He reached out towards Maddalena's sex, desiring to touch her moist flesh. She smacked his hand away and then ran her fingers along the springy softness of her pubic hair.

"Do you see my cunt when it's not in front of your face? Do you imagine my cunt when you're tailoring the king's clothes?"

He smiled a weak smile. "Oh yes, my Queen, my most perfect creations have emerged from pondering your sweet cunt all day."

"Liar."

Maddalena smeared a film of cream over her pubic hair and then daubed some on her nipple. Her thumb and forefinger lingered on her nipple, pulling and twisting it. She pulled the razor from the scalding water. "I think you need some new inspiration to create your tailored masterpieces," she said, giving an ecstatic little cry as the hot razor pressed against her sensitive flesh. She dragged the razor over her mound, wiping the tangled mass of black hair from the razor and then eagerly dipped it back into the hot water. The razor was the width of her little finger and she carefully scraped away more hair. Even working slowly and carefully, small nicks emerged. Trickles of blood ran down her leg, red drops fell onto the floor.

"You're bleeding," Santo said, slightly horror struck.

"'Tis nothing," she said, wiping between her legs with the towel. She admired her newly shaven skin, only a small amount of hair remained nestled between her legs where the razor could not reach.

Maddalena climbed on top of Santo, pinning him between her legs. Her nicks continued to weep blood. She moved her face close to his and, darting her tongue out, penetrated his mouth and encircled his tongue. She felt his cock stiffen and rubbed her sex against his. His head in her hands she kissed him savagely, barely able to restrain the frenzy rising inside of her. He tried to ease her over his hardened cock, but she resisted.

She leaned forward for the razor, one of her breasts falling into his mouth which he nibbled like a mouse.

"Someone once said to me 'order is the foundation of success'," Maddalena said grabbing the razor and cream from the table. "We're about success, Santo, you and I. An orderly, clean body is akin to holiness, don't you think?"

"You're still bleeding."

"Do you fear a bit of blood?" Maddalena rested her rump on his thighs and smeared some cream over the pubic hair encircling his erect penis.

"I don't know about this," he said, a slight quiver in his voice.

"Blood is so messy."

"Yes it is. Could you put that razor down?"

"Blood is never tidy. But if you fear it, you have lost. I don't ever intend to lose."

She swiped the razor across his skin, roughly pulling it off in the last instant. Santo gasped as a small pool of blood gathered in his groin before flowing over his leg. Maddalena turned around and straddled his chest, her buttocks near his face. She continued shaving all around his cock, over his balls. Occasionally she sucked his cock in between swipes with the razor. She could tell he felt delirious for her body and he pressed his thumb into her ass. She rocked back and forth and sucked him more firmly. But then flung his hand away from her rump and continued to shave him.

Santo remained lying perfectly still. She knew what he was feeling. That acute sense of both arousal and fear each time the hot razor touched the skin. And every time the razor was removed he let out a groan of relief.

When she finished, Maddalena dropped the razor

onto the floor, spread the cheeks to her buttocks apart, and pressed her body over his penis until he was deep inside her. They both groaned deeply, a sense of release at finally reaching this point. Maddalena reached up and rested her hands on the top of her head, watching her reflection in the mirror across the room. She basked in the spectacle of her body, her jiggling breasts, her long black hair, her firm round belly. She reached down between the folds of her flesh and rubbed, coming a while thereafter with a violence that matched her bloodied body. As she was crying out, she felt Santo shake and shudder beneath her. And she continued to cry out as warm life leapt inside her.

When her body started to cool down, Maddalena removed herself from Santo's embrace and got up off the bed. It was mid afternoon and the sun was at its hottest. Lying naked and doing very little seemed like the most sensible thing to do under the circumstances. She would love to linger, but it was becoming increasingly difficult. The castle felt particularly crowded at the moment in the lead up to the wedding. People seemed to be milling about everywhere. How relieved she would be when this wedding was over. She pondered that thought for a moment as she started pulling on her clothes. She'd miss her boys terribly, but she'd find new playmates, wouldn't she? Playmates were easy enough to find. None in the league of Santo and Joshva, though. She had gone through times when neither of them would be able to be in her arms for a week, sometimes two. Those were times of darkness in her opinion. It was like her skin turned to sand, her hair became limp, her eyes dull. Food tasted differently, like everything had been boiled too long leeching out all that was good and flavoursome. In their arms, she felt whole. She was the person she liked being. She felt fully erotic. In their arms, her mouth wasn't just for taking in food and water, it was an extension of her sex, moist and ready. Her hair became that of a wild animal, ragged and bristling. Her eyes became alive to all that was happening around her. It was as though she could see things with a greater clarity, like a cat in the dark, even at the very anticipation of seeing her boys.

Maybe Justen would be a decent lover for a while? Although he wasn't Joshva or Santo, maybe he would be enough? She wondered if he already had lovers in his home city that he was no doubt keen to get back to. And if he could have lovers, why couldn't she? Maddalena had tried to glean this out of him when they rode off together after the dance practice earlier in the day. As his horse slowed to a walk in the royal forest, she had said to Justen, "You're a very handsome man. I imagine you've had many lovers to keep you warm in your icy northern land. Still have them, don't you?"

Justen stifled a laugh. "Not the kind of conversation I was anticipating on the eve of our wedding."

"You may jest, but I do believe I am right. I am simply preparing my heart for the inevitable grief that awaits me when my husband finds comfort and solace in the arms of another."

Maddalena wished for a moment that his back wasn't facing her and that she could see his eyes.

"You talk like you already know my character and have an expectation of what I'm likely to do in the future."

"I've been married before, which I'm sure you've been

made aware of. I'm simply speaking the truth as I know it to be."

"How about we both start with a clean slate and not have expectations."

"How convenient."

"What do you mean by that?"

"What I mean is the slate is never clean. The slate is in fact very grubby. I expect why you're marrying me is wrapped up in some sense of duty. You're honour bound, otherwise, why would you be doing this? But you still want what you want. You just don't want people to know. Believe me, I understand. So how about we…for the sake of our blessed matrimonial union…acknowledge that some things just need to be." Her hands moved from his hips to his thighs, where she gave him a gentle squeeze.

He didn't respond at first, and then said, "I think I'd better take you home."

"Come now. We're alone in the forest. Two people just days away from being husband and wife. You're not bound by tradition too, are you? I mean, I'm soiled goods anyway." Her hands moved between his thighs.

"Let's…let's be bound by tradition on this occasion."

Maddalena released a slight snort and moved her hands away.

"I'll take you home," Justen said.

"I have business to attend to at the castle, if you don't mind taking me there." Then she added, "In the spirit of tradition, you should tell me whereabouts in the castle you are staying. We can't run into each other before the wedding, can we?"

Justen described the location of his and Pieter's rooms on the third floor of the castle, which Maddalena was pleased to hear. As far as she knew, no one else was occupying a room on the fourth floor. Which is why, on this day, she was surprised to hear voices out in the corridor. Santo was watching her get dressed and seemed oblivious to the chattering outside their door, but Maddalena felt instantly uneasy.

She moved over to the door and motioned with her finger against her lip for Santo to remain silent. Maddalena pressed her ear hard against the wooden panel.

"The road particularly needs improving at Tors Ravine. The mountain pass is so narrow there we had a team of four horses and a cartload of goods go over the cliff three weeks ago." The voice of Viggo was instantly recognizable to Maddalena.

"Mmm, it's perilous indeed," replied a wheezy, breathless voice that also seemed familiar.

"Plans are already underway to improve the port facilities at Marius."

"At Marius?"

"It's a strategic move," Viggo could be heard saying. "We're looking to decrease our reliance on the River Albo over the long term."

"Mmm, very wise."

They had stopped outside the room where Maddalena and Santo remained inside. Maddalena knelt down silently and looked through the keyhole. She saw Viggo standing with two other men. One of the men was whom she suspected the wheezy, raspy voice belonged to: Pieter. He was leaning over, struggling for breath after the steep climb to the fourth floor. The other man was one Maddalena had not seen before. He wore an oilskin jacket, his hair was red and his face somehow disfigured as though he had been in a fight recently.

"Such a shame we can not progress these ambitions through diplomacy alone," Pieter said.

"That's what marriage is for."

"Well, yes, that's what I was referring to. It seems to take the binding nature of a marriage to effectuate important arrangements between our kingdoms," Pieter said dryly.

"An alliance linked by blood is always preferable. We were unlucky with the untimely passing of Renatus's son. The availability of Seigneur Reiner's eldest daughter is fortuitous in order to see the alliance through." Viggo then added, "Now you wanted me up here for a reason, Pieter?"

"Yes, yes. Down here is a room we can discuss things in."

"You seem to know the castle well…" Viggo said, before his voice trailed off as the three men walked further down the corridor.

Why was Pieter having a private meeting with the king's financial advisor on the deserted fourth floor? And who was the other man? She had never seen him before in the company of Viggo, so presumed him to be an associate of Pieter. The presence of the three men only confirmed that she was not the only one seeking a secluded space free from prying eyes and ears. She stood up and looked enviously at Santo lying on the bed, seemingly without a worry in the world.

Maddalena said goodbye to her naked friend and surreptitiously stepped out into the corridor. She closed the door gently. In a few hours she would be back in the castle having dinner with the king and her husband-to-be. The sensible thing to do would be to walk towards the steps and make her way home.

Her feet lightly padded along the floor in the direction

the three men had gone. She pressed her ear against each door as she went, listening and occasionally peering through the keyhole. Mid-way along the corridor she stopped with a sense of excitement when she heard voices on the other side of a door. She lowered her body and peered through the keyhole.

"…mining side of things with this venture."

"Yes," she heard Viggo say.

The back of the red-headed man blocked her view of Viggo and Pieter.

"How splendid. I see future opportunities. Much to gain, wouldn't you say?"

"Certainly. Although Redshade is in its infancy. Gedion has established strength in mining. But it will not take much time for Traegos to catch up."

"Hmmm," crooned Pieter, "you're quite the crusader, aren't you."

"I am the king's financial advisor. I see it as my duty to provide the best possible economic outcomes for my kingdom."

"Oh yes, yes, yes. You won't hear an argument from me. It is very admirable what you are doing for your kingdom. Great even. You strike me as a man who understands the need to take action. You are a gambler, are you not?"

Viggo didn't respond straight away. "Yes."

"You don't have children?"

"What's that got to do with anything?"

"Correct me if I'm wrong, Seigneur Vennamo, but your penchant for wealth and power are understandable and, in my opinion, commendable qualities. I don't believe I am entirely different. But what I find most interesting about you is that you have a gift for calculating odds that makes you quite dangerous."

"What is your point?" Maddalena detected a note of irritability in Viggo's voice.

"If there's any point to be made, it's simply that it's quite fortunate for you to be the king's financial advisor. Few questions would be asked. Few people to answer to. Just the king really and his cognizance of late has been in doubt, has it not?"

"If you're referring to Redshade, I keep Thormund Reiner fully informed. And together we keep those in the advisory up to date."

"What exactly are you letting them know? What is there to inform them of?"

Maddalena pressed her ear even harder against the wood.

"I suggest your friend leaves the room."

"Oh no, I insist he stay."

"Well then I shall leave."

Maddalena saw through the keyhole the figure of Viggo walking around the red-headed man and making his way to the door. She quickly stood up ready to flee, but then she heard Pieter say, "So incredibly courageous of you. Acting when other men are too timid to act."

No more movement could be heard inside the room and she peered back through the keyhole to see that Viggo had stopped walking towards the door.

Pieter continued, "Everyone else talks about Traegos's reliance on other kingdoms for raw materials. You're doing something about it."

"I'm grateful for the flattery."

"There surely must be something underneath that cruel earth. Iron Steppes I believe it's called? Yes, something to bring grown men to their knees. After all, people want something to hope for even when they don't know what they want. There's money to be made in hope. That's where you see yourself fitting in. A crusader galloping into the vast space of uncertainty."

"I believe I've heard enough."

Pieter seemed to have not heard Viggo's comment. "And paper currency as well? Ingenious really. You have been very busy indeed convincing those around you of your brilliance. There is a problem though, isn't there? If word gets out there is nothing to be mined at the Iron Steppes, things could get a little rocky for you. And if Redshade collapses and all that investment into paper money collapses…well, who knows? We could be witnessing the first kingdom to go into bankruptcy. You carry a great burden on your shoulders indeed."

"You know nothing," Viggo said. But even Maddalena could tell there was a edge of shakiness to his voice.

"I know everything. Mining exploration is a great strength of mine. Another strength of mine in providing the best possible economic outcomes for my kingdom, which I believe you claim to share."

"What do you want from me?" Viggo said, his tone icy.

There was a long pause before Pieter finally said, "I need you to do what you do best."

"What's that?"

"Manipulate people."

Silence.

Pieter continued, "Let me explain."

"Oh my Queeeeen! What are you doing down there?"

Maddalena turned her head to the side in disbelief and saw Santo standing outside the room where they had spent time together. Through gritted teeth she mouthed the words "shut-up" and sliced her hand menacingly across her neck. In the next instant she raced down the corridor. She had never run so hard in her life. She heard a door open and footsteps racing towards her. She grabbed Santo roughly by his arm just as she was about to pass, and started pulling him along.

"Go! Go!" she growled.

They leapt down the steps three at a time.

"Just get to a safe place," she said between breaths. "Don't repeat this to anyone. Understand me?"

Maddalena didn't wait for him to answer. She turned right off the stairwell on the second level, and gave Santo a nudge to head left. She could still hear footsteps in pursuit and sprinted ahead, frantically looking from side to side in the hope of seeing a door ajar. She had to get into a room and soon.

She turned another corner and started to feel disorientated. Up ahead she saw two people walking towards her. She slowed down to a brisk walk. The couple looked her way as they passed. The man smiled and the woman remained expressionless. She hurried further along the corridor until she came across and enormous doorway. She walked into the chapel and sat down heavily in one of the seats. She had never felt so grateful for religion. Four other people were sitting in the room, scattered amongst the pews. Above her the ceiling soared to such an immense height she momentarily thought birds with giant wing spans would be at home in the space. She looked back down at her lap and leaned forward, trying to make her body small.

Her mind was racing. Just a couple more minutes listening at the door and she'd have so much more understanding of what Pieter and Viggo were up to. Maddalena had never heard Viggo with a tone of vulnerability in his voice. Usually the man was supreme confidence, if not outright insolence. He had an unwavering belief in himself and everything he did. But if Pieter was to be believed, it was all a sham. Redshade, the mineral wealth to be found there, printed currency. All of it. A big, monumental lie that could have terrible consequences for her father, for her.

Her heart was thumping loudly, ringing in her ears and making it difficult to think straight. She had to tell her father, but how? The man was hardly open to discussions questioning Viggo's honour. Maddalena had tried on so many occasions over the years to do this, backed up only by her gut-feeling, to find herself firmly shut down. It was quite difficult to love the man sometimes.

In a few hours she would be back in the castle having dinner with the king. Her family would be present. And so would Pieter. It would be one of those affairs where everyone is so excruciatingly cordial. Maddalena cringed at the thought. The man who had chased her had only seen her from behind. But he would no doubt report to Pieter what he had seen. She noticed her dress and felt the need to strip off right there in the chapel.

More than anything, she wanted to get her father alone. It was unlikely to happen tonight.

People came and went over the next hour. She stood up and made her way to the door, gingerly looked out into the corridor and then started her way back home.

7

Leap of Faith

The carrier swayed and rocked with the muscle of the two horses. Inside was luxurious and tactile. Large fringed cushions embroidered with elaborate patterns, velvety furs and sheepskin rugs draped the wooden seats. The canvas roof reached up to a point in the centre giving the confined space a feeling of openness.

Ever since they entered the carrier outside their home, the three passengers had been silent and pensive. Thormund fixed his gaze out the side, his hand peeling back and holding onto the red and white striped curtain. Maddalena was seated beside him looking ahead, her sight trained upon Aaliya, who was facing her. They looked at each other without uttering a word. Every now and then a blink, a subtle shift, or a rubbing of forefinger and thumb would take place and momentarily ease the troubled atmosphere. It was as though wire had been wound around the small space and was gradually being tightened.

"You've changed clothes today," Maddalena said mockingly, ending the long silence.

Aaliya looked down at her long green dress and then looked up at Maddalena. "Not like you to notice something about my appearance."

Maddalena leaned forward. "Anyone would think you're out to impress someone."

Aaliya smiled. "I'm out to impress everyone."

"Funny."

"It wasn't meant to be funny. It's simply about time I dressed like a woman of my position, isn't it, father?"

Thormund turned and glared at her, then tilted his head and looked back out the side of the carrier.

Aaliya looked back at Maddalena. "What's going on?" she asked.

"What do you mean?"

"You're not looking your usual tidy self," Aaliya continued.

Maddalena's eyes narrowed. "Nella wasn't available." She tucked some loose strands behind her ear.

"Nella wasn't available to groom you on your first formal evening with your betrothed?"

"The woman's a cumbersome burden who spends more time dusting than tending to my needs." Maddalena turned to face Thormund. "She should go, father."

Thormund looked at his eldest daughter and then returned to looking out the side. Deep in thought, it seemed that only an event as cataclysmic as a fire underneath them would break his focus. Aaliya was relieved of her father's indifference on this occasion and a wry smile spread across her face. In her opinion, Nella was a constant scapegoat for Maddalena's misdemeanours.

"You'll be leaving soon anyway," Aaliya said. "I hope your new maid in Gedion is as…um…discreet, as Nella has been."

"My new maid will be exactly what I want her to be

because I'll be the mistress of my household. And if I don't like her, I'll get rid of her," Maddalena said with a click of her fingers.

"Madame Laus might have a say in that. I've heard she's quite the dominating matriarch."

"What would you know?"

Aaliya had heard rumours over the years about Justen's mother. She wasn't sure what was myth and what was reality, but she simply couldn't let go of this opportune moment to unhinge her sister a little. "Word is she prowls the corridors of the Laus home like a she-wolf, sniffing out any hint of rotten meat that might harm her clan. She hears every uttering, sees every gesture, no matter how subtle or innocent. A chair out of place, a cup left on a table, a wave of a hand, nothing escapes her notice.

"And that's just within her home. Out in the city she is known as The Black Mamba. She comes across as shy, demure, but she will lash out viciously at anyone who harms her or her family. She's said to have considerable power in Gedion but it's not well known..."

"That's enough," Thormund said staunchly, releasing his hold on the curtain. "It's bad enough we don't know what to expect from tonight, let alone from this alliance with the Laus family."

"Do we even know if King Renatus is going to turn up tonight?" Maddalena asked.

"I have certainly strongly urged him to do so," replied Thormund.

"I don't know why you insist on him being present when he disappoints you so much whenever he is," Aaliya said.

Thormund leaned forward and tilted his head slightly.

"How we behave is scrutinized by all. If the king is seen as weak, if his life is perceived to be chaotic, that filters down and touches everyone in this kingdom. I've worked hard to help Traegos to thrive, to ensure Renatus and his family have all they need to take on Gedion and Rone and every other bloody wayward state around us. He owes me now. I need this to be a night without incident. Our Gedion visitors will be watching closely."

Aaliya thought she saw a look of concern on Maddalena's face. Her sister's expression of haughty defiance present only a moment ago seemed to have disappeared. Thormund leaned back in his seat and the three travellers returned to their stony silence, the activity outside their carrier on the balmy night providing just enough interest to get them through the remaining distance to the castle door.

They were lead through the cloisters to the entrance of the Great Hall. Thormund stood on the threshold, Aaliya and Maddalena behind him. At first he hesitated upon seeing King Renatus seated at the end of the table. He gave a shallow bow, and then proceeded to a chair at the king's side. Queen Viktoria was pacing beside the window. The chiffon of her dress rustling with each subtle movement she made. Her long hair, streaked with grey, had been savagely pulled back and coiled above her shoulders. Her discomfort appeared like a symbol between her eyebrows. As if needing something to hold onto, her long fingers nervously ran over the brocade feature on the curtain. She looked up when the three guests entered the room, and lowered her hands to her side.

"Come and sit down now," the king urged his wife with a flap of his hand. His other hand was firmly gripped on a glass of wine, which was brought to his wide mouth and emptied in one smooth motion. He was already as glazed over as a stuffed pigeon. His eyes were boiling, red and raw.

Aaliya looked at the portraits lining the walls. At the far end of the room was a painting of a man who was known as the 'peasant knight'. Alvaro Clausen, the founder of the Kingdom of Traegos some three hundred years before. The portrait featured a young man with long brown hair, neatly trimmed beard and steady, brown eyes exuding assuredness. He sat in his white long sleeved smock thick with embroidery of turquoise and gold beside an open window through which one could see the flat plains of Traegos with the peaks of the Great Anjar Range in the distance.

Aaliya's eyes rested on the portrait of the current king. Renatus Clausen had been painted during the Battle of Barmer. Decked out in his shiny finest. A proud expression on his face. Clutching his helmet to his side. His hand resting on the hilt of his sword. Red gloves. Aaliya wondered if he had insisted on red gloves. No other portrait featured the shock of red. Perhaps he wanted eyes drawn to him. To his hands. His doing hands. His commander hands. His hands dipped in blood.

People spoke in whispers about the Battle Of Barmer. For the first time ever, Traegos was defeated. And it happened under Renatus's watch, his command. Aaliya didn't need to be a general to imagine the humiliation. It would become all you're remembered for. Your supposed weakness, your perceived lack of courage.

The king clutched his wine a little tighter as if he himself had also just become aware of the situation. Victors from that conflict were here in his castle. He ran his large paw-like hand around his beard, as if suspecting it may appear shabby and needed to be smoothed down. He seemed to suddenly have an awareness his meaty shoulders were slumped like a man disappointed. He sat up a little straighter. He waved his hand and a servant made his way to the table and started pouring wine into the glasses. Thormund guided the servant to fill his glass only half full.

Maddalena sat down next to Princess Dea. Aaliya took her place at the end of the table. Although just two years older than Princess Dea, Aaliya felt she walked a different landscape entirely from the young woman. Princess Dea's composure, her seemingly conscious blindness to the scene around her, struck Aaliya as sad. Aaliya had grown up listening to her father repeatedly compare her to Princess Dea, "Why can't you just do as you're told like Princess Dea?" or "Princess Dea understands full well what's expected of a young woman, why can't you?" She was refined and proud. Aaliya suspected she played her part a little too well, to the point that she was utterly out of anyone's reach. Aaliya certainly had never been able to get close to her. Princess Dea remained silent as guests filled the room. Her long ginger hair immaculately pulled back, her blue eyes open but dull with incuriosity.

It was too warm in the room, stifling. Each person sat with their mouths closed. Eyes searched other faces, then quickly looked away when furtive glances met. Aaliya swung her legs under the table vigorously. Footsteps at the entrance made her heart leap. Justen and Pieter stood briefly at the entrance to the room and then bowed to the king. Pieter's grey and green jacket was as flouncy as a ball gown. His pale dainty hands, upon which he showcased rings featuring gemstones the size of eyeballs, rested at his front. Justen, by comparison, seemed unencumbered. He stood a man who appeared wholly comfortable with himself, his presence much older than he actually was. His thick hair slightly dishevelled, the navy jacket he wore bore a utilitarian quality that Aaliya imagined could be worn all the way back to Gedion. They were lead to their chairs on the other side of Thormund. Justen sat down, and when he looked up he smiled and nodded his head. All four women seated on the opposite side of the table smiled back, with varying degrees of enthusiasm. Even if this man had his own private encumbrances, as Aaliya believed everyone did, they seemed to have been left at the entrance to the Great Hall.

"A truly historic moment indeed," King Renatus said once everyone had settled. He raised his full glass. "Traegos and Gedion seated side by side. Raise a glass with me, good people, to lasting union between our two kingdoms."

Everyone raised their glasses and toasted the occasion. Some mutterings of "unity" could be heard around the table. The king was first to empty his glass, and brought it to the table with a thwack where it was hastily refilled.

"May this marriage bring wealth and prosperity to our kingdoms," the king continued. "Show Rone we mean business, eh?"

"We are honoured to be here, Your Grace," said Pieter politely.

"Trade routes," the king said, seemingly oblivious to Pieter's comment. "Yes, we could do with more of those." He raised his glass in Pieter's and Justen's direction. "Buy more wool and wine, my good men. The River Albo is a fucking costly thing to defend."

"Your Grace, I'm sure our guests would appreciate

hearing how we're on track for this wedding in six days. Madame?" Thormund said, looking at Queen Viktoria directly. "Do tell us how things are coming along?"

The Queen nervously talked about the preparations that had been taking place throughout the castle. The food choices, the fit-out for the Ceremonial Room, all the people that would be attending. It was going to be lavish and spectacular. No expense spared. Pieter and Thormund seemed to positively glow talking about the wedding. Maddalena seemed somewhat bored. Aaliya was uncertain what to make of Justen. He said all the right things. Acted with dignity and pride about his upcoming nuptials. She wanted him to appear devastated, but he wasn't letting on.

The food was brought to the table by experienced hands. The volume of silverware was so large it seemed to reflect extra light around the room. Turkey and quail, pies and galettes, cheese and candied fruit smothered the white damask.

The king spooned large amounts of quail onto his plate and then hastily shoved portions into his mouth. He ate like a lion might eat its prey, crunching on all the flesh and gristle in an orgy of feasting, then surreptitiously removing only the largest bits of bone.

Queen Viktoria turned away from her husband, mildly uncomfortable. "Enjoying our warm weather?" she asked, looking towards Justen and Pieter.

"Most certainly," Pieter offered.

"Ansgar is said to have the finest summers of all the capitals."

"I can see how that would be said. The days have been magnificent."

"Better than when you last visited?" The king said,

after wiping grease from his beard.

"Indeed. I recall a cataclysmic storm during our trip two years earlier," Pieter said.

"Yes," responded the king, "anyone would think you'd brought the calamity with you."

Silence. People went back to eating, not sure what to make of the comment.

The king continued, "What say you, young Justen? Likely to be any storm fronts coming through that you know of?"

"Your Grace, that would surely depend on circumstances over which I have little knowledge or control." He attempted a wry smile to soften the delivery, but Aaliya wasn't sure the king was buying it. The two men looked directly at each other as if locked in a silent conversation.

Pieter announced briskly, "It seems, with each visit, the food in Traegos gets better and better."

"We make the most of our seasonal produce," responded Princess Dea, apparently happy to have made a contribution to the conversation.

"Yes, it's quite delicious," said Pieter.

"It's our wine, in particular, we're famous for." The king snapped his fingers and servants moved towards Justen and Pieter and filled their glasses. He leaned over the table and turned his attention to Maddalena. "You might even be popular when you arrive in Tashker with a crate of wine in your cargo."

"I'll drink to that." Maddalena said raising her glass and taking a deep slug.

"Madame Reiner will be popular regardless, I assure you, Your Grace. Gedion is thrilled with this alliance." Pieter briefly looked assuringly at Maddalena but then turned towards Aaliya with an odd expression. If she wasn't mistaken, she thought his eyes had narrowed slightly as though momentarily harbouring a degree of wariness.

"As we are," said Thormund.

For a while the table fell silent. Princess Dea coughed, and whispered her pardon. Queen Viktoria raised the plate of potatoes and seemed intent in offering the food around, but then changed her mind and placed the plate back down. The king poured himself another drink. He waved away the servants like they weren't needed on this battlefront. He was getting hammered. That much was plain for all to see. Queen Viktoria's furtive sideway glances in her husband's direction hadn't stopped all night.

Aaliya became aware she was staring. After two years of existing only in her mind, she wanted to soak Justen up. She watched his mouth intently. Every gesture seemed wild and seductive. She felt as though he was luring her in like a tethered beast pulled slowly towards its captor. And yet, he was doing so little. He was simply chewing his food. But she was sure that wild mouth of his was really telling her to kiss it, and kiss it deeply.

His mouth formed a subtle smile when he looked up and noticed her. He was feeling it too, she was sure. She looked at the other people seated around the dining table. They were eating, loading up their plates with food, swilling their wine into their mouths. There was some chatter going on in the room that Aaliya had completely tuned out of. It was like hearing muffled voices from behind a closed door. Something about rebels on the western frontier of Traegos.

"So what does King Arav make of these…developments in Alvira?" slurred the king.

Before Pieter had a chance, Justen quickly said,

"Concerned. But quietly confident it won't affect Gedion."

"But your border..." suggested Maddalena.

"Yes, we share a border. We don't share a culture. The new government wouldn't take hold easily in Gedion," said Justen.

"What makes you so sure?" asked Thormund.

"Our long term planning. Our history. Our people. Our way of doing things."

"The Gedion way of doing things!" scoffed the king, laughing. "Now there's a book of instruction I'd like access to."

Justen went red as though sensing trouble, and opened his mouth to speak when Pieter said, "It's about values, Your Grace. And we are most fortunate to have our two kingdoms share a number of values that will see us through adversity."

The king looked at Pieter, a puzzled expression on his face.

Pieter continued, "Order, responsibility, duty to name but a few. I've travelled to distant lands. I've seen many people. And I've observed the chaos in other places. Places where people have given over to their baser instincts. Traegos is a proud country. An orderly country. Gedion holds enormous respect for your land."

"Yes," the king managed to say. "Order...will be maintained. In Traegos. And those damned insurgents...keep stirring up trouble. Nearly everyday I receive news. They're stealing horses. People are going missing. Missing, I tell you. Yes, order...they have no idea who they're dealing with. I round them all up. Get rid of them, I do."

"Traegos is fortunate for your firm hand in dealing with this matter," quipped Pieter enthusiastically.

"Yes, yes..."

"We've come a long way since our days of conflict, I'm sure you would agree."

"It's all behind us," King Renatus said barely audible.

The remainder of the meal was eaten with fraught politeness. Everyone was quietly relieved when the evening came to and end. It hadn't been a consummate disaster, but it hardly rated as a successful attempt at bridging the divide. The king stumbled out of the Great Hall with the assistance of a servant. Queen Viktoria soon followed. The remaining men made their way to the drawing room.

The three young women walked towards the Solar. Just as they arrived, Maddalena hovered for a brief moment near the door, provided a flimsy excuse about needing air after the distressing dinner events, and then shot off down the corridor without looking back. Princess Dea quickly settled into a large chair, picking up a cushion cover from a basket to her side. With needle and yarn she started carefully planting her stitches. The process looked rather palliative. The needle went into the fabric, left its mark, and then came out again. She embroidered the next stitch and the next until a pattern emerged, lucid and beautiful. She held it away at arms length and smiled, admiring her workmanship.

Aaliya felt as lackluster as a lead weight. She pulled a book from the shelf and spread out on the settee and tried to read. The same paragraph was read over and over again. She moved onto the next, but the same thing happened. She skipped a page and tried to persevere. But she wasn't absorbing it. Her thoughts kept wandering to Justen. She wouldn't be seeing him again tonight. That opportunity was over. Maybe tomorrow.

She put the book down and got up and walked to the window. A soft light illuminated the grounds outside. Aaliya didn't come to the window expecting to see anything. It was more out of habit. Looking out of the window was what she usually did to find clarity, even when it was dark outside.

Feeling the light breeze on her face seemed to awaken her out of her drowsiness. Her thoughts turned to Justen, once again, and she couldn't shake the idea that she had to see him tonight. It wasn't particularly rational. He might still be in the drawing room with Thormund and Pieter. If he had returned to his chamber the quest was no easier. She didn't know where in the castle his chambers were located. There were four levels to Ansgar Castle, three of which held rooms for guests. But she had to give it a try. Aaliya didn't want to wait until tomorrow with this restlessness surging through her body.

"Your sister was quick to take off," Princess Dea said looking down at her needlework, but sensing Aaliya's intentions.

"Yes, you could imagine seeing Seigneur Laus would have really unsettled her." Aaliya couldn't believe she was still covering for her sister after all these years.

Princess Dea barely stifled her laugh. "From what I could see, Maddalena was about as unsettled by Seigneur Laus as my left toe."

"I guess then she just wanted some fresh air."

"You look like you're about to leap yourself. The Reiner girls…you two are so alike."

Aaliya raised her eyebrows. "We are nothing alike."

"Denial. You two will never admit to it, but you need each other."

"I don't need Maddalena. We're barely in each other's lives as it is. It's been that way for so long I can't remember it ever being any different."

"You care. Why else would you lie for her just now."

Aaliya didn't respond.

"It's been quite an eventful evening," Princess Dea said, placing the embroidery back in the basket and standing. "But you'll have to excuse me, I must go to bed. I'm sure your father and sister will be along soon. Good night."

"Good night."

What a strange girl. She rarely attends gatherings and is prone to such extraordinary conclusions, Aaliya thought. She was right about one thing though. Aaliya wanted to get out of the room. When enough minutes had passed for Princess Dea to return to her chamber, Aaliya grabbed her shawl and left.

She made her way to the drawing room first. Just as she was a few steps from the doorway she could hear her father's voice. A servant, who recognized Aaliya, came out of the room.

"Could you tell me," Aaliya asked, "who is in the sitting room with my father?"

"A man, Madame. I believe his is the gentleman who arrived from Gedion the other day."

"Two arrived from Gedion. Does the man in the sitting room have a large moustache and fair hair?"

"Yes, Madame. Another man was in there, but he left ten minutes ago."

Frantic for more information, Aaliya asked which way the man had gone, and was told that he had made his way up the grand staircase. Aaliya thanked the servant and ran up the stairs. There were very few people about on the next level. Lamps lined the corridors and a haunting stillness enclosed her. In her haste she felt like a bumbling beast tearing up the night. Aaliya didn't know what she was looking for. Only that she had to at least look. Door after door was closed. She thought how nice it would have been to have some sort of sign indicating which room he was occupying. But there was nothing. Just blank wood greeted her at every turn.

She left the first floor and made her way up another coil of stairs to the second floor. She passed all the guests rooms, pressing her ear against some of the doors to see if she could pick up anything that might indicate his presence. But the castle wasn't revealing its secrets tonight. Aaliya encountered only the hush of the sleeping hour. She walked briskly to the stairwell. Although she knew her chances were slim, she still wanted to look on the top floor. She felt like she couldn't return home having not exhausted all options.

Eyes down, Aaliya scurried up the steps. She wasn't looking ahead. She didn't see anything or anyone other than the steps before her. And then she felt it. Her body has smacked into another person. Aaliya looked up. It was Justen. For a moment, they both just stood there. Utterly shocked that they should meet like this, at this hour, in this place.

This was what Aaliya wanted, but she hesitated. She didn't know the rules. She wasn't sure of his feelings for her. She tried to say something, but the words wouldn't come out.

She grabbed hold of Justen's face between her hands and brought his lips to hers. She kissed him, her tongue slid over his lips and parted his mouth, hungrily searching. Justen responded, tenderly at first and then with a possessive hunger. His lips explored her face. He kissed her eyelids, her neck. He was feverish. Aaliya felt drunk with desire in his arms. She wanted more and reached for his belt, fumbling to undo the buckle. She let her hand slide beneath the belt and felt his desire.

Suddenly he pulled away. It was as if she had caused him pain.

"I'm so sorry, Aaliya," he said, "I can't do this."

"Justen…" was all she could say, utterly lost for words.

In the next instant, Justen buckled his belt and briskly walked down the steps. Just a disappearing silhouette. Aaliya leaned back against the cold stone wall. She didn't understand it. She had taken a leap of faith, bounded in where normally she would have cautiously crept. She stood there feeling as ridiculous as a blundering court jester. She made her way back to the Solar, her head felt swathed in a fog. She collapsed in the large chair and stared into the darkness until sleep finally rolled over her like a warm hand.

8

Mad River

Maddalena paused at the door to Thormund's study. She went to knock, then stopped herself. It never got easier, this knocking on her father's door. She wanted to just lightly tap and say "it's me father" and hope that he would hear. Entering his study felt like walking into a gladiatorial arena. One had to place on armour and prove oneself. Maddalena swallowed loudly and did three loud raps on the door.

"Yes," a voice from inside the room said.

Maddalena opened the door. The early morning light was shut out by silk damask curtains pulled tight across the windows. The fabric featured a large circle enclosing a rosette, the pattern in gold thread drawing her attention as she cautiously entered. An enormous oak desk was in the centre of the room. Thormund was seated behind it in an absurdly high backed chair looking down as his quill scraped over a piece of parchment.

Behind him was a towering bookcase, laden with old tomes, jutting out from the wall and partially segmenting the room into a separate space. It was there, on the wide carved table that occupied the space at the back of the room, that Thormund contemplated strategy and empire building.

Maps of the realm were laid out as permanent fixtures. Flat palm sized rocks were painted with the various totems for each of the six kingdoms: the single, cresting wave for Rone; the mountain and river for Gedion; the shifting sands for Elkha; the wide, rolling land for Alvira; the triangle of strength and autonomy for Asturia; and for Traegos, bands of light encased in a crescent moon. The rocks were placed along borders, points of interest or locations indicating pockets of resistance.

The room held so many memories. But there was one in particular that she was able to recall with ease. She had come into the study one day to see her father running his finger along the map, tracing the path of the River Albo as it cuts through the heartland of Traegos from the snow-capped peaks of the Great Anjar Range to the port city of Marius on the Mindano Sea. Her father had talked that day using a language different to the way he normally spoke. He described the landscape almost as having a personality of its own. But it was the river, in particular, he wanted her to understand. "No other feature on the Traegos landscape," he had mentioned, "has the emotional pull as that waterway."

He went on to describe that for the inhabitants of Traegos, the river was not unlike the thread linking a child to its mother in the womb. It had been said that Traegonites were inflicted by a certain unsoundness of mind, an irrational obsession with *their* river, as they affectionately called it. Many across the realm, from Asturia in the deep south to Gedion in the north, labelled it "Mad River". Countless legends and myths were borne from the watery hold it apparently had over those who lived in its vicinity.

Thormund had pointed on the map a place where the river dissects the lands of Traegos and Rone. The place was called the Murrhand Frontier, but had become an area simply known as "The Fist". It was a place once known for abundant fields of barley. The harvests from the region so bountiful, the river boats laden with grain from the Frontier were said to have barely moved even in full sail due to the weight of their cargo. The past fifty years, however, saw increasing conflict between the neighbouring kingdoms and the fields once a haven of honey transformed into an expanse of grey. "The Frontier is now little more than a smeared rag," Thormund explained. "Dirty, crowded military camps along the banks of the river as far as the eye can see."

Maddalena had placed her own finger on the map, and heard her father say, "For our kingdom, losing control of the river is simply not an option. Everything comes back to the river. It reminds us to return home. There always needs to be the return."

The conversation left Maddalena feeling as though she had been wounded. It left such an indelible mark she was sure it rested on the surface of her skin. There was a place on the inside of her arm that she would inadvertently scratch sometimes and be reminded of what was said. As the river cuts through the landscape, so too her need to make something of herself threaded through her whole being and shaped her choices the following years. She wanted to make sure neither Traegos nor her family could ever be compromised.

And she thought often about 'the return'. For much of her early life, she was sure her father was right and that everything did lead back home. But after her first marriage, she was less sure. Maybe the journey could go on in a different direction that was not homeward bound? She started to wonder if she had it all slightly wrong, if she was wrong about him? It felt ungrateful just thinking it. But she couldn't help feel that at this point in her life that she was just another fixture being of some 'use' to him. That he had in fact invisible aims and motives that he increasingly kept to himself. He was entitled to a private life after all. Her own private life was something she guarded with unfailing zeal. But it was enough to convince her on the eve of her second marriage that she had to build a future for herself that was separate from him.

Standing in the doorway of the study, however, it was difficult to contemplate separateness. Thormund had a strange habit of sitting in darkened rooms during daylight hours when he was concentrating. At least until midday, almost everyday, he could be found in his study writing letters, managing his business affairs or plotting his next moves to secure more power. Maddalena had once asked him why he needed the room dark and he responded that darkness helped shape the quality of his decisions, like the well-timed swoop of an owl at night. And the dark room did seem to wrap around his thoughts. Shut out distractions and enclose him in his macabre vision for the future. The only illumination in the room came from the dancing flame of the lamp beside him, which he would occasionally look at as if seeking an answer or some sort of confirmation.

The desk was covered with leather held firmly in place by numerous studs. Ink pot, quill and parchment, wax and the Traegos seal were the only items Maddalena ever saw on his desk. It had rarely changed since Maddalena's first memory of coming into the room as a young girl. In fact, the whole scene seemed so fixed in time Maddalena briefly forgot why she was here. Then she noticed there was one other item on the desk. A key.

She closed the door behind her and walked onto the large deer hide resting in front of the desk. To her side the cedar cabinet stood with its doors open. Maddalena peered into the cabinet. She calculated there must have been about twenty neat bundles of brick sized paper sitting on the shelves.

"Is that what I think it is?" She remained standing, waiting for her father to look up and acknowledge her. But he kept writing, seemingly oblivious to her presence.

"Yes, another letter," he said, head down.

"I was referring to what's in the cabinet."

He finally looked up and saw what she was noticing. "Quite a thing to behold, isn't it? Printed money. Who would have thought?"

Maddalena moved towards the cabinet and picked up a stack. Each pile was wrapped in a strip of parchment, sealed into place with wax. She pulled a note from the bundle and held it close to her face. It featured the outline of a man, unmistakably King Renatus. She turned it over and saw the other side displayed a motif of the Traegos seal.

"The king would be loving this," she said.

"It's quite an achievement."

"I meant his image on the note."

"He's deservedly proud, yes. This hasn't been done before."

"The '100' is what?"

"Equal to one hundred krones."

She raised her eyebrows and tilted her head sardonically. "This," she said waving the bit of paper, "this, is the same as a hundred krones?"

"Yes."

"A hundred krones is equal to one dom of gold. A

month's wage for a skilled craftsman."

"Yes."

"Gold! Father."

"It's high level commerce. No one else is taking such an innovative approach that we know of."

"But gold is so…valuable. How can printed money ever be of equal value to gold?"

"It can be of equal value and even greater value if the king devalues gold and makes printed money the standard currency. Which is what has been happening. Viggo has got the full support of the king to have money printed. Renatus has already prepared an edict to encourage people to bring in their gold in exchange for printed money. Traegos is slowly moving away from reliance on krones. Metal coins are expensive to produce. We have been importing nickel and copper and ore from Gedion and other states to manufacture krones and to make steel. It keeps us reliant on them, it makes us dependent. Redshade will not only move us away from importing so much raw materials, but it frees up our economy as paper money is so versatile."

It sounded simple enough. But after overhearing the conversation between Viggo and Pieter the other day, she was no longer convinced by simplicity. Maddalena was sure an intelligent man such as her father would have investigated this notion of paper money. But she also knew, for all his good prudent business sense, he was vulnerable to the persuasiveness of Viggo. So desperate was her father to bury his past as the son of a shepherd, to be worthy in the eyes of someone whose whole heritage was wealth and power, that it was like there was some invisible thread wrapped a little too tightly around his finger, causing a degree of numbness when it came to making rational decisions.

She had come into her father's study with the intention of talking to him about Viggo, but a plan had never formed in her mind prior to entering as to how to approach the topic, and one certainly wasn't presenting itself now. She recalled an earlier time when Thormund had discussed Redshade with her. Thormund had claimed that you just had to scratch the surface at their secret location in the Iron Steppes to see the copper under the soil. It was going to change everything for Traegos. Fund the venture with capital, her father had said. And lots of it. But not just our own money. Other people's. Get the king on side. Everyone has a stake in the new Traegos, a more powerful Traegos. It was the new battlefront. Paper currency hadn't been discussed at the time and she thought that to be an interesting omission.

"It sounds as though when you set up the Quadsun Bank with Viggo you actually had paper money as a goal," Maddalena said.

"You could say that," Thormund said.

"Both of you or just Viggo?"

"It was Viggo's idea."

"Why doesn't that surprise me."

Thormund leaned back in his chair. "What's that supposed to mean?"

Maddalena breathed a little deeper, aware there was a fine line here between loyalty and doubting his good sense. Maybe that was why he trusted her so much, and not Aaliya. She went along with his schemes so compliantly, bolstered his faith in himself, in his vision for the future. For all she knew, he was as much a well of insecurities as she was. He was just so determined to not let any of it see the light of day. What a laugh! Chip off the old block she was.

"It means nothing. Forget about it," she said.

Thormund seemed happy enough with the response. Didn't care to pursue the issue. He picked up the key from the desk and stood. "I've changed my mind on the dancing troupe for the wedding. We'll just stick with the musicians." Thormund secured the cedar cabinet. He pulled a green covered book from the bookshelf and placed the key inside, before pushing the book back into place and then said, "I was writing to let them know they wouldn't be required."

"Never like dancing troupes anyway," she lied. Light entertainment was exactly what this wedding required, she thought.

Thormund returned to his chair. "Take a seat, Maddalena. Your hovering is making me uncomfortable."

She sat down opposite her father.

"Your groom-to-be is an interesting character," he said.

"Last night was quite the celebration of merriment."

"I thought it went well under the circumstances."

"At what point do we bury the past?"

"It's not just about our two countries."

"There's more?" she sniggered. "Here I was hoping there would be some acceptance of me."

"That will come with time."

"So what else is it then?"

Thormund linked his hands and rested them on the desk. "Ten years ago Justen's father was killed during our incursion into the Barmer Valley. Different stories have floated around as to what exactly happened. But what is certain is that King Renatus was there at the time and ordered the execution."

Maddalena hesitated. "No wonder you were uneasy during the trip there."

"Quite relieved when it was over. Now we just need

to keep them separated until the wedding."

"That shouldn't be too hard." Maddalena wanted to tell him that Justen's attention was likely to be occupied elsewhere for the next week, but it seemed trivial. Nothing she couldn't handle. Aaliya's gooey-eyed expression whenever Justen was near was about as well-concealed as a blacksmith's ass. And Justen's lust for her sister was equally obvious. Nothing had changed that she could see. She could warn Aaliya. But she knew full well that they'd find a way to be together regardless. She certainly would. Wasn't it the impossibility of love that drew lovers together? Let it be, she thought. Her father had enough to worry about.

"Doesn't come across as the revenge type, anyway," Maddalena said.

"You've had experience with the revenge type?"

"I'm just saying…oh, doesn't matter." Maddalena sat quietly then asked, "will you be in here for most of the day?"

"No. Very soon I'll be heading out. Hunting with the king. He wants to take out his falcon. I'm going to ask Aaliya to join me."

"She may not be open to that right now."

"It will do her good. She's not going to move on if she stays in that workshop all day."

This was getting ridiculous. She was here for a reason, and all she was doing was wasting time and putting off the inevitable. She took a deeper than usual breath and said, "Father, we need to talk about Viggo. I overheard a conversation between Viggo and Pieter the other day. It concerns Redshade, and it's not what it seems. The company is - "

"Stop right there, Maddalena. We've been through this before. Countless times. Just a moment ago in fact."

"No, you have to listen to me this time, father. I think

Viggo is being bribed by Pieter, and Pieter has Viggo in this situation because he knows there's nothing to be mined at the Iron Steppes. Pieter says it's just empty space. And Viggo is worried. I could hear it in his voice. Pieter talked about Redshade collapsing. Collapsing! The investment in paper money collapsing too. And how Traegos would end up bankrupt. Pieter wants Viggo to do something for him."

"Do what exactly?"

"I didn't get to hear any further."

"I see."

"I know that tone. I know what you're thinking. I heard this, it's not something I conjured out of my head."

"This is all very interesting, but it's not new to me."

"…Not new?"

"Viggo has always been forthright with me about the risks. And we've talked at length about management of those risks. I know what is to be found at the Iron Steppes. I've seen the reports. Do you think Pieter is really the first one to try and bribe Viggo or myself if that is indeed what took place?"

"I don't know. But Pieter knows mining better than us."

"Does he now. Greatness inspires envy, Maddalena. Have you ever thought about that?"

A knock sounded at the door. Maddalena and Thormund both looked quizzically at each other expecting a reason for the interruption.

"Seigneur Reiner," Fin said from the other side of the door, "Viggo Vennamo is here to see you."

"Expecting him?" Maddalena asked softly between her clenched jaw.

"No."

"Why would he see you here?"

"I don't know. But I'm going to find out." Then added, "if you don't mind."

"Father, we need to sort..."

"Maybe later."

She stood and opened the door.

Fin promptly stepped aside, Viggo hesitated then said, "greetings, Madam."

Maddalena mumbled a response, moved past him, then looked behind. The last thing she saw was an expression of forced geniality on Viggo's face before the door was closed.

Fin walked away and could be heard descending the steps. Maddalena stared at the closed door, her arms hanging rigidly down by her side. What was Viggo playing at? Meeting Pieter recently and now meeting her father here in his private study. Outsiders rarely came to the Reiner house to see Thormund. Her father always met for business in the warehouse at the dockyards. Who was she kidding, though? Viggo was hardly an outsider. He was practically family. The thought made her clench her fists even tighter.

She leaned down and peered through the small keyhole. She could see Viggo walking in and out of her viewpoint with a menacing aura. He seemed clearly agitated, but Maddalena was sure he was trying to prove he was above visual displays of personal disquiet. He slipped out of sight and a moment later light flooded the room.

"You really ought to let more sun in," she heard Viggo saying. "I was talking to a fellow, a doctor actually, the other day and he was telling me about an ailment known as darkness nausea. One gets moody, irritable. Lack of sun, apparently. Particularly affects our northern neighbours."

Maddalena stood up, thought for another moment about staying and listening, before walking down the corridor. She had just turned the corner and was starting to walk down the stairs when she heard what sounded like a door opening. A moment later the sound of a door latch fiercely clicking into place. Maddalena arrived in the kitchen and reached for some almonds. She placed a handful of the nuts in her mouth with an exaggerated crunch. That was Viggo opening and closing the door, she was sure. He was checking to see if I was listening, she surmised. Her desire to return back to the study and listen at the door gnawed at her. But she knew it was flawed. If she was discovered, Thormund would lose all respect for her. There had to be another way.

9

The Hunt

Aaliya found herself back in the workshop the next day. She had barely any recollection of making her way down there. Her feet had found their own way to the workshop as though pulled along on a great tide. But truth be told, there was simply no place she'd rather be. The smell of burnt leather as she walked through the door instantly relaxed her. A clear reminder that it was here she belonged. Amongst the tools and the threads, the sculptured wood blocks all shapely and graceful, and the endless fiddly bits crowded into rows of tins. She found it oddly comforting to be amongst these things.

Prior to making her way to the workshop, she had been sitting in her room trying to piece together the events of the night before. She had made an utter fool of herself. She longed for her mother with an ache that left her trembling. Helena would know what to say, she would know what to do. Helena knew the world wasn't black and white. She'd forgive Aaliya for dipping into the sea of grey that swirled around everyone and everything. It was a rare day that Aaliya didn't think of her mother. Helena's face was so burned into her eyes. She saw her in everything. Every tack she pressed into leather was a berry she had placed in the hand of her mother. Shining up a completed saddle with a bit of grease and Helena's face would be there smiling back at her. Being in the workshop for Aaliya was about sitting with her memories and her visions, yet still feeling mildly functional.

And Olle was simply there for her. Aaliya was grateful for his natural ability to talk to her as a companion. He had been doing that for as long as she could remember. Over the years, Aaliya had loved coming to the workshop to listen to stories of his own life: riding a camel through the Sayan Desert and being chased by rampant bulls; coming down with pneumonia as a boy and nearly dying; falling out of an olive tree as a young man, breaking both his arms and suffering the humiliation of his mother wiping his bottom for three months. He talked extensively about the idea of beauty. About the balance between simplicity and complexity. That functional doesn't have to be at the expense of elegance. And the skills one acquires from crafting something to that next level is what sets one apart. Even opens doors. Olle also finally admitted that making items of great beauty proved to be a good way to win the affection of women.

Olle had told her about how he watched his father for hours mold leather into the most beautifully crafted things he had ever seen. He took the skills taught to him by his father even further. He tried new things. Remolded and carved the saddle trees to be even more comfortable; sourced exquisite lorimers from as far away as Maghrib to give his saddles a unique appearance. He became known as 'Othalepo', a Maqibahian word for 'subtle warrior'. He told her about how his father scraped together the meagre savings left over after feeding the family of eight boys and one girl to send Olle and the eldest boy, Lorens, across the Amistar Strait to Asturia to learn new techniques from those considered the best in the realm. ("I resisted at first. My… there were scenes in the Lohr household. I had fallen in love and nothing, but nothing, interested me more than to stay in the Tilwara Valley to be with this girl.") The journey took place and Olle told Aaliya about how it changed his life forever, the people he met, their lives, what they were fighting for. It left a significant imprint on him. And the girl? Aaliya wondered. ("She married and moved on. So that was that.")

Aaliya wished her father would send her off to Asturia to study saddle making. But she wasn't being entirely truthful. The idea was incredibly daunting. How would she get by? She'd only ever known life in the capital albeit with occasional wanderings into the woods behind the castle.

Aaliya felt grateful for Olle's teachings and felt incredibly lucky to have had such a fine teacher who never held back because she was a girl, never treated her like porcelain because she was a daughter of a wealthy merchant, never talked down to her because she was younger. She saw in him someone who genuinely enjoyed her company as an equal. She wasn't sure she had this equality with anyone else in Ansgar. Her relationship with her sister had been fraught for so long. There was connection there but it was like a frayed piece of string.

Her friend, Catja, could be shameless good fun but too much time in her company felt as unsatisfying as eating hollow bread. For Catja, every interaction with other people seemed like a networking opportunity to the point that Aaliya wondered if she valued anyone simply for their companionship. Catja was interested in anyone who could advance her ambitions ("to be rich"). Aaliya certainly wondered if she herself meant a great deal to her. But she wasn't losing any sleep over it. Any doubts she had were assuaged by the authenticity of her relationship with Olle.

They both took up their tools a little bleary eyed on this day, but thankful to be in each other's company. For a long time there was no conversation, just the subtle, muted sounds of metal against leather.

Aaliya looked up and watched Olle, his face in deep concentration as he stamped a succession of holes into the leather along his pencilled outline. "I'm thinking of leaving Ansgar," she blurted.

Olle stopped what he was doing and looked at her. "Bold statement but I'm not entirely surprised."

"Things…are going on. I just want to get away."

"I know this is a difficult time for you, Aaliya, but - "

"It's not just because my mother's gone," she interjected. "There are…other things going on. And I just want to go away for a while."

"Does Thormund know?"

Aaliya bit her bottom lip, not responding.

"You won't get far on your own," Olle said soberly.

Aaliya tried not to show that she was hurt by Olle's comment. "My grandfather just walked away. I don't know why I can't."

"He would have had good connections."

"I don't think he had connections."

"You probably don't know as much about his story as you think you do. Maybe he knew quite a few people who were able to help him. Maybe he was incredibly lonely. Maybe he gave up because he had no purpose and stopped seeing the point of what he was doing."

"Well, at least he had the opportunity to work that out."

"You haven't planned anything."

"I've been planning it my whole life."

"Is that so? You ready to leave this?" Olle waved around the room. "You ready to leave the comfort of your home? You'd be leaving me, your father, Catja, Maddalena –"

"Maddalena is moving on anyway. She'll be gone in a week and then I'll be next. Carted off to fit into someone else's life."

Olle nodded his head. "Just think about it some more, eh? There's tension all around Traegos. There are thousands of men down on the border with Alvira. And along the River Albo, Traegos and Rone soldiers stare at each other every day waiting for the inevitable. A poorly told joke could set off conflict there."

Aaliya swallowed and folded her arms. "I still want to go, Olle. There will never be a perfect time."

Olle didn't respond. Went back to punching his holes. He eventually put his tool down. "Consider then going for just a couple of months. Head down to Blackrock Canyon for a while. I know some people there. You could stay with them. Still make saddles even."

"But it's still in Traegos," Aaliya responded.

"Aaliya, be sensible. Don't go too far, just far enough. You've just buried your mother. I know you want to run, but you've got to keep your head."

Aaliya took this in. "A brief trip."

"Yes, just a brief trip," Olle said. "And if it goes well, we could look at something longer. Keep working on your apprenticeship out there for a bit and believe me, you'll get to the stage of being a journeyman and your world will change. One other thing, I'll ride with you out there."

"Olle - "

"Aaliya, this is the only way your father will cope with your decision to do this. And it's also for your safety."

"Alright. But I will tell my father," she said.

By the afternoon Aaliya felt she had the first genuine smile her face had known for the past couple of weeks. A warm energy seemed to course through her blood and every task felt gratifying, joyful. She was so absorbed in thoughts of riding out to Blackrock she didn't hear the creak of the door as a man entered the workshop.

Thormund walked in as Aaliya was shoving great handfuls of horsehair to the underside of a saddle. Aaliya gave a jolt as she saw him out of the corner of her eye. Olle was in the backroom working with the apprentices. She knew her father had a profound dislike of the workshop and the sight of greasy hands. Respect for the activity was always there, though. A sense of pride at seeing an industry that he had chosen to invest in continued to thrive when other contributions to the king's coffers had slowed to a trickle.

Aaliya picked up a rag and wiped her hands. "Father, I wasn't expecting you here."

"Of course your weren't. Why would you?"

Aaliya looked around for a seat to offer Thormund. The stools were all grubby. She wiped one down and gestured with her hand for Thormund to take a seat.

"No thank you. I shan't be long," he said.

She waited for him to say something more, but he stood in silence, his eyes darting around the room. His attire was different to the lush brocades and exquisite buttoned jackets he usually wore. Today he wore a thin leather jacket, close fitted olive pants and long riding boots. His shoulders were forced back, his body rigid. Thormund didn't lose any opportunity to stamp his elegant authoritarian presence on whatever room he entered.

"You're going riding?" Aaliya asked, at last breaking the silence.

"Yes I am. You'll be joining me today."

Aaliya stared at her father blankly. She just wasn't up for it today. The familiar smells and tasks offered in the workshop were all she was up for. "I'm not feeling well today, father. I can't go riding."

"You can, and you will."

Aaliya looked around in the direction of the backroom in the hope of seeing Olle and catching his eye.

"Answerable to your saddle maker friend, am I?" he asked brusquely.

"Of course not."

"Well come now," Thormund said, giving a nod in the direction of the door. "We're hunting rabbits today."

"Why do you want me to come hunting?"

"You're good at it, Aaliya," he said, and then added, "I like to do activities with my daughter. Is there a crime in that?"

Aaliya made her way to the backroom and informed Olle. The pair left like awkward strangers.

Thormund had always loved the bow and arrow, the thrill of the hunt. The synergy of mind and hands working in flawless unison. The bow and arrow were his choice of weapon. He saw little skill in the sword. As far as he was concerned, men flailed their iron around like wanton barbarians. Aaliya thought that was what the attraction was. But to Thormund there was little skill in this, no finesse. Just a heavy sharp instrument effective in butchering anything in one's way.

Thormund had become excited when he observed her promising skills with bow and arrow many years before. She had taken to practicing regularly, enjoyed the 'thunk' as the arrow sunk into the target. But more than anything, she was grateful to finally have something over which she could connect with her father.

He insisted on taking her hunting, testing her abilities on real targets. Aaliya did have a talent for shooting at great distance. Aiming at what seemed like an inanimate object. But then when she would retrieve the dead animal, hold it and smell its blood, the senselessness seemed shocking. Killing for pleasure never took hold of her core the way it did others. She knew this disappointed her father but by then, things seemed beyond repair.

Aaliya normally loved an afternoon ride, but this didn't feel good. She wasn't a hunter and why her father would insist on having her alongside him like this left her feeling an imminent sense of foreboding.

Thormund and Aaliya were joined by Viggo. The party rode away from the woods to the bare hills and rocky outcrops that spanned out like a desolate wasteland all the way to Alvira. A somewhat unbidden landscape, it was awesome in its own bony, rugged way. Although trees had been removed en masse beyond the royal forest, there was still a life-affirming quality to the place. And there were birds everywhere. Finches and flycatchers, skylarks and sparrow-hawks, warblers and wagtails. The branches on the few trees that stood on the plains were dense with the feathered creatures. Their amplified song seemed to carry across the valley.

A horse could be heard behind them noisily running to catch up. All three turned around, Aaliya aghast to see Justen getting closer. Thormund brought his horse to a stop, and shifted in his saddle. An austere look passed between Thormund and Viggo. Aaliya longed to back away, to return to the workshop where she had been content before this moment.

"I would have thought your archery session this morning would have worn you out," Thormund said.

"Absolutely not," Justen replied. "I wouldn't miss this for anything. What finer way is there to spend an afternoon in Ansgar?"

"And Pieter?"

"He encouraged me to go on my own. Said he wasn't feeling the best. Sends his apologies."

Justen was positively radiating. There was not the slightest hint in his demeanour that he felt awkward over the previous night's events.

"I see you're fully equipped," Thormund said, noticing the bow slung around Justen's body and his leather canister of arrows.

"We're hunting, Seigneur Reiner. It would be foolish of me not to come with my bow and arrows," Justen said with a faint mocking tone.

They continued riding, stopping once the lake came into view. A bird flying high above the lake was being eagerly watched by a gathering of thirty or so men on horses at the water's edge. Aaliya saw the king amongst the group of men, his guards nearby. The falcon soared so high it appeared as little more than a blemish against the clear blue backdrop. Suddenly, it tucked in its wings and began to dive, its speed catching many of the ducks and shorebirds on the lake unawares. Some of the birds began to disperse, wings launched out in a frantic attempt at fleeing. A young bird, not sensing the imminent danger, was caught in the talons of the falcon. Clutching its prey, the falcon soared across the lake. The king shouted for joy, the men surrounding him began cheering and clapping.

Thormund clapped, followed by Viggo and Justen. Aaliya looked at them all and kept her hands firmly on her reins. They watched the raptor drop the prey by the king's horse and return to the gauntlet on its master's outstretched arm.

Thormund lead the way riding down to the lakes edge.

"Impressive, Your Grace," Thormund said as his horse pulled up alongside the king.

"Our seventh kill this afternoon. It's been a stellar day for hunting," said the king.

A young man came and collected the bird lying in a bloody heap on the ground. Aaliya recognized it to be a sandpiper. Its feet were bound with rope and it was then attached to the same long rod as six other birds. Upside down, their wings fanned out like they were in full flight. It looked macabre to Aaliya. She remembered wandering around the Great Market as a young girl and coming across a trader selling exotic birds. Most were in cages, but four were perched on a ledge with a thin chain attached to each bird's leg. The birds were able to flap their wings and fly momentarily, but the chain would always pull them back into position. Aaliya watched, transfixed, as the birds repeatedly attempted to fly away. Their instinct was to be free or die trying, and Aaliya saw them grow weaker and more exhausted with every attempt.

The next day she returned with a sharp rock she had found in the woods. Filled with a jumbled mix of both fury and joy, she smashed the chains shackling the birds, and watched as all four immediately leapt into the sky and flew out of sight. The trader reported her to Thormund, from whom she received a caning of monumental proportions. But it was worth it.

Aaliya was relieved when she heard King Renatus announce that his falcon had done enough for the day. She even started turning Providence around to head back.

"Where are you going, Aaliya?" Thormund said. "We haven't even started."

"But I thought…"

King Renatus directed his falcon to move from his gauntlet onto the arm of his nearby aide. "My dear girl," said the king, "I am merely having my friend here take Hanno back to the castle safely. Aren't you a lucky girl to be out here? I surely would not have Dea present at a hunt. No, I would not."

She didn't feel lucky at all. In fact, she felt bile churn in her stomach.

The king's aide rode off at a gentle trot. The falcon perched contentedly on the man's covered arm, while his other hand controlled the reins.

"Gather round men," the king shouted. "I have only one short thing to say to you all, and that is, don't miss. Now, go forth and hunt."

The men gathered near the lake immediately launched a spray of arrows into the enormous beech tree nearby.

Another round of arrows sprung from taut bows within seconds. Then another round. It literally started raining birds. Some fell on top of Aaliya, one landing in her lap, its wings beating and struggling as it clung onto life. She looked into its black unyielding eyes and the thought that lodged in her mind was one of essence. The core, the pith, the meat of all of us. And how quickly, how easily, we can be brought undone. Providence became jittery and started moving around in a circle, trying to find a good direction to turn.

Aaliya looked up and saw Justen's eyes boring into her, telling her something, but she couldn't read it. And then he was off, manoeuvring through the melee to catch up to Thormund, Viggo, Renatus and several other men who had taken off around the lake. When they arrived at a part of the lake that had not been disturbed, they launched a series of arrows across the water, striking numerous birds resting and feeding. The birds not struck on the water flew up into the sky where they inevitably met their fate from arrows poised at the ready.

"Stop this!" Aaliya screamed racing towards them. "Father, stop this now! You didn't say anything about hunting birds." Her heart was beating hard in her chest. Blood had risen to her head, she felt fervid with anger. She wanted to lash out, pull an arrow from the case on her back and shoot it at any one of the men before her. Aaliya frantically moved through the crowd screaming and hoping to startle the birds to flight.

Thormund looked a little awestruck at the situation. As for Justen, she couldn't believe he had chosen to be a part of the carnage, had willingly come along. She didn't want to see him, didn't want to see her father. Thormund and the others were moving back in her direction and all she could think about was getting away from here. Aaliya braced her reins and kicked Providence hard, leaping back towards the castle at a gallop.

She leaned low in her saddle, her horse pounding the earth, dirt and dust flying in its wake. She could hear someone coming up behind her then the voice of Thormund bellowed, "Tell me what's going on! Tell me!" His words erupted from his body with such violent force, his voice was broken and hoarse.

Aaliya didn't look around. Just get me back, Providence. She maintained the frantic pace and ripped up the ground. Thormund was following close behind her, and then she sensed something had changed. She turned around and saw that her father had dropped back. Aaliya eased back her horse, the wind no longer howling past her ears.

Viggo was calling out for Thormund to stop. There was a commotion of shouting and frenzied movement as most of the expansive party rode up to the location where a man had fallen off his horse. It was one of the king's guards. For a moment Aaliya didn't know what to do. She gingerly rode closer towards the forming circle of men. The man had taken an arrow in the back and lay on the ground, his mouth frothing with blood.

Rambling chatter moved through the crowd. Viggo bent down beside the wounded man, whose lungs were pitifully trying to take in some air. The group quietened down, and then there was complete silence. Viggo grabbed hold of the shaft protruding from the man's back. The man flinched with pain as the iron tip was ripped from his body before whimpering like a child and slipping into death.

The king began jabbering, his face white, his eyes

bulging. "Behind me…he was behind me…he called out my name…the arrow was meant for me."

10

The Wine Bearer

It was an enormous room, spacious as an open field yet as cluttered as a cook's pantry. She had sat in this chair untold times, but couldn't recall any other moment where she had really noticed the space around her. The four-poster bed could have fit a family of five in it. The summer cover draped her bed in royal blue, a phoenix embroidered in gold at its centre. The ebony dressing table loomed against the wall like a large black horse. Trinkets and lacquerware, jewellery and ornaments seemed to clog up every surface. How did she come into possession of so many things? She only knew that she needed them. There was some comfort to be found there.

From where Maddalena sat, with her head fixed forward while having her hair prepared, she could see the oak side table with glassware and candelabras. Above the table hung a painting of a woman with long brown hair and a yellow gown. The woman in the painting was standing beside a stone tablet, the ancient text *'neblo von senna arem'* visible on its side. The text was the old Angari version of Traegos's motto: through darkness comes light. Maddalena had requested the painting when her grandfather passed away. It was said to feature Queen Nissine, the wife of King Alvaro, a woman greatly admired for her fortitude and perseverance during the early years of the kingdom. Maddalena liked to think of the woman in the painting as herself: graceful, resourceful, powerful.

Thormund had told her recently that only her finest gowns and jewellery would be accompanying her on her trip to Gedion after the wedding. That she would acquire new possessions in her new home. Maddalena wanted to take all her things. But at the very least, she would not be parting without her painting of Queen Nissine.

Maddalena's awareness was drawn to her scalp as Nella tugged her hair roughly into a braid. At least if I had some decent company this tedious process could be bearable, she thought. As it was, Nella, was her father's choice so functional and steadfast were the company she had instead.

"Are you nearly done?" Maddalena asked grimacing.

"I'm getting there, Madame."

"It's only dinner with my father and sister for God's sake."

"Still, you want to look your best I'm sure."

"Nella, you endlessly talk like you know what's best for me."

"Maybe I do."

"I admire your enthusiasm for your job, but believe me, you don't know what's best for me." Maddalena pulled her head sharply to the side forcing Nella to let go of the strands she was holding. This know-it-all had been in their home for much of her life. A saving grace of leaving soon would be to see the back of this lumpy, self-righteous old hag.

"I have served royal women - " Nella said, attempting to grab at Maddalena's hair again.

Maddalena kept her head turned. "Yes, I know. You're highly regarded and I should be eternally grateful. Now please, just finish my hair in silence."

Maddalena straightened herself and through gritted teeth allowed Nella to continue the braid. It was late afternoon. Aaliya didn't turn up to dance practice earlier in the day. Again. And she had seen little of her father since yesterday morning in his study.

Through her open bedroom door, Maddalena heard a knock coming from downstairs. The front door was opened and Thormund's manservant, Fin, was heard having a conversation with the person who entered the house. The sound of bottles clanking together rose up the stairs.

"Is that the wine boy?" Maddalena asked.

"Yes, I believe it is. Fin was expecting him about this time today."

Maddalena hadn't always been curious about this young man who delivered wine to her home once a month. She knew his name to be Jakob, but preferred to call him 'wine boy'. He was just another person who performed a task, but otherwise, meant little to her. But lately he had piqued her interest. On countless previous occasions he would come into her home and she wouldn't even turn her head to acknowledge him. But lately she had taken to watching him intently. Maddalena knew him to be several years younger than herself. That would surely put him at an age of desiring the experience of a woman, wouldn't it?

"Send him up," Maddalena demanded.

"Miss Maddalena, I don't think that's - "

"Nella, send him up. Thank you."

Maddalena watched through her mirror as Nella left. She leaned closer to the mirror and ran a finger under both eyes, removing wayward traces of kohl. She licked her lips and focused again on the reflection of the doorway through the mirror.

Jakob's frame appeared in the mirror and Maddalena turned around. Nella followed behind him.

Maddalena pointed to a table across the room. "I have an empty decanter that needs filling, if you don't mind."

She watched him cross the room. She didn't find his sandy hair or his plain face to be particularly attractive. And his tall, lanky body and hunched shoulders looked awkward to her. She watched him fill the decanter of wine on the table, holding the bottle with a slight twist in his wrist. It was those hands. They looked almost oversized for his thin frame. She imagined those great animal paws grabbing her ass.

"Nella, leave thank you," Maddalena said.

"Your hair, Madame. I haven't finished."

"I can finish it. It's a braid for goodness sake. Out!" She said waving her hand.

Jakob noticed the maid being asked to leave and quickly finished what he had been asked to do. "Madame," he said, slightly bowing his head and walking towards the door.

"Pour me a drink. And pour yourself one too." Maddalena smiled her beatific smile. She knew it to be one of her winning assets.

"Madame?"

"You heard me."

Jakob returned to the table and poured two drinks.

Maddalena rose from her chair and approached him. She picked up the glasses handing one to him, making a point to rub his fingers. "To discovery," she said, downing the contents of the glass in one fluid motion.

Jakob took a sip and then another.

Maddalena poured herself another glass. "How long have you been doing this job?"

"About five years, Madame."

"What else do you do? Surely this isn't enough to fill your days?"

"I deliver wine around the castle too. It keeps me fairly busy. Sometimes I help my mother in the castle kitchen."

"It's good to help your mother. You've been almost a permanent fixture of Ansgar Castle since you were born, haven't you?"

"Yes. I was born there."

"Really?"

"Yes, Madame."

"And now here you are, all grown up." Maddalena drank from her glass.

Jakob lowered his glass. "I'm sorry, Madame, but I'm not allowed to drink on my rounds."

"I won't tell anyone anything," she whispered. "And I insist you share a glass of wine with me. I'd be insulted if you didn't."

Jakob nervously brought the glass to his lips and took another sip.

"I remember you as a boy," Maddalena said, standing close to the young man, "running around the grounds. Tearing along the hallways. You used to play a lot with my sister. You two would get up to no good and your mother would come after you, screaming at you to get back into the kitchen. You were quite the terror.

"I'll never forget the time you brought a toad into the castle. It was Princess Dea's eighth birthday, wasn't it? The

Great Hall was adorned with ribbons and candles. Hordes of young girls were carted in so it looked like she had plenty of friends to mark the auspicious occasion. The feast, the music. Everything was going along brilliantly until a great big toad jumped from nowhere into the pot of pea soup."

Jakob started chuckling.

Maddalena felt spurred on, only pausing to drink more wine. "Great sloshes of pea soup spread over the table. Girls started screaming. That toad jumped onto the potatoes, onto the fish. It was pandemonium! But oh, that mulberry pie. It's like he saved all his energy, prepared himself for the leap of his life, and dived into that mulberry pie with the force of a fired cannonball."

"It went everywhere!" Jakob said in between peals of open, relaxed laughter.

"Absolutely everywhere!" Maddalena said loudly, before bursting into hysterics. "I swear they were scraping mulberry pie off the ceiling the next day."

They both drank more, giggling in between sips.

"Oh, I so wasn't laughing that day though. My pretty dress was covered in muck."

"I got in so much trouble. Whipped raw."

Maddalena wiped away the tear that had formed in the corner of her eye from laughing so hard. "And here you are. Still getting yourself into trouble."

"Madame?" Jakob said, suddenly abashed.

"Don't be alarmed. You're not in trouble. Yet." Maddalena removed his glass from his hand and placed both glasses on the table. "I think you're the kind of young man who likes a bit of trouble though." She kissed his neck and then let her lips move around, gently tugging on his ear lobe with her teeth. Maddalena took his face in her hands and brought her lips to his, parting his lips with her tongue. There was a momentary resistance, as she suspected might be the case, before he parted his mouth and drew her in.

But it didn't last long.

"Ah, Madame," he murmured.

"Maddalena," she purred, "please call me Maddalena."

"Madame. Er…Maddalena. I really must go. I have more rounds to do."

This wasn't the first time this had happened. She wasn't fazed. They usually started off coy and reserved, but in no time she was sure, he'd be knocking on her chamber door.

"Very well," Maddalena said, as she moved back to her dressing table and proceeded to braid her hair. "You know, you have a very important job."

"I do?"

"Wine delivered all over the city, including to the castle. Am I right?"

"Yes, that's right."

"Very important. And potentially very useful."

"Useful?"

Maddalena was always struck by how little faith people had in their own power, their own cunning. Every-one had something to offer. Most people just couldn't see it. They needed to have it pointed out to them. Maddalena had learnt to give just enough to make them hungry for more. These people were so beaten into submission, made to believe that they were worth less than a jester's lame joke. Give them a small taste of self-pride and they were like putty in your hand. Remarkable things could be achieved when people were allowed to experience dignity. Thormund and his cronies just didn't understand this. In their minds, it was always and only about maintaining fear.

"You ask many questions. I'll put this to you. Everyone drinks wine. Everyone seems to need it around here like they need Gods to pray to."Maddalena secured her hair and got up out of her chair. She approached the young man, and standing beside him, ran her fingers around the collar of his shirt. "It can be dangerous to be so needy, can't it Jakob?"

Jakob didn't answer. He stood for a moment longer, Maddalena's breath close to his neck, before gently stepping back and bowing politely.

"Good evening, Madame," he said picking up his crate of bottles and leaving the room, quietly and discreetly.

Maddalena walked back to her dressing table, a smile wide across her face.

11

Willowmead Inn

Aaliya looked around the dining room. The day's events were swimming around in her mind. The birds. Justen. Flight. Alarm. She longed for something to look at, a painting or an ornament, but the walls were blank, whitewashed limestone. The flickering candlelight the only distraction in the room. Maddalena and Thormund were being equally silent, politely eating their meal with their mouths closed.

Aaliya took another large gulp of wine. She had eaten so little tonight. The carafe was in easy arms reach, and she had been extending her arm in that direction much of the evening. Much to her surprise, she hadn't been admonished for drinking so much, as now she was well on the way to having the cognizance of a goldfish.

Maddalena placed her spoon on the table. "This dinner has about as much good cheer as a dog burial."

"Do you have to say things like that?" said Aaliya slowly, concentrating on the delivery of each word.

"Well, at least now we're talking."

Thormund finished his mouthful of food and wiped his mouth with his napkin. "There was an attempt on the king's life today. All suspects have been taken in for questioning."

Maddalena looked at her father incredulously, willing him to provide more information. "Who?"

Thormund listed off four names of men Aaliya had never heard of, paused, then announced, "and Justen."

Aaliya almost spat the contents of her mouth across the room. She hadn't seen who they had rounded up. Thormund insisted they return to the stables straight away and make their way home. In the fog of her mind at the time, she didn't have the ability to put up an argument.

Maddalena's eyes widened. "What happened out there?"

He described the hunt in simple, prosaic terms. One overhearing the description would possibly mistake the afternoon's events to be little more than an inconvenient tea party. To Aaliya, the day was a massacre. She listened and considered rebuking her father's irksome testimony, but was too weary, too inebriated to say anything effectual.

"…and your sister took off, and I tried to catch up to her. So I didn't see what happened next. Then Viggo started calling out, and I turned around to see Erno Kerola lying on the ground with an arrow sticking out of his back."

"And Justen…Justen is a suspect?" Maddalena asked.

"He was near the king at the time. I don't know more than that."

"There were arrows flying around everywhere," Aaliya said, waving her arms around dramatically. "It's likely to have been a stupid accident. And now, these poor bastards are going to be tortured for it."

"Accident?" Thormund scoffed. "This was no accident. There are plenty of witnesses. The right man will be found."

"Should I be concerned?" The words came out flippantly, but Aaliya had a feeling Maddalena was being utterly serious.

"I don't know," responded Thormund.

Maddalena took an uneasy gulp of wine. "Four other men were taken in for questioning, you said. I'm sure it will come out he had nothing to do with it."

"Viggo will let me know the outcome tomorrow."

The room went silent. Each face at the table became slightly glazed over, pensive. Thormund finally took a long drink of wine, having avoided drinking all night. Normally Thormund would keep the drinking of wine at the table in tight check. With what happened out there today, he seemed content to let Aaliya drink herself into a stupor. Her bowl of food sat in front of her, barely touched.

Thormund wiped his mouth on his serviette. "I received news earlier today." Then added, "positive news."

"Well, that could be nice to share right now," Maddalena said.

"Redshade is doing exceedingly well."

"With all due respect, father, Viggo will never tell you otherwise."

"Are we going there again?" A hint of resignation to his voice.

"He..."

"The news that I wanted to share," Thormund said loudly, "is that myself and many other merchants, as well as members of the royal family, have for some time been exchanging our gold for paper money at the bank. And now it's out in the wider community. More and more people are coming into the Quadsun to exchange gold for printed money. And everyday, more and more people are buying shares in Redshade with their new printed money. Viggo has just informed me that the shares in Redshade issued recently have been bought faster than a snowball melting in hell. This shows no sign of ending."

Maddalena sat a little higher in her chair. "What if it is just sand under the Iron Steppes? What if Pieter does have Viggo in a difficult situation? It's hardly a secret that Traegos has long been desperate to acquire raw materials. And all of a sudden Viggo announces this blight on our terrain holds the very thing Traegos has desperately wanted since that mess in the Barmer Valley ten years ago." Maddalena paused, as if expecting Thormund to have a strong retort by now, but continued after noticing his continued silence. "Pieter asked Viggo to manipulate people. I don't know any more than that but I wish I did. In light of events that took place earlier today, a different way of looking at Viggo needs to be considered."

The mention of Pieter forced Aaliya to put her glass down and try her best to concentrate. Aaliya didn't understand much about the conversation, but the crackling energy around the table was almost assaulting her.

"Are you saying he had something to do with the attempt on the king's life?" Thormund asked.

Maddalena went stony, silent.

Thormund continued, "Just think for a moment what you are implying."

"If Redshade isn't going so well…assassination attempt…could be good distraction." Aaliya wasn't sure she had said what she was trying to say, but she thought it came close.

Thormund looked at Aaliya for the first time all evening. "Enough. From both of you."

"She might have a point. This is all hugely ambitious, even by your standards. What if this whole scheme goes wrong?" Aaliya had never heard Maddalena speak with a pleading tone in her voice. She sounded genuinely worried.

"What could go wrong?" Thormund replied.

Aaliya leaned forward, her glass in her hand. "Maybe someone could just walk into Viggo's bank and…and ask for their gold back in exchange for a barrow load of paper money."

Thormund reached over and grabbed the glass from her hand, bringing it noisily to the table. "You've had far too much to drink," Thormund retorted scathingly, "you don't know what you're talking about."

Aaliya knew she was drunk, but sensed an annoyance in her father that she had actually been following the conversation. Maddalena and Thormund ceased their discussion. Aaliya finally started spooning the stew into her mouth, chewing slowly. The orange flavour of the stew was so sweet she wondered how she could have let it sit in front of her all evening and not eat it. She thirsted for more, suddenly feeling ravenous. It seemed to bring some vigour back to the blood plodding around her body. In her haste to eat, Aaliya started shovelling food into her mouth, barely finishing a mouthful before taking in more. It started to drip down her chin. Sauce splashed onto her clothing. And then she mistimed the spoon going into her mouth completely, and a saucy, meaty mess dribbled down the whole front of her dress.

"Will you stop that!" said Maddalena, a look of disgust on her face.

And with the suddenness of a bubble popping, the wine started taking its toll on Aaliya's emotions. She wanted to cry, but tears wouldn't come. The thought of grabbing the whole pot of stew and pouring it over herself didn't seem like an entirely unreasonable thing to do. Just to feel something.

"What's going on?" Thormund asked Aaliya. "This is disgraceful behaviour."

Aaliya was struck by the simplicity of her father's question. What was going on? He wanted a simple response back. But after what she had heard this evening, things were far from simple.

"Excuse me," she said, "I need to go." Aaliya didn't wait to hear if this was acceptable or not. She got up, and started to walk to the dining room entrance, dragging half the tablecloth with her as she passed the table.

Aaliya trudged up the stairs to her room. Once inside, she removed her soiled dress and plonked it on the floor. She walked over to the window, and there in her undergarments, she looked out at the street scene below.

The Vysarq was dark and subdued. She watched over the street, entranced by the scene below. A Night Guard walked past, whistling a tune. Three men, who looked as though they were returning from a bout of drinking down at the docks, shared a joke with the guard and then broke out into peals of laughter. Humming music accompanied a man as he emerged from the darkness. When the small amount of streetlight fell on him, Aaliya could see the man was cradling a zanfona in his arms, a wide strap draped over his shoulder to support the weight of the instrument. He tinkered with some notes as he walked. He had on a long cloak and Aaliya wondered if he had just finished playing somewhere or was walking to a place to play his set.

Aaliya recalled Catja's offer the day before. "The dance," she said quietly.

She moved away from the window, quickly dressed into a plain dark dress, and pulled a cloak over her shoulders.

Aaliya gently shut the door behind her and crept down the stairs. She could hear the muffled sounds of Thormund and Maddalena talking in the dining room located at the back of the house. She paused on the bottom step and pulled the hood up over her head. Then, concentrating hard so as not to make a noise, Aaliya eased open the front door and walked out into the night.

Slightly uneasy on her feet, Aaliya walked briskly along the darkened street, her head facing down. She turned off the Vysarq into a side street, walking a short distance north along Rowan Lane to Catja's home. It was a narrow semi-detached stone house, blue shutters framed each window and a brass lion knocker was set like a large jewel on the blue front door.

Aaliya looked up and saw light coming from Catja's window. She set about looking for a stone on the ground to throw and alert Catja of her arrival, but in the darkness none could be seen. She got down to her knees and felt around along the cobbled street until she gathered a couple of pebbles into her hand. Catja's shutters were wide open and Aaliya aimed high for her window. Unsuccessful at first, she kept throwing the pebbles until Catja came to the window. Aaliya gestured frantically for Catja to come down. Expecting her friend to take some time getting ready, Aaliya moved into the shadows to wait. To her surprise, Catja leapt from the front doorway only moment's later.

"What?" Aaliya exclaimed, aghast. "You're ready?"

"Come on, let's go," replied Catja.

The two young women linked arms and dashed down

the side streets. The potency of the wine had eased, and with each block Aaliya walked, a satisfying sense of unrestraint grew inside her. Her heart was pounding in her chest, her stomach fluttering with a delightful mix of heedlessness and fear.

The music could be heard three streets away. Deep, rhythmic beats thumping out, vibrating the air. This end of the city felt like a different town entirely compared to her world on the Vysarq. The night was warm and sensual bringing people out of their homes, milling about on the street, relaxed and open. There was no judgment. No one cared who you were, or where you came from.

They approached the entrance to the Inn. Catja pulled back her hood and Aaliya did the same. Three horses were fastened to posts down the side of the Inn where a solitary lamp secured on the wall softly illuminated the narrow area. Aaliya instinctively walked towards the horse at the front. Reaching out to stroke the beast's nose, she heard murmurs further down the darkened alleyway. Soft, panting noises being made by a woman. She looked in the direction of the sounds. Squinting to focus more, she could see the dark shape of a woman standing against the wall, one of her legs over the shoulder of a man who was kneeling. His face seemed to be in her crotch, and by the sounds emanating from her lips, he was pleasuring her with his tongue. Aaliya couldn't see the proceedings clearly, which made the scene even more sensual to her. She imagined his tongue licking between the woman's folds of flesh. Her own loins started pulsing at the thought. The woman let out more audible gasps, bearing resemblance to the sounds of pain if one didn't know the context. Aaliya watched her lean forward and grab the sides of the man's face, before leaning back against the wall, her chest visibly heaving. Aaliya stood transfixed, her own body feverish, as she listened to the woman release a guttural, animal sound. Aaliya blinked and shook her head in an attempt to wake herself up from this state of voyeurism. She started to feel a wave of embarrassment for standing there watching.

"Your turn, sweetie," the woman down the alleyway cried, before releasing a sexy, shameless laugh.

Aaliya turned around feeling suddenly exposed and self-conscious. Catja was standing nearby, watching her.

"Enjoy that?" Catja asked.

Aaliya laughed a nervous laugh. But the truth was, she did.

Aaliya pushed open the large oak door to the Inn and hovered at the entrance, taking in the scene. It was the smell that struck her foremost, a heady blend of spice and hot blood. It was a pungent scent, but not at all displeasing. Aaliya breathed it in deeply, let her being be flooded with the sensual richness. Bodies coiling around one another, hot and slick in the torchlight, seemed to be everywhere. What few tables and chairs were in the room had been pushed up against walls. The cavernous space was for dancing and welcomed all, regardless of ability. Stairs at the back of the room were heaving with people…onlookers, drinkers, lovers embracing.

The musicians were situated on a platform at the back of the room, overlooking the crowd. The four men on the platform seemed utterly immersed in their music, barely noticing the teeming masses before them. One of the men appeared to be playing a zanfona, the other a guitar. The remaining two musicians were pounding a series of naqqarat drums situated around them. There was a violence to the drumming Aaliya had never been privy to before. The animal skins stretched taut across the hollow bowls of baked clay were being thumped and slapped frenetically. People seemed possessed by the music, their bodies answering the rhythm with seemingly little conscious control. It didn't take Aaliya long to understand how the music was having this effect. Even in her state of shocked awe, she found herself moving.

Aaliya felt overdressed. Many of the bodies in the room were distinctly unencumbered. Women bared their breasts, their bodies open, on view. They seemed to be relishing in this, like they were being caressed by the whole world not just their dancing partner. Most men were shirtless, their chests slick with moisture. Couples openly kissed, their bodies dancing like they were devouring one another. She felt like she had walked into something incendiary, like the heat in the room could light up the building and annihilate everyone contained within it.

"Catja, did you say you've been here before?" Aaliya asked, incredulously.

"A couple of times."

"I don't know whether to hug you or…hit you. This is…this is…amazing," stammered Aaliya.

"The Willowmead is legendary."

"I can see that. Legends would be born here, and dare I say it, probably end here as well. Oh, what am I doing? I don't need more trouble."

"You were the one who dragged me down here. You must need something this place provides."

Catja was right. Desire. Anger. Grief. Wanting to throw herself from the nest and see where she would land. This was exactly the place she wanted to be. Even the simple act of standing in a forbidden place felt transformative. And if nothing else happened tonight, that was good enough. It was like being a young child and discovering a secret hideout for the first time. She saw how easy it would be just to throw off caution and care little for consequences in a place like this.

"When were you planning on telling me about you and Justen?" Catja asked.

Aaliya really didn't want to talk. Not here. Aaliya partly felt shame, a sense of embarrassment over her recent incident with Justen. The man was marrying her sister in a couple of days. She should just let it go. Aaliya opened her mouth to say nothing was going on, but in the last instant she blurted out, "He doesn't want me, Catja. I tried."

Catja smirked. "I find that hard to believe."

"I kissed him. It all went wrong."

"There's a timing for everything," said Catja.

"It's not just a matter of timing. And I'm not trying again."

Catja let this comment settle before saying, "Brave for trying in the first place. The brave are always rewarded in the end."

"Believe me, it has nothing to do with bravery," Aaliya replied. She could think of a thousand reasons for her actions, but feeling brave was not one of them. "It was stupid and dumb. What was I thinking?"

"Don't be hard on yourself. We all do dumb things."

"Not like this! I just…I just want to put it behind me."

"Well, you're in the right place to do that."

Aaliya nodded her head in agreement. Yes, she was going to have some fun tonight, she thought. "You were fully ready when I came by your house. You weren't going to come down on your own, were you?"

"No, of course not."

"Come on. Who is he? Who are you meeting here tonight?"

Aaliya had seen Catja play these games before. She always extracted intimate details of other people's lives, but kept her own world intensely private. She sensed Catja had been planning to come to the Willowmead Inn tonight all along, and no amount of coyness was going to dissuade her.

"So what does he look like? At least give me a hint."

"I don't know what you're talking about," Catja said smoothly.

"Oh, *please*, Catja."

This wasn't going to be easy. The room was full of men who were perfectly Catja's type. Aaliya craned her neck and scanned the room, her gaze resting a moment longer than it should have upon a bare-chested man with deep olive skin. His hair was black and the sharpness of his cheekbones were such that he looked as though he was carved from wood. At the very least, he clearly wasn't an Ansgar local and Aaliya suspected he came from the tribal lands of the south. He swooped over to Aaliya and placed a hand on her waist.

"Come," he said, leading her away from the doorway.

"I'm a terrible dancer," she said uneasily. As they moved through the throng of writhing bodies, Aaliya turned around towards Catja and shouted, "I'll get more out of you later."

Out in the centre of the room, tribal man placed his knee between Aaliya's legs, a forceful, direct gesture like opening a lover's mouth with one's tongue. He held her firmly and started guiding her body to the music. Aaliya had tried dancing on many previous occasions, but realized she had never felt it before this moment. She was amazed to understand that her body was capable of responding to the power of music. The rhythm was hypnotic and expansive, and she felt it was there for her and for her alone.

The two dancer's loins locked together like joined by some force of gravity. It was from that central place all other moves flowed, their legs, their arms, their hips. Tribal man insisted Aaliya keep looking him in the eyes. Even in the dim light she could see they were a deep brown, almost black. They pierced her like two stones pushing through her self-doubts and insecurities. Aaliya felt demasked. Even with clothes on, she felt naked.

When she relaxed into the man's capable hands, she began to feel the same freedom that was guiding so many in the room. A wave of immense joy overcame her, and for a while, all her worries left her like a drift of smoke.

Aaliya looked around the room. Women were being thrown over men, their bodies as pliable and resilient as rag dolls. One bare-breasted woman had mounted her man, her legs wrapped around his waist. Her loose skirt had a deep split at the front and provided a thin veil of modesty from what surely was sex taking place. Aaliya tried to turn away, to look back into the eyes of tribal man but she was gripped by such blatant eroticism. Repulsed and aroused at the same time.

Surrounded by such sensuality, Aaliya started to feel feverish. She could feel tribal man's desire through the thin material of his pants. Her own juices were flowing, her nipples had hardened like stones under her clothing. She started to feel incredibly anxious at the erotic charge coursing through her body. She tried to pull away a bit, give herself a bit more room. Tribal man firmly pulled her back close, his desire pressing hard against her.

"Please," Aaliya said, moving a fraction away.

"No talking," he replied, guiding Aaliya's hip back to his and holding it there.

She let herself continue with this physical lock for a moment longer, but she couldn't shake a sense of discomfort from all the conflicting things doing battle with her emotions. The wanton lovemaking in the room, the forcefulness of tribal man, the heavy smell of sex in the air. Gasping for air, she placed her hands on his shoulders and firmly pushed him back. "I need to go outside." He reached out for her as she hurried away. Aaliya pushed through the crowd and leapt at the door, flinging it open.

Outside Aaliya took a deep gulp of air, bringing it down deep to her core. She bent down and squatted, resting her head between her knees. Looking up she saw a handful of people play-acting the scene inside the Inn. They were obviously drunk and revelled in their own bawdy renditions, laughing and rolling. Aaliya smiled at their playfulness, welcoming the lighthearted relief from the fervour inside.

She eventually stood up and opened the door, the smell once again hitting her like a huge fist. She pushed her way through the crowd, craning her head in the hope of finding Catja. She could be anywhere in this room, with anyone. Aaliya looked at the tables near the walls. Nothing. She reluctantly ventured amongst the dancing bodies. She saw tribal man had found a new partner for which she was grateful. Aaliya made her way back to the edge of the room, where she saw someone seated whom she recognized. It took a moment to register, as he was not someone she saw often. Pieter. That long pointy nose, the groomed moustache as thick as a baby's arm. Aaliya was sure it was him. He had a free chair beside him, and wasn't talking to anyone. He was looking at the dancers, and seemed somewhat transfixed by the entertainment before him.

His eyes wandered in Aaliya's direction and eventually locked with hers. They looked at each other. Saying greetings was not an option. One came to the Willowmead Inn with little desire of being discovered. A hand clapped onto Aaliya's shoulder causing her to jump.

Catja: "Where have you been? I've been looking for you."

Aaliya wrapped her arms around her friend. "Likewise. Are you alright?"

"Yes, everything's fine. Why wouldn't it be?"

"You haven't been mauled yet?"

"Sounds divine. But no, I haven't been mauled. You clearly have, you're panting."

"Look, I've had a wonderful time, but I want to go home."

Catja released a tiny sound of disappointment.

"We have to go together," Aaliya insisted.

"I'm not ready to go."

"Catja, I'm not leaving without you."

Catja looked over Aaliya's shoulder. Aaliya turned her head. Catja seemed to be looking at Pieter.

"Do you know Pieter?" Aaliya asked.

"What? No. I mean, we met at dance practice the other day, remember?"

"I'm just worried he might tell my father about me coming here tonight."

"I wouldn't be too worried about that. He'd have to admit that he was at the Willowmead as well, and that's not likely to happen." Catja glanced again in Pieter's direction. "Let's go."

They walked back silently in the direction of Catja's

home. Away from the Inn, quiescence hung in the air as heavy as overripe fruit. The few torches lining the streets were burning low. There was no one around.

Aaliya said goodbye to Catja near her friend's home, and started making the journey down Rowan Lane towards her own. She kept her face concealed by the hood. She found a wondrous beauty to darkness. The way torchlight would throw shadows onto walls making strange dancing creatures.

Arriving at her home, she looked up and saw only darkness in the windows. She tried the front door but it was locked. When she stepped back away from the door, she cocked her head slightly, sensing a presence nearby. She gingerly looked around her but saw no movement. Aaliya started walking down the side of the house towards the back. A small stone shed stood at the rear of the Reiner property as a storage facility for excess wool products from her father's business. She had slept out there a couple of times before, rising early to sneak back into her room when Nella unlocked the door early in the morning.

She reached for the handle on the shed door, and felt a hand clasp over her own. In an instant, a scream escaped her mouth. The person behind her quickly placed his other hand over her mouth.

"It's me," the man whispered hard, "Justen."

12

Walking Through an Open Door

Justen removed his hand from Aaliya's face and turned her body to face him. For a moment they both stood there, wary, unsure. In the darkness, little of each other's faces could be seen. Other things emerged which hinted at their feelings. Raspy intake of breath, slight shaking of fingers as blood pounded to their extremities. Based on recent experiences, Aaliya didn't think her senses were something she should heed. She had been here before, and maybe her trembling hand was nothing more than a shiver from the cool air. His turning up here like this was surely little more than a trick of the night. Her deepest desire befuddling her and leading her back into confusion.

Aaliya managed to gain some composure. "Did you do it?" she asked frantically.

"No, Aaliya, I didn't."

"Why did this happen? I don't understand?"

"Don't worry, shhh. Don't worry," he whispered, stroking the side of her face. "They have their man." Justen hesitated stepping closer to fully embrace her, as though sensing her turmoil.

Aaliya didn't withdrawn her hand from his. She

slightly squeezed his palm, wanted to let him know without words that she did know him. Justen took Aaliya's face in both hands. He held her face with a sureness as true as sun and wind and water, and brought her lips to his.

All fear left her in an instant, as effortlessly as walking through an open door. Her back against the shed door, she relished the sense of being enclosed as Justen settled his weight into her body. She ran her fingers around the back of his head and held him close. This kiss, the intensity and savagery of it, was instantly familiar yet as new as an infant's skin. She had ached for him many days and nights during the past two years. There was no recovering the time that had passed. And finally it felt as though there was some sense of redemption.

There was a richness to his mouth. Aaliya didn't hold back. She drew him eagerly in, hungrily curling and twisting her tongue around his. She felt her blood rising, a surge of warmth to her eyes, to her fingertips. She gripped him harder, her hands tugging at his hair and then ran her hands down his sides. She craved every bit of him.

Justen's hands moved over her body, caressing and inciting, pinching and teasing. They worked their way to her ass where they held and kneaded her flesh. Still leaning against the door, Aaliya lifted a leg around his body, his hand encouraging her to do the same with her other leg. She sensed an unbearable itch building up inside her, a deep longing to go down on his hardness out there under the night sky.

Aaliya released her arms from his body and brought her dress up over her head, flinging it to the ground. Her breasts bared, she felt as wanton as the women from the Willowmead Inn she had seen earlier in the night: consumed by desire, uninhibited and free. She almost craved for somebody to walk past and witness their passion. She imagined that someone was there beyond the shadows, watching their every move. He cupped her breast and brought the nipple to his mouth. Shots of pleasure tingled through her body.

One of Justen's hands fumbled for the doorknob. He was relieved when it turned. Still carrying Aaliya on his hips, he shuffled into the shed, kicking her dress in as he went.

The interior of the shed was as dark as coal, but warm and dry. A mere slither of moonlight illuminated the far end of the space where the one window was located. The shed was brimming with stock which they felt as their bodies knocked and fumbled around the space. Wooden crates were piled high in the corner filled with rolags of wool, hessian sacks sat bulging with oily raw fibre, and copious sheep-skin rugs climbing so high up a wall the stone work all but disappeared.

The rough wooden floor, combined with the oily smell from the fleece, gave the room a subterranean scent, earthy and pungent. It seemed just right to Aaliya, and it some-how calmed her. The feeling of being down low. Being one of the earth. Tears started in her eyes, but she blinked and they were gone. Together they bumped into the tall pile of sheep-skin rugs, knocking some to the floor. Aaliya started laughing, she couldn't believe this joy was happening.

They lowered to the ground. Aaliya fell back onto some of the fallen rugs, her legs still wrapped around his body. She unhooked her limbs and Justen removed her undergarments, leaving her completely naked. Her sex now bare, Justen breathed the scent in deeply. He threw her legs over his shoulders and brought his face down between her knees.

The feeling of Justen's soft hair against the inside of her thighs was of such inexplicable beauty she skipped a breath. His tongue lightly touched her sex, gentle but deliberate. Little pauses, like a cat first testing the water from which to drink. His tongue then made soft quick motions before moving around and exploring all the folds of her flesh. She reached for her nipples and squeezed them between her fingers. Aaliya felt herself descend to a place of deep sensuality, a wild magnificent place. A great tide began engulfing her and a deep animal sound, she barely recognized as her own, escaped from her mouth. Her whole body shuddered and shook, her legs clamped tight around his shoulders.

Aaliya reached for the buckle of his belt and began undoing it. The darkness heightened her awareness, making every gesture, every nuance, alive and vibrant. All feelings were crashing and colliding in the heady mix of hardness and softness, smoothness and ruggedness, silence and thrumming. She pushed his pants down to his ankles and he bent down and pulled the clothing away from his body. He removed his shirt and Aaliya reached out for him and touched the back of his thighs. She went to put her mouth around his penis but he took a step back.

"Justen," she said, softly, "move closer, I want you."

Justen grabbed hold of his penis and massaged it. Aaliya could hear the soft tugging sounds and she again started to feel a throbbing sensation between her legs. She felt in the dark for his body, leaning in towards the pleasant bitter smell of his naked sex. When she reached out and found him, she ran her hands up the back of his legs to his ass, before he stepped back again.

"No, Justen, I want you in me."

He stepped out of her grasp and resumed touching his

own flesh. Aaliya started to fear he didn't need her. Why was he doing this? She had waited for this for so long, thought it over and over in her head about that sweet moment when Justen would enter her body. This was not what she was expecting. It reminded her of their interaction on the steps in the castle the other night, and she couldn't bear the thought of the night ending the same way.

The darkness became disconcerting. There was little illumination to yield clues or hints, to read the expression of her lover's face. Aaliya drew nearer again and, finding his body, wrapped her hands around his buttocks. Justen withdrew his hand from his cock, which Aaliya took in her mouth before he could change his mind.

She nibbled on the tip of his cock, the velvety softness of his skin as it touched her lips arousing her instantly. There was a sense of control that was previously absent before, and it turned her on enormously. A hunger to take charge pulsed through her. Playing and sucking, she lingered there at the tip of his cock a while longer, before drawing more of him into her mouth.

He was slowly abandoning himself. Small sighs escaped his mouth, and every now and then he breathily muttered her name.

Justen suddenly pulled out of her mouth. "Lay down," he said, gently nudging her shoulder.

"But I want to do this," she said.

"Lay down," he repeated.

Aaliya fell back onto the soft pile of rugs. She arched her back in the sweet anticipation of his body entering hers. But he did not do this for her. His head fell between her knees again, his soft curls brushing her thighs. Aaliya murmured softly, joyous to be experiencing such bliss but aching to have Justen inside her.

Her breath became laboured. Justen slowed down, his tongue only softly caressing her nub. He was teasing her. She knew it. He wanted her but he wanted to unravel her too. Make the itch unbearable. Weren't these the games they played last time? She started begging, pleading for Justen to fuck her.

Justen sat up and spread Aaliya's legs wide. She eagerly awaited Justen's next move. When finally his cock touched the mouth of her sex, Aaliya gasped. It was like being scorched. His shallow, teasing penetration gave way to long, deep thrusts that left her trembling. The two of them tearing at invisible shackles.

It was as though they were riding a chariot behind a troop of harnessed horses, headed only for the edge of a cliff. Flesh charging, manes flapping like flags, urgency and power the only guide. And as the cliff edge approached, there was no slowing down to respond to the danger. Only a leaping over the edge into weightlessness, nothingness. And then, just the sublime sense of freefall and not knowing where one would land.

13

To Have and Not To Hold

Aaliya ran her hand down the length of his arm as he lay coiled around her. "You're alright," she whispered, the quiet words concealing how utterly relieved she felt.

Movement in the room had almost stilled. Aaliya's head rested in the crook of his shoulder, her leg nuzzled between his parted ones. Outside the world was quiet, becalmed. The night air was slowly cooling down, but Aaliya felt wrapped in warmth. Enclosed in enormous wings, safe and content.

"I'm fine," Justen said at last, on the cusp of slipping into sleep. "Someone's not though. I believe his name is Mark."

"Why, though?"

"The rumour is he's an insurgent. I was about to be strung up on the rack but the message came through that they had their man. Your father's friend, Viggo, looked disappointed indeed when he had to let me go."

"Viggo was the one questioning you?"

"Yes. He kept telling me all the things he was going to do to me. It occurred to me that he has practiced those same words on others many times. He seems to take a keen interest in inflicting misery."

Aaliya shuffled, feeling suddenly uncomfortable. "I don't like the man. I never have. My father literally worships him." A mutual disregard for the man seemed to be the one thing in common she shared with her sister. She had watched him for much of the past ten years as her father's business partner, systematically acquire all that he wanted, with little thought for the consequences. She was certain he had even acquired a wife simply because a man of his status must have a wife, yet Aaliya was sure the thought of sharing a life would have been abominable to him. Acquiring wealth was an absolute necessity, no matter how it was done, and any man who didn't hold this view would have been considered lower than a rat's belly. It was his lofty sense of right to acquire that seemed to persuade him to try and get what he wanted physically from Aaliya one day when she was fifteen. What he wasn't counting on was her screaming the place down. Which convinced him to not try it again, although he threatened her often that he would have his way with her one day. Aaliya wondered if he had tried it on with Maddalena as well, but it was yet another topic left untouched during the intervening years. "He places more trust in Viggo than anyone," Aaliya said finally, shaking her head.

"How can you trust a man who would willingly torture another? Your father will pay a price for that one day."

"Perhaps," she said. There was little doubt in her mind that the longer her small family remained tethered to Viggo, that harm would surely come their way. "And Mark? Did he confess?"

"I don't know. I doubt it. Do insurgents ever confess?"

"I guess not."

"If he is guilty, pity he missed."

Aaliya propped herself up on her elbow. "Justen, you can't say things like that."

"Renatus has many enemies, Aaliya."

"Don't all kings?"

"Comes with the territory."

"Just be careful."

Justen didn't respond.

"Tired?" she asked.

"Yeah."

They lay silent for a while. Justen suddenly propped himself up on an elbow. "I know the way these men work."

"What are you talking about," Aaliya said, sleepily.

Justen suddenly seemed energized. "You need to be careful too, Aaliya."

"Careful…of what?"

"Trusting."

"I'm getting the feeling you want me to know something, but you're just not telling me."

"I can't do it to you," he muttered, slumping his body back down.

Aaliya sat up. "What? Can't do what?"

"You've just lost your mother. I know that feeling. You don't need my wretchedness as well. Not now. Not with so little time to share."

"Justen, it's not just about sharing happy thoughts. That's not what we're about, is it?"

"No…no, of course not."

"What happened with Viggo today? Tell me."

She didn't understand what was going on and wanted to scoop him up in her arms, soothe him and tell him everything would be alright. Eventually he talked. Slowly at first, quietly. And then his voice lifted from a whisper and hardened. He talked about being interrogated and threatened with having his bones dislodged from their sockets. He talked about the cold fear in him, but if there had to be physical pain he was prepared to go there. The scene of blood cascading down his father's throat was firmly in his sight when he had looked into Viggo's eyes. He mentioned how he said nothing during Viggo's verbal assault. Merely returned his gaze. As much as he wanted to let those thoughts go, believe that it was possible to move on and have a different life, Justen told Aaliya that he simply couldn't forget. And he wasn't willing to forgive. Things like that just don't go away. He tried to shake off the thought but it was even there now, the whole bloody stage production of it, going over and over in his mind.

Even once they had finished talking, sleep didn't come. Aaliya assumed Justen was sleeping, or at least trying. She looked over at him, the thin light in the room indicating his eyes were closed. She rolled onto her back and closed her own. For a while she rested, relaxed. Slipped ever closer to dreams. And then she felt something wet touch her nipple. She didn't open her eyes at first, hoping to feel it again. But this time a whole mouth pressed over her nipple. An unhurried gentle, rhythmic sucking. She opened her eyes to see him sit up. He started placing long, languid strokes down the whole of her body, from her neck, across her shoulders, over her breasts, her belly and down her legs. Aaliya didn't take her eyes off him. And when he looked into her face, his eyes gripped and tortured her. She could see his lustful madness.

Dull grey light was now peaking from under the door. She had no idea what time it was, but from the stillness outside, she sensed the sun was yet to shine its rays on their city. She felt groggy from lack of sleep. Justen stood and started gathering his clothes. Aaliya remained on the sheep-skin rug, flecks of wool sticking to her damp skin, looking at the fuzz of light.

"What do you think will happen?" she said, watching him pull on his trousers and button up his shirt.

"I don't know. It's never good to be accused of something. It means there's a doubt. Doubts don't just leave in an instant."

"No, I can't see that happening either."

"Maybe you should be telling me? These are your people. What are they likely to do next?"

Aaliya sat up and cradled her legs. "Be careful of Viggo. I've seen him destroy men before for simply being late with payments. He has little regard for anyone, I believe. As for the king. Well, he's..." she lowered her voice to a whisper, "...he's clinging by his fingernails. He sees threats everywhere. Some warranted, others not so. Maybe that makes him more dangerous."

"And your father? Should I be wary?"

"My father doesn't cope well when things don't go according to plan."

"I'll take that to be a yes."

"One other thing, should you be wary of Pieter?"

"My mother would be throwing daggers in your direction if she heard you say that."

"Oh, I didn't mean..."

"She's got a thing for Pieter. Regards him as some sort of saviour of the family. He got me off the Range which she has never stopped being incredibly grateful for. I was too young to fight in the Battle of Barmer, but when I was fifteen, mother couldn't hold me back any longer. I joined a militia force as a mounted cavalryman. I remember being asked my age and telling the officers I was eighteen. They laughed. Thought I was a child. But they didn't mind. Said they'd be happy to have me along. Mother was grief stricken. I knew what she was thinking. She couldn't bear to lose another loved one. I tried to assure her I'd be back, but to be honest, I wasn't sure. I wanted to get away. Somehow find my own identity. Work out who I was."

"And did you?"

"Yes…yes I believe I did. I was sent to an outpost high in the Range. I remember seeing those mountains for the first time. They were like walls that seemed to close around the land below, and it was as though those walls could at any moment crush the land and turn it to rubble. The sheer sight of the mountains in those parts terrify some men. The thought of perishing in such an unforgiving landscape too much to bear. For me, the mountains were the preparation for the moment I knew was coming.

"I'm sure you know the history. Traegos forces came over the range. The blood, Aaliya, you never forget the blood. Those soldiers just kept coming and I hated them. I hated their…their willingness to die. For six months, through the rain…it was endless…the fighting showed no signs of stopping.

"But then it did. Quite suddenly. They just seemed to disappear. Traegos retreated and the outpost emptied. I stayed on as long as I could rebuilding the roads and the military bases. And then I returned home not long after my seventeenth birthday to an offer of employment.

"Pieter was a pivotal player in successfully establishing trade routes across the realm for Gedion's raw materials after the Battle of Barmer. Even back then, his entrepreneurship gained the attention of our royal family. My mother was grateful to have such an influential person somehow overseeing her family, providing security. But I believe there was more to it. I simply believe she felt indebted to Pieter for returning me to her. It has always been made clear to me that I was to heed whatever Pieter advised. And here I am."

"Here you are," Aaliya said.

"About to embark on something that will change my life forever."

Aaliya stood and did the remaining buttons on his shirt. "Don't do it. Let's just go, Justen. You and me."

He looked at her, briefly turned away, and then faced her again. "You know, I've heard of people doing that. Just leaving, just walking away from it all. But I've never heard how it goes for them. Whether or not it works out. Does it destroy them? Do they somehow thrive?"

Aaliya gently held his face. She knew that feeling. That familiar knot of competing thoughts, working out what one wants, what's realistic.

"I wish I could do that. I really wish I could. But I can't," Justen said.

"You won't be alone."

"No, I'd have you. I think about us all the time. How we could make it work. And for me it comes back to somehow planning it out."

She smiled. "You will get along with my father."

"I don't think my kind of planning will put me in his good books."

"What have you got in mind?"

"Going through with the wedding. Give it a couple of years. And maybe, just maybe, that might turn out to be a better time for us. To be together."

"Years? Anything could happen in a couple of years."

"I know. Anything *could* happen. But that's the only way for me, Aaliya. I still want to go through with this wedding. I want the alliance to take place."

"Why is that so important? We'd have each other. Isn't that enough?"

"It should be enough. But it's simply not. There's nothing romantic or normal about my life. I can't easily remove the politics I'm involved in. And I don't know that I necessarily want to. I want to see my family again. I'm sure you do too, even if you don't want to admit it. There are things I need to see to that I can't even begin to explain. Not right now, anyway. But in time. Be patient, Aaliya. I truly believe that with time, anything is possible."

"You're talking like you can have some sort of control over future events. You can't. You never will. I want to be with you now. Whatever problems you think lie ahead, we'll work through them. Whatever you need to see to, I want to be by your side. My mother actually encouraged me to forget about love altogether and stick with friendship. But what I know is that it is possible to meet someone who you are drawn to so deeply, so inexplicably, that even when the world of family, expectations, even politics… tries to spin you in the other direction, you come back to this one thing that is so rare and so special it needs to be heeded."

Justen closed his eyes and shook his head. "I'm sorry."

Silence.

Aaliya stared up at the roof of the shed. What had been a black void ten minutes ago was changing. She now noticed the cobwebs up high draped across the wooden beams. She looked back at Justen. She truly could have looked into his eyes forever. "So…this is all we have?"

"This is all we have," he repeated, softly.

"Until…"

"Until when, I don't know. We waited two years before."

"Yeah, what's another two? Is that what you're thinking?"

Justen shrugged.

"Anything could happen," she said. "No promises."

"No promises."

"So, I guess all we've got is a few more days?"

He nodded.

"I don't think I can bear to see you marry my sister."

Justen grabbed her hand and stroked it. Circled her knuckles, ran his finger over the back of hers and then turned her hand over and traced the lines of her palm. "If I could see you again, I would be a happy man. If I can't, I'll understand that as well." Justen wrapped her cheeks in his hands and brought her lips to his.

He left a short time later, leaving Aaliya to remain basking in the pleasant warm fug of the morning for what seemed like another hour. Before he left, they made arrangements to meet near the giant oak the following day. All she could think about now was passing time until she could see him again.

Aaliya sat up, passing her fingers through her matted hair. Would it be obvious to anyone who saw her that she had not spent the night in her own bed? Did she care? Not particularly. Although she knew this could land her into trouble, the need to get up and walk held a potency she couldn't ignore. The sensible thing would have been to go inside her home, tell Nella she had gone for an early morning ride, have some breakfast of rye and honey. But she didn't feel hungry. Thoughts were swimming through her mind giving her energy, making the need for food seem excessive. We found each other again. Time had not diminished anything at all. The connection felt stronger than ever. And now it was time to let go.

But how could she let go of something that made her feel whole, that brought her deep joy, that somehow shaped her to be the person she wanted to be. There was a helplessness in letting go, a stark, solid reminder that she couldn't change things that she wanted to so badly.

When he was in her arms, everything felt simple and right. An act of truth. A swim in the sea of rapture. And yet, it was far from simple and was wrong in so many ways. When Justen had got up to leave in the fuzzy early morning light, it wasn't so much that he was walking out. He was walking towards his family as surely as if they had been standing in the doorway waving him towards them. Walking towards some calling he could not let go of, not for her, not for anyone. She wished now she had asked more questions, tried to understand what he was going through. She could control Justen no more than she could control Helena and her spiral into death.

Aaliya stood and gathered up her clothes. She quickly dressed, pulled on her boots and started running her fingers through her knotted hair. She gathered up the sheep-skin rugs that had fallen onto the floor. The ones she and Justen had made love on top of were shoved to the bottom of the pile. Aaliya ran her hands down her clothes, hoping she looked acceptable enough to walk out. And then without giving it any more thought, she opened the door.

She briskly walked away from the Vysarq and headed down side streets until she got to Stohl Road. Her head remained down for much of the journey, heeding little of her surroundings. She could smell freshly baked bread, and sensed the growing movement of the Ansgar population. The morning traders were out crying their wares, cloaks and long garments were swooshing around her, their hems captured in her lowered sight. Underfoot the cobblestones were worn smooth, eroded from hundreds of years of frenzied foot traffic. People were everywhere. Rushing around, performing their errands, walking with a sense of purpose, a destination in mind.

Aaliya felt a hard bump against her shoulder. She looked up to see an old woman, her face red from exertion, or heat, or both. For a moment the woman looked as thought there was a glint of recognition in her eye. Aaliya contemplated running back to her house. The woman slipped back into the crowd, a bundle of freshly killed pheasants dangling by their feet in each hand. It was then that Aaliya noticed that a man was standing not far from her, looking directly at her. His hair was short cropped and red. Aaliya turned around and continued to walk.

Many people around her were laden with goods: sacks of flour, crates of candles, melons, pears and pomegranates, linen and furnishings. Wine barrels and wooden carts were being pushed in every direction heavy with flagons and tankards and plates, and enough firewood to keep kitchen furnaces going night and day for weeks. The wedding was in four days, and although preparations had been going on for some time the frenzied activity around her jolted her out of her incognizance. Perhaps some of these provisions were heading to the castle in preparation for the event?

The aedes was located close to the western city wall at the end of Stohl Road. The spire and the tops of the grand trees gracing the grounds came into view. Aaliya wove through the headstones and monuments, lined up neatly facing east. She headed for a copse of yew trees at the edge of the walled grounds. Knowing she was getting closer, she breathed a little deeper. When at last she was under the shade of the trees, she stopped and knelt down beside the ornate marble headstone.

Helena Annestine Reiner
Loving mother and noble wife

She thought she had been going well, moving on as she had been encouraged to do. But sitting there beside her mother's grave she felt broken. She thought she had it all worked out – life, love, people. But she realized she knew so little. She knew the affair with Justen was wrong, a betrayal, but she didn't want to put a stop to it. It was the one thing that made her feel alive. He had made it clear that he was going through with the wedding, and yet she still didn't want to walk away.

She looked up and turned her head. A man was standing a distance away, leaning against the trunk of a tree staring at her. The man she had seen earlier on Stohl Road. The sight of him gave her a start. She returned her gaze to the headstone, and when she turned her head ever so slightly back in the man's direction, she saw that he was no longer there. Aaliya gave a great sigh, like she had been holding in her breath all that time. The words 'loving mother' were read over and over, each line in each letter traced with her eyes. A tear ran down her cheek. A solitary, lonely run.

14

The Tannery

The Vysarq on this summer morning was a raucous and bustling thoroughfare. It was a road lined with fabric shops, bookshops, apothecaries and butchers. Although the Great Market was a daily event in Ansgar, the morning seemed particularly chaotic. Children were running to-and-fro brandishing their hoops and sticks, bread-sellers were hollering loudly their wares, and men and women were pushing their carts of meat and grains with such belligerence one was lucky to escape a physical shove. The road seemed to follow like a tedious discussion, noise and obstacles Maddalena would prefer to shut out.

Banners and bunting marked the entrance to the Great Market, the fabric stretched across the buildings in the square had faded over time, the threads worn thin. Where tables used to heave with the iridescence of fresh food, the produce now seemed imbued with a pale hue. Goats stood tethered and bored, chickens and roosters squawked in their cages. To the side was an open-air kitchen where giant cauldrons bubbled over fire-pits, barley and cabbage simmering incessantly in weak broths. People hovered in the darker recesses of the square, their faces blank as if in some sort of trance.

Maddalena passed through the square, thinking about recent events. Her fists slightly clenched, she walked with a sense of urgency, great strides leaping across the cobblestones. The lack of control over her own life was starting to wear thin. There were only a couple more days to the wedding and the last thing she wanted was sleepless nights contemplating a murderous husband. The news from her father was playing havoc with her peace of mind, even rudely inhibiting the wantonness of her lovemaking with her boys last night. Justen a suspect, for God's sake. She didn't know this man she was about to marry at all. For all she knew, revenge could be exactly what he had in mind. But it somehow didn't seem to fit. Recalling the scene of Viggo and Pieter together on the fourth floor of Ansgar Castle three days earlier, Maddalena couldn't help but feel that the events seemed a little muddy, even sinister. Pieter told Viggo something he didn't want others to hear. Pieter, more than anyone, would know, or have ways of knowing, what his nephew was up to. Why would Pieter knowingly implicate his nephew in such a serious crime if it wasn't true?

She could just go and extract a confession from Justen. She had ways and means and the very thought of them brought her a twitch of delight. But he would just deny it. So close to a wedding, people barely resembled human beings anymore. More like bumbling, single-minded fools incapable of honest, independent thought. So what could she do? When she woke up this morning, she lay in bed staring at the underside of the canopy draping her bed. Her mind wandered in many directions, but always came back to one person. Her sister. She could just ask Aaliya what she knew, but this would reveal that Maddalena strongly suspected the affair between her sister and Justen, and spark a train of events she would have little control over. But Aaliya did have a confidant. Maddalena had always found Olle to be slippery to deal with. He knew so much more than he let on. His impoverished tradesman underclass persona had never fooled her. Although she didn't know exactly what his motivations were, she had always suspected him to be a man of wide and far-reaching connections.

Maddalena had long been envious of Aaliya's relationship with her saddle making friend, and had long wondered if she would be the same woman if she had a man such as Olle in her life. Although she rarely saw the two of them together, Maddalena couldn't help but wonder and speculate over the subtleties of their connection. That friendship, that overarching sense of looking out for each other, was clearly very real. But Maddalena was sure there was a whole additional element underneath the surface. Not necessarily a sexual thing, but definitely a power thing. Although, she was sure sex was still a part of it, even if it was simply an assessment being made.

Was Olle grooming Aaliya for something? Gently and patiently unearthing something submerged in her that would cause alarm if revealed in haste?

Maddalena reached the saddle workshop at the northern end of the Vysarq and walked in to find the front room empty and quiet. She cried out and looked around. An apprentice emerged from the backroom and informed her that Olle had left half and hour ago to buy hides from the tannery at Qlots Creek. A visit to a stinking tannery was not what she had bargained for. Great masses of grey clouds were heaving and colliding and she feared it could rain anytime soon. A tannery was not the kind of place she wanted to get caught in the rain. However, with the wedding looming, she didn't have the luxury of time. She thanked the apprentice and left the workshop, fighting her way back through the crowds of the Great Market until she arrived at the stables. She wasn't dressed for a trip to the tannery. Her dress was too long, the fabric too delicate. And on her feet were silk flats--fine for a small errand around the city, but potentially useless for the muck she would likely encounter out at Qlots Creek. With the help of the stable hand her horse was promptly saddled up. She rode up Floran Road, keen to avoid the madness of the Great Market, and headed in the direction of the city walls, her long dress flapping around her ankles like wings.

Maddalena knew she was close to the tannery when a meaty, pungent smell hung in the air like soupy fog. The creek running alongside the ragged track was a brown clog. It moved slowly downstream, death and blood and shit seemed to be the main things making up the liquid composition of the flow. Maddalena grimaced as she looked sideways at the creek from her horse. She was sure she saw bits of flesh in there. The creek hardly resembled a waterway but more a cesspool of waste.

The trees began to thin out and the outermost structures of the sprawling tannery came into view. It was an expansive enterprise, and appeared like a village upon Maddalena's approach. A group of men and women, some kneeling near the creek edge, others knee high in the water, were scrubbing down what appeared to be freshly butchered animal skins. The water flowing around their legs resembled a grim soup. Cleaned hides were tossed to the side where they were loaded onto a cart and wheeled to large vats. A team of men with red raw hands then dunked the hides in a noxious concoction using long poles. Nearby, a group of women seemingly oblivious to the smell, had hides laid out on the ground like carpet, scraping the loose hair off the cleaned hides with single edged knives. The atmosphere was miasmic. Maddalena covered her nose with her sleeve, but the effort didn't remotely alter the profundity of the stench.

Maddalena looked around for Olle, hoping she would see him and not have to go searching through the grounds. Large oak trees dotted the landscape, all completely stripped of bark around the trunks. She reluctantly dismounted and secured her horse to one of the trees. Near where she stood, a man peeled off freshly butchered animal skins from a pile on a cart. One-by-one the remaining flesh and hooves and horns were cut off and discarded onto the ground creating a great macabre pile of bone and gristle. She walked past the large vats of lime solution feeling the grit underfoot seeping though her thin silk shoes. She hitched up her dress and crossed over the makeshift bridge spanning the creek.

She approached a man standing near one of the oak trees, drying his bloodied knuckles on his navy apron. Only brief questioning was required. Of course he knows who Olle is, he assured her. Everyone knows Olle. The man directed her to a brick shed at the eastern edge of the grounds. Maddalena thanked the man and began walking in that direction.

The red brick shed came into sight. Two men were standing out the front. Even from the distance she could see both were of considerable height. She imagined their bulk would consume much of the space in the small shed they were in front of. As she got closer, she recognized Olle. It didn't matter that he had a belly, his face somewhat awkward, inelegant. He was a man in his prime, and Maddalena was sure he knew it. He was standing beside an enormous man dressed in black, under the awning of the brick shed. A flash of recognition came across Olle's face, and then softened into a somewhat bemused expression. He motioned her over with a tilt of his head.

"Maddalena, this is Salomon Ezcaroz. He runs this establishment," Olle said, smiling, as she stopped beside him. "Salomon, Maddalena Reiner."

Maddalena expected Olle to introduce her as the 'daughter of Thormund Reiner', but he didn't. She held out the back of her hand and Salomon reached for it and brought it to his lips.

"A pleasure, Madam Reiner," said Salomon.

"And you, Seigneur Ezcaroz."

"You are brave to venture to the tannery. Not the most pleasant place for a morning's outing," said Salomon.

Maddalena looked behind her. "No. The word pleasant doesn't come to mind. But I am impressed, Mr Ezcaroz. You run a thriving business."

"Yes, I was just discussing here with Master Olle that nearly five years ago this was a very small venture indeed. Demand for leather has risen considerably. I am only just managing to secure the materials I require to process the skins and meet demand."

Discussing business was something Maddalena felt comfortable with. It was a skill she had developed through endless debate with her father and reading reams of parchment on the personal memoirs of merchants throughout the ages. She watched as Salomon's face lit up with delight when she recounted the story of Pav Eilmar whose profitable dye business went bankrupt when his former lover went on a scathing campaign to discredit him claiming he was riddled with syphilis; or how Villars Paldeen established the first shipbuilding enterprise out of the Port of Tshane and is now operating with two thousand men and an annual turnover of three hundred thousand krones.

When at last they finished their discussion, Maddalena and Olle farewelled Salomon and walked towards Olle's horse, secured to a nearby tree.

Olle unhitched the reins from around the branch. "My condolences for your recent loss, Maddalena. Helena was a fine woman."

"Thank you," Maddalena said.

"Young people should not have to bear the agony of losing a mother."

"It happens to many. Death is everywhere. We're walking on it right now." She turned her head and looked around. She felt as though she had lost her mother years ago, and that what happened a couple of days previously was merely the final adjustment, the lowering of the flag at the battle's end.

Olle's eyes followed, as if noticing something for the first time. "Were you ever told the story of the reed and the tree as a young child?"

"No."

"Well, a reed and a tree were disputing about their strength and powers of quiet endurance. When the reed was reproached for being weak and easily bent by wind, it answered not a word. And then a great storm came through. The reed took being tossed about and bent by the gusts, weathering the storm; while the tree, which resisted the wind, is broken by the storm's violence and tumbles to the bank to lay amongst the reeds. It's just a story, but you seem to be bending with the wind, wouldn't you say?"

"Bending with the wind," she repeated, softly. "You know, I actually just really feel like I'm sinking in animal excrement."

Olle laughed. "I love this place too."

"That's impossible," Maddalena said, stepping over some stray bones.

"Why not? It's as good a place as any."

"It stinks. It's filthy. And it's…just…repugnant."

"It's business, and a man's strange and wonderful role in that. You of all people should understand."

"Why? Because of who my father is?"

"No, because of who *you* are. You're on the king's counsel. You provide advice about strategic affairs, do you not? The knowledge required to do that is immense, in my opinion, especially for a young person."

"I read a lot. And talk to my father."

"Well, you can't go off hearsay your whole life. You've got to see things for yourself."

"The way I've done things has got me this far." As soon as she said it, she regretted it. She did want to hear what he had to say, did want some guidance above and beyond what her father had provided her. Her father had helped lead her to the point of marriage to a young man with valuable connections in a foreign land. It was what she had always wanted. But now she wasn't so sure. Was there further she could go, in a different direction? "Ezcaroz seems an interesting man," Maddalena said, embarrassed at her previous outburst and keen to change the topic.

"He seemed impressed with you."

"He would have to be very wealthy to run an establishment this size."

"He runs it. He doesn't own it. The wealth lies with the

Manegold Abbey of Everarda. Monasteries, as a rule, run exceptional businesses and tend to amass incredible wealth."

"You seem to know a lot of people, Olle."

"Perhaps for a saddle maker, yes I can see this. But compared to your father, I probably know very few."

"Oh, I don't know about that. My father has always lived in Traegos. He's travelled, yes. He's a merchant after all. You though, you're from elsewhere. Your accent is different. Where are you from?" Maddalena asked.

"I have been in Traegos for fifteen years."

"I know."

"But yes, I am from elsewhere," Olle replied, his eyes fixed ahead of him. "I was born and raised in Rone. But spent many years in Asturia."

"The Land of the Maqibah. What could possibly take a man from Rone to a land of poor ethnic tribes?"

"Wealth," Olle said, unassumingly.

"How so?"

"High demand for weaponry and other tools of war."

"Tools of war being saddles?" Maddalena said with a slight scoff to her tone.

"You say saddles like they are of little importance. You won't win the war if you fall off your horse."

"So you got rich from this venture in Asturia?"

"Clearly not rich," he said, pulling out the front of his ragged shirt like it was an emblem. "But a certain wealth, I do believe, was acquired."

"There's rich and there's poor in our world. No in-between."

"You see wealth only in terms of riches. I see it in terms of abundance."

Maddalena's eyes narrowed. Her confidence suddenly

unhinged.

Olle continued. "Monetary wealth and the ownership of beautiful things have their place to be sure. But we only own something while people agree that we do. And if people stop agreeing, well…let's just say, you will need a good pair of boots."

Maddalena instinctively looked down at his boots. They were not those of a poor man. His clothes may have been soiled and ill-fitting, but his boots were immaculate: high-grade tan leather, rising above his ankles, snugly secured with long leather thread. What it would feel like to be a man of little wealth, each day slipping ones feet into the most beautiful boots available; ones that would normally be reserved only for princes and noblemen? She imagined it would feel exceptional, rare even. And that rareness would create a sense of abundance.

They arrived at the tree where Maddalena's horse was secured. She pulled the reins loose and turned to face Olle. "And this is what you tell Aaliya, is it?" she said. "I've always found it interesting why a young woman, the daughter of the most powerful merchant in Traegos, should choose to work like a pauper in a grubby workshop for much of her life."

"Maybe you should ask her."

"I have. She's not very forthcoming."

"And this is why you're here? You're not satisfied with her answers so you track me out to this place you find so godforsaken, urgently wanting to understand your sister's motivations before you run off to Gedion?

"Yes. Partly."

"A woman, like a man, has to be something. I believe, for Aaliya, it is that simple."

Maddalena wasn't so sure. "What do you want from

her?"

"Do you think there is an exchange going on?"

"There's always an exchange."

He mounted his horse and seemed to focus on some point in this distance. Maddalena climbed onto her saddle, the edge of her dress now caked in mud.

He turned to her and smiled. "I wish you well in your marriage." He lightly tapped his horse on the neck, getting ready to move.

"Justen Laus," she said, reaching out to stop him, "the man from Gedion I'm due to marry in a few days. Do you know him? Has Aaliya mentioned anything about him?"

"I know nothing about him. Aaliya hasn't mentioned him at all."

15

The Bunker

Aaliya couldn't remember picking herself up from beside her mother's grave yesterday afternoon and getting herself home. Something inside her directed her where to step, which roads to follow, without her knowing much about it. She had a faint memory of seeing Nella on the stairwell as she climbed the steps to her room. Were words exchanged? She didn't know. She only knew that it was late in the day, and she had woken to the smell of Nella's cooking drifting around her, and her father standing in the doorway of her room. He didn't say anything, just stood there, as if sensing she was slowly being pulled back from a place that was foggy and amorphous. Aaliya brought her parched lips together and strained as she moistened the inside of her mouth and swallowed. She hadn't drunk anything or eaten all day. Her body now ached with hunger.

Thormund crossed the room and poured her a cup of barley tea. He handed the tea to her, and she took the cup, shaky with disbelief at the warmth of the gesture. She gulped down the cool liquid, and waited for it. It was surely coming. The disappointment, the humiliation of it all, what the hell was she thinking? Maybe the whole household knew she had not returned to her room last night. Maybe Nella had told Thormund she saw Aaliya stumbling up the stairs looking ragged and spent. But the recriminations didn't come. Instead, they both remained still, she on the edge of the bed, he standing beside her, silently looking at each other.

Was he finally feeling it too? That sense that something inside had shattered, the shards now scraping along everything underneath the skin. A thought came to Aaliya's mind of a time when her family had made a concerted effort to do something together. Aaliya recalled that she would have been around eight at the time, a point when her father was increasingly working long hours. On that blistering summer day, Thormund had suggested taking a small boat upstream along the river, just the four of them. There was little wind to fill the sail that day. Thormund worked the oars, and seemed to relish the physical challenge of it. When they were far enough upstream and the sprawl of Ansgar had eased to a few farm houses, Thormund rowed close to the embankment. Without warning, Helena stood up and dived into the water. The remaining three in the boat watched agog as she laughed and kicked, and threw herself around like a contented seal.

"You must all come in," she called out, "you can't miss this."

Although not the strongest of swimmers at that stage in their lives, Aaliya and Maddalena had been taught the basics to keep themselves afloat. Learning to swim was unusual amongst the inhabitants in the city, but Helena saw it as an essential bodily function. As important and natural as walking.

While Thormund was demanding his wife to get back in the boat, Aaliya stood and jumped in. Aaliya could remember that feeling as if it were yesterday. The tingle of the cool water hitting her hot skin felt restorative, like she had stepped into a forbidden world, a world that would at any moment close back up and thrust them all back into reality. With some coaxing, Thormund dived in and finally, Maddalena. They were all in. Together. No one else was around to suggest it was irresponsible or inappropriate. For a brief while, expectations and status didn't matter. It was the rarest of moments, which is why it remained so vivid in her mind.

As Aaliya looked into her father's face, she wondered if he thought about these things as well. Families are funny things, she concluded. So much left unsaid. She knew full well Maddalena was her father's favourite child, just as she had been her mother's favourite. Taking favourites was some-thing, she was sure, took place in most families, though would often be denied. Aaliya had to admit that while her mother was alive, she had loved her mother more than her father, as well. And now with her gone, she wondered if it was possible to put aside these conscious choices and be open to something new.

Thormund opened his pursed lips, and breathed through his mouth with a sharp intake of breath. He paused, holding his breath for a moment. Aaliya was sure he was about to say something. Something that had to be said. Something she had to hear. But he exhaled noisily without uttering a word.

After another long pause, Thormund did finally speak, "It's supper time. I'll see you downstairs."

Aaliya didn't have to be here. She knew she could just turn and go home. Even when she made the arrangement with Justen, an uncomfortable feeling overcame her. What good can come of this? Yes they'd kiss, hold each other, take each other's clothes off. And that would feel good. Hell, it would feel great. But then what? That journey into loss and despair would follow as certain as fingernail growth. That cycle of being alone with her thoughts. Grappling with her jealousy and hurt. How could he not change his mind if he loved her? What an imbecile he was! What a complete tosser!

She shifted in her saddle, her horse still and content with its head lowered to the ground under the large oak tree. Aaliya's eyes scanned the landscape before her. Her gaze rested on the open grassy area where only days earlier she watched Justen and his uncle riding towards her and the group of women practicing strange moves in the midday sun. So little time had passed but such large things had happened. A destabilising mix of contempt and desire charged through her. Why did she want to fuck him so much when he made her so angry? She imagined telling him how she felt. Yes, she would do that today. When he rode up alongside her she'd be prosaic and sensible and tell him that she just couldn't do this anymore. It was wrong and stupid and mentally wrecking her. She could be strong. Everyone seemed to think that she carried herself with a certain robustness. She didn't know why. Sometimes she thought she had the strength of a day old fawn. A mere delicate critter bumbling through the wilderness.

One thing was for sure, getting drenched was not the way Aaliya imagined a meeting with Justen. She thought herself reasonably perceptive to the changing patterns in the sky. But the change that came over during the day was violent and sudden. One minute the was sky was blue. Next, great thundering clouds bustled and mustered across the late afternoon sky. Aaliya felt uneasy. With each minute the clouds got angrier and darker. He'll come, she told herself. She looked in every direction anxiously. Where was he? Providence shook his head and redistributed his weight, as if sensing her solicitude and getting ready to move.

A fat drop of rain landed on her hand. Then another and another. And then the sky opened up and whole creatures of water poured down saturating the earth. Her shelter under the oak tree started to struggle under the pounding from above.

Aaliya kept looking in the direction of the castle from where she expected Justen to come. Only an empty expanse of ground before her, and trees sagging under the weight of water. She couldn't stay out for much longer.

A slight movement to her right drew her eye towards a thicket of pines. A flock of birds launched into the sky. And then a man emerged from the concealment of the trees on a dappled grey. When she saw the figure in the distance her big defiant stance melted into liquid. Everything just feels better in those arms. Her hand reached up to the top button of her dress and tugged at it. Gods of Life and Death, Justen, I love this, I hate this! Do you know what you're doing to me? Why don't I have the strength to walk away?

The horse was walking slowly. Aaliya squinted her eyes to try and get a better look.

"Justen?" she whispered.

The rider moved closer, seemingly untroubled by the sheets of water pounding down on him.

When at last he came into focus, Aaliya could see it wasn't Justen. She recognized him to be the man she had noticed the afternoon she visited her mother's grave. She thought it strange to be walking the horse slowly though the rain. Aaliya did another scan around her, but there was no one else. What had happened to Justen? What did this man want with her?

The rider moved closer under the expanse of the oak. Aaliya could see he was in leather pants and a long leather jacket that covered his body down to his knees. This was expensive outfitting. He was a man of importance to someone. His flame-coloured hair was extremely short. At first it looked as though two long scars were slashed down his face as the creases in his cheeks were so deep. His eyes were as dark as cold furnaces. Aaliya felt a raw, menacing feeling. She tried to tell herself that this feeling was due to being out in the grey wet, but as the rider edged closer, it simply felt all wrong.

The man pulled his horse up alongside Aaliya. "Strange for a young lady to be out in weather like this," he said.

"It's as good as anything we get," Aaliya replied.

A grin went across his face. "Wouldn't it be better to be inside by the warmth of a fire, doing your needlework or whatever you ladies do?"

"I'm happy enough out here," Aaliya said, a caustic taste in her throat.

"You under this particular tree for a reason, miss?"

Aaliya looked hard at the man. "You have a lot of questions."

The man edged his horse closer to Aaliya and leaned in towards her. "Now I'm thinking you're out here to meet someone. Someone you shouldn't be meeting. Am I right?"

Aaliya told herself not to show fear but the slight tremble in her hands as she gripped the reins revealed her self-deception. "I don't know who you are. Just turn your horse and walk away."

To this, he didn't reply or move. He remained still, a weird smirk on his face. Eventually he spoke. "Like listening to private conversations, do you?"

"I don't know what you're talking about."

"You run fast. I'll give you that."

"Go!" she demanded.

He clutched her arm in his large hand, a grip so strong Aaliya feared he might pull her off her horse. "Let's make our way back to the castle together shall we?" he said in a low, growling voice.

Aaliya didn't have the strength to remove the man's grip from her arm, but she knew her horse did. In one swift movement she leaned low from her saddle, gripped the reins firmly and kicked her horse hard in the ribs. Providence bolted, his ears pinned back as he charged across the field. She looked over her shoulder and saw that the man was racing to catch up to her. The rain came in sideways and lashed her face. If she could get to the woods, an area she knew well that offered her concealment, she may be able to throw the man off track.

But he was a fine horseman. He tailed close behind, the hooves of both horses pounding the wet ground, a loud thrumming sound reverberating in their wake. Both raced through the clearing. Aaliya veered in a loose direction, but he matched her every move. Just have to get to the woods, she told herself.

Up and over the ridge, she rode Providence at a sustained, feverish pace she had never experienced before. It was the closest she could imagine to flying. The edge of the woods came into view. There was no direction but forward now. And with a last strenuous dash, Aaliya lead her horse into the tree filled world.

The dark of the canopy was instant relief. It felt familiar and safe, like she could call on the natural environment to help her. Aaliya weaved between trees, guiding her horse through the thicket as she had done many times before. Aaliya sensed the man was still close, but she believed she had at least gained a stride or two ahead of him.

It was like time had stopped and her and Providence were as one. All that mattered was the short distance she could see ahead of her, and getting there as quickly as she could. The uneven ground spurred her on, madly jumping over fallen logs and avoiding low hanging branches by a whisker. She rode on. She had a sense she was covering an enormous distance, probably the whole length of the royal forest. She looked behind again and saw no movement. She knew she was alone. She listened hard but there wasn't much to hear other than the raspy breath of her horse and his hooves hitting the ground.

She tugged at the reins and eased her horse to a gait. He's gone. Aaliya looked around once more in every direction. The only movement the leaves bouncing in the rain.

A dull light was all that remained in the woods, barely illuminating her own skin. She had no idea how much time had passed. It felt like hours, but it was probably only minutes. Although she knew the woods well, the run had disorientated her. Aaliya suddenly felt cold to the bone and knew that if she didn't get herself back soon, she would have a long, miserable night ahead of her outside.

Aaliya guided the horse back in the direction she had come. Her body remained rigid, expecting the man who had followed her to reappear at any moment. With the little light she had left, she took in every tree, every rock. The sky offered only thick cloud so it was not possible to be guided by the setting sun. Fear continued to ripple through her, coating her every thought. She recalled the man's cold, black eyes as clearly as if he were standing in front of her. Aaliya knew now she had completely misjudged her ability to follow her heart free from scrutiny.

For now, keep going in a straight line she told herself. She wondered if Justen was alright. What had stopped him coming to their arranged meeting place? And how did that man know where to find her? Justen wouldn't tell anybody, would he? So many questions needed answering.

Aaliya finally came across a recognizable feature. Large granite boulders loomed before her. It was all she needed to confidently nudge Providence to a gentle run in the direction of the castle. Emerging at last from the forest, she started riding towards the stables. As much as she wanted to discard the wet clothes clinging to her, she craved connection. More than anything she wanted to see Justen, but that was simply not possible.

After crossing the bridge straddling the River Albo, she changed her mind and kept moving up the Vysarq. Olle would have a cloak to wrap around her. And she needed to see him.

The last of the day's light gently touched the walls and windows of the great street, retreating at the edges to cool blue shadows. Torches were being lit on the outside of buildings. Bodies were moving about street, a certain weariness from the day's work.

Aaliya arrived at the workshop. There was no torch a-flame on the outside of the building, but that wasn't unusual for Olle. He would often stay around long after the other saddle makers had gone to clean up or sometimes just to sit with a drink in hand. She looked up and the quarters above where he resided were also in darkness. Aaliya dismounted and stood beside her horse. A woman at the end of something and on the cusp of a beginning.

She tried the handle of the door but it was bolted from the inside. A dog with a wary expression watched her as she tried the front window, but it was also locked shut. C'mon Olle, she thought, I know you're in there, I just want to see you. The wet clothing hung heavily on her, dragging down her shoulders. The dampness worked its way under her skin and she shivered. There was a small window around the back where the apprentices worked. She thought for a moment that she should go home, not bother with this. But a niggling feeling gripped her and she walked around the back, her feet squelching in her boots.

The alleyway at the back of the workshop was dark. She shuffled along the cobblestones expecting to see someone as the hour was not yet late, but the street was empty. The window was open slightly and she prised it wider. Aaliya had seen Olle lock it on occasion, his heightened need for security amusing her. She wriggled in headlong and landed on the bench below the window. The room had a pleasant mustiness from the recent rain. Once she got herself to the floor, she realized she had no plan. It was dark inside the workshop and she didn't know where Olle kept the striker.

She quietly walked towards the door when she heard what sounded like a person coming up a flight of steps. She stopped. There weren't steps in the workshop that she knew of. It started raining again outside, a great downpour that rung like bells in Aaliya's ears and drowned out every other noise. At the doorway, she peeked around the corner to peer into the adjacent space, the storage room.

Lengths of hides and completed saddles hung on hooks around the windowless space. It was a room she didn't go into often but she knew the layout all the same. On this evening, the space was different. The large hide that normally lay flat on the floor was rolled up. A square hole cut into the wooden floor was exposed, a trapdoor with a steel ring in the middle was pushed to the side. A man emerged from the dimly lit space below him. There was a bunker under the workshop. All these years coming here and she had never known. Even in the dark she could tell that it wasn't Olle. This wasn't what she was expecting.

More footfall on the steps. Another person was coming up through the hole in the floor. And then a third person could be heard noisily striking the steps synchronously. Aaliya didn't try to look. She remained hidden in the dark, her body pressed hard against the wall. The rain came down in great unravelling sheets and Aaliya was thankful for the pounding from above.

The three men hovered near the bunker opening, cursing the weather in stilted mumbles.

"The bugger's bloody lucky he avoided the rain tonight," one of the men said forthrightly.

"Listen to you, ya big girl."

"S'alright for you. I've got to get out to Caser-fuckin-gillie."

"Tavern's just around the corner."

"Gawd, that'd be the death of me. She'd murder me for sure."

"At least you'd be so off your face you wouldn't know what hit yer."

They all laughed. "Damn right. Bloody perfect way

to go."

"Okay you lot." Olle's voice was clear and sharp as his feet thumped on the steps. "Get outa here."

Olle reached the top and all the men silently walked through the workshop to the front door. Aaliya heard the heavy bolt sliding across the frame. The sound of rain hitting the cobblestones outside suddenly got louder before becoming muted again. The bolt creaked back into it's secure position.

Footsteps padded back to the storage room as Aaliya remained cowering in the dark. It was Olle, she was sure. But she didn't want to alarm him. No one likes surprises in the dark. She heard Olle descend back down under the workshop. Aaliya moved towards the hole in the floor and peered down.

"Olle, is that you?"

There was a pause and then Olle shuffled into view. "Aaliya?" He stood frozen, looking at her questioningly. A man weighing up his options. "Come down," he eventually announced.

16

The Gift Half Understood

When she reached the bottom, Aaliya looked around the room, wide-eyed and curious. For a while no words were spoken. The lanterns flickered light around the space, and Aaliya was struck by how much larger the room was than what she had imagined. It was wide enough for up to forty standing men. The room was lined from floor to ceiling with wooden shelves and an impressive array of items clogged their surfaces: flints and water skins; hooded cloaks were neatly folded and stacked high in rows of ten; beautifully constructed light-weight armour made from the finest chainmail hung from hooks; and in a dark corner a large wooden crate sat overflowing with boots of all sizes. On the other side of the room, glinting and shining in the lamp-light, was the most impressive collection of weaponry Aaliya had ever seen. Displayed neatly on purpose built stands were rows of daggers and knives, bows and arrows. She attempted to take in the sheer volume of the weapons in the room and guessed there to be over a hundred daggers. Bows and arrows were so plentiful they were close to falling off the shelves. But it was the quality of the weaponry that caused a leap inside her. The items were beautiful, timeless. Obviously crafted with the finest materials in the hands of masters. These were serious weapons for people with a clear purpose.

She had so many questions about the bunker and it's contents, but didn't know how to frame her words. Instead she turned to the man she thought she knew so well and simply asked, "Who are you?"

"Aaliya, you know who I am."

"Clearly," she said, turning her head to look around the room, "I don't know you at all. Just a hobby collection, is it?"

"Alright, then. I am more than a saddle maker, yes."

"You didn't want me to see any of this," Aaliya said turning to face him. "Why didn't you just tell me to go?"

"Because you wouldn't have. Here, give me your cloak. You're soaking wet."

Aaliya eased off her cloak and handed it to Olle. He placed it on the shelf and handed his jacket to her, which she declined.

"You know, Olle, right now things are going through my mind…things like… insurgency. Treason. Can you see how I might be thinking that?" Aaliya said, anger rising inside her.

"I like to think of us as freedom fighters."

A nervous laugh leapt from her mouth.

"We just want fair government," Olle continued. "People want to live with self respect."

"How…how long?"

"How long have I been doing this? Five years or so."

"Right under my nose."

"Surely you can understand I needed to protect you."

"I'm not understanding anything right now."

"Some things are simply worth fighting for."

"This is dangerous, Olle."

"I'm not denying that. I guess you could say I want this more than being afraid of it."

"Want what exactly?"

Olle didn't say anything.

"Olle, want what?" she repeated.

"This was a mistake," he said, more to himself than to her. "Aaliya, it's best you leave."

"The other day. That was real, wasn't it? I thought it was just unlucky."

"I mean it. Out." He pointed at the steps.

"But it was real. It was an assassination attempt. And you know who did it, don't you?"

Olle still didn't respond.

"This is treason," Aaliya said, the tendons going hard as rods in her neck. "Someone very dear to me was questioned over this. He could have found himself in a very bad situation over something he had no part in. And you stand here not answering my questions. You're a fucking coward."

Olle's face went grave. "Aaliya, the men you saw here tonight. This room. Everything in it. You are to let it go."

"Now you're sounding like my father. I can't unknow what I now know."

"No, you can't. Everyone at some point in their life comes across something, a piece of information they've seen or been told, and it's what they do with that information that sets the course of their life. What path they'll travel on, who they'll surround themselves with. A choice is in their hands."

"Well, that's exactly right, Olle. If you hurt the king, you hurt my father. If you hurt my father, you hurt me."

"It doesn't have to be like that."

"I don't see that you would have much control over

the events that would come from your involvement here. You just said so yourself."

Olle nodded. "True. Who's to say that the events, or any consequences for that matter, would not be good? Even for your father."

"You're clutching, Olle, and you know it."

"No, I don't know it, Aaliya. I wouldn't be in this business if I knew it would devastate Thormund. I respect the man. I actually believe Thormund is clever enough and prudent enough to thrive in the world no matter who is in power."

"The status quo suits him right now."

"Perhaps someone within the status quo is working to undermine him as we speak. A successful man such as your father ignites flames of jealousy in many men. Status is a burning, seething thing."

"Is this your underhanded way of saying that you know someone is out to ruin him?"

"No, I'm not saying that. It was merely my observation of the way people work."

"Really? That's the way people work?"

"Not all people."

"Thanks for that clarification."

Aaliya's mind reeled. How could it be that she'd known Olle for most of her life and yet he stood before her now a stranger. She felt a fool for her blind loyalty all these years.

"Do you know the situation this puts me in? Do you?" said Aaliya, hotly.

"Yes."

"Whatever I do, from this moment on, someone I care about gets hurt."

"I'm sorry you had to find out. I don't know with any

certainty that this is right," Olle said, motioning his arms through the air. "All I know is the world is changing. And it will never stop changing. There's only the possibility that it is more right than what we currently have in place. I liken it to walking down a passage you didn't even know you were walking, towards a door that's never been opened. I want to open that door."

Aaliya turned away from Olle. She closed her eyes. It was useless to try to empty her mind of thoughts. Not at the moment, anyway. When she opened her eyes, she looked directly at a row of daggers on a shelf. Her trust in Olle was teetering, but maybe her faith in herself was too. Who was she to suggest an idealized notion of trust had just been broken? Her recent actions were hardly beyond reproach. Perhaps she should be thankful that he had kept this to himself all these years. Maybe if she found out when she was younger she wouldn't have hesitated going straight to her father and telling him. Olle would have been executed in a heartbeat. She wouldn't have had him in her life all these years to talk to, learn from, craft beautiful objects with. Would she be the woman she is now? Probably not. Her life would have taken a different course. He was her dearest friend, her mentor, her confidant. He had been there for her like a rock of stability for many years. And he still guided her forward in ways he knew she needed to go without the need for discussion. He seemed to know her better than she knew herself.

And it wasn't only that she would lose Olle. Revealing the existence of the bunker would end her world of saddle making as she knew it. The workshop would cease to exist. The cluttered space within these walls was her centre of stability. And although the workshop was merely stone and mortar, it was here she flourished. If the memories ran deep, the emotional pull was as mighty as a crashing wave being sucked back out to sea. The workshop meant everything to her. It was more a home to her than the red roofed house at the southern end of the Vysarq. Although life would go on if it was destroyed, a part of her would be buried with it.

But her family had to be protected. Family. It was just one word, but it was a whole story.

"Keep it," Olle said.

So immersed in her thoughts she hadn't even noticed she had picked up one of the knives and was tossing it between her fingers. The blade caught the light with each turn, shining light into her eyes. The blade itself was simple and small. No markings, no engravings. The hilt, however, told the story of its origin. The grip was wrapped in threads of leather the width of an ink mark scraped across parchment, one dyed red, the other white. The leather had a slightly compressed appearance as though it had been held many times before. An intricate rose had been fired into the iron pommel at the end of the handle.

It took a moment for Aaliya to register what Olle had said. "This? I don't want a knife." She put it back down on the shelf.

"Go to Blackrock as planned. Put this behind you. At least for the time being. Take the knife."

"What do I need a knife for?"

"If anything, you'll need it for food. For skinning rabbits."

"I've never skinned a rabbit before. I've never even grown a vegetable. I wouldn't know what to do with it."

Olle barely repressed a chuckle. "Believe me. When the moment arrives, you'll know."

Aaliya continued tossing it around in her hand. She found it incredibly beautiful. "I can't just walk out of here with a knife, Olle."

Olle grabbed the lantern and bent down to kneel. The lower shelf had numerous leather products. Satchels and scabbards, book covers and mugs. He pulled a scabbard attached to a slender harness from the shelf and stood up. He asked her to raise her arms slightly and guided her through how to attach the harness and scabbard under her arms and fasten it across her chest. The blade sat in its sheath between her shoulder blades with the tip facing down. An easy reach behind her neck, Aaliya was able to effortlessly release the knife. With Olle's help, she practiced over and over removing the knife and replacing it, until the movement became fluid and fast.

When they finished the instruction, Olle climbed out of the bunker and left Aaliya downstairs to conceal the dagger in it's scabbard underneath her dress. She climbed the stairs and made her way to the front part of the workshop, where she found Olle sharpening some of his tools. He turned around when he saw her.

"I know what's going through your mind. But you can trust me. You've got to believe that," Olle said.

She nodded weakly.

"Look after yourself, Aaliya. I'll always be there for you. But look after yourself."

17

The Fall

Aaliya arrived back to a house languid and quiet. The emptiness was disconcerting and it occurred to her that in a few more days the sense of hollowness would become a standard feature of her household. Maddalena was a giantess in their home, her presence large and emboldening. It would hardly feel like a home anymore. Just a place of shelter. Aaliya felt a longing to see her sister, a burning need to talk to her. Finally have that sisterly discussion they had both put off for so long. Find some common ground, open up the closed books of their hearts even just a little. It suddenly seemed wasteful to have not made better use of time. Their lives were now destined to go in separate directions.

Maddalena's door was ajar and Aaliya gave it a tap and pushed it open. Nella was inside folding clothes and told her that both Thormund and Maddalena were involved in last minute preparations at the castle. Aaliya made her way to her room, closed the door behind her and slumped down on the edge of her bed. She removed the knife from the scabbard. Stared at it, somewhat bewildered. She wanted a person but instead had a weapon. She tossed it between her fingers for a while then placed it down. While it had been in her hand it distracted her, sabotaged her. She got up and went to the door, opening it with a force that made her hair dance around her face. Just go and find him again, she told herself. You did it once before. It could happen again, couldn't it? Standing at the threshold she stared at the darkened wall opposite. Dim light flickered on the surface. Her shoulders went limp. It was madness. They had been found out somehow. To do anything now was simply insane. If only she could ask him why he didn't turn up. The not knowing had her mind racing. Maybe he had second thoughts about what he was doing? Maybe he couldn't face her anymore? She thought hard about how she could get a message to him. A person to deliver a message. But who? And what would the message be anyway? She may as well wear a breastplate featuring a large red snake-like 's' for scarlet woman.

Aaliya closed the door and made her way across the room to the window. She roughly drew the curtains and pulled out a dress from the nearby closet. A treasured object. A loose drape across the shoulders in a muted, smoky pink. Layers of fabric flowing all the way down to the ankles. Aaliya recalled every occasion her mother had worn the dress: Maddalena's first wedding, dinner with the king on the eve her father acquired vast land near Lake Ilm, Prince Jonas's eighteenth birthday. So imbued with memory was the dress, the shifting sounds it made as she brought it to her bed, seemed to whisper to her.

She shuffled over to the sidetable and poured herself a drink. The wine tasted rich and sweet. She smiled at the thought of going to the wedding a slovenly mess. She took another deep gulp, and then another. It took every bit of her power to resist the dark feelings that were bubbling to the surface. Justen…the marriage…Olle and his bloody bunker. Surely Helena didn't raise her to be like this. What had happened? When did it start to go horribly wrong?

The glass was emptied and slammed down onto the table. Her face appeared as a silhouette on the shiny surface. Violence. She had never felt the need to lash out the way she wanted to now. Maybe Justen smelled the desperation in her and wanted to have no part in it. Pathetic neediness. Aaliya picked up the glass and threw it against the wall. It smashed into a thousand pieces. The shattering sound rang in her ears. She raised her arm ready to wipe the bottle off the sideboard in one swift motion, but stopped herself and lowered her arm.

She stumbled to the bed and picked up the dress. Pressing it to her face, she inhaled deeply, weeping and sobbing as she exhaled in spurts. It smelled of lavender, of summer, of her. She lowered her whole body until she was lying on the floor, the dress covering her face. Just fall for a little while, she told herself. Just fall.

The next morning, she woke to a rod of light scalding her face. Dazed, she levered herself upright and had a look in the direction of the window. Outside were the sounds of carts being pulled, horse hooves clomping, shouts amid the hum of chatter. It had to be late, but just how far into the day it was she had no idea. Not like Nella to let her sleep in, she thought. It was intensely hot in the room. Her tongue lazily swirled around the inside of her mouth trying to spread some moisture. Her head ached, even her feet hurt. Gods, what was she thinking last night? But that was the thing.

She didn't want to think. Glad for a messy distraction.

Beside her on the bed, almost rolled up into a ball, was her mother's dress. She reached over and squeezed the fabric. She'd need it looking reasonable for the wedding. A panic swept over her. Was the wedding today? She forced herself fully upright and dangled her feet over the side of the bed. Her head thrummed and churned with the simple action. One more day. One…more…day.

On the carpet was a large, dark stain. She nervously felt under her bottom, fearing she had let go of all dignity during the night. But she was still dry. She leaned closer to it. It was a bit more innocent than something from her body but it still wasn't great. She'd have to clean it up at some point, but not now. Right at this moment, movement felt monumental. Whatever was encased in her skull seemed to sway with the effort of her getting up off the bed. She picked up the dress and hung it back in the closet. She needed food, something healing, nourishing. Down the stairs she stomped, tightly gripping the balustrade, not quite ready to start the day but mildly determined to at least give it a try.

It was early afternoon when she finally made it to the workshop. She hauled herself in and slumped heavily onto a stool. Sweat lay thick over her skin. She didn't want to think about the state of her hair. The workshop provided instant relief from the smothering heat.

Olle entered the room carrying a saddle tree. His expression changed to a grin when he saw Aaliya. "You're here?" he said, clearly surprised.

"Only just."

He placed the saddle tree on the bench and stood beside her. "Why did you come back?"

Aaliya shrugged her shoulders loosely. "Right now, I

don't really know where else to go."

"Rough night?"

"You could say that."

"Aaliya, I didn't mean to…"

"Olle, right now…I don't want to think about it. Yesterday…is yesterday."

Olle nodded his head.

"There's more to it…" Aaliya said, trailing off.

"I know."

She raised her eyebrows in surprise, but then convinced herself that he was simply referring to the recent loss of her mother.

Olle suddenly looked remorseful, like he had said something out of place. "I've got an errand to run today. I'd like you to come with me."

"Need to get leather or something," she said, feeling slightly more coherent.

"Not exactly. Just something I should have shared quite a long time ago."

While Olle made arrangements for the horses, Aaliya looked around for something with which to busy herself. She carefully began cutting the leather for the billets. Normally she was prone to working energetically but on this day she lingered, like she had given herself permission to just enjoy the task.

Eventually, the time came to put down her tools. They mounted their horses and headed in the direction of the city gates. Once outside the city, they leaned low in their saddles and put the walls of the capital a widening distance behind them. The stony road was empty, not withstanding the few making their way on foot to Ansgar after their days work in the outlying districts. Sheep could be heard in the distance, a soft blithesome sound that made Aaliya feel good to be out of the city. The air smelled of pine and oily wool. After a while they slowed their horses to a walk. A strange landscape stretched before them. The grass and low plant life were all ochres and washed out greens that appeared almost grey.

"You know, you could be a queen one day,' Olle said, ending the silence.

Aaliya continued to look straight ahead. "So I've been told."

"Queen Aaliya…very regal."

"You're giving me shit."

"You don't want to be a queen?"

"Not particularly," she responded.

"Surely you're curious? All the things you could do…"

"All the things I *couldn't* do."

"Come on, Aaliya. Who doesn't want to be pampered, to live amongst beautiful things, to wear beautiful clothes, to be admired by many - "

"To be possessed," she suggested firmly.

"Yeah, there would be that too. But there would also be power."

Aaliya laughed. "You've previously told me how strongly you disagree with power being in the hands of a few."

"Yes, but I'm just a grumpy old stalwart – correction, a stalwart – who's lived too long, seen too much, and believes, probably hopelessly, that things could be different. You're fresh and young. And optimistic. You could take what comes your way and never look back. You have the connections, the family to set yourself up and be comfortable for the rest of your days. You'd have nothing to feel guilty about."

"I think I can do better than that."

Olle smiled. "I think you can too." After a long pause he said, "You would make a great leader. Not one of those leaders that rules by fear alone. One that's compassionate, but firm. You follow through. You are responsible, even though you probably don't want to be. You do things that inspire others –"

"Inspire? Really?"

"You don't think what you do is inspiring?"

"Not really. I guess I've never thought about it."

"Well, it gets noticed."

Aaliya shrugged. "I've never seen myself as the type of person who could be a leader."

"The good ones often don't."

"I'm in the workshop making saddles most days."

"You won't be in there forever."

"Maybe I will. I'd like to."

"There's what we like and want, and then there's the stuff that just happens. The strange happenstances that come along and turn everything on its head."

"And maybe those strange happenstances won't come along. In which case, you'll be stuck in that workshop with me until they cart you, or me for that matter, out to Dreadfield."

"You're still young," said Olle, smiling.

The late afternoon air was thermal. Olle and Aaliya encouraged their horses to a trot as they approached the village of Torrany, the sunlight illuminating the scattering of thatched homes fanning out from the thin road.

Olle looked around, appearing satisfied. "We are here to visit a man I know as Ranger Elric. I was here only a couple of days ago…after the attempt on the king's life."

They pulled up alongside a stonewall. Olle hitched his horse to a tree and walked towards a small earthen cottage with a gnarled pomegranate tree out the front, its branches sagging with heavy fruit. Aaliya secured her horse, her long skirt brushing past rosemary and thyme, casting a sweet scent into the air. She wiped her brow, the late afternoon sun unrelenting in its heat. A small bell hung near the door. Olle reached for the cord and struck the metal once. Dogs started barking at the back of the property. They walked around the side of the cottage towards the sound of the yapping dogs and waited by the tall stonewall.

A minute or so later, a man could be heard menacingly snarling at the noisy animals. The heavy wooden gate was pushed open and a man with long grey hair and drooping eyes looked into Olle's face.

"You always come at my supper time," Elric groaned.

"I apologize. Occupational hazard."

"Who's this?" Elric said, turning to Aaliya.

"Aaliya Reiner. An apprentice of mine. Trusted apprentice of mine."

The dogs leapt up to Olle's thighs and were snarled at again and given a sharp whip with a thin stick of bamboo. The old man's eyes were moist, and even in the dry afternoon heat, he appeared silvery, venerable. Olle closed the gate and they walked towards a rounded structure in the middle of the yard. It was not much smaller than the size of the mud brick dwellings in the district and looked like a thimble that had been turned upside down.

Elric opened the door of the dovecote and the three of them went in. Inside was teeming with homing pigeons, cooing in their nesting holes carved into the mud. The pigeon holes reached up to the dome shaped ceiling. Elric lit the lamp and placed it on a hook. Shadows bobbed and quivered against the orange walls. The old man reached for one of the pigeons and petted it gently between his hands.

"Where do you need a message to go?" Elric asked.

"Sune Birk at Blackrock."

Elric placed the bird back into its hole, moved a stool into place and stood on it. He looked amongst the nesting holes and started whispering affectionately to the birds. "Not the best time of day," he quipped.

"You told me that last time."

"Earlier in the day, Master Olle."

"Closer to the hours of darkness are best."

"Hmm, occupational hazard indeed."

Elric began looking amongst the birds. The confined space was stifling. Outside only the assuring sound of sheep beyond the ranger's garden could be heard.

"Yes," he uttered, "here we are." Elric pulled a pigeon from its nesting hole.

On a small table, the bird was placed in a wooden box.

Olle took a tiny piece of tightly rolled parchment from his pocket. He handed it to Aaliya. The words read 'Gracious Phoenix arrival five moons'.

"Gracious Phoenix?" questioned Aaliya.

"You'll get used to it."

Elric picked up the pigeon from the box and Olle tied the message onto one of the legs of the bird.

"Is this the best bird you've got?" Olle asked.

"Oh yes. Just don't expect a message to get to Siwaqas and you'll be right. Shy Lotus gets a little off course. And Humble Wrangler. Dear bird ended up at the Voups Bog instead of the Pleasant Slough a couple of moons ago. Extra training for that girl."

Olle showed a prick of anguish.

"Don't worry," Elric continued, "Aching Volcano won't let you down."

The three exited the dovecote, the box containing the bird in Olle's arms. The dogs paced around their knees and then lay down on the dry grass when commanded. Olle lifted the lid of the box and the bird rose up to flight. Aaliya watched as it soared over the thatched roof tops, and thought of that tiny piece of parchment tied to its leg.

"You're a messenger," she said to Olle.

"Yes, I am. I brought you here today to see what I do. To understand that no matter what happens, no matter where you go, you will have help. You only need ask."

Arriving back through the city gates upon twilight, Aaliya farewelled Olle and set off in a different direction on her own. The sky was aglow in the east. The rippling clouds unfolded across the sky alight with colour. She hadn't travelled beyond the city gates before and a pleasant feeling continued to buzz and corrugate under her skin. The entering of the city from outside made her realize the oldness of her home town. There was something undeniably ancient here on the outskirts. The buildings marked by weatherstains, the rust upon the iron work, the small homes hand built. And there was a buzz in the air, some sort of primordial hum permeating the stillness. Beholding extreme longevity made her think that maybe some things were permanent, unchanging.

She knew this to be false though. Everything changes. Nothing remains the same. Some of it within ones control, most of it outside. And of course picking what one wanted to control wasn't so simple. Nothing ever was.

She continued to ride through the city and into the royal forest. She wandered through, glimpsing the darkening sky above. The air felt instantly cooler, denser. Aaliya veered from the forest track to where the ferns bristled and teemed. In here, she felt sufficiently free from observation. There were no more eyes watching her, only the comforting sense of being enclosed by giants. The horse walked on, deeper into the forest, until she tugged at the reins in an area resembling a small dell. She slid off the horse, the animal gratefully commencing to nibble at the grass.

Aaliya lay down on the ground. It was where she had wanted to be today. The place where Justen and her had made love two years ago. They had come to this place on numerous occasions and felt so wholly free here. It was as though the forest wanted to provide them with a sanctuary, a place for their bond to flourish. Lying on the leaf-strewn ground, Aaliya childishly longed for some magical power that could lure him to her at this very moment. The day before his wedding. She could only imagine what was going through his mind. Perhaps he longed to meet her in the forest as much as she longed for him. For a while, be in a place where rules and laws did not exist.

She closed her eyes and tried to quieten her mind. She was going to move forward in a different way. In the distance she could hear a small stream, the faintest babbling of water flowing over rocks. It was a soothing, gentle sound and, although she was tired, it failed to lull her into sleep. Instead, with her eyes still closed but feeling immense wakefulness, she thought of the water as the current of her own life moving through the shadows into a place of mysterious light, as wide as an ocean.

18

The Wedding

She remembered the last time she had been here. This place in her head before vowing unending union to a man. The previous time, Maddalena had hardly been one of those frightful, dainty creatures who actually thought their lives were about to begin. But it did unhinge even the hardy, she had to admit. She had found herself throughout the day stopping and simply staring into space. It was tomorrow. All those lovely vows will be uttered, but what really was a marriage? Those other women her father insisted she while away the time with prior to her first marriage foolishly believed it was all pretty simple. "Romance" they had said. Love. Loooove. In no time, they were complaining about the lack of affection. Lack of gallantry. Lack of romance. What was romance, she had asked them. They had looked at her incredulously, their eyes soupy with pity. "Watching the sky together on a summer's night," one had said. "When he just stops what he's doing and tells me how much he loves me," said another. "And what about…er, matters of the flesh," she had implored. Oh yes! Some spoke in mischievous tones about the forbidden things they did with their husband. Others would rest their chin in their hands and sigh as though listening to a carpenter preach the seven uses for wood. "He doesn't want anything 'strange'." "Just wants it kept simple." Simple? It was anything but simple. What she came to realize was this marriage thing was as complicated as calculating distances to stars. The best she could do was find a place within her own marriage where she could be herself.

Like everyone else, she had hopes and expectations. He was a swordsman, after all. Images of a man valiantly riding into battle, one arm raised brandishing heavy iron like it weighed little more than a teacup, came into her mind and pleasantly filled her days. And there were certain physical features she considered 'swordsmanlike'. A strong, straight nose. Sharp blue eyes. A defiant jaw that looked as though it had been carved out of stone. She hadn't met the man, but she put her mind at ease that her father who had arranged the marriage wouldn't let her down. Thormund surely wouldn't have invested so much time, and dare she say it – love – into their relationship over the years only to have her carted off to the household of someone mediocre, would he? Surely he would want the best for her?

She finally met Bruno Staffin the day of the wedding. She recalled that feeling of her insides turning to water. No part of her having anything to grip onto. It wasn't so much the lack of stature that concerned her. That had never been an issue before with her previous lovers. It was the mouth hanging open in a perpetual state of dumbfoundedness. The yellowing, crooked teeth vying for space in the small, oval mouth of his. The corners of his eyes slightly pointing down, as if concerning himself with the world was all too much. As for the colour of those eyes, she couldn't recall whether they were brown or blue, green or grey. She had never looked into those droopy eyes long enough to determine their hue.

What was her father thinking? Why would he do this to her? She had looked his way in the process of avoiding Bruno's eyes during the wedding ceremony. Thormund was wearing a stern expression, a look that said focus on the task and get on with it. Her father's jaw had set a little firmer when she didn't look away and he had motioned his head in the direction of the groom. Maddalena had little functioning of her body at that point. She was sure she inadvertently turned her head from side to side, hardly caring that the whole congregation had witnessed her disapproval.

Maddalena hoped his mind would make up for the lack of physical attraction. But it was an empty, vacuous space where the scope of his curiosity extended about the length of a fingernail. He would wax lyrical about his finest sword fighting moments, go on about his bravery during times of adversity. Maddalena's agreeable responses quickly became a parody he sadly didn't have the ability to decipher. "You are so brave, my love, like a lion. No like a wasp, a great roaring wasp." How could he not tell that she was being ridiculous? Was the man that starved for compliments he would take whatever he could get? Humankind mystified her. People and their neediness, it was all so desperate.

She told herself constantly to not be that way, to rise above it. Find a place of her own. Her marriage was a farce. She felt shoved into a small box and forgotten about. The boredom of it ate at her. She found a willing lover in the town and for short stabs of time each week she momentarily forgot about the world she had mistakenly joined.

Then it was as though some ray of light from a distant star shone down on her for the inexplicable happened. Bruno Staffin (bravely) put his name forward to fight for his kingdom of Marius in the Broken Mountain Rebellion. And was killed on the first day of battle. A widow so suddenly. She asked the maid bearing the news to repeat herself three times. Maddalena hurried to her room finally convinced her ears were not playing tricks on her, the maid no doubt expecting her to grieve in private. But far from it. She launched herself onto the bed and looked up at the canopy with a sense of bewilderment. Hours passed, and she continued to lie there thinking, contemplating, plotting. Never again, she vowed, would she find herself in this situation. Never again would she willingly launch into another marriage that did not meet her own terms. It was an institution and she would treat it thus. It was a vehicle for accumulating wealth and providing her with the level of status she was worthy of. And the arrangement could only be with someone with whom she had the greatest chances of power and influence. She'd find her passion elsewhere. Nurture her dignity away from the flawed arena of love. Be finally away from her father's watchful gaze. Her restlessness would be reserved for striving to be someone remembered, someone in the history books she knew and loved.

The door of the Ceremonial Room creaked loudly as it swung open, causing everyone inside to turn their heads to the rear of the room. A young boy began slowly walking down the aisle between the throng of onlookers, a sword resting in his outstretched arms. Behind him was Thormund, his tall frame clad in a fine silk green brocade jacket and black dress pants. Linked into his arm stood Maddalena, her long black hair twisted to rest across her shoulder and threaded with bejewelled ribbons. On her head rested a fine wreath of hawthorn, the life giving elements of the plant forgotten about as the thorny branches maddeningly dug into her head. The bodice of her blue dress was studded with hundreds of glittering beads, making her seem luminous, opalescent. Maddalena wasn't nervous, she had done this before. But she could feel an uncomfortable twitch in her neck, and try as she might, she couldn't get rid of the slight strain between her eyes as she focused only on what was ahead of her.

Two enormous sculptured columns – the robed androgenous forms of the God of Life and the God of Death – stood formidably either side of the altar, as if overseeing the proceedings in the room. A stone frieze above the columns was intricately carved with a scene of Traegos sacrifice in a time of conflict. Justen stood before the priest at the altar, his hands resting on the hilt of his sword. The sword of his ancestors. His father's, perhaps? Maddalena briefly wondered how he was feeling at this moment, knowing he had to present his sword to her, to part with his former self, to unite them in matrimony. Would it be a sweet release, or would his soul be aching? He looked around, as if sensing her thoughts were directed at him. His expression was impassive, there was nothing to read, and then he looked back down at his sword.

The thurifer standing beside the priest was gently swinging his censer. Clouds of myrrh floated around the altar and slowly spread across the vast space. Beside the thurifer stood a narrow table, upon which all the pre-signed documents outlining the handover of Tyln Bluff from Traegos to Gedion and the trade agreements rendered binding by the marriage, were on display.

Thormund and Maddalena slowly began walking the length of the room. Supporting the soaring gable roof above them was a row of hulking arched timber beams that gave one the feeling of being pulled through the space by an invisible force. Hanging down from the top of each timber arch were wheel-sized wrought iron pendants, each heavy with flickering candles. At the altar, the young boy handed Maddalena the sword and left to join the crowd to the side. Thormund took his place beside Aaliya. Aaliya looked at her father, and he looked at her. Maddalena saw her sister smile, and to Maddalena's surprise, she saw her father return a soft grin in Aaliya's direction. The significance of the moment was not lost on Maddalena. It was Aaliya and Thormund now.

The priest commenced his solemn words of matrimony. Of sharing a life together blessed by the four cardinal directions for a long and successful union. "Blessed be this union in the East," he explained, "for your gifts of communication and understanding will help you to grow together. Blessed be this union in the West, for your gifts of fidelity and honour with strengthen your union and embolden your hearts. Blessed be this union in the South, for your warmth and generosity will ensure solidarity in troubled times. And blessed be this union in the North, for your fertility will provide your union with the foundation from which all the richness and plenitude of life will flow. Side by side, shoulder to shoulder, take this opportunity to declare yourselves for one another."

A veiled woman approached the couple at the altar and dipped a fir-twig into the bowl of verbena and water she was holding in her other hand. She gently flicked the liquid onto the betrothed couple and conferred the blessing and protection of the Gods. She moved back into the shadows and the priest announced the exchange of gifts.

Maddalena and Justen turned to face each other, their hands gripped the hilts of their swords and pointed them to the ceiling. They carefully passed their ancestral swords to the other, and then turned to face the priest.

"Do you, Justen Laus, son of Laszlo, before the witnesses gathered here today, take Maddalena Reiner, daughter of Thormund, as your lawful wife, to have and to hold, from this moment until the God of Death invites you forth?"

"I do," Justen said.

"And do you, Maddalena Reiner, daughter of Thormund, before the witnesses gathered here today, take Justen Laus, son of Laszlo, as your lawful husband, to have and to hold, from this moment until the God of Death invites you forth?"

"I do," Maddalena replied.

A young boy came forward and Justen plucked a band of silver from the small cushion resting in his hands. Justen reached for Maddalena's hand, and placed the ring on her finger. Maddalena looked at her hand, stretched out her fingers, and retrieved the other ring from the cushion. She rolled the ring back and forth between her fingers before placing it on Justen's finger.

"Let these rings be a sign that you both are united in holy matrimony, in the eyes of the people gathered here today, and in the eyes of the God of Life and the God of Death who gather around us. You are now man and wife."

There was a slight hesitation then Maddalena leaned in to receive Justen's kiss.

The Great Hall provided welcome relief from the oppressiveness of the Ceremonial Room, if only because here Maddalena had vast quantities of comforting food to soothe her anxiety. In here, the balmy evening was invited in. Window panes were pushed back. Warmth and fading afternoon light filtered in and touched the colourful canopies draped across the ceiling, making the space seem kaleidoscopic. Candles around the walls were all alight, the dancing flames dribbling wax onto the floors.

A group of four musicians occupied a plinth in the corner of the room where an area had been cleared for dancing. The flute and harp were already being played as people streamed into the hall and took to their seats. Once the room was filled, they were joined by violin and lute, creating a warm, generous sound.

The enormous oak tables were laden with offerings: fig encrusted quail, pickled cherries, marinated octopus. Jugs of mead were already being sloshed around.

The high table was situated at the far end of the room, draped to the floor in a heavy white damask. Three green hawthorn branches, each embedded on a wire stand and decorated with violets, stood on the table. It was the enormous pie, however, placed prominently in front of the married couple that was the showpiece of the banquet.

"What's in it?" asked Justen, eyeing it suspiciously.

"A whole roe deer. A couple of chickens. Maybe some pigeons and a rabbit or two," replied Maddalena.

"Extraordinary. I've never seen anything like it."

The large golden pie formed a centrepiece, with dozens of smaller pies surrounding it. The top of the large pie was adorned with a gilt-like layer of pastry resembling a crown.

Maddalena briskly downed a cup of mead and then

stood, and without hesitating, sliced open the large pie. "Here, you must try some," she said, spooning some of the pastry and pink flesh into Justen's bowl. "It's a delicacy here."

"Back home, my mother makes an incredible pie with broad beans and tomatoes and turnips."

"Turnips. What kind of meat is that?"

"Well, it's not from an animal. It's a vegetable."

Maddalena spooned some pie into her mouth with a twitch of bafflement. "Well it's not a pie then."

"Of course it's a pie. It has pastry on top, a filling in the middle."

"No meat, no pie. The whole point of eating a pie is to eat meat."

Justen made a slight sarcastic grin.

A servant rushed over to continue serving the meal to the other people occupying the high table. Pieter sat to the right of Justen. To Maddalena's left sat Thormund and then Aaliya, followed by King Renatus and his family.

"Your mother. She couldn't make it?" Maddalena enquired before taking a mouthful of food.

"The mountain pass makes for a hazardous journey. Her health isn't particularly strong," said Justen.

Maddalena was sure there was more to this than Justen was letting on, but with both Pieter and Thormund in earshot, it was a pointless conversation to have. In fact, just about all the things she wanted to ask Justen, she felt she couldn't. *So are you here to kill the king? What are you really getting out of marrying me? Do you have any reason to suspect your Uncle Pieter is a wolf in sheep clothing?*

"Well, I look forward to meeting her," she lied.

"Both my sister and mother are looking forward to meeting you. As is the King of Gedion. You will have a good life in Tashker, you will see."

Maddalena washed her mouthful down with a large gulp of wine. "A good life you say? My last marriage bored me senseless."

Thormund grunted.

Justen paused and brought his cup of mead to his lips. "Were you married long?"

"Long enough," she replied.

"Was it really such a misery to endure?"

"It lasted four months. Like I said, long enough."

Justen suppressed a laugh. "Ideal really. Anything beyond that is just being greedy."

"Seigneur Staffen of Marius," Maddalena said, haughtily. "Stupid man got himself killed in battle. Sword through the neck I was told. He was generous enough. He had no common sense though." She poured more wine and drank from her cup. She hadn't thought about her former husband for the past two and a half years, and now she couldn't get him out of her head. "Couldn't make a decision on his own. What jacket should I wear riding? Should I insist on mead or ale at the wedding? Should I go into battle or continue to write my exposition on the preferred sailcloth for the lateen-rigged caravel?" Don't even get me started on what went down in the bedroom, thought Maddalena. It was like guiding a donkey through open pasture.

Justen nodded in uneasy agreement. "Nothing to hide behind in a marriage."

She leaned in closer and lowered her voice so her father wouldn't hear. "So maybe we should just put it on the table right from the start? Save ourselves the pain of working it all out over the course of months and years. It would be nice if you were to inform me of which variety of suffering I am in for so I can go to Gedion a little prepared."

"This is not the conversation I was expecting to have tonight."

"So what is it? Hmm? What is going to appal me? How are you going to disappoint me?"

Justen didn't respond, instead he tossed down another nervous glassful.

"Gods, if you dared to think about it for a moment," Maddalena continued, "you wouldn't do it, would you?"

"This needn't be a disaster. I can't believe I'm even saying that at this point in time."

"I'm appreciating the honesty."

"For all my own reservations leading up to this point, I'm determined to get this right. Or as right as I can get it."

Maddalena watched his eyes flicker in the direction of Aaliya.

"In other words, you're going to stick to your own belief in what is right and what is wrong and follow your own self-assuredness, which I'm probably not too far from presuming correctly is forced and fragile." As soon as she said it she was embarrassed.

"Are you talking about me or you?" Justen replied through a clenched jaw.

Maddalena smiled, respecting the retort she had received. "I'm sorry. I'm…I'm trying to deal with this. And clearly not doing a good job."

"Let's just eat, shall we?"

They fell silent and resumed delving into the feast. Maddalena ripped apart the quail drenched in syrupy figs. Justen heaped more great spoonfuls of pie into his bowl. Thormund stood with his cup in his hand and hushed the crowd. The musicians stopped playing and the room eased into a state of quiescence.

"I would like to thank everyone for coming here today," Thormund announced, his voice loud and clear. "There is no greater event worth celebrating than the union between a man and a woman."

The crowd chorused their approval, and then Thormund continued, "This marriage also unites our lands. It will ensure prosperity and security for all. I am deeply proud of my daughter, Maddalena. So steadfast and so loyal. And welcome Justen into our clan. May the Gods truly bless this marriage. Before your king, join me in raising your cups and toasting the bride and groom. Neblo von senna arem."

Cups were raised and Thormund's final words repeated around the room. A hundred thirsty bodies then drank their fill and cheered. The musicians returned to their instruments and launched into an almighty melody that filled the room.

Thormund turned to Maddalena. "Out you go." He nodded his head in the direction of the dance floor.

Maddalena looked at her father, her eyes begging him to let this go. She drained her cup. "Come on," she said to Justen with a slur. Unsteadily she got to her feet, thankful to have a hand to hold and guide her to the floor.

The vibrant galliard seemed to decrease in momentum. For the past two weeks Maddalena had been practicing the dance. On each occasion she had tried her utmost to transform it into something resembling grace, and she believed she had gotten close. On the evening when it mattered she was hoping for divine intervention to get her through the ordeal. Being back on her feet forced her to confront just how much she had had to drink. She wobbled and fumbled through moves that required a significant degree of composure, some sense of control. Why couldn't they just play something faster? At least then I could loosen up?

"You're doing just fine," Justen said, as he firmly supported her back.

If he didn't maintain a firm hold of her, she was sure she would be on the floor by now.

"Does this end anytime soon?" Maddalena asked.

"Just a couple more minutes."

"Do you think they can hear us?"

"No, I don't. But I certainly feel as though there are a hundred pairs of eyes on us."

She thought for a moment if there was a way to ask the next question with any sort of sensitivity, but in her inebriated state, she settled on directness, her words close to his ear, "Are you here to kill the king?"

Justen stopped dancing. Frozen. He then fumbled through the next couple of moves in an attempt to synchronize again with the music. "Let me make this clear," Justen said, his mouth close to her ear. "I am not here to kill your king. Is that understood?"

"Yes." She looked in his eyes and saw a man firm in his need to be believed. It is often said that from looking into another person's eyes you can tell when they're lying or telling the truth. Eyes will supposedly always betray the liar and reveal their treachery. But Maddalena wasn't so sure. Hell, she'd done her own fair share of lying and, so far, she was sure her eyes hadn't betrayed her.

The remaining chords seemed to go on for an eternity for the dancing couple. When the song finally ended, Maddalena and Justen bowed to the crowd. Maddalena's head was spinning and she hastily returned to the table. Justen remained on the dance floor, where he was joined by many from the crowd, including all the guests of the high table. When the men and women had formed their lines, the music sang out, clear and vibrant, and the whole room seemed to be moving.

At the high table, Maddalena grabbed the jug of mead and filled her cup. She toasted the dancers before bringing the cup to her lips and draining the contents. The music had become frenetic. The pace of the dance had changed. Cups and bowls were moving with the thunderous stomping of feet. She couldn't be bothered joining the formality of the dance floor. Instead, remaining near the high table, she stood in front of it and started spinning around, laughing like a child rolling down a hill. Maddalena thought it to be the most fun she'd had standing up in quite a while.

Her spinning became so energetic her feet couldn't move out of the way of the other fast enough. She tumbled over, fabric and hair spilling across the floor. At first the shock of the fall caused Maddalena to shake her head in disbelief, before she launched into peals of laughter.

She propped herself up on an elbow. "Someone bring me a cup of wine. It is absolutely divine down here. I urge you all to join me."

A servant approached Maddalena and helped her to her feet.

"Oh my, you are returning me to my seat. How boring of you."

Guided back to her seat, Maddalena plonked down heavily in the chair. She leaned over the table and rested her head in the palm of her hand. The room seemed to take on a darker shade of grey to her. She didn't want to be here. A sense of need started to creep into her soul. She hated feeling needy. She could almost taste the bitter, acidic taste it left in her mouth. She felt as though she were a neglected animal. She just needed lots of preening and physical love to make her feel kindly towards others.

She looked up to see Justen standing beside her. He filled a cup with barley tea from the earthenware jug and offered it to her.

"Leave me alone," Maddalena said, pushing the cup aside.

"Are you alright?"

"Just leave me alone."

Justen sat down and squeezed her shoulder. Maddalena couldn't look him in the eyes, preferring to keep her gaze on the dancing before her. A minute or two sagged by, the silence awkward and unwieldy.

Justen took her hand. "Come back and dance with me, Maddalena."

"No."

He didn't move.

"Go!" Maddalena insisted. "Go!"

Justen stood up, running his fingers through his hair. He continued to stand near her for a while before turning and walking in the direction of the dance.

Maddalena took another sip of wine and leaned back in her chair. People talked and ate, the music played on. She looked over at old woman slumped in her chair, snoring and farting. She thought the old woman had the right idea.

It was in this state of inertia Maddalena felt something touch her between her legs. At first she thought it was her wicked mind playing tricks on her. But she felt something again. This time, a rub of her sex through her dress that was quite deliberate. Maddalena did a cursory look around her before lifting the tablecloth to see who, or what, was underneath the table.

Leaning back in her chair she could see the face and hand of her beloved Joshva. Without hesitation, she dropped the tablecloth back around her lap, and spread her legs as wide as she could manage. "What a glorious wedding gift," she whispered.

While everyone else went about their banal chatter, their haughty, stilted moves on the dance floor, Maddalena relaxed into the sensation of her body being erotically touched. She didn't want to lift her dress too soon. The feeling of it, even through her fabric, was exquisite. The pleasure heightened by the sheer naughtiness of it. She could feel her loins turn to liquid. Oh, to reach down and touch his hardness. She couldn't hold off the need for skin on skin for much longer.

When at last she relented, her hands dropped beneath the tablecloth to hitch up her dress around her lap. She slid down in her chair a little further. Wearing no undergarments, her sex was now wide and gaping for her friend.

Round and round his tongue went, circling her labia before lapping again at her nub.

"Ohhhh," she moaned through clenched teeth. Keeping quiet throughout sex was never something she had mastered. She spread her legs even wider, if that was possible, in the hope of yielding even more of her body to the pleasure. Softly undulating into his face, she started to become breathless and looked around. She didn't know what she was looking for. She was beyond caring. All that mattered was the feeling, the feeling of being on the tip of abandonment.

"Finger fuck me darling, please," she whispered, breathlessly.

His fingers plunged into her, again and again. The

thumb on his other hand continued to work on her nub. Her body felt like it was going to explode with joy. With one final push into his outstretched fingers she came in a mad, feverish climax.

She stayed in this state of pleasurable weariness for quite a while, the wine still swirling through her body like an analgesic. Joshva removed his fingers. Moments later, out of the corner of her eye, she watched him emerge from under the table at the far end, and blend into the crowd like a jaguar fading into foliage. She pushed her dress back down to her ankles and leaned back in the chair.

Oh the beauty of it! How deliciously indecent of me! She started laughing. Weddings are not so bad after all.

19

The Twelve Freedoms

The day after the wedding, the absence of Maddalena from the house was disconcerting for Aaliya in a way she couldn't quite process. There was the obvious conflict she felt knowing that her sister would be in the arms of Justen. The churn of envy almost engulfed her as she lay on her bed and the morning sun filtered in through the curtains. But there was also a stranger sense that the deed had been done, the moment had arrived and passed, she had jumped across the chasm where she had long been hovering at the edge, and it was as though some fears had left her mid-flight to the other side.

There was still her father to tell about the impending trip to Blackrock, but she was sure she could do that now. Olle had been insistent she tell her father, admonishing her like she was a small child when she last confessed she was yet to tell him. Olle had told her he had received news from Sune Birk that arrangements had been made. Aaliya's lodging was ready, basic yet comfortable. She would spend the days during her visit working with Master Saddle Maker Birk and his small group of apprentices, after which, if all went well, she could stay longer with the view to becoming a journeyman with her father's consent.

Olle and Aaliya made plans to ride out at dawn on Aerinday in four days time. The ride to Blackrock, Olle had explained, would take a bit over a week (or three moons by the ancient Zurian calendar) and would involve riding south through the heartland of Traegos where villages were few and the country opened up, wide and ageless. By day six of riding, he went on to say, they should arrive at an area that resembled a natural amphitheatre. An area where they would ride down into a vast depression in the landscape, where dazzling white cliffs, as glossy as porcelain, would encircle them and sting their eyes. And from there the thin blue ranges of the Tempest Mountains would shimmer in the distance. It was unimaginably beautiful, he had expressed, surreal and unsettling.

It was silly to contemplate taking many possessions, but the thought of leaving her home even for a short period forced Aaliya to look at her belongings in a way she rarely contemplated.

She got out of bed and pulled the cover across neatly. She went over to her dresser and started brushing her hair. There on top of her dresser was the small leather bird she had made as a young girl. She picked it up, noticing it fit comfortably in the palm of her hand. It was a strange looking creature. Randomly cut pieces of leather were hand sewn together in a slipshod fashion. The form, however, was unmistakably of a bird. Longer lengths of stiff leather at the back indicated the tail feathers, and larger pieces on the side resembled the wings. Aaliya remembered how happy she had been with the little project, proudly presenting it to Olle one day when she was a young. In her hand, it felt pithy, like a turning point that was solid enough to touch.

Aaliya put down the bird and crossed the room. The woollen cloak was hanging amongst her dresses in the wardrobe. She pulled it off the hanger and spread it across the bed. There were few things she wanted to take from the room. Most of what she cared for in terms of possessions was in the workshop. But she would need some things to get herself through the upcoming weeks. She grabbed boots, simple dresses, woollen undergarments and threw them on the bed. She caught a glimpse of her image in the mirror and pulled her long hair towards the back of her head. She contemplated cutting it all off, but the moment passed and she let her hair tumble again to her shoulders. Rummaging through draws she found her enamel cup, candles and her precious maps. It was all thrown onto the bed. And then there were things she simply couldn't part with. The leather bird, her first leather satchel, some books, a small pot of ink, a quill and some parchment.

She walked around the room. There was still so much remaining. She stood near her dresser, her eyes scanning every surface. All her jewellery tucked away neatly in ornate boxes. Hairbrushes. Cushions and sheets. She didn't need any of it. Or did she? She went to her box of silver and lifted the lid. Her fingers searched through the jewels. Some of the pieces she had not taken the time to look at for years. She picked up one of the necklaces and stretched it across the palm of her hand. It featured six emeralds encased in a filigree of silver. It was beautiful, but she had never worn it. Maybe it was meant to be in Maddalena's collection as it didn't resemble anything of importance to her. She placed it back in the box and continued to forage amongst the jewels, until she came across something that instantly made her still.

A pendant of twelve discs of silver, each no bigger

than a small fingernail, soldered together to form a circle the size of a mouth open in surprise. Each silver disc had a word engraved in old Elkhani, the original language of the South. Aaliya brought the necklace closer to her face, inspecting every detail. She had been given the necklace from her mother on her sixteenth birthday. "This had been given to me on my sixteenth birthday by my father," her mother had said. "My father told me that the pendant was forged in Elkha many, many years ago during the age of the Four Gods. It has been recorded that people across the realm also worshipped the God of Justice and the God of Mercy and unlike our Gods, were represented by male and female. The God of Justice being a man, and the God of Mercy a woman. Each disc contains an Elkhani word for the twelve freedoms: temptations and burdens, abandonment and restraint, flight and confinement, wants and needs, unruly and tame, present and future.

"Legend has it that the True God of Life touched the Great Rock of the Blazing Canyon at full moon over the course of twelve phases, and on each occasion a piece of rock turned to silver and fell into his hands with the words inscribed. And although some words seem contrary to the notion of freedom, the wisdom is that they are all integral to the whole. It's just the way you look at it, and what you wish for. The twelve freedoms were forged together to form this pendant.

"But understand this, my girl. It doesn't provide the owner with special powers. It doesn't indulge the owner with the ability to make their hopes and dreams come true. It simply reminds the owner they are on a path, and that you had better be prepared for some startling changes along the way."

For the first time since receiving the necklace, Aaliya placed it over her head and the pendant rested on her dress between her breasts. She expected to feel different, maybe feel a slight jolt, some sort of new power entering through her skin. But there was nothing. She touched it, running the tip of her finger over the words and wondering what each word was. What were they again…flight, wants, needs, temptations…Aaliya couldn't remember them all. Maybe that was the point, she wondered. If they were easy to recall she might cling to them like they were answers that could materialize. Instead she wore it as a necklace, an ornament, an offering from her mother.

Standing beside her bed, she lifted the pillow and uncovered the knife still wrapped in its sheath. For three nights she had kept it under her pillow, too nervous to secure it to her body. Just as she picked it up, a knock sounded at the door. Aaliya quickly placed the knife back under the pillow and covered the sundries on her bed with the cloak.

"Nella?" Aaliya said as she peeled open the door.

"Catja is here to see you. She's downstairs in the drawing room."

Aaliya quickly took off the pendant before closing the door behind her and following Nella down the stairs.

Catja rose from the sofa when Aaliya walked in. She was wearing a long apricot coloured dress with fabric pulled up to her shoulder and secured with a pin. Her long fair hair was pulled back into an exquisite braid. She looked radiant. Catja walked towards Aaliya and they kissed and hugged.

"We didn't get a chance to speak at the wedding," Catja said.

Aaliya smiled. "No, I was on a leash you could say. You looked pretty busy yourself."

Aaliya recalled Catja flitting between numerous men at the wedding. She had the ability to draw in male company like ants to honey. Her personality was a giant thing, a great thundering chariot of mirth and vivacity. Her laugh would boom out like an exotic bird. And those touches on the arm or hand made one feel as though they were connecting with the divine. Aaliya didn't envy her abilities so much as find her difference refreshing. She treasured Catja for being herself.

"I remember catching a look your way at one point," Catja said, as they sat down together on the sofa. "You looked as though your face had been stretched from here to Lagos it was so long."

"Here I was thinking I had done really well."

"About as well as a midwife extracting teeth."

"Am I that serious?"

"Yes. I don't mind, though. I quite like having a nana in my life."

"I'm a nana now, am I?"

Catja nodded.

"I quite like that," responded Aaliya proudly. She then quickly reached for a cushion and swung it at Catja's face. Catja was startled for a moment before grabbing a cushion of her own and clipping Aaliya's chin with it. "Right," said Aaliya, grabbing a cushion in her other hand and laying into Catja.

In the next moment, legs and arms and hair filled the space around them. The two women started laughing, squealing as wildly as happy pigs. The pillows were tossed to the side, and in one swift move, Aaliya grabbed Catja around her middle and wrestled her back down onto the sofa. Jabs in the ribs and more wrestling ensued until they fell off the sofa still holding each other and clutching their stomaches in their hysterics.

"Aaliya!" came a firm woman's voice, and Aaliya peered through the hair sticking to her eyes to see Nella standing at the doorway, her hands on her hips.

Aaliya stood up, sweeping her hair off her face and tried to suppress laughing, but it boomed out of her with a violence. Catja got up off the floor and leaned against her friend, smiling.

"Now that I have clearly won this fight," Catja said, as Nella disappeared back into the hallway, "I wouldn't mind a drink of something."

"You landed like a sack of potatoes."

Catja plonked herself back down on the sofa while Aaliya left the room. She returned with two cups of barley tea and handed one to her friend, sitting down beside her.

"What were we talking about again?" Catja said, reaching for the cup.

"Nana pride."

Catja laughed. "The wedding, that's right."

"That fine display of might just now, was my best effort to change the subject."

"Well, you have a lot more practice to do, girl, because that hasn't even come close to shutting me up."

Aaliya laughed nervously.

Catja took a sip of the tea. "I watched you and Justen and although you two were rarely within arms reach throughout the night, there was clearly something going on. Are you going to tell me, or not?"

"What's to tell?"

"You are in love with him. Am I right?"

"Well…"

"Aaliya. Geez."

"I don't know. I guess I am. I mean, I just can't get him out of my head. But I don't know. It's all just…" Aaliya threw open her hands in exasperation.

"Oh for the love of the Gods, that was the most depressing account of love I've ever heard."

"What were you hoping to hear?"

"I was hoping you were going to tell me what a wonderful, passionate, joyous thing it is."

"Joyous? That's a nice thought but no, joyous doesn't seem like the right word. Intoxicating, exciting…yes. Early days though. But from my experience, love is… confusing. All that control and loss of control. Maybe my mother was right. She said once "love is a terribly jealous thing" and I didn't understand her comment at the time, but I certainly do now."

"This is getting worse!"

"Seriously, Catja. Hear me out. It is a jealous thing. That's what's so irresistible about it. Friendship by comparison is so… simple. You want to be here, I want to be here. It's equal, it's steady."

"It's not enough."

"Maybe it could be."

"Not convinced," Catja scoffed. "Well, the reason I am asking is because I think I'm in love."

"Oh. Well that's lovely. That's wonderful, Catja."

"Based on what you were just saying I should run for the hills and find a cave to hide in."

"That is absolutely what you should do! No, I'm kidding. It is probably what I would do, but that's just me." Aaliya smiled. She briefly looked in the direction of the window, before turning back at her friend. "That feeling of connection with another is worth the effort, worth every risk. Truly Catja, I'm happy for you. Do I know him?"

Catja licked her lips and smiled. "Pieter. Pieter Laus from Gedion."

"Pieter?" Aaliya said, disbelievingly.

"Yes."

"But you've only known him a few days." Aaliya instantly felt like a hypocrite. She knew that whirlwind feeling herself. Being swept up into something that felt larger-than-life. It was heady, maddening. She hungered for Justen just thinking about him. A tingly feeling of pleasure that was as unmistakably real as it was elusive.

"I just know," Catja exclaimed.

"Know…what?"

"That he's the one."

"The one?" Aaliya tried to recall if she had spoken about Justen the same way. Coming from someone else it seemed so irrational.

"The attraction between us is amazing."

"He's…quite a bit older, isn't he?"

"Irrelevant."

"He hasn't proposed to you, has he?"

"Oh no," Catja said, waving her hand, "but it's a matter of time. Anyway, what if he did propose? That's good, isn't it? Why put off the inevitable?"

"Is that what you want?"

"Well, of course," Catja replied.

"He's heading back to Gedion in two days."

"It doesn't have to end. We'll write letters." Catja eyed the decanter of wine on a sideboard in the corner of the room. She got up and poured two glasses of wine. "This is the drink I had in mind, by the way." Catja raised her glass and handed the other to Aaliya. "To victory!"

The two women clinked their glasses together.

"You make it sound as though you've won the war," Aaliya said.

"Absolutely. It's a battle out there," Catja said bringing her glass to her lips.

Aaliya followed and took a long, soothing drink. "So why are you so taken by him?"

"His scintillating conversation."

Aaliya raised an eyebrow.

"Actually his sunny, cheerful demeanour," Catja said with a smirk.

Aaliya continued to stare at her friend incredulously.

"I jest of course. Truth be told he has wealth and connections that would put your father to shame."

"It's not a bloody competition."

"Ha! There's a lot at stake for us women. It's absolutely a competition."

"Count me out."

"You won't be able to avoid it forever. And you can't spend your life pining for someone who's going to be spending their life with another."

"I don't intend to put my life on hold, Catja." Aaliya took another sip and then attempted to take the topic away from any focus on herself. "So, you mentioned Pieter has connections." She paused before adding, "I was just wondering - for Maddalena of course - what those connections might be?"

"Well, your sister has done well. The Laus family is very close to the King of Gedion."

Aaliya thought to herself that would please Maddalena. She didn't believe her sister had ever let go of her childhood longing to become a queen. "Justen mentioned the king is impressed by Pieter. His apparent flair for negotiation…or was it mining exploration?"

"Yes, yes," Catja said, as though brushing the comment aside. "But there's something else."

"What?"

"He told me he stands a chance of inheriting the Isle of Pike."

"Really impressing the king by the sounds of it."

"Well, it's actually got nothing to do with royalty. The Isle of Pike belongs to Justen."

Aaliya looked hard at her friend, her face screwed up tightly. "That island is one of the most sought after pieces of land is the entire realm. Are you sure you heard correctly?"

"Yes, I know what I heard, Aaliya," Catja retorted, rolling her eyes.

"And you heard that from Pieter?"

"After quite a lot of coaxing, yes…"

"But I'm not following. If the island belongs to Justen…"

"Pieter is only ever to inherit it in the likelihood, how should I put this, the likelihood Justen dies. It's really just a long shot of course. People have their silly dreams, don't they?" said Catja, attempting to sound flippant. She paused for a moment before continuing, "Justen's sister, Carly, is not in the running. I'd be incensed if I were her, wouldn't you?"

Aaliya nodded feebly, still a little dumbfounded by what she was hearing.

Catja took a deep lungful of air and then went on. "We'd had a bit to drink the other night when we were talking, but from what I recall, Pieter and Justen's father…Laso or Laszlo…I believe his name was, were quite close. They were brother's of course, but that's hardly a given they're going to get along. But Laszlo being the older son inherited the Isle of Pike when their father died. Pieter was starting to make headway in the discovery of minerals across Gedion at that point. Really making an impact. And then he did some prospecting on Pike, and you wouldn't believe it…copper! But it was difficult to retrieve, the island is so far from the nearest Gedion port at Elisus.

"The way Pieter told it, it was a massive operation. Getting materials to the island to set up the blast furnaces. Shipping in skilled craftsmen. But he did it. And in the process, created wealth for himself. But what's particularly interesting is how he created wealth for his brother. Without Pieter, Laszlo would have been overseeing a useless rock in the middle of the Mindano Sea."

"So the island went to Justen after Laszlo was killed?" Aaliya asked.

"Yes, in the Battle of Barmer."

"I heard…" Aaliya stopped herself, not sure that it was wise to mention that Justen had disclosed to her that it was in fact Renatus Clausen who had killed Justen's father.

"You heard what?" Catja prompted.

"I heard that Justen was only ten years old when that happened."

"Yes. So young."

"Sorry…it's just that…" Aaliya tried to grasp the scope of the information she just heard, but it was too big, too inexplicable. "What else do you know about Pieter? I don't know…everyday, ordinary things about him?" She softened her tone, "the way he treats his pets? How does he like his tea?"

Catja shrugged, an expression of disinterest upon her

face. "I know enough. The rest I will find out."

"You've only known him for a week or so and Justen has mentioned so little about him. I find it odd."

"Maybe Justen never talks about much at all. Maybe Justen's mouth has been occupied with other activities."

"I'm clutching a pillow very firmly…"

"Come on, Aaliya. I want details."

Aaliya took a sip of her wine. "You know what I'm like. It's a timing thing with me."

"Lousy excuse."

"Sorry." Aaliya could sense she had let her friend down. "I just need some quiet for a while. Is that alright? Please don't mention this to anyone."

"My lips are sealed," Catja said, running her finger across her mouth.

"It's over now anyway. For obvious reasons."

"Well…not necessarily."

Aaliya eased back further in the sofa, her body soft like a rag doll. She took another sip, closed her eyes and enjoyed the feeling of smooth warmth gliding down her throat. Aaliya placed her hand on Catja's knee and, for a while, silence enveloped them.

"You're right, you know," Aaliya said quietly. "When is it over? When is there closure? When do you actually know?"

"It's only over when it's truly over."

"When you're dead in other words."

"Yes, that's another way of putting it."

"My Gods, the fumbling around we do."

"A lifetime of it."

Aaliya looked across the room, at nothing in particular, and she suspected Catja was doing the same. She then turned to face her friend. "I do want to see Justen. Just one more time," Aaliya said.

Catja looked at Aaliya and nodded.

"It's stupid…I know…"

"No…it's not."

"Do you think you could you get a message to him? He leaves the afternoon of Phenday."

"I think so."

"Please tell him to meet me at ten o'clock tomorrow morning at our place in the forest. He'll know the spot I'm talking about."

"I'll do that," Catja replied.

"Thank you."

They stayed that way for the next hour. It was the most relaxed Aaliya had felt in weeks. The tension seemed to slip away with the lightness of silk. Aaliya was incredibly grateful for the moment, the uncomplicated tenderness of what she was sharing with the person beside her.

When at last the time came to part, the pair stood and held each other again.

"Goodbye, Catja," Aaliya said.

Catja nodded and left the room.

Back up in her room, Aaliya stood beside her bed and lifted the pillow. She undid the buttons on her dress and placed the knife in its sheath snugly between her shoulder blades. She reached for the necklace and placed it over her head. She considered having the pendant exposed, but as she buttoned her dress back up, she tucked it under her clothing, letting it rest close to her skin. It felt right there, an extension of herself. She rolled her shoulders, aware of the feeling of leather wrapped around her body. It was a good feeling, firm and secure.

20

The Sudden Fury

The morning leapt into the afternoon. Aaliya stood outside the stable, brushing long strokes down the side of her horse. She was so close to leaving now, a nervous trembling bubbled under the surface of her skin. She felt as though fiddles were playing in her stomach, vibrating out to her fingertips and making her hands a little shaky. She smiled at the thought of leaving to go to Blackrock in four days time.

After Catja had left around midday, Aaliya had made her way to the workshop. As soon as she stepped into the room, that familiar feeling of comfort rippled through her being. The smell of singed leather wafting through the air, the sight of leather offcuts strewn across the floor, the gentle sounds of hide being sliced and punched. It all contented her so much she had to resist picking up an awl and starting on a project. Half finished saddles hung around the workshop like portraits having a conversation with her. She wondered about the horses whose backs they would soon lay upon. The places the creature had been, the distances it was yet to travel. She moved a little closer to a saddle she had been working on for the past couple of weeks. She ran her fingers over the skived ornate surface of the pommel, took hold of a strap and brought it close to her nose so she could smell its richness.

A part of her wanted to keep the beautiful saddles she made. So much time, so much of herself went into every detail. The parting with the finished product never became easier. But the parting always took place. Aaliya never mentioned to Olle that she kept a journal of every saddle she made. She'd faithfully write down the main elements of the saddle, any new features that were added and the skills she learned along the way. She even gave them names like they were unearthly beings: Brilliant Emblem of the Wolf, Pledge of Grace, Crest of the Supreme Guardian and countless others.

It was this sense of a parting that she had felt when standing in the middle of the workshop earlier in the day. A part of her would always remain there. The magic of it all couldn't be explained easily. The room, what was made there, what was used. The creaturly quality of everything in the space. It was death yet it was so alive. What awaited her at Blackrock, she didn't know. Certain things would remain the same. The same tools would hang from boards in the next workshop. The same comforting smells would fill the air. But it wouldn't be Olle's space. It wouldn't be Olle she would see each day. The history wouldn't be there. Memories were yet to be made.

She had gone through tools with Olle to work out what she could take. How could she not take the saddler's awl and stitching awl in addition to her round and closing awls? And although the half moon knife was an awkward shaped blade to pack, she used it all the time. Nails, hammers, lanolin, not to mention buckles, lorimers, metal mountings. It all had to fit into her duffle bag.

As she stood in the sun brushing, she thought about what other things she may be able to do. She imagined whole days of magnificence. Mornings busily making, the comforting feel of a metal tool in her hand. Afternoons riding out across a wild and stark landscape. Just her and the mountains, birds soaring above, the wind, the sun. In her mind, how could it not transform her life? Surely this was the moment she had been working towards all along?

"Enjoy the wedding yesterday?" a staid, low male voice asked.

Aaliya suddenly plummeted back to earth. She looked up. Her thoughts splintered into a thousand pieces until there was nothing left but fragments of dust. Not now, she thought. Not ever really, but certainly not now. Viggo sat high on his horse, his body blocking out the afternoon sun. He looked like a dark mass to her, she didn't notice his features or what he was wearing. Simply that he had cast a shadow over her. She momentarily stopped brushing. She instantly felt tense, uncomfortable. It wasn't that she was scared of him. It was simply that he was bad for her. A negative force in her life. Whenever he approached she felt like she had to quickly don armour to repel him.

She didn't want to respond. Didn't want to discuss anything with this man. Just act boring but congenial and hopefully he'll leave me alone, she thought. "Yes," she finally responded.

He waited, as though expecting her to say more. "It was a spectacular affair indeed, wasn't it? The music…the dancing. And that pie was remarkable."

"Yes, it was," Aaliya said, bringing the brush back along the flank of the horse.

"Have you been to many weddings?"

"Not really."

"They're intriguing events. I can't help but wonder what goes through the minds of the bride and groom."

"To hurry and get it over with, I imagine."

Viggo laughed. "You're probably right. They certainly looked to me as though they didn't really want to be there."

"It's my sister's second marriage. It's business to her."

"It's business for everyone. But to marry again does seem a desperate leap of optimism over rationality."

"She knows what she's doing."

"And the groom, do you think he knows what he's doing?"

Aaliya shrugged. She momentarily stopped brushing, and then quickly resumed upon realizing her faltering had been observed.

"What brings you down here? All too much to bear?" he asked.

Aaliya smirked. "It was a wedding."

"Of no great importance whatsoever, right?"

She remained silent.

"He cuts a luscious figure, doesn't he? Justen…Justen the great noble of House Laus of Gedion. Quite the catch, I'm sure you'd agree. Marries your sister, and in a few days they'll be riding off rarely to be seen again. You'll be palmed off soon enough, probably not under such an auspicious arrangement. Which leaves just Thormund. With Helena gone, House Reiner is but a name no more significant than leaf or chair. Your family as you used to know it has gone."

Aaliya gripped the brush tightly, her fingers like wire. "Do you need help unsaddling your horse? Benj will be back in twenty minutes or so if you want to come back then."

"We're having a conversation. Expanding our capacity

as human beings. Making a contribution to civilization."

"Nothing civilized going on here."

"Speak for yourself."

"This is the thing, isn't it? You're all talk."

"Said by someone who struggles to put two words together most of the time."

"You seem to confuse my lack of interest in talking to you with a general lack of interest. Thought you were smarter than that."

Viggo didn't have a quick retort to follow. He looked momentarily displaced, unmanned. To Aaliya, you could see him processing his next move, how to get back on top of the situation. She didn't wait for him to work it out. She put down the brush, picked up the reins and hoisted the saddle into her arms. Her tools were sitting in the open duffle bag on the ground. A shot of nervousness swept through her at the thought that Viggo might see them and think something of it. She walked into the tack room carrying the saddle. Behind her, she heard Viggo dismount and follow.

The room inside was long and narrow. A dozen saddles rested upon wooden trestles. Coiled reins and ropes hung from hooks along the windowless walls. Horseshoes nailed into the mortar held up cluttered bundles of bridles and halters. The stable hand regularly did battle with the elements of summer. The wooden floor was swept regularly and a good degree of order maintained in the room. But by the end of each day, dust crept in and coated everything.

Inside the room, Aaliya placed the saddle on a trestle. She made a move towards the wall to hang up the reins. Viggo quickly stood in front of her.

"Does this look like just talk to you?" Viggo said.

"Get out of my way," Aaliya said, looking down at

her feet.

He put a finger underneath her chin and attempted to tilt her head up. She shrugged him off and backed away. A long moment passed. He smiled, waving his arm as he stepped aside.

She hesitated then stepped forward and hung up the reins. This was what she hated. This assertion of physical presence. She hated his power. The way he could just stand in front of her knowing that was all he needed to do to silence her. She knew she had to leave. That was the sensible thing to do. Admit to herself that she was intimidated and remove herself from the situation.

But she couldn't shake the need to get a word in. That was what uncoiled him, so it seemed. She was going soon anyway. Not likely to see him again for quite some time. Would he end up thinking she left because of him? That he had successfully come between her and Thormund? She hung up the reins. "Like I said, all talk." She turned to face him. "And as for my father, he'll be around long after you're gone. He's smarter than you. You were just lucky to have been born into it."

"I almost detect a threat in there."

Aaliya sniggered and walked outside to retrieve the last of the horse tack. "I've been opening my mouth for eighteen years. You've been trying to close it for eighteen years. So typical of you to cry threat." She awkwardly brushed Viggo as she squeezed back through the door frame into the room.

"Oh dear, I believe I am seeing just how unhappy you are now. I guess the wedding really did affect you, not to mention the loss of Helena. Well, at least Thormund seemed happy at the wedding, even if the remaining Reiner women weren't," Viggo said, still standing at the threshold, his arm raised and resting on the door frame.

She rolled her eyes. What would he know about her happiness anyway? Did she have to parade around with a big smile on her face to please him, to please anybody for that matter?

"I do believe a burden lifted for him when Helena passed away," he said.

"A burden?" she replied.

"Her long illness was a drain on Thormund's quality of life. But what I've seen recently is that he's put all that well and truly behind him. He's very eager to move on. I'm not complaining. He's making me a very rich man. He has considerable influence amongst merchants in this land."

"I think it's fair to say you'd be nothing without him."

"We're back there are we? Who's the smartest of them all?"

"You said it."

"He's not as smart as he thinks he is."

"What makes you say that?"

"I think you'll find in time he'll be nothing without me."

"What are you doing? Swindling my father?"

He laughed. "I wouldn't call it swindling."

"So what is it then?"

"Answerable to you, am I?"

"I know about Redshade. Maddalena isn't the only one Thormund confides in," she lied. She tried hard to recall what Maddalena talked about with Thormund at the dinner table several nights ago, cursing herself now for getting so drunk. She was clutching, but drew on every filament of information she had heard. "I know about the printed money. People buying and trading shares with this printed money. Father thinks you're a genius."

"So he should."

"And the Iron Steppes. Just a wasteland for so long. A blight on our terrain. Suddenly it holds all our answers. Holds the very thing Traegos has desperately wanted since the Barmer Valley mess ten years ago."

Aaliya waited for Viggo to interject, to clarify, to add some smarmy element and make the dialogue go his way. But he didn't. Aaliya knew then that he was holding something back. 'Power is largely about perception' her father had once told her. Perhaps Redshade was nothing more than a ruse to make people believe Traegos had this highly desirable commodity that would cease its vulnerability forever. "I'm sure you're busily spreading the word everywhere that Redshade is the solution Traegos has been looking for?"

"Indeed. I have the king's ear no less."

"And people want a solution to cling to."

"It has been said…yes."

"People don't like uncertainty. It's hard to prosper with uncertainty."

Viggo hesitated. "Yes. It is."

"But there's no mineral wealth under the Iron Steppes is there?" Aaliya said, wondering if she could truly bluff this man. "It's just sand, isn't it, Viggo?"

He grabbed her by the neck, the suddenness and force of the gesture making her gasp. Viggo slammed her against the stonewall, pinning her like she were a rag doll. Aaliya pulled at his arm to try and get him to release the pressure, to grant her a slither of an opening through which she could draw breath. His hold was vice-like. She could feel warm blood matting her hair where her head had hit the wall. Her body was suddenly drenched in sweat. His power was so great she couldn't get his arms to budge. She had to get some air, very soon she had to draw breath. She looked into his eyes and saw something hateful, menacing. Would he really kill her? As one hand of hers continued to pull at his own wrapped around her throat, her other reached up to his face. She plunged her thumb as hard as she could into the corner of his eye. It seemed to slide into the wet socket with the ease of a knife into butter.

Viggo let out a blood curling cry and reeled back, clutching his eye. Wheezing and spluttering she tried to draw breath. She couldn't get enough air in. It was like breathing through a straw. Clutching her throat and still trying to draw breath, she stumbled towards the door. She had to get out of here.

"You fucking whore," he growled, launching at her just as she had passed.

Aaliya fell hard onto the ground under the man's weight. She writhed and squirmed and fought. Don't, under any circumstances, get pinned to the ground. He was strong. But so was she. Aaliya screamed as hard as she could. Last time Viggo had tried this, the power of her bellow had worked for her. But this time, only a raspy, broken, pathetic sound came from her mouth.

Viggo laughed. "I told you I would have you one day."

He pushed her hard onto her back. She felt the back of her head open up more. I'm not going to let this happen. And then she felt it. The thin blade wedged so neatly between her shoulder blades. Her mind was racing. If only she could get to it. Her arm reached up to try and get her hand behind her neck. Viggo slammed his hand down, pinning her arm into place. She couldn't move. As a last resort, Aaliya turned her head to the side and took his thumb into her mouth and bit down hard. Viggo let out a howl of pain and Aaliya bit even harder.

"Is everything alright in there?" said a voice from outside.

She couldn't believe it. Someone was near the stable and had heard Viggo. The voice of the stranger had clearly alarmed Viggo and she kicked him off her forcefully.

"You…you touch me again…I will kill you," Aaliya whispered, hoarsely, struggling to get to her feet.

"You think this ends for you? You think you can walk out of here and go back to your sweet life? This will never end. I'm only getting started."

Aaliya turned away, unable to look at him any longer. She stumbled out into the open, correcting herself against the wall as she walked. She felt dizzy, depleted.

Outside, the stranger looked surprised to see a woman emerge from the tack room. She considered saying something, but instead kept walking.

21

Duty and Honour

It was late afternoon, and Maddalena could see through the window the sun outside was weakening. The room she sat in was sparsely furnished. A table, a chair, a closet, a dressing table. Grooming aids had been brought in at her request. The bed was kept excessively neat with the sharpest folds in the linen she had ever come across. She longed for a messy bed, a sensual bed, but suspected this would not be the case where she was headed.

At the dressing table she repeatedly ran a brush through her hair. The gesture seemed to take on a life of its own and was done over and over with little conscious thought. She was officially a wife again. So convinced she had been that somehow it wouldn't happen, some chance event would stop it from taking place, that she sat in the room feeling slightly altered. In a short time she would be having a small, intimate dinner with her new husband, his uncle and her father. It would be her first time in the company of her father since the wedding. She was now independent of him yet couldn't shake the notion that until she was on the other side of the Great Anjar Range, he would still yield some strange power over her.

The walls were void of paintings and she longed for her picture of Queen Nissine, still gracing the wall of her own room. The expression of the woman in the painting in her elegant yellow gown rarely left Maddalena's thoughts. In the painting, the Queen looks out in the distance. Her eyes fall on something situated above ground level, but not too high into the sky. It's achievable, Maddalena thought, all of it. As soon as she returns home today, she would take the painting down off the wall. There would be no trip to Gedion without it.

In the bath on the other side of the room lay her husband. She had bathed first, alarmed at how cool the water was. Surely it must be so cold by now to be of little comfort at all. But when she had passed by him a moment ago he looked as deeply relaxed as a cat in the sun. She shivered a little at the thought of him. She actually held a deep longing to incite his fury. She indulged herself in a fantasy: keeping him at a distance until he is driven into a rage, and then, in an act of abandonment he lashes out at her, yells at her before yielding to her embrace, the security of her generous arms. And then they would fuck. They would fuck without restraint until their loins became sore. He would want to be her protector, her rescuer, and the inability to do so would cause him endless turmoil.

The fact that she didn't need rescuing made the fantasy all the more potent. She came to the conclusion he was a decent man, restrained and somewhat haughty in his sense of duty and honour, but nonetheless decent. Justen wanted to do the right thing by his family. A man who didn't shirk his responsibilities. It was clear from their brief discussions together that he adored his sister. Carly was seven years younger than him and still had a winsome and lighthearted outlook that Justen admired and (had to admit) wished he could be more like. Justen had laughed as he spoke of Carly who, on the eve of his parting for Ansgar, derived some sort of weird pleasure from the turmoil he felt around his familial responsibilities. Maddalena had laughed along with the story but knew with absolute surety that Carly would have to buy in to the madness everyone else had to one day.

Maddalena looked over and saw Justen stand up out of the bath. He reached for the towel nearby and wiped himself down. They had made love during the previous two nights, a strange mix of the perfunctory and the pleasurable. In her mind, he was clearly an experienced lover which ensured awkward fumbling was kept to a minimum. Titillation and emotion were largely absent. Maddalena wondered if that would change with time. If they could ever remove themselves from prying eyes and the governance of their bodies, but she doubted it.

He walked across the room naked and threw himself down on the bed. His face pressed hard into the mattress, he let out an almighty groan. Maddalena turned back to the mirror and watched her reflection as she swept the brush over her hair.

22

Anchor

Aaliya watched her father from a distance as he stood on the quay looking up at the ship moored before him. She knew he marvelled at ships, their possibilities, the way they opened up the world. The ship was a three-masted square-rigged beauty, the masts standing naked whilst cargo was lead into its impressive hull. As many as ten other ships lined the long jetties poking out into the river, their sails also folded away, though none as remarkable as the one vessel in front of him. Watching the large boats sail in and out of the quay was something he never tired of. He had mentioned once that he would like to see the river take an even bigger ship, some sort of monolithic beast that could sail right out of Marius all the way to distant realms.

He had been doing this ritual ever since he was a young boy. Although the putrid smell rising up from the river forced those of delicate constitution to cover up their nose, Thormund would inhale the smell by the river as deeply as his lungs could cope with in the hope the salty dampness would linger in his head days after his visit. He had told both her and Maddalena about standing close to the very spot he was now as a young boy, watching the boats dock at the quay. Back then, the boats were much smaller but they were still the most beautiful things he had seen. He would have gone everyday to the quay to watch the boats if he could. As it was, once a month was all he could manage.

Thormund had once told the story that before his father brought him to Ansgar to work, he had never seen a ship before. His home was a tiny village called Alderfi, two days on horseback south-west of the capital. As a young boy, Thormund thought that he would train to become a shepherd like his father. Instead he was sent to the capital as a boy of ten to work as a servant for a tailor, doing all the jobs the tailor's apprentice didn't want to do. He could still remember the watery sludge dished up nightly in the year before he was sent away. "You'll be better off," his father had told him. "Work hard and you might get an apprenticeship."

But he knew even as a young boy he would never get an apprenticeship under normal circumstances. His family were poor farmers of no repute at all. He knew that to be noticed, he had to offer something more than his name and his ability to sort scrap fabric. He had to offer something special. He couldn't read or write, but he was fast and he was meticulous. He would observe the way the tailor and the apprentice did their stitching, and he would lie awake at night thinking about how he could do it better, faster. In his small cavity under the stairs at night, his hands would make motions in the air as he imagined cutting and threading the fabric. And he kept telling himself to never accept it, only to rise above it. No matter what.

It wasn't even an apprenticeship with the tailor he wanted (although he was sure his father would have thought that was the pinnacle of high achievement). A mercer would visit the shop occasionally to inspect fabric and the garments being made for export. Every now and then, Thormund heard snippets of conversation between the tailor and the mercer. Words of 'trade' and 'silk' and 'voyage' were mentioned, piquing his interest and encouraging him to work even harder.

Watching the ships moored at Ansgar Quay, he began to understand what the words meant and their power. His visits to the quay took on a new urgency. Every chance he could, he would ask whoever was present "Where is the ship going?" "What's the cargo?" or "Who are the goods for?" Thormund's recollection was that for the most part he was swatted away like a nuisance bug, but occasionally a seaman would stop, even briefly, to have a chat with him and explain the world of trade as he knew it.

For the first six months after Thormund turned fourteen, he didn't see the mercer at all. Then one bitterly cold afternoon, the mercer walked into the shop. Thormund recalled with ease the way the sky outside was a coalescence of greys yet the man that entered the shop looked as though he could turn grey to gold. The mercer was wearing a long, plum-coloured velvet cloak draped heavily around his shoulders. On two of his fingers, above his knuckles, sat gemstones of such enormity, Thormund wondered where he acquired the strength to even lift his hand.

Thormund waited until the mercer had finished his business with the tailor and left the shop. He then leapt out from behind his table and raced out the door. Thormund told him all that he knew: the burgeoning wool trade, who was making the finest silk, markets across the realm for fabric, the growing demand for furs. He knew he had this one moment to convince the mercer to take him on. Whether it was sheer luck or simply that Thormund's preparation had paid off, the mercer didn't walk away. The mercer eyed him with suspicion, challenged him on his family connections, on how he had acquired such valuable knowledge. Thormund explained how he had acquired his information and then took a gamble. "You will be able to place your trust in me and know that the only thing I want is for your business to succeed," Thormund said to the man.

"Trust, you say. How do I know I will be able to trust you? I don't even know who you are," the mercer responded.

"You need someone to tell your secrets to. To get to where you are you have guarded your knowledge. But you can't go much further without sharing it with someone else. I'm that someone you've been looking for."

As he had explained it, the time the mercer took to weigh up Thormund's suggestion was a gnawing kind of agony. He remembered the way the mercer looked down the street, before eventually turning back to him and announcing that he would give him an apprenticeship. "You'll need to take the guild's oath and vow to keep secret all that you learn." The mercer went on to explain that arrangements would be made to ensure he learned to read and write, and learned basic arithmetic. It was also firmly suggested to Thormund that under no circumstances would unruly behaviour be tolerated.

The mercer's name was Axel Bak. With Axel's guidance, Thormund gained skills and knowledge he never dreamed he would be exposed to. He learned how to assess the quality of goods, who the best sources for various goods were, the preferences and tastes of customers in different provinces. After years of establishing trust, Axel imparted to Thormund his greatest trade secrets. Thormund learned how to deal with (and sometimes manoeuvre around) import and export regulations of the jurisdictions through which their goods passed. It was essential to keep shipments moving smoothly and Thormund was guided through which customs officials to bribe and with how much money. Thormund had been right all along. He stressed in his retelling to Aaliya and Maddalena that it wasn't enough to be wealthy and powerful. Axel needed to impart his knowledge to someone; he needed a witness as a way of surviving in the world.

Her father went on to say that if he had stayed in Alderfi he would not have had the opportunities he had. He didn't want to dwell on what his life would have been like if he had not been sent to the tailor as a young boy, but he knew with absolute certainty that his parents had done him a favour. He continued to carry a certain pride from making the same decision for his own daughters. Aaliya knew that Maddalena's loyalty and political cunning from a young age left no doubt in her father's mind she would help grow his empire. Nurturing Maddalena to understand her power and potential was an instinctively natural act.

Watching her father from afar, Aaliya knew she was a different scenario entirely. She had qualities that Thormund found admirable. But her nonconformity was problematic. Her father had noticed the beautiful things she made, the way she lovingly transformed items found into wondrous creations. But to request to see her at the quay, a place she knew defined his place in the world, sent a strong message that they were not here to discuss craftsmanship.

From afar, Thormund cut a grand figure as he stood framed by the enormous ship. With every step she made towards him, however, she began to see that was nervous too. He appeared to be simmering with strange unrest as though he were a captain unsettled at the prospect of his next voyage. She had hardly slept and the sockets of her eyes felt as though they had been filled with sand. Her body was shaky, her guts in a knot. Last night had been a long and wretched one emptying the contents of her body into a bucket. She didn't know if she could tell her father about Viggo attacking her, but she knew she had to. The intended visit to Blackrock seemed like a trivial side-issue by comparison. Aaliya had been looking forward to seeing her father again now the wedding was over, but as she walked ahead, the air seemed leaden and heavy.

"I've been waiting here a while," Thormund said.

"I'm sorry, father."

"Let's walk, shall we?"

They started moving along the dockside. The hulls of the moored ships created a strange tune as they walked. The smell of bilge in the water rose up and assaulted their senses.

"You must be very pleased for your sister," Thormund said. "Married again at last."

"I am," she lied.

"Do you think she'll keep this one longer than the last one?"

"Why wouldn't she?" she asked, not sure if it was a rhetorical question.

"I'm no fool, Aaliya. I could tell she didn't want to get married." Thormund turned to look at Aaliya directly. "The Reiners get married and we have children, that's what we do. Maddalena knows this. It's the right thing to do."

Aaliya wanted to suggest otherwise, but kept her mouth shut.

"She will have a son," Thormund continued, "I'm sure of it. Your mother couldn't though. After you were born she was heavy with child on three more occasions. But each time her body yielded only a tiny, strange creature which the doctor took away and had buried."

"That would have been heartbreaking for her."

"A woman shouldn't become attached to a child until it is well grown. She shouldn't have allowed her heart to take over."

"It's not something over which one has much control."

"Nonsense. We can control just about anything."

Aaliya released a small sigh. She was sure it was her mother's ability to feel heartbreak that made her so human to her. There was an essence to Helena that transcended perfectionism, this notion of winning in the game of life.

Thormund stopped. "I brought you out here for a reason, Aaliya. See those crates over there?"

Aaliya looked in the direction Thormund had jabbed the air. The piles of crates stood like a grand monument. Seamen were working in teams to carry the hulking items up the gang plank and onto the ship.

"Reiner wool. Reiner cloth. Rugs loomed in Reiner workshops. Hell, even some of your saddles are in those crates. Bound for Ports of Lagos, Tshane, Maghrib. To far reaches of the realm. The scale of what's at stake is immeasurable. The legacy is great. As a Reiner, you have a responsibility. Not a choice. A responsibility to make sure all this endures.

"During the past nine months I have been having discussions with the Langen family of Elkha. You are betrothed to their eldest son, Aldrin, and will marry at autumn's end."

Aaliya's mouth felt like it had been filled with ash.

Her knees started to sag and she tried to say something but couldn't make her voice carry.

Thormund continued, "Whatever fanciful notions you've been entertaining you are to put an end to forthwith. I know you'll work hard to make this marriage a success, Aaliya. Grace without hard work is no path for you. I know you will do this for our family."

Aaliya tossed her head from side to side. This talk was what he used in his business dealings, making the client feel they were utterly privileged to be connected to the Reiner name.

As though sensing her reticence, he went on. "Maddalena didn't know Justen before their wedding. I didn't know Helena before marrying her. You won't know your husband before marrying him. You don't need to know the person who is going to give you a son."

"Father, stop."

Thormund raised an eyebrow. "Stop?"

"Viggo…" Aaliya stammered, "if all this is so important to you, you've got to look at Viggo. He'll destroy everything you own. Everything that's important to you."

"Convenient, once again, to deflect away from your responsibilities. This has nothing to do with Viggo."

"It has everything to do with Viggo."

"I won't hear of it, Aaliya. You, and to a lesser degree your sister, have been trying to discredit that man for years. We've come so far with his guidance and we've got much further to - "

"He tried to rape me!" Aaliya growled, looking around in the hope her raised voice did not attract the attention of people nearby.

It was as though a great club had slammed into his

chest and knocked the air out of him. Aaliya watched uncomfortably as her father processed what he heard, the neatly arranged compartments of his life suddenly cracked and fissured. "Are you saying that to hurt me?"

"What? No! It's the truth."

"Truth," Thormund mumbled so quietly it was almost a whisper.

"It happened yesterday. We were talking about Redshade… the Iron Steppes. I challenged him as to whether there truly is anything to be mined there, and he just snapped. He became violent."

"I'm not surprised he became angry."

"No. Not just angry. He was violent. He hurt me. Your daughter," she said, aggressively pulling aside the fabric of her dress to reveal the red marks around her neck.

Thormund pursed his lips and furrowed his brow. He looked over Aaliya's shoulder at the ship. "I'll address this," he said.

"You will? How?"

"I *will* address this. But it doesn't change anything for you. You'll meet your betrothed at month's end. You'll do what is being asked of you."

"Yes," she replied. She didn't have the will to refuse. She just wanted the conversation to end. Just wanted to see Justen one last time and then head for Blackrock.

23

Time, Real and Imaginary

A strange heavy heat lingered over the forest like a wet cloak. Aaliya could feel trickles of sweat run down her back, down the inside of her legs. The rock she was sitting on still held some of the coolness from the night before, but the air was oppressive. She was desperate to relieve herself but told herself to calm down, stop fidgeting and everything would be alright.

She forced a brittle smile onto her face in the hope that it might make her feel better. Anyone seeing her would surely find her to be an odd sight. She let her expression go slack again. Catja had asked her a simple question the other day about being in love with Justen. For the sake of the Gods, she couldn't even answer it simply. Had to go on about complexities and impossibilities. Of course she loved him. Did he understand he had this power over her? She was just so scared to acknowledge it knowing it inevitably meant heartbreak.

The remaining hours of the day after visiting her father at the quay yesterday had tumbled by as a series of harried moments. She couldn't tell her father about Black-rock and the decision to withhold such an enormous bit of information weighed heavily on her. He would never support it and yet, the thought staying and just biding her time during the next couple of months pending her duty to marry filled her with such dread she could barely speak anyway. But wasn't he guilty of holding out too? Didn't he say he'd been in discussion with the family from Elkha for nine months about the arrangement? And then to just spring it on her and expect her to comply! Their respective notions of family and honour seemed to have the common ground of quicksand.

After leaving the quay she had made her way to Catja's house, only to be told of her absence. Aaliya longed to receive some sort of confirmation that Justen had received the message. But she also wanted to say goodbye properly to her friend. Her determination to leave was now hard-set and unyielding. If she couldn't have closure to her life in Ansgar, she at least wanted to leave without regrets. After Catja's house, she visited Helena's grave again (for good luck she told herself) before making her way back home. Maddalena was still away from the house and Aaliya had to fight with every fibre of her being the sickening sense that she had missed her opportunity.

She had barely slept and now here she was, sitting alone in the forest on a warm morning, wondering what this last visit would be like, if indeed it did happen at all. Would he be a man of self-control and not embrace her? Would they talk perfunctorily about the long trip ahead? She loved his honour, and she hated it. It's funny how the trait you start off admiring the most becomes the one you desperately want to change.

It was a death of sorts. Not as harrowing as the loss of her mother. But it was there all the same. A deep gash into her heart that would take time to repair. And it wasn't just Justen. Basking in whatever attention came her way over the past ten days she had literally been too blinded to notice Maddalena and consider her feelings. But she was losing her too. For all their mutual strangeness, Aaliya was fully aware now that she needed her sister more than ever in ways she couldn't explain. She contemplated telling Maddalena everything when she returned to the house after this visit. She certainly hadn't ruled it out. Just get through this one first.

Aaliya looked around at the trees surrounding her. The conifers and sycamores didn't seem to be straining under the summer heat. The trees rose tall and strong, an umbrella of shade that allowed only thin spears of light in. The ground a patchwork of browned grass with smatters of new shoots from the recent soak. Ivy crawled over remaining earth, twisting up and around the giant trunks. She had loved this forest ever since she was a small girl. The king loved the forest too so its future was preserved for the time being. But what then? When Aaliya looked at trees she saw feminine forms. Branches seemed to coil and interlock in a graceful, loving exchange. She felt nurtured and safe in a forest the way a child feels in a mother's arms. It could be a place of darkness too, a space where one is forced to confront anxieties and fears. Aaliya wondered if this was part of the reason men like her father cleared forests, preferring the unimaginative practicality of farmed fields. Remove the mystery, the solitude.

She heard a soft padding sound and looked up.

"Hey," Justen said, as he approached.

"You're here." Aaliya stood up and wrapped her arms around him. He smelled of figs and honey, of nervousness.

His hair was soft against the side of her face and she reached up to run her fingers through the wayward curls at the back of his head. Any lingering worry that he was going to pull himself free from her arms simply evaporated. They steadied themselves and held each other even closer.

Aaliya leaned back a little to look at his face and ran her thumb across the beads of sweat resting in the stubble above his lip. The moment was one of grace. One that could have easily not happened at all, but for which both were deeply grateful that it did.

Aaliya blinked furiously to hold back tears. "I just wanted to see you again. Before you go."

"I wanted to see you too."

"I know it's not easy for you being here."

"I want to be here. I wouldn't have come if I didn't want to be here."

She was relieved. She needed some sort of confirmation that she hadn't dragged him to this place, with all the risks that it entailed, against his will. They sat down together on the large rock, Justen's arm wrapped around the back of Aaliya.

"The other day…why didn't you come? I waited for you," Aaliya asked.

"I am so sorry. Don't think for a moment I didn't want to. My uncle dragged me across to the other side of the city to visit the Guild of Silversmiths, of all places. He insisted. I told him I had something else I had to do but, as I was riding out to see you, he caught up to me and insisted again. He was not going to leave my side. I just couldn't do anything about it. It was our last opportunity. I'll think about that forever."

"A man found me at the oak tree."

"Who?"

"I don't know who he is. I've seen him before, though. The day…the day after our night together, I visited my mother's grave. I saw him then."

"What did he look like?"

"Very short hair, shorn short, and red."

Justen's face went pale.

"He knew I was there to meet someone," Aaliya continued. "Said something about listening to other people's private conversations. I tried to leave and he chased me."

"That's Zar, I'm sure of it."

"How do you know him?"

"He's my uncle's servant."

"Justen, this doesn't sound good. Pieter…"

"Pieter has kept an eye on us, that seems quite plain. Gods, I suddenly feel sick. You tried to tell me." He leaned forward peering down at the ground. "I just want to be with you, Aaliya. I just want to be…with…you. But I don't know how to manage this situation."

Aaliya had so many questions she wanted to ask him, so many things she wanted cleared up before they parted. But with so little time left it suddenly seemed indulgent. She didn't want to end their time worrying about the motivation of others or lurching in anxiety over events she had little control over. Every bit of time felt so utterly precious.

He sat back up and smiled, and she smiled back. She was going to miss his smile, the way it soaked her up and made everything good.

"Are you ready to go? Have you packed?" She cringed at the idiocy of her question.

"There really isn't much for me to pack. I didn't come with much."

"Yes, of course. Maddalena, I'm sure, is having a hard time of it."

"Probably. You are…you are seeing her before she goes?"

"Of course I am."

"Good."

"I'm going to miss her."

"You two are funny. You can't live with each other, can't live without each other."

"Sounds like a marriage," Aaliya said soberly.

Justen laughed. "Yeah, you're probably right."

A solemn look passed between them. They both knew they couldn't stay out here much longer.

"What's going to happen?" Aaliya asked.

"I don't know."

"So…" Aaliya didn't know what else to say. Silence enveloped them which normally was a comforting feature of time they shared. But now it felt strained, abashed. "A tale could be written about us, you know. Included in some weary tome about lost love," she said.

"What could we call it? How about, 'People Pleasing: The advantages and disadvantages'."

"Ha! What about, 'Rejecting Posterity: Tales of friendship and fornication.'"

"Now we're getting somewhere. Okay. 'Everything I know about women I learned from my horse'."

"Your horse?"

"You look unconvinced. A horse just really wants to please you. Make you happy."

"Your book title wins. I think we could all learn a bit more from horses."

"Yes, our most companionable beasts are onto

something. But, truth be told, friendship and fornication is *the* title."

She gave him a whack on his waist and smiled.

"I'll miss you," he said.

They were simple words, but they were what she needed to hear. That she was valued and her absence would be felt. "I'll miss you, too. My Gods, I will miss you."

"You know, every time I'm with you I have the time of my life."

Her fierce composure went and she wrapped her arms around him again and sobbed. She rested her head on his chest, her tears dampening his shirt. The gentle rise and fall of his chest a wonder of comfort. She breathed in his scent. She breathed in the expansive smell of the forest. The two mingled together to form a heady scent that she would never forget.

Finally, when tears stopped flowing, she looked at him.

"Tell me something, Aaliya. Where to next for you?"

Aaliya looked through the trees and told him about how she'll be riding out to a rare and beautiful place called Blackrock in a couple of days. How she would be staying in a little hut and working alongside a master saddle maker. How she planned to make a saddle in honour of her mother, an exquisite piece that would make her father proud. She described for him a place to recover and heal, a place to learn who she was, a place to immerse herself in beauty and craftsmanship. She told him how after Blackrock, she didn't know, couldn't possibly know where her life would lead. But that she would try to be as authentic to who she was as she could possibly be.

And then time stilled. The soundlessness between them a gift. They interlocked their fingers and sat with no expectation of the other or of the moment other than just to be.

"Travel safely," Aaliya said.

"I will."

"Keep warm at night."

Justen smiled. "I surely will, Aaliya."

"Sorry, but I've probably got another fifty sentimental expressions to get through before you leave."

"I'm patient."

She laughed. "You'll regret it. Wait until I get onto personal hygiene."

"What's that?"

"You're not convincing anyone. Man of beautiful hair and sweet smelling skin, you've got that more covered than me."

"Your horsey, leathery smell is part of your charm," he said, giving her shoulders a squeeze.

"Okay, I've had enough of you now." She smiled. "One more thing. I've seen your saddle. It's got a particularly high cantle. Get yourself to a decent saddle maker when you return and have that fixed. Or better still, get yourself a better saddle."

"Trust you to run your hand along a surface where my ass spends a lot of time," he said with a grin.

"It's strictly a professional observation."

He brought her face to his and they kissed. It was the briefest of exchanges, yet it was rich and life affirming. She swallowed knowing that particles of him would always remain with her.

Justen stood up and held out his hand. "Goodbye, Aaliya."

"Goodbye," she said, taking his hand and standing.

She squeezed it again and then let it go.

Justen turned and walked. And he kept walking. And Aaliya stood feeling as though she were going to burst. Because she wanted to shout. She wanted to scream 'Come back to me!' But he kept walking. She knew she couldn't reach him. What they shared would have to be enough. Justen's hope that in a year or two they'd find a way through the murky world of family and politics to be together was just a fanciful dream. It was nice to have dreams, and it was something she found attractive in him. But her feet were too firmly planted on the ground. It was over. And was now a beautiful memory. And it was futile to hope for anything else.

It was when he reached the edge of a small clearing she heard it. The sound of horses galloping towards their location. There was something foreboding about the sound. Too urgent, too purposeful, for a hot morning in the forest. Their meeting place was a fair distance from the main track and yet the riders were getting closer. If she wasn't mistaken, it sounded as though they weren't on the track at all and were riding through the thick of the trees.

Aaliya looked in a panic all around her. Nothing. But it was so loud now. Her fear became sharp, useful. Run, she told herself. "Run, Justen! Run!" she screamed so loud her voice cracked.

Justen turned around and looked at her briefly, his mouth open in confusion. He then launched into a sprint and got little more than the length of a drawbridge when two riders emerged from the trees and stopped him in his tracks. Aaliya almost stopped breathing. She stood staring in Justen's direction, knowing she had to flee herself. But her feet felt as though they were weighed down with lead.

What were they going to do to him? Should she try to help him? Within the next instant, the choice was made for her as another five riders descended on the scene. She became encircled herself. Instantly felt bilious. Sweat ran down her arms and legs, her toes curled in her boots trying to get a better grip on the earth. The harness strapped around her back concealing the knife felt like it was being tightened. She thought she might pass out from the constriction of it. Do I use it now, Olle? Is this what you meant when you said 'when the moment arrives, you'll know.' Their swords rested on the flanks of the horses. Her knife was no match for theirs.

Her eyes slowly moved up to their faces. The sweat dribbling down her body stopped instantly and was replaced with a cold, goosefleshed feeling. A man sat high on a grey horse, short red hair flanking his pale face . And on the horse beside him, a man with the familiar dark eye. The other concealed by a leather patch.

"We meet again, Aaliya," snorted Viggo. "You and your lover have been very bad. I told you this would never end."

24

The Memory Room

Aaliya ran her hand across the stonewall. She did it again the other way. As stone should feel: cold, solid, impenetrable. It wasn't yielding anything intuitive. She brought both hands and her forehead to the shadowy surface. It was damp and smelled slick and oily. She knew there was no window but she looked up anyway. It was as though hope rested above like a cloud when reality on the solid earth became too much to bear.

The cell had a wooden slab for a bed. Iron bars ran across one side of the small enclosure. A chamber pot in the corner. It was funereal. A torch burned night and day by the first step leading out of the cell. Or at the last step before you came in. Whichever way you looked at it, it was a hellhole of a space and Aaliya was desperate to get out of it.

She knew exactly where she was. There was a bittersweet triumph in that, even if she couldn't go anywhere. As they marched her down to the cells, she observed every feature, the location of every guard along the way.

The dungeons were a labyrinthine confusion under the castle. One of her more daring exploration jaunts with Jakob as a young girl took Aaliya through these dark tunnels. Even as a girl she found there was something strangely impelling about stepping into the unfamiliar no matter how scared it made her feel. The feeling of blood rising into your eyes, your stomache churning, heart beating so hard in your chest it hurt. Aaliya found it uncomfortable, but necessary.

Jakob and Aaliya had been daring each other to go to the dungeons for weeks. One day they finally plucked up the courage to do it together. They tried to casually walk past the guards at the entrance like it was the most normal thing in the world, but were stopped. One of the guards told them to "piss off". The other one, his enormous oval face ringed by dark hair and a nose like a giant shelf, thought it would be a right laugh to introduce the two children to the wretched stony hell in the bowels of the castle. Jakob and Aaliya looked at each other, as if to give permission to opt out. It was okay to admit that they'd taken things too far and that this was something they didn't actually want to do. But Aaliya took the first tentative step behind the guard as he walked down the dark corridor, and Jakob followed.

It wasn't long before the stench became overpowering. Aaliya looked behind her at Jakob, screwed up her face and waved a hand in front of her nose. Jakob nodded, covering his nose with the collar of his shirt.

"Fuckin' stinks down here, don't it?" said the guard.

It was a smell of shit and death and Aaliya wondered how the guards could bear to work amongst it. They walked past several openings, dark as wolf's mouths. Only a few of the openings to the side were lit with a torch, where rough hewn steps could be seen curving out of sight.

They walked a few more steps, Aaliya reached behind and clutched Jakob's hand dragging him beside her. Her fingernails found his skin and he winced. She wanted to go back to her mum, her dad, anyone, but she also wanted to know what was up ahead. Jakob's hand felt clammy in her own. How could it be that the stench was getting worse?

As the guard moved through the dark corridor, he flung out his boot to kick a small wooden door down around his ankles. The clang made the children both jump. Aaliya was sure her fingernails must have almost drawn blood but Jakob didn't complain.

"If your bum's lucky enough to sit on one of those fancy garderobes upstairs, this is where your shit ends up," the guard announced.

Aaliya looked at the small inconspicuous door, her eyes watering from the smell. They turned around and walked back the way they had come. At a narrow opening where a guard in light armour stood beside a flickering torch, they all came to a stop. The two guards exchanged some words, had a laugh and looked in the direction of the children. Aaliya couldn't hear the exact words, but there was nothing warm in their banter. It had a menacing tone which convinced her to take a slight step back. She looked again at Jakob for reassurance. He looked terrified, unhinged.

"Come," said the guard they had been following.

He lead them down the stone steps. Aaliya still clung to Jakob as he trailed behind. She started counting the steps simply as a distraction to the fear she felt every time she put one foot in front of the other. Eighteen…nineteen. The torch below shined light on the last couple of steps, and as she rounded the curve, the bars from wall to wall came into view.

The children peered through the bars with trepidation, as if at any moment a monster was going to spring from the darkness and eat them. But, of course, there wasn't a monster. The light from the lantern picked up the shape of a man in tattered clothes cowering at the back of the cell. He was desperately thin, open sores covering his legs. It was his skin which unnerved Aaliya. It was grey and seemed to render him a part of the stony backdrop.

"Ivar, you fucking dog, get up. You've got some guests," the guard snorted.

The prisoner didn't move.

"Get the fuck up!"

The prisoner shuffled out from the dark corner. He moved to the centre of his small enclosure, each step a precarious battle to remain steady. Aaliya could see his face more clearly. His eyes were fixed on hers. The light captured the moisture in his eyes: hope and fear, terror and longing in one long, dreadful gaze. Even at a young age, Aaliya was acutely aware of this look in a creature's eyes. Horses had this same look in their eyes when they were injured. Like they knew they were about to be slaughtered.

Aaliya wanted to say something, but words wouldn't come out. The man looked wrecked: beaten, starved, damaged. She remembered leaving the dungeons and feeling something, but not knowing what it was or how to articulate it. Reflecting on it now she knew that feeling to be shame. Shame for treating the man as a curiosity. Shame for her privilege while so many were in desperate situations. And shame for not doing anything.

Aaliya and Jakob ended up going back a few more times, each occasion going a little further along the weaving, darkening corridor. A secret world revealed itself. Nooks and pockets in the labyrinth that seemed to serve no function other than in delighting their curiosity and sense of discovery. Word got out about the two children being allowed past the guards to explore the dungeons, and it was stopped forthwith. But she still remembered it all. Those moments of being truly scared could always be recalled with ease. They were so very present everyday.

Nothing had changed in ten years down here. She knew she was in the third cell on the left at the end of the last tunnel. She knew there were twenty-nine steps leading down to her cell. She knew a guard was stationed at the top of the steps. And by the sheer stench of it, she knew the sewer was close.

Viggo had personally thrown her in several days ago. A hard shove that tripped her up. She spread across the filthy floor like a tossed rag. He locked the iron door and padded down the fabric of his jacket as he slipped the key into the breast pocket. Aaliya quickly got to her feet and lurched at the bars.

"What's happening?" she asked. "Tell me what's going on?"

Viggo laughed sourly. "It's not looking good for you."

"What's not?"

"Look around you, girl." Viggo indicated with a wave of his hand for the other two men who had escorted Aaliya to her cell, to leave. When they were out of sight, he grabbed hold of the bars and stepped closer. "Is this a place you ever thought you'd end up?"

"Get me out of here. You know I've done nothing wrong."

"Oh dear," he said, raising his eyebrows, "are you that deluded?"

"You…you know what I mean."

Viggo shook his head. "No, I don't know what you mean."

"It was a mistake. A bloody stupid thing to do. But I

shouldn't be locked up for it."

"Well, you can tell that to the king at your trial."

"Trial?" Aaliya grabbed hold of the bars. "What the hell are you talking about?"

"Come on, you've known all along. You may have been able to fool those closest to you, but it will all come out."

"What will? Will you just tell me what's going on, Viggo?" Aaliya rattled the iron. She felt a sudden urge to do him harm.

"Will you stop playing games and admit you knew Justen's plans."

"I'm still not following."

"My, you are good at this. His plans to kill the king."

Aaliya let go of the bars as suddenly as if they had scorched her. She recoiled back and tried to take in air. The torch by the steps danced and flickered, making Viggo's shadow seem a giant presence in the room.

"Father…" she mumbled, "I need to see my father."

"Oh, please. The man has taste. As if he wants to mar his good name visiting a traitor."

"The man is my father and I am not a traitor."

"Well, that remains to be seen. You'll need more than statements of denial to help you out of this."

Aaliya moved close to the bars again. Defiance was getting her nowhere. He probably wanted to watch her beg. Didn't men like Viggo revel in their power? Didn't they literally go about creating situations that boosted their control over others?

"Please, Viggo. He respects you. And I know you respect him. You want what's best for him. My father needs to see me. No one wins if this is not resolved fairly."

"Wins, now there's a word."

"Viggo, please!"

He looked at her hard, and then his eyebrows softened. He moved in closer and held the bars. "You know, something could be possible. I'm your only connection with the outside world now. I'm sure we can come to some arrangement," he said, the smirk widening across his face.

Aaliya backed off to the wooden slab against the back wall and sat down. She wanted to be as far away from that man as possible. She closed her eyes but could hear him laughing as he left.

The first couple of nights in the cell she couldn't stop thinking about Justen. She screamed out his name in the hope that he was nearby. She just wanted to hear his voice. Hear that he was alright, that he hadn't been harmed. But she heard nothing from Justen. Only the guard at the top of the steps telling her to shut-up.

Days of not knowing left her gasping for air. She craved oblivion, longed to slip into sleep and leave awareness behind. But sleep barely arrived. And when it came it was a tormented, restless experience and she'd wake up more exhausted than ever. Her mind raced trying to understand what had happened. She had been watched all along. She foolishly thought she could have one last week in her lover's arms before their lives were separated forever. What a blind moron she was! What a naïve little girl! What did she think was going to happen once the door was opened? Did she seriously think she could simply close it once she had had her fill?

Aaliya found herself lurching again towards thoughts leading up to her capture. It must have been Catja who told Viggo about her planned meeting with Justen. No, not Viggo. She must have told Pieter. Catja had talked about being in love with the man. Aaliya could understand Pieter wouldn't want his newly married nephew meeting another woman in the forest. But Viggo made it clear that the affair wasn't their crime at all. Justen was being accused of attempted regicide and she, some sort of accomplice. They were embroiled in something far murkier than their illicit liaison. Aaliya thought back to the morning they had spent in the woolshed. Justen had talked about a man called Mark being the prime suspect. An insurgent. A couple of days later she watched men emerge from Olle's bunker. Olle refused to confirm or deny any of them were involved. This man known as Mark may have been one of them, and yet, what possible reason was there for him being released and Justen now finding himself accused? There was no doubt in her mind Justen was not involved. He was too bloody honourable, too exasperatingly responsible. He possibly would have thought about it. But who didn't harbour desire for someone to meet an unfortunate event at some point in their life.

It was all wrong. A twisted, convoluted scenario that was not going to simply 'sort itself out'. Maybe if she was to have one visitor, maybe her father was not the best choice. Maybe it had to be Olle. Olle would know what to do.

Every morning she was thrown some muddy water and some cold slop in a bowl through a small slot in the bars. The repugnant taste of it made her gag at first. What was she eating? Dirty ditchwater combined with some-thing rotten, something incomprehensible. It would take her hours to get through her bowlful. By the third day, she was ravishing every morsel. This life business was a bloody fight to the death, she told herself. She knew she wouldn't survive long in here. No one did. Over and over in her mind she thought about escape. How can I get myself and Justen out of here? What did I have that could help me out of this predicament? Amongst the flurry of thought she also tried to quieten her mind. Just get through each moment.

25

Under the Surface

Boredom was an effective weapon if they were looking to unravel Aaliya Reiner. Having nothing to do was as good as a death sentence. Her hands were used to making, her mind was used to planning the next steps. And although she had the time to plan and think, it felt fruitless, meaningless. Her neck ached carrying the load of pressure between her mind and her body. There were times when she'd gaze at the torch and see something good in the light. A rescue mission. The workshop. Riding across a ridge. But most of the time bad thoughts like poison seeped in and consumed her. Days were spent staring through the bars in a numb stupor, occasionally scratching in the dirt for something to do.

She had no idea where in time she was. With no window to watch the sun rise or the sun set, she didn't know whether it was night or day, whether days or even a week had passed. She slipped in and out of sleep, uneasy, troubled affairs that failed to provide her with the rest she so badly needed.

Aaliya woke one day to find Maddalena standing on the other side of the iron bars. At first she couldn't make out the figure, her eyes were swollen and her vision blurry from looking into endless darkness. The red of Maddalena's dress seemed shocking. She looked immaculate with her hair twisted into a long braid that snaked over her shoulder. Her wrists and fingers heavily laden with jewels.

Aaliya waited for Maddalena to say something. Aaliya was sure she looked like the imprisoned man she had seen over ten years ago. Wild eyes, dirty clothes, gritty unkempt hair. She moved forward close to the bars wanting Maddalena to see her.

Eventually, Maddalena managed something like a smile. "The dull light in here is doing terrible things to your skin."

"My complexion offends you?" Aaliya replied.

"Not as much as the stink of this place. I'm not going to be able to stay too long down here before I pass out."

"I haven't had a visitor since I was locked up. Seeing you…I don't know if I'm dreaming."

"I'm very real. *This* is very real," Maddalena said as her eyes moved around the wretched space.

"I'm so sorry, Maddalena. I'm so sorry," Aaliya blubbered. "I couldn't turn it off….what I was feeling. Mum died. I felt so angry. I felt reckless. I just wanted someone to take the pain away. I'm so sorry!" She held onto the bars, feeling at any moment her legs would give way under her.

"Stop. You're not going to have me preaching the 'how could you' guilt thing. People can. And do. And do it all the time. Fallibility is a close friend of mine."

"My head is spinning. It's all such a mess."

"You can say that again. My plans are totally fucked up."

"I'm so sorry, Maddalena."

"Will you stop saying sorry. I mean it. Stop it."

Aaliya blinked away the tears pooling in her eyes. Maddalena was so good at being steadfast and strong. But maybe anyone could be on the other side of iron bars.

"Is father going to visit me?" Aaliya asked nervously.

"He will. He's just…dealing with things. Anything less than winning is failure. You know how it is. This…this was not a part of his masterplan to success, you could say."

"I see."

"Give him time."

"I don't know that I have much time."

"Well, have faith then. Have hope."

Hope. There was that word again. Aaliya felt as though she'd been battling with it her whole life. It had a hold over her and refused to let go.

"Tell him I love him," said Aaliya. "Nothing changes that. No matter what happens, I'll always love him."

"I'll let him know."

"Is Justen alright? Has anything happened to him? I've been calling out for him but I haven't heard anything."

"He's in the tower. I don't know how he is. Even I can't see him."

"You're his wife."

"The nature of the crime. Strictly no visitors."

"And the crime is attempted regicide? Have I heard that correctly?"

"Yes."

Aaliya sighed. "It's madness, Maddalena. You do know that, don't you?"

Maddalena remained silent.

"Don't you?" Aaliya repeated.

"I asked him at the wedding and he denied it."

"He's telling the truth."

"You know, I don't tend to trust people on face value. Most people have things they're desperate to hide. They'll say what you want to hear, what they feel you can cope with hearing. I'm not sure about his guilt or innocence. If anything, I'm leaning towards innocence simply because I saw Pieter and Viggo having, let's call it, a clandestine conversation in the castle one day. And then all the stuff conveniently emerged that Justen was intent on assassinating the king."

"Oh."

"Pieter had to have been the one to tell Viggo about Justen's alleged plans, but why, I have no idea. I have never trusted Viggo. But Pieter is something else entirely. I thought I understood these games. I thought I could sniff them out, uncover them. This…this has surprised me."

"Will he get a fair trial?"

Maddalena laughed. "This is political, Aaliya. They had someone else, they let him go. They just want this tidied up now. Could you imagine the collective humiliation for all those men if Justen was found innocent."

Maddalena's words crashed in her head with the force of a boulder dropped from the sky above. She was right of course. They had their man, but it was Justen they wanted. Aaliya finally wept, enraged. Her stomache was in a knot. Yes indeed, what a question to ask. A fair trial was about as likely as an oasis in the Sayan Desert. Her poor love. What he must be thinking now? What was he feeling? If they hadn't already broken him, she suspected his loneliness, fear and grief must have come close to shattering his spirit. Their last brief kiss in the forest came into her mind. How fleeting that moment was. How utterly massive it was as well, the way it carried their souls forward through dark times.

"The person they let go was an insurgent. His name is Mark," Aaliya announced unwaveringly.

"So?"

"So?" Aaliya repeated with a tone of incomprehension.

"What do you want me to do with that information?"

"Maddalena, I've just told you something that could free Justen. You yourself said you believe he's innocent."

"No, I didn't say I believe he's innocent. I said I'm leaning towards innocence. Big difference. And anyway, you've told me something they probably already know. Do you really think that's going to save him?"

It was on the tip of Aaliya's tongue. Tell her about the bunker, tell her about Olle. Tell her everything she knew. But as she paused to take a breath, she came to the realization that she actually knew very little. Olle had held out on her. He failed to confirm or deny he was involved, even indirectly, in the assassination attempt. And the miserable reality was that she was now complicit in the plot to overthrow the king. She had failed to come forward and tell somebody about what she had seen and heard in the workshop that night. Who would believe her now? Any attempt to tell what she knew would simply be seen as a last desperate effort to save her lover. And if she was listened to and believed, Olle would go down. The workshop would go down. Even her father would go down. Their name would be in tatters. It would destroy him. The knife still strapped to her back started to feel heavy, irritating. It felt as though the blade were unsheathed against her back and was sawing through her skin with each small movement she made.

"His trial is tomorrow," Maddalena said.

"Please help him, Maddalena. Please!"

"What can I do?"

Aaliya didn't have an answer. "He can't die for something he didn't do."

"He betrayed me. You betrayed me. I understand people are capable of pretty fucked up things but right now, Aaliya, I'm not feeling a burning desire to save the man. And I simply can't, even if I wanted to."

Aaliya's eyes stopped being sad and pleading and set into a gaze that was direct and purposeful. She breathed deeply. "What about me? Do you think you could help me though?"

"Probably not." Maddalena paused. "Maybe. I don't know."

"Are you scared?"

"Well of course I'm scared."

"And I'm shitting myself. Quite literally. I sit in here day after day, talking to the rats, scratching in the dirt, shitting on the ground where I eat and try to sleep. I don't know what's going to happen. But it looks bad for me. And I can't do anything about it on my own. The only person I have is you. You're the one that came to me. I have to believe that a part of you came because you want to help me."

Maddalena looked down at the ground and then walked around, menacingly. She stood and took hold of the bars. "I don't have to do anything. If I'm caught, then I'll end up like you. I kind of like wearing nice dresses. Anyway, getting out of this cell is just the beginning for you, Aaliya. Then what?"

"I don't know. I'll work out the rest. Maddalena, I'll die in here unless I get that key. If I don't die in here, I'll have my head on a block at Bria Trela in no time. It's that simple."

"I'm aware of the urgency of the situation."

"We're blood."

"Don't give me that blood is thicker than water rant. That all for one, one for all bullshit. I'm thinking of self-preservation here. That's my only concern."

"I don't think it's your only concern for one second. We're not so different. You need me, too."

"How could I possibly need you, Aaliya?"

"Justen has been compromised and this was the case from the moment he set foot on Traegos soil. I have had nothing to do with it. You've had nothing to do with it. Yet we're both pawns in this mad business. Your hopes and ambitions have been thwarted. Mine are going nowhere fast. We need to look after each other. Because, sure as hell, no one is going to look after us."

"You self-confident, righteous little rat. You prance through life with your armour of self-worth wrapped neatly around you. Justifying yourself and believing wholeheartedly that people will be there for you no matter what you do."

"We're not so different."

"Stop saying that!"

The silence passed by maddeningly. Maddalena kicked at the ground, muttering to herself. She finally said, "Which guard has the key to your cell. Describe him."

"Viggo. It's in the breast pocket of his jacket."

"Viggo. Why doesn't that surprise me."

"Maddalena, there's something else I need to tell you."

"Now is not the time. We need to stick to tactics."

"He tried to rape me."

Maddalena cursed under her breath and shuffled uncomfortably.

Aaliya whispered hard, "I don't want him to harm you."

"You're right. This is looking bad for you."

The two sisters looked at each other. It was as though

the masks had finally been removed. There was nothing left to hide behind. All those wasted years withholding love, lashing out. And for what? It became simply a way of being which they didn't know how to undo. And now they felt stripped bare, standing on the surface of themselves. Here I am. Offering up all their vulnerabilities, hopes, fears. I know I'm a messy package but it's all I have to offer.

"I'm not making any promises. Your trial is in four days."

"Thank you, Maddalena."

"I haven't done anything yet."

"You've done so much. You came to see me. No one else has."

Maddalena turned and walked towards the steps. Aaliya watched her go and felt like a child standing on a wharf watching loved ones leave on a ship with no destination. She suddenly felt goosefleshed, her skin prickled, her knees went soft. Her thoughts went everywhere and nowhere. Please don't leave me.

To Aaliya's utter amazement, Maddalena leapt from the steps towards the bars and thrust her arm through. Aaliya desperately grabbed her hand and kissed it hungrily. Even though darkness was across Maddalena's face, Aaliya was sure she could see moisture pooling in her eyes. Aaliya didn't want to let her go. She squeezed and kissed her sister's hand again, before Maddalena slowly pulled her arm back. She then leapt up the steps until she was out of sight, the red fabric swirling around her ankles as she left.

26

The Trial

Bria Trela was situated like a grand carpet between Ansgar Castle and the River Albo. The castle loomed behind a great monolith, and across the treeless space one could see the royal forest that circled the castle like a leafy halo, the ships moored down at the quay, and the whole great tapestry of the city unspooling north and south along the river. The largest open space in the capital, Bria Trela had been the scene of some of the most significant events in Traegos's history. Newly throned kings and queens took their first steps amongst their subjects in the enormous square on the riverbank. Armies had, on occasion, amassed and formed in the square prior to battles. But, for the most part, Bria Trela was known throughout the kingdom as the site for public executions.

The crowd gathered across the large gravel area. A ring of guards maintained the circle around the man kneeling in the centre, his wrists and ankles shackled, his head covered with cloth. The sun was sitting low in the western sky, pale and benign. The cool breeze rising off the river seemed to have enticed a larger number of people than usual to leave their homes, their workshops, to make their way to the square to watch the death of the man that had tried to kill their king.

The large crowd moved and heaved like expanding lungs. Maddalena stood beside her father on the inner perimeter of the circle. Guards maintaining the circle were hopelessly outnumbered as the crowd continued to expand with each passing moment. She looked around with a strange mixture of fascination and fear. She had seen a few die before in this very spot, and had thought about dying on many occasions. She wondered often about how it felt, whether it was painful. But most of all, she wondered about *that* moment. That slippery moment right before dying when you know you are going to die and you let go of hope and invite death in. She wondered if Justen, who was kneeling on the dirt ground blind as a mole, but painfully aware of what was going on around him, was still clinging to hope.

"This crowd is getting out of control," Thormund mumbled, steadying himself from a shove from behind.

"Clearly there haven't been enough public executions of late," Maddalena responded.

"Maybe the people are also aware that the death of this man may cause a reaction from Gedion."

"It seems that we just can't keep away from creating enemies."

Thormund made a wry sideways glance at his daughter, then looked ahead again. "The enemies are always there. You have enemies the moment you have success. Our job is finding a way to do business with them. Everyone wants something."

"It would be a whole lot easier, don't you think, if we didn't go around executing their noble men."

"We need punishment, Maddalena. There was a crime,

punishment must follow. Justen knew the risks and took them regardless. The trial proved his guilt. This is a setback for the Reiners. But we'll move forward again. We always do."

"What if he's the wrong man? What if he's innocent?"

"You have so little faith in our judicial system."

"What if, though? That means this could happen again. Doesn't that worry you?"

"Maddalena, what I heard in the Throne Room two days ago has left no doubt in my mind of his guilt. I understand your predicament. This is a tremendously unfortunate event. All I can do is assure you that we will get through this."

"Does the 'we' include Aaliya?"

"Well, that depends on what's revealed at her trial, doesn't it? I'm not responsible for her actions."

"No, but you're certainly responsible for your own."

"I'm quite aware of that."

"Well go and see her. If you wait until the trial, it will be too late."

Thormund's jaw set as rigid as a plank of wood. Maddalena knew the expression well. It was the closed and mercurial side of her father. His speech became clipped, evasive. He used words that ultimately told you nothing. It may have served him well to this point, but it wasn't good enough anymore. There was too much at stake.

Maddalena spoke eloquently. "Easy to make assurances, father. Much harder to deal with the problem."

"You're not telling me something I don't already know."

"The problem never goes away. It just changes shape. I'm telling myself that as much as I'm telling you."

"You've made your point."

King Renatus sat perfectly still, his large, meaty frame slumped back, his arms outstretched along the armrests of the throne until his fingers curled over the edges. The Throne Room was slipping into darkness. He looked from Justen Laus, seated shackled in the temporary wooden dock, to the crowd perched along the benches with a look of weary reticence. It was once said that he used to have a killer instinct for authority. For the first ten years of his reign, it never seemed to fail him. Maddalena wondered if it wasn't instinct at all but more a case of embracing the circumstances that presented. When he became king at age eighteen his whole world would have expanded overnight. What would that do to a young man, she thought. All of a sudden he could eat off gold-rimmed dinner plates, he would win every argument even when his reasoning was flawed. All of a sudden, he had control over life and death.

Although it wasn't openly talked about amongst the citizens of Ansgar, Maddalena knew there were ripples of conversations taking place discussing his waning authority. A trial was the perfect opportunity to take a stand. The king had been in this game long enough to know that this would only incite Gedion to take revenge on his kingdom. But the expectation was there. Take action.

Justen sat in the dock facing the king, the witness box to his side. Only a rustle could be heard as the spectators sat in a tormenting silence. It was late afternoon and the torches around the room provided warm light around the vast space where past and present mingled and overlapped. Wide planks of blackened oak covered the floor. The draperies were rich, heavy velvet of crimson, cobalt blue and gold. Curtains were hardly required but suggested the personal taste of its ruler. The eye-like windows surrounding the perimeter of the towering walls gave the unsettling sensation of always being watched. Dark and light, light and dark. It was easy to dichotomize so purely and simply in a space like this.

Darius sat beside the king in a high backed chair, the back of his thumb running over a fingernail. He turned his head slightly and his eyes scanned the profile of the king. What to make of his expression? Was it a slight disregard perhaps, wondered Maddalena. The king's lips moved silently as if telling himself something, and then he stood. Everybody in the room joined him in standing.

"I, Renatus Clausen, King of Traegos, am judge of this trial. This man standing before you is accused of murder and attempted regicide. If found guilty, he will die by the sword. The Justiciar for this trial is Darius Liikanen. He will oversee proceedings until guilt or innocence is clearly established today." Renatus slumped back into his chair and the whole congregation noisily followed.

After a moment's pause, Darius stood again, his great legs like tree stumps taking a few steps closer to the dock. He waited for the crowd to settle. He seemed to relish these opportunities to perform, demonstrate his loyalty and skills at showmanship. He turned slightly, encouraging his long dark robes to ripple across the oak floor. "Justen Laus, you stand accused of murder and attempted regicide. The God of Life and the God of Death is your witness. How do you plead, guilty or not guilty?"

"Not guilty."

Darius continued. "A man by the name of Erno Kerola, a distinguished King's Guard, was brutally murdered at a hunting expedition in the month of Hynara, on the day of twelfth Ierial, attempting to protect his king. Were you there at the hunting expedition on the fateful day?"

"Yes, I was."

"It is understood you weren't invited."

"My uncle Pieter told me about it. I thought it would be fun."

"Fun?"

"The hunt, yes."

"And was it fun?"

"No, it wasn't actually. As it so happened, I didn't want to be there after all."

"How so?"

"It was just a distressing day."

"Distressing?"

"Birds were being killed."

"Did you not know it was going to be a bird hunt?"

"I did."

"Then why the change of heart? Have you not participated in bird hunts before? I would have thought in Gedion that would be a regular practice for a man of your standing."

"Yes, they are familiar to me. It was the reaction of someone present on the day that changed the way I felt."

"Who?"

There was a long pause before Justen said, "Aaliya Reiner."

"Ahh, the woman you were found with in the forest when you were arrested."

Justen didn't say anything. He moved in his seat as though uncomfortable.

"Was she your lover?"

He remained silent.

"Answer yes or no," Darius said as light bounced off his shiny head. "You are before witnesses and the eyes of the Gods."

"Yes," Justen murmured.

"She was your lover. The sister of the woman you married just a week ago was your lover. My, you are not very trustworthy, are you? What a shameful thing to do behind the back of your betrothed. How long had it been going on?"

"Not long enough."

The crowd broke out into loud chatter. Movement swept amongst their bodies, tired of sitting still for so long.

"You two surely would have had intimate conversations?"

Maddalena watched as Justen's eyes moved from Darius to the king. His eyes then wandered a little higher to the symbol of the moon and bands of light which seemed to be sucking the air out of the room. "No, we just fucked," he said at last.

"Excuse me," gasped Darius.

"That's all we did. We just fucked. No words were exchanged."

"No words. Just…fucking…as you call it."

"That's right."

"I find that hard to believe."

"Just got lucky I guess."

"Silence!" Darius demanded of the awakened crowd.

Justen looked to the side where Thormund and Maddalena were seated. She glanced sideways. Her father looked as though he wanted to tear out Justen's heart and eat it. She turned to face Justen and he met her eyes. A devilish smirk widened across her face. She realized she didn't have him worked out quite the way she thought she did. If he managed to get out of this alive, she silently vowed to stop making assumptions and get to know her husband a little better.

Darius walked over to a table and picked something up. "Is this your arrow?" He raised it high so the crowd could see.

"I don't know."

"Look closely." Darius made his way to the dock and held the arrow a short distance from Justen.

"I don't know," repeated Justen.

Darius shuffled towards the crowd. "This arrow was the one pulled from the back of Erno Kerola. It was the arrow that killed him." He briskly walked back to the table. "The accused had in his possession these arrows," Darius announced, picking up a canister containing several arrows. Standing back in front of the crowd, he theatrically presented them like they were sacrificial offerings. "I'm sure you will agree, they look exactly the same." Darius slid up beside the dock. "What do you have to say to these arrows being in your possession?"

"They look like mine. But they may not be mine. They were made by a craftsman who makes arrows for a living and exports them far and wide across the realm. They could belong to anyone."

"Oh, but they don't belong to anyone. This canister has the initials on the bottom 'JL'. These arrows belong to you."

"The canister belongs to me. Anyone could have planted those arrows in my canister."

"It was kept in your room."

"Most of the time my room wasn't kept locked."

"Was that so your lover could easily make her way to your bed?"

Justen said nothing and kicked at the wooden bollard near his shackled feet.

"It's time for the first witness, Your Grace," Darius announced to the king.

King Renatus nodded.

"Viggo Vennamo," said Darius.

Viggo rose from the front bench. He walked tall, with a sense of purpose. Great, confident strides towards the witness box. An undercurrent of sanctimonious energy fizzled and crackled in his wake. Every strand of his glossy, silver hair was slicked back. A perfect curve featured at the tips of his moustache, held in place neatly with a little balm. His normally black cravat had been replaced with one of red silk, the significance of which could only be assumed. Blood perhaps? Victory?

Darius took Viggo through the oath and invited Viggo to share his testimony. Viggo sat with cold-eyed detachment and recounted the events leading up to the death of Erno Kerola.

"…At this stage most in the hunting party were riding across the field," Viggo explained. "I was riding alongside the king. I looked over my shoulder and noticed the accused behind. I thought it strange that he hadn't lowered his bow."

"Strange?"

"Most of the other riders had lowered their bows by that stage. I didn't think much of it at the time. Well, to be honest, there was a greater distraction. I noticed Thormund Reiner racing up ahead in an attempt to catch up to his wayward daughter, Aaliya, who was leading her father away from the scene."

"What did you do next?"

"I decided to assist Thormund and tried to catch up

to him. Just as I started doing this, I heard the king's name called out. I stopped and turned around, and saw the man I know to be Erno Kerola slip off his horse, clutching his chest."

"So you didn't actually see who released the arrow that killed Erno Kerola?"

"No, I didn't. But I know Erno Kerola was riding behind the king to protect him and I know it was his voice who called out the king's name."

"Could it be that someone wanted to kill Erno Kerola and not the king?"

"Preposterous suggestion," Viggo spat.

"What makes you say so?"

"Because I interviewed the accused after the incident. And the accused was the most incorrigible, the most self-assured, of all the suspects. He had the most to hide. It took a great deal of time and skill but I was well on the way to extracting a confession when I was requested to stop interviewing the accused."

Justen laughed. "Torturing, you mean."

"Silence," quipped Darius. "So another suspected man was found to be responsible immediately after the incident?"

"Yes. Another man was thought to be responsible. That was until new evidence emerged indicating Justen Laus was the correct suspect all along."

Justen clearly looked confused. He screwed up his face and stared hard at Viggo, a man to whom Justen had never caused any harm and yet seemed utterly determined to see the end of him. Further witnesses came forward, painting a picture of Justen as an assassin with a heart as cold as a stone plucked from the icy depths of the Mindano Sea. People she didn't know and had never seen before took to the witness box and recounted how they had actually seen him release the fatal arrow that pierced Erno Kerola's heart. Justen sat in the dock staring at whoever took to the witness box. His eyes piercing, the muscles in his jaw clenching. She didn't know Justen well, she wasn't present on the day of the hunt, but her internal gauge for a flagrant set-up was on the verge of boiling over.

His expression loosened and he appeared to be somewhat heartened when he saw Pieter rise from the crowd and make his way to the witness box. Pieter's shoes were too big for his frame and gave him the appearance of a penguin shuffling. Pieter's body was so lacking in power that his jacket hung from his shoulders as limp as a wet towel. Justen leaned a little more forward in his seat. When Pieter sat in the witness box his two small arrogant eyes darted around the room, looking everywhere but at Justen. He appeared to be ready and willing, and the supercilious manner with which his eyes rested on Darius suggested that the proceedings had best get underway. Immediately. Darius took Pieter through the oath and then requested for Pieter to announce himself.

"I am Pieter Laus of Gedion. Chief Miner of the Sunavigations Mining Company." Pieter's thin voice expressed with a slight lilt.

"It is understood the accused is known to you?"

"He's my nephew."

"Your nephew stands here today accused of murder and attempted regicide. If found guilty he will be sentenced to die by the sword. Do you have anything to offer which could point to his guilt or innocence for the crimes of which he has been accused?"

"I do," Pieter remarked decisively.

Justen's eyes bored into Pieter, willing for him to continue.

Pieter's adam's apple tweaked. "Sadly, I have known for some time of my nephew's intention to kill King Renatus. I just didn't think he would go ahead with it."

The whole shape of Justen's face changed in an instant. The muscles in his face contorted into an angry knot. He clenched his fists as they rested, shackled, in front of his body.

Pieter continued, "Justen's father was killed during the Battle of Barmer. King Renatus, as I'm sure you know, was the reigning monarch during that conflict. I believe Justen, who was a boy of ten at the time, witnessed the incident. He came under my shadow after the death of his father. And he vowed, during the whole time, he would one day have his revenge and kill King Renatus himself."

The crowd released a collective sigh and shuffled in their seats.

"People talk all the time of avenging those who cause harm to their family," Darius said dismissively. "This is hardly unusual. We could all be on trial for uttering thoughtless words about harming someone at some point in our lives. Don't you agree?"

"No, this was different. These weren't just flippant words. These were words that went hand in hand with a premeditated plan."

"He told you of his plan?"

"No, not exactly. He wrote it down for me." Pieter paused, and for the first time, shifted his eyes from Darius to Justen.

Darius motioned quickly to the table and picked up a piece of parchment, creased and damaged.

"Is this the plan you're referring to," Darius remarked,

bringing the letter close to Pieter's face.

"Yes it is."

"Your Grace, I have before me a letter written and signed by Justen Laus. I would like to read this to you and all the witnesses here today." Darius stood to the side so his back was not facing the king.

Renatus nodded, willing Darius to continue. Darius cleared his throat.

"Dear Uncle Pieter,

I hope this letter finds you well. It hasn't been possible to have contact with the outside world for so long, your letter was quite a surprise. Your offer of employment, while most generous, is not something I can consider at the moment. There's still so much work to be done here.

I've been a part of something I can not easily walk away from. I shan't put it in a letter in detail other than to say I've seen men reduced to meat. I am convinced the fiercer and more terrible the fighting has become, the more satiated the generals sit in their warm tents. Men are shutting their horrors up in their hearts, acting merry and priding themselves on their ability to survive. But no one's convincing. Not in the slightest. We're all changed forever. The fighting may have stopped for now, but I still have so much rage inside me. That's not likely to change for a while. I think of Traegos and all I see are the limbs of my countrymen severed from their bodies. I think of my father too. King Renatus will surely meet his fate one day for his crime. I will get myself to Ansgar one day and do it personally if need be.

Give my love to mother, and Carly. I miss them so much and think of them daily. Yours, Justen Laus."

"I wrote that when I was sixteen!" Justen cried incredulously.

"So you don't deny you wrote the letter," asked Darius.

"Why should I? Were we not at war four years ago? Was I the only man to express hatred for the enemy at the time?"

"Based on many accounts here today, it wasn't just a point in time hatred of the King of Traegos. You have carried your contempt through to the present day."

"I didn't do it…" Justen mumbled, shaking his head. He looked up and turned to Pieter. "Why? Why are you doing this? What are you getting out of it?"

Pieter sat still, not offering a word. His lips remained pressed together, his body upright and belligerently leaning forward.

"Do not address the witness," Darius demanded.

"Well it's a bloody good question to ask, don't you think?" Justen scoffed, hotly.

"Silence!" Darius stood in front of Justen like a mountain blocking out the sun. "The letter completes a picture. A picture that has been formed fully by the testimonies heard here today. By the arrow that killed Erno Kerola being matched to others found belonging to you. You've disclosed to Pieter Laus over a significant period of time your desire to seek vengeance for the death of your father. And you finally saw your chance to complete what you've always longed to do. You saw an opportunity through the marriage arrangement with the daughter of Thormund Reiner, one of King Renatus's closest confidants, to insinuate yourself into the Clausen family. And you saw an opportunity with the hunting expedition and planned your execution. As you stated in your letter, you would 'do it personally if need be'. Your desire to kill King Renatus has been a simmering, festering ambition of yours for many years. A desire that has never gone away. A desire that has willed you to this point where you murdered a man whose purpose was to protect the king. This is the truth, isn't it?"

"I did not attempt to kill the king. No arrow of mine went into the back of any man." Justen's voice lowered to a growl. He looked directly at Renatus. "Someone is out to get you. Someone other than me. I'd like to shake their hand."

The crowd erupted like angry bees. Loud murmuring and chattering filled the space. Agitated movement swept amongst the rows of bodies seated on the benches. Some stood, at least one person yelled out "Traitor!"

Justen looked around him with apparent disgust. Maddalena shook her own head. The burden of believing that he could possibly be innocent was too much to bear for these people. She watched Justen examine the face of his uncle, as though trying to find a slither of the man he thought he knew. Her own eyes turned to Pieter and she saw only coldness, damp mud set hard. She felt the eyes of various people around the room on her, gauging her reaction. All she could think about was the exchange she heard between Pieter and Viggo. The great burden on Viggo's shoulders…economic outcomes…manipulating people. Every interaction with another person is a transaction of sorts, no matter who they are. In Maddalena's mind, Justen trusted. But did that make him a fool? Or did it simply make him a man? A man who took a risk with another. A man who had the same struggles as everyone else, battling selfish needs against selfless ones. Short-term needs against long-term sensibility. Darkness against lightness.

Darius moved to the side and spoke to the king. "Your Grace, the time has come for your verdict in the matter. Do you declare Justen Laus to be guilty or not guilty of attempted regicide, and guilty or not guilty of the murder of Erno Kerola?"

"Guilty of both," he said immediately, leaning back on his throne.

"Justen Laus, you have been found guilty by King Renatus of Traegos, of attempted regicide and the murder of Erno Kerola. Your punishment for your crimes is to die by the sword, one day from now at sundown. May the God of Life and the God of Death have mercy on your soul."

The guards attempted to make way for the wide form of Darius with his swishing black robes, and the masked man behind him. But the pair were hustled in roughly, knocking bodies as they walked. The stirring crowd had become feverish around the man on the ground, kneeling. People moved and jostled about in an effort to get a better look. A steady flow of people broke away from behind the guards to get closer to the inner circle.

Maddalena felt pushed away from her father in the melee and became surrounded by strangers. For a moment, she lost sight of Justen. With her elbows out, she fought her way back to a position where she could see him. Bodies were pressed up hard against her own. She could see the top of her father's head. He seemed oblivious to the fact that she was no longer by his side. His gaze was fixed on Darius as he spoke of Justen's crime and the punishment that awaited him.

She felt pressed up against bodies at every angle. It was a feeling she would normally consider to be a pleasant one, but which she found instead to be incredibly disconcerting. The bodies around her seemed to devour the air, leaving her with little to breathe. A sensation caught her attention. A man behind her was pressing his hardness into her backside. She felt disgust and longed to burst from the crowd. What the Hell, she thought. The man she had exchanged vows with just a week ago was about to die, and someone was trying to get his dick inside her? She wanted to turn around and hit him hard, but it was too difficult. She was wedged in with the crowd as tightly as a dovetail joint.

Justen was made to stand and the cloth removed from his head. His head was coarsely shaven, his eyes bloated and raw. He looked around the crowd, but he didn't search hard. Maddalena knew there was nothing left he wanted to see. Probably didn't even see people in front of him, just movement. And then a smile grew across his face. Justen's gaze rested on a point on the ground ahead of him, and although she wasn't sure, she thought she saw his mouth silently form the word 'Aaliya'.

The man behind Maddalena started undulating his hips, pressing into her with a noticeable rhythm. A great turmoil started to build inside her. This disgusted her, but at the same time, her loins were throbbing. She instinctively started moving her own hips with the man. She planted her feet a little further apart to strengthen her grip on the earth and invite more of the man's desire between the folds of her body. She wasn't interested anymore in turning her head. She didn't care to see who was doing this, only that she didn't want it to stop. Her hands ran down the length of her dress. Anything shorter and she may not have been able to resist the urge to hoist up the layers and allow the man to enter her from behind. She moved her hand to the front of her dress and discretely started rubbing herself through the fabric.

Justen was forced to kneel once again. Darius asked him if he had anything left to say to which Justen replied, "Fuck the king."

Maddalena didn't remove her eyes from Justen. She didn't know if she had imagined it or someone was hurting her, but a sharp pain gripped her and made her gasp. But it felt right to have it present. It felt right to feel pain while she was standing, a complicit spectator, watching the ruin of a man.

The executioner raised the great sword above Justen's head. He paused. The iron captured shards of sunlight from the setting sun. Maddalena started trembling, ashamed at how she was feeling. And then the sword crashed down onto Justen's neck, his head coming loose with one violent strike. The crowd pushed forward, trying to see the head as it rolled to the side. The man behind Maddalena placed both hands on her hips and started pressing his body into hers with a renewed frenzy.

He was no longer alive, and for a moment, she wasn't sure if she was either. She no longer felt the ground beneath her. She started to fall. Be free, Justen, she thought as she leaned heavily forward and slipped into sleep.

27

Taste of Royalty

Viggo's eyes were boring into hers. Dead eyes. Fish eyes. Eyes open but not seeing. He was heavy on her, as weighty as a tree trunk between her legs. And the pain. Sharp, agonizing. Like his cock was a broken bottle slashing into her.

Maddalena woke up, moist and startled. The room was dark and still. The curtains hung limp on their rods. She gave a slight shiver, sensing another presence in the room. She had never got over her childhood fear of ghosts but didn't know now whether her intuition could be trusted. Her fingers twisted around her hair, nervously. There was nothing more she wanted than to hide away and lay with her violent thoughts. She had never felt the need for solitude until now. And the moment she needed it, she couldn't have it. Time was ticking. Aaliya's trial was in two days. And there it was again. Justen's head coming away from his body like he was little more than a broken doll. The key….the key. She pressed her eyes tightly, tried to block out other thoughts and think only of how she was going to get the key. But there behind her lidded darkness she saw Viggo harming her.

She eventually managed to sit upright and dangle her legs over the side of the bed. She teetered a moment and then stood, dragging whatever clothes on she could muster. The door squeaked as she edged it open. She padded down the stairs to the kitchen and poured herself a small cup of cooled tea. In the dining room, she lifted a chair out from under the table and sat down. The wall was satisfyingly blank. Maybe there was another way. Hire enough sellswords to kill and maim her way through and then break the iron door down. But leaving a bloody trail just wasn't her style. She wished it was. Hell, it would have to be easier. That's why people used violence, wasn't it? When you don't know another way to deal with your problem? That bloody trail would lead right back to her, though. Not for her sister, not for anyone, was she going to find herself hooded and awaiting her fate at Bria Trela.

She hadn't seen Joshva or Santo in over a week. The recent events were playing havoc with her physical needs. That gangly wine boy had come by on his rounds. He so wanted to do naughty things she was sure, but kept up the responsible persona painfully well. He averted her eyes when she caught him looking at her. He'd tremble ever so slightly as she drew close. It was doing her head in how much she wanted him. The apothecary on Floran Road had supplied her with a concoction of opium and henbane nearly a year ago. There was never a set plan of what she wanted it for, other than that it could come in handy one day. As it turned out, she had never used it. But she thought about that sinister little vial sitting in her draw whenever she saw the wine boy. The chase being so much more gratifying than an easy conquer.

Maddalena started walking back to her room. Maybe she could get Jakob to deliver drugged wine to Viggo, to the guard outside Aaliya's cell. The guard would take to the wine. That part would be easy. It was catching Viggo in a vulnerable moment alone. That was the hard part. The man was so damn cautious. She thought about Viggo's weaknesses: gambling, sex (not going there), money, sex (urgh!), vanity, status, fine clothes. She rolled the last two notions around her mind. His beautiful jackets, the shiny leather of his boots, his neck adorned with silk cravats. How does one flatter a man who has access to the finest tailoring in Traegos. Almost the finest. *The* finest tailors belonged to the king. And they tailored for the king and the king only. Her dear, saucy tailor boys. She stopped still on the last step before reaching the top, her hand gripping the balustrade. They'll know how to handle this. They make her feel like a queen whenever she's in their arms. Viggo, you're about to get a taste of royalty.

The instructions were simple enough. Formally invite Viggo Vennamo for a fitting to take place in the evening for a new jacket to be handmade by the king's personal tailors. When Viggo removes his jacket during the fitting and measuring, (discreetly) remove the key from the breast pocket and keep it safe until Maddalena arrives.

Joshva wrote out an invitation and was pleased when, half a day later, he received a response from Viggo. Yes, the message declared, I would be happy to visit the tailor's workroom in Ansgar Castle this evening at seven o'clock for a fitting.

Joshva and Santo both tried keeping busy throughout the day, but there was something decidedly exciting about being a part of Maddalena's scheme. Not to mention the thought of a long overdue session with their favourite lady.

Santo presented the beautiful silken whip he had finished making. They both discussed exultingly the chastisement they wanted to try with their new toy. Smacking and biting had long been a sensual delight for them all, relishing the secret bruises and marks left on their bodies. Joshva feared needing to tear off his breeches straight away at the mere thought of the flaying he was to receive in the evening.

The sensuality of their workspace did little to calm their brimming excitement. Spools of coloured thread formed a mosaic along the wall. The vast mahogany table in the centre of the room was covered with pieces for a new gown for the Queen. The fabric, an exquisite indigo blue silk, featured a silver leaf brocade of the moon and stars as they appear in the night sky.

The pair were renowned for not only their sumptuous tailoring, but also their commissioning of prints that were otherworldly. They sourced embroiderers and fabric printers whose grace and skill in designing and making were unparalleled, who pushed the boundaries with what could be done with fabric. After discussions with a notable weaver just outside the capital, a rare chintz was presented to the pair, gold dust sprinkled onto the sticky pattern of peacock feathers.

The brilliant hues of the dyes used, the sumptuous contexture, contributed to a luxury economy unmatched by other kingdoms in the realm. A gift from King Renatus made by his tailors was so highly prized it couldn't be worn.

Gold and silver wrought silk brocades were a favourite of the king and queen. But it was the delicacy of muslin and its use for undergarments that gave them both a charge. The muslin they sourced was as delicate as a spider's web. Each roll of muslin was called a different name depending on the fineness of the fabric and the valuation in which the fabric was held by the king: 'woven air', 'morning dew' and 'flowing water'. They once made undergarments for the Queen using 'flowing water', the words of Oemada, the book of Life and Death, woven into the hem in gold thread.

Joshva pulled from the shelves a range of fabrics he believed their customer arriving later in the day may like: velvets, leather, wool stiff with embossed silver leaf. They continued to work on the Queen's silk gown throughout the day, only pausing to eat. Outside, as the sky darkened and stars began to appear, they looked at each other in a state of wretched anticipation for the night ahead was surely to be one of playful wickedness.

By half an hour past seven, Santo was stroking his silken whip incessantly. They paced around the room performing basic tasks, but unable to manage anything of significance. The Queen's gown was left unattended. Bits of fabric were picked up off the floor. Spools were corrected and made perfectly level in their formation. By eight o'clock they couldn't even manage small talk. Santo whacked his thighs with his whip. Joshva, in response, hurled a large reel of wool at his head.

It was all going according to plan. Jakob had willingly taken her small vial of the apothecary's concoction, and reported back at dusk that the delivery had been made to the guards in the castle's dungeons. She handed him a small gold ingot for his troubles, though kept insisting she had gifts to bear far more delightful than a pebble of gold. He smiled. The warm gesture had her leaping towards the castle in high spirits. Around ten o'clock she knocked on the door to the tailor's workroom, giddy with excitement.

Joshva came to the door, solemn, unsmiling. "He didn't come. Viggo didn't turn up."

Her laugh was low and indignant. "Fuck."

28

Red River

Aaliya wasn't sure if three or four days had passed since Maddalena visited. She had given up screaming Justen's name. What's worse, death or not knowing? Although she resisted, she allowed her mind to go there. She knew little of what was going on, but at least she was alive.

But only just. The food seemed to have gotten worse. Some hideous grey gruel that didn't represent anything edible, could only have been someone's idea of a sick joke. They wanted her weak. Did they fear that when they opened the door she'd put up resistance? Keeping her body reasonably capable was a struggle. She tried to avoid just sitting, anything to maintain a degree of strength. She'd move around, stretch. But it never lasted long before she'd be back on the cold floor, consumed by thoughts.

Repeatedly, she'd pull out the necklace from under her dress and rub it between her fingers. She'd go over each freedom, one by one, not knowing the order, not caring, but being thankful for a small ritual to pass time. There were only a few items in the cell: the chamber pot, the bed, the dirty bowl not collected. She was desperately hungry, and the hunger seemed to fuel a wild imagination in her. She would stare at the items so fixedly until they would animate into her mother or Justen. She saw them as clear as day. Her mother standing before her throwing berries into her mouth. Justen running into her on the stairwell, opening his arms wide to embrace her. The moth dancing amongst the firelight at her mother's funeral.

It was in this state of part delirium, part starvation, Aaliya heard a familiar voice at the top of the steps.

"You are fucking kidding me!" Viggo boomed. "You hopeless drunk. After this, you're done for."

He continued to mutter cursed words as he descended the steps.

"You behind that?" he hissed.

"What?" she said from the back of her cell.

"Up there."

"What are you talking about?"

"Don't shit me, Aaliya."

She wanted desperately to see someone, but not him. She didn't respond. The knife strapped to her back stopped her leaning flat against the wall, but the coolness still found its way under her skin.

"It's going to be like that, is it?"

Silence.

"Do you know why I came down today?"

"To set me free and allow me to live the rest of my days a content woman."

Viggo smiled viciously. "Sorry, not on the menu today."

She waited for him to continue.

"Justen's dead." As if his words weren't clear enough, he leaned his face through the bars and repeated himself.

Aaliya knew it was coming. Told herself not to hope for anything different. Over and over she had said to herself that if she kept her expectation low enough, then anything remotely good would feel like capturing a comet to another world. But how hard does one have to make their heart before it stops beating? She hated him. Sorry mother, she thought, but I hate this person. You never wanted me to be a hater and I'm going to disappoint you.

"The trial proved beyond a doubt that he had tried to kill the king."

"He was innocent," Aaliya said quietly, without expression.

"Is that what you're going to say tomorrow at your own trial? That you're innocent?"

"My trial's tomorrow?"

"Yes. Aiding and abetting a murderer. It's going to be a miserable life for you. That's if the king let's you live. Attempted regicide doesn't put him in a good mood."

"You know, the funny thing is, you've been done over. You, Viggo." She moved closer to the bars and into the light. "Justen may have lost his life. I might as well. But you're also about to lose. A lot."

"Said like a true defeatist who's got nothing left to lose." Viggo bared his teeth and raised his eyebrows. "Let me see, next you're going to tell me that we've got it all wrong and my bank is going to collapse, I'm going to go bankrupt, and my marriage is going to breakdown. Hmm, really? It's tedious."

"Tedious it might be. Someone once said to me there's what we like and want, and then there's the stuff that just happens. The happenstances that turn everything on its head."

"Well, I'm sure that person didn't own an empire or have the ear of the king."

"You're so sure of yourself," she said. "Are you sure you know Pieter and his motives as well as you think you do?"

"Pieter Laus? He's history. Left the day after Justen's trial. Believe he left with that ditsy fair-haired friend of yours. Didn't even wait to see the executioner's blade come down."

"How convenient."

"As a matter of fact it is. A treaty was still signed thanks to the marriage. We still gained valuable trade routes. Rone will be by-passed. We're secure."

"I'll tell you what was gained. Nothing. What was discussed at your private little meet ups with Pieter, eh? What does a man like Pieter tell the man who has the 'ear of the king'? He tells you what you want to hear, that's what. And whatever he tells you gains momentum. Treaties are signed at a wedding. They get Tyln Bluff, which, for all we know is the most valuable land we've ever held. And with Justen out of the picture and Maddalena remaining here, Pieter also conveniently ensures Traegos has no influence in Gedion. So we gained some trade routes. How long do you think that's going to last?" Aaliya said decisively, gripping the bars and rattling them before stepping back.

"You seem to be struggling to come to terms with the fact that your lover was a traitorous swine."

"You seem to be struggling with the fact you've been done over."

Viggo sniggered. "You have no idea."

"We'll see."

"Although, your analysis might provide some light relief at the trial tomorrow."

She didn't know if she had it in her to tell her story at the trial. Even if she was right, even if what she was saying was true, she wasn't sure she lived in a world that could hear it. There was a chance that tomorrow everything would turn out fine. She had Maddalena, her father. They may not like what she had done, but she had to believe they would still find it in themselves to stand by her. There was a chance.

"We're all good and bad," Aaliya said for her own benefit.

Viggo laughed. "Is that what you tell your Gods when go to sleep at night?"

"I see it all around me."

"Have you thought perhaps to conceal these flaws a bit better? Have you not noticed it has landed you in trouble?"

She wondered how the man standing opposite her now, saw her? A silly girl that wasn't worthy of the father she had? An outspoken botheration? A troublesome recalcitrant? A defeatist, he had labelled her before. She thought about how she recognized herself. She knew how to live in this world. She could be sagacious when she wanted to be. But defeatist, no. Not now, not ever.

Aaliya made her way close to the bars. "You're good and bad too, Viggo. All that darkness swirling around inside you. There are terrible things you want to do, aren't there?"

Aaliya moved her hand to her crotch, and gently started rubbing herself through the fabric of her dress. "Did you watch Justen and I?"

He didn't respond.

"You would have loved it. It was carnal."

"Would you have liked me to watch? Is that where this is going?"

She thought she saw a flicker of fear in his eyes. A faint admission that he was afraid of what was coming next, but also had to know. It encouraged her to keep going, to follow through.

Viggo's eyes went from Aaliya's face to where her hands were rubbing. He swallowed hard and checked around himself involuntarily. "Do you think I'm stupid? Do you think I'm just going to unlock the door and we'll fuck out here? I can have you anytime."

"I'm not going to be around for much longer. Why wait?"

His hard-on was obvious through his pants.

"Why deprive a girl of a bit of pleasure before she goes, eh?" Aaliya squatted down by the iron bars, lifting up her filthy dress. She had nothing on underneath, her sex bare and exposed. She held onto the bar with one hand and plunged the middle finger of her other hand deep inside her, unleashing her honey and spreading it over her sex.

Although the light was dull, Aaliya's sex appeared moist and glistening, like overripe fruit. Aaliya had always loved touching herself. What she wasn't counting on was how hot it felt to do it in front of someone she hated. The bars separated them, but seemed to heighten the exhilaration she was feeling, and she suspected Viggo felt the same. Aaliya knew there was still a likelihood Viggo could hurt her, but she let that fear in. She let it course through her veins and coalesce with the power she was starting to feel. Her body was in a fever.

Aaliya pulled her finger out and presented it through the bars to Viggo. "Suck," she whispered.

Viggo didn't hesitate. He knelt down and sucked her finger hard. His mouth wrapped around Aaliya's finger and he sucked like it was supplying the oxygen he needed to live on.

Viggo undid his trousers and kicked them to the side.

He then lowered his breeches, his large, hard cock flopping up as the garment was moved down. He left his breeches dangling around one ankle, not bothering to remove them fully. Viggo knelt down and presented hungry and ready. "This is just the start, Aaliya. I'm going to have you again and again before you go."

"I want nothing more," Aaliya said, shuffling close to the bars. She spread her legs as wide as she could in a squat position. In her mind, she was thankful for her years of riding. The sides of her knees jammed hard against the bars.

Aaliya held onto the iron rods. Viggo's hands reached through and grabbed her ass and pulled her towards him. Without further hesitation, he plunged into her as deep as he could. After weeks of darkness and loneliness, the raw sensuality of it all was overwhelming to her. Viggo's cock was hot and firm, pulsing and ravening. Didn't bars keep two people away from each other? This shouldn't be happening. The grittiness of the cell, the darkness of her feelings. Aaliya knew she shouldn't have been enjoying this. But she was.

The sound and sight of the sex through the bars was making them both delirious. For Aaliya, this trembling inside her was something so wonderful. On the cusp of certain death, every fleshy interaction seemed to give her more life, more power.

She closely watched his face. She could see pleasure rising in him like a storm. He was close to the tipping point, as was she. Aaliya chose this moment. This crucial moment. Life and death. She reached down the back of her dress with one of her hands and unsheathed the knife. With no warning at all, while his eyes were closed feeling the urgency of his pleasure, Aaliya plunged the knife hard into Viggo's neck. His eyes popped open and he let out a stunned whimper.

She then plunged the knife hard into his chest, swiftly doing it again and again. She quickly snatched the keys from the breast pocket of Viggo's jacket before he slumped back like a sack of grain onto the floor. Blood pulsing from his veins in great red rivers.

Her body started to tremble. The ecstasy was still coursing through her body. She couldn't shut it off. She had reached short of climax, but a different feeling was rippling through her body now. Different, but no less intense. I'm alive, she thought. She was alive while the man she hated lay dead in front of her.

Aaliya grabbed the bars with both hands to steady herself. She was still clutching the knife. Slow drips of blood started running down her hand. She tried to slow down her breathing but she just couldn't stop panting. The air seemed like hard, impenetrable matter. She just couldn't get it into her lungs. Aaliya let go of the bars and looked at her hands. They were shaking furiously. She could feel panic rising inside her like a fever. She tried again to take deep breaths. She knew she had to regain some control or she wouldn't get out of here.

Aaliya reached through the bars and wiped her hand and the blade of the knife on Viggo's shirt. Just keep breathing, you can do this, she said to herself. With the keys in one hand, and the knife in the other, she stood up. Aaliya poked her hand through the bar and jiggled the key through the front of the lock and turned it. A metallic click. She had never heard a more beautiful sound. She pushed open the door.

There's something about experiencing freedom when you don't know you're ever going to have it again. At first Aaliya didn't know what to do with it. It felt decadent, like eating the last slice of the cherry pie. She stood at the first step before the ascent towards the light above. Twenty-nine steps. She didn't know what exactly awaited her at the top of the stairs. Only that she was ready to face it, whatever it was.

29

Somewhere In-Between

Aaliya's body hugged the wall as she silently climbed the steps. The knife was kept out in front leading each move. Her shadow moved across the wall as the torchlight ahead peaked around the curve. Her heart a great aching muscle in her chest. Up ahead, a figure came into view, seated on a stool with his back to her. She clutched the knife even tighter, almost seeing the whiteness of her knuckles in the dull light.

She knew a guard would be situated at the top of the steps. Something had turned in her. She felt ready for anything. She was with them now. The soldiers, the executioners, the cold-blooded killers, the hapless folk who find themselves in situations in which there's no other way to turn. She had blood on her hands. It felt sickening, this power. Sickening, and dare she acknowledge it, useful. Like severing an infected finger. The figure before her was purely an obstacle to her freedom. If she could just creep up behind him, quiet as a sparrow, and slit his throat, he wouldn't even know what had happened to him.

Aaliya took a few more silent steps, her heart making leaps in her chest. Somewhere was a soft tapping sound.

Dripping water. The chamber reeked of damp, of rotting waste. The guard still hadn't stirred. She was so close now, just five steps away. Her breathing became shallow, a tiny film of air slipping in and out of her open mouth. Her body was silent, predatory.

And then the noise happened. It must have been a tiny stone, but treading on it seemed to unleash a sound that reverberated off the walls like the blasting of a war horn. Aaliya held her breath and got ready to lunge.

But he didn't move. Was he asleep? Was he drunk? She didn't know what to do. Should I just kill him anyway? She took another step and edged her body a fraction away from the wall. Aaliya bent around to try to look at his face, his chin slumped heavily into his chest. Frothy spittle was running down his chin and glistening in the light.

Warily, Aaliya stepped to the side of his body, then stepped again. She kept the knife out pointing in his direction, her arm rigid, braced and ready. Only one more step to go. He wasn't responding to her presence at all. He wasn't even stirring. Aaliya noticed a cup laying empty in his hands. She looked at his face to see if he was breathing, but didn't stay long enough to work it out. She took the twenty-ninth step and then ran down the tunnel that took her deeper into the subterranean belly of the castle.

The knife was promptly returned to the sheath between her shoulder blades. The tunnel continued straight, a couple of fire torches lighting the path. And then the light stopped, only the blackest of darkness before her. Her eyes took a moment to adjust to the blackness. There was nothing to see, no feature to guide her. Only the feel of the wall as she ran her hand along it.

So complete was the dark she was sure that at any

moment the ground underfoot would just give way. She paused a moment just to grip one of the protruding stones from the tunnel wall and steady herself. Time is a strange thing. She felt like she was her ten year-old self again. The feeling was so potent, it felt like no time had passed at all. Aaliya closed her eyes, she couldn't see anyway, and let the walls and her instinct guide her along.

The air around her became cooler and clammier, the scent moist and musty. The walls started to feel rockier, less brick like beneath her touch. The tunnel narrowed until it was little more than the width of her body. It felt like the walls were closing in, trying to push her out like an unwelcome visitor.

Aaliya continued to run her hand along the wall, and kept it low. Eventually she found what she'd been searching for. The protrusion on the rock was distinctly shaped like a hammer-head. She ran her fingers over it again to make sure. She knew she was close now.

The tunnel took a sharp turn. It was around here somewhere. Aaliya desperately wished she had one of those fire torches now. The tunnel widened and Aaliya spread out her arms as she walked. The narrow tunnel had finally given way to a wide space. This was the cavern she had been searching for.

Aaliya squinted and looked hard around. Ahead was the faintest variation from the blackness enshrouding the space. It was dull, but to Aaliya it was as wondrous as looking into the light of a hundred fires. Arms out, fingers flared, she tried to keep herself steady as she fumbled over the slippery uneven ground. Her shins crashed into rocks. She gasped, shrieked, with each unexpected dip.

The ground suddenly gave way. Aaliya staggered into

a deep pool of water. Breathless with shock, she steadied herself and clambered on. Excited mutterings escaped her mouth. Gentle light from the night sky filtered into the cave casting a shade of dark grey near the opening. Water rose up to her hips. She saw a star. A shimmering, glittering pinprick of light. She noticed another, and then another, and felt a shocking surge of heat rise up her spine. It took all she had not to feel overwhelmed.

She leapt towards the opening, her body crashing into something solid. She wrapped her hands around the familiar shape of iron bars. "No! No! Please no!" she wailed.

Aaliya dived under the water in the hope the obstruction didn't reach the rocky floor. She felt around, running her hand along the whole bottom of the iron structure. Nothing could get in, and nothing could get out, except the tide of the river.

She came to the surface of the water and wanted to scream. Wanted to let out a blood curling cry that would shake the place down.

It can't happen like this, she thought. This didn't use to be here. She held onto the bars and looked through to the outside where a hundred stars filled her eyes. For a moment she let herself be bewitched by such a beautiful sight. The bars just seemed to fade away. Or was it that she was fading away. She didn't feel present. She couldn't even feel the coolness of the water anymore. Just a sense of drowning in the sight of the night sky. She felt sure it was looking back at her, offering a veil of protection.

Aaliya turned her back to the starry night and lurched her way back the way she had come. Once back at the mouth of the tunnel, she wrung out the bottom of her dress and took a deep breath. She had to do something, she just didn't know what.

Up ahead Aaliya could see the flickering light of a lamp. She was getting closer to where she had started. The smell as she approached the cells became more putrid. But there was another scent wafting around, something metallic and corporeal. It mingled with her head. Her breathing became shallow, her hands started to fumble and shake. In her head she saw blood and shit and gore and suddenly felt fear rise inside her, violent and disturbing. The silence was unsettling. At least if she had some noise, she thought she might have a better idea what to do. Feel galvanized into some sort of action. Instead she felt like she was walking towards the edge of a deep chasm.

More careful steps. She edged closer to the second lamp, close now to the entrance to her cell. Light was bouncing around her now and she felt exposed. She knew she could be discovered at any moment, and within minutes find herself back in a cell. Just her and her gut-wrenching loneliness before certain death.

Up ahead she heard the uproar. Her body froze. A voice bellowed out, "She's escaped! Alert the king! The prisoner Aaliya Reiner has escaped!"

Aaliya immediately threw herself to the ground. She didn't know why, she just knew that she had to get low. Bit down on her tongue. Her jaw locked shut.

She saw movement ahead. Other guards running to the cell.

"Find her! Search every part of this dungeon. Go! Go!" screamed one of the guards.

She knew she had less than a minute before they would find her cowering there on the ground. She scurried forward on her knees like a rat, her heart pounding so loudly in her chest all extraneous sound was blocked out. That smell. It hit her again as powerfully as a charging bull.

The first guard emerged from the stairwell that lead to her cell. He leapt down the corridor back towards the main exit. She wouldn't be so lucky with the next one.

She found the small door to the latrine pit and kicked it open. In about ten seconds she would have guards passing this very spot. She had nothing left to loose. Aaliya threw her body through the opening.

30

Means Without Direction

It was a kind of madness. The sheer lunacy of the situation almost had her laughing. "Shit lake," she cried before covering her mouth and nose.

Aaliya held her breath but the desperate gasps that followed seemed to make things worse. However unpleasant, the air in here was all she had. "Just breathe like a normal person," she muttered, "a normal person experiencing a normal event on a normal day."

The door was placed back into position. That innocuous item had convinced her it was a pointless piece of furnishment. It's ability to stifle the stench coming from the cesspool seemed utterly rudimentary. But situated now on the other side of the small wooden door, she realized she should have been more grateful. Here in the dark, she felt profoundly assaulted by the power of the fetid odour.

She heard the sound of stamping feet on the other side of the door. She wasn't safe yet. They would surely look in here too. The flies were aggressive, eating into the corners of her eyes. There was a good chance of an opening somewhere. She just had to find it.

The feeling of god-knows-what squishing between

her toes almost had her fainting as she waded through the cesspool. The cloak of darkness was slightly redeeming. Each moist lump that touched her skin had her recoiling in disgust. She focused her eyes directly opposite on the far side of the cavernous space. A faint circle of light revealed itself. There was an opening out of this slimy hell.

Each step was carefully placed. The thought of losing her balance filled her with dread. Mutterings of encouragement escaped her mouth. It was all she could do to keep herself from going under. She tried thinking of Justen, but it put her off balance. Too confronting, too traumatic. Instead she thought of wings. Papery wings. Feathery wings. Enormous spans that block out the sun. Swift, tiny ones as delicate as a decomposed leaf. Wings on insects. Wings on birds. Wings on horses. Flying. Flying.

A loud bang behind her caused her to lose her balance slightly. She quickly regained her footing and turned around. The wooden door had been kicked in and a lamp was being shined through the opening.

"We know you're in there, Aaliya," a hoarse voice howled loudly.

Terror reached deeply into her core. She couldn't breathe. The noxious space seemed suddenly devoid of oxygen. Bile rose up from her stomach with such ferocity she could feel the metallic tang of sick at the back of her throat.

Her careful steps changed to desperate, clumsy floundering through the watery sludge. Just get the hell out of here no matter what it takes. She didn't know whether she consciously numbed herself or if her mind went there of it's own accord. All she knew was that she was doing something she never thought she was capable of doing.

Behind her she could hear the guard alerting others, the sound of their alarmed cries and stamping feet booming in her ears. She edged closer to the portal to the outside world. Every emotion at once seemed to be charging through her body: hope, fear, exhilaration, anger.

Some poor man had been ordered to chase after her. Aaliya briefly looked over her shoulder as the shadowy figure powered his way through the molasses thick sludge. She panicked and pressed on as hard as she could, grunting with each step. At last her hands gripped something solid. Her fingers wrapped around the hardness of rock, and she held it firmly heaving herself out, the bottom of her dress weighed down by the clinging muck.

She leapt for her life through the portal and slid down the rocks on the other side. Like a scuttling cockroach, she scrambled over the last rock and sunk into the soggy marsh below. The mud instantly wrapped around her legs as firmly as a cast. Each step taken had her sinking up to her hips in the sodden muck. It was a despairing moment, she felt like she wasn't gaining any traction. That she was sinking deeper into helplessness. There was nothing to grab onto. Mud and faeces covered her whole body.

The man tailing her had hauled himself up to the ledge. He'd have her under the mud in a moment or two, she'd be dead a minute after that. Aaliya grunted like a mad animal and pressed forward, lifting her leg high for each step. Bit by bit, the mud gave way to more water.

She tried to keep panic at bay but it was starting to well up and take hold. Her face felt hot, the blood vessels in her neck as taut as bowstrings. In the distance Aaliya could hear cries of alarm. They were calling her name. The word was out already. In no time, the castle grounds would be overrun with bodies looking for her. With every last bit of strength Aaliya lifted her legs through the mud. The river was so close now.

When the water level finally reached her waist, Aaliya threw herself into the river, her legs coming free of their muddy confinement. Thrashing in the water, she swam away from the riverbank as fast as she could. The man behind her dived too, but mistimed. His heavier body remaining stuck in the thick mud.

It was cold, frigidly cold. But unlike the mud, it was silken and yielded to her body. The water kept getting deeper and at last provided the cover she needed. She took a great lungful of air, dived under and swam swiftly into the middle where the current was strongest.

Every so often she came to the surface for a gulp of air before gently descending again. The river was wide and powerful and cut through the land like black ink. On and on she went, each dive taking her further away from the castle, further and further away from her old life. When she felt as though she had created enough distance, Aaliya stopped and tilted her face to the sky. It was vast and black. The moon and stars above heaving and shimmering like wild lights of the night.

She remained in the middle of the river, her body submerged and gently paddling. Guards were running out of the castle, dozens of them. The hunting dogs had been released, their barking a cacophony of angry sound echoing across the land.

A voice hollered, "Get to the boats. You lot on foot, search near the river. Every bit of the river is to be searched. Every bit of ground. Behind every rock, every tree. Get moving!"

Aaliya took one last look at the castle. There standing at a window on the third floor was the silhouette of a person. A woman. She couldn't be sure, but she felt it was Maddalena. She stopped paddling, took a deep breath and went under.

31

Beyond the Boundaries

The outlying districts seemed to unspool endlessly along the river. Aaliya had heard about caves where critters would cling to the rocky black walls and produce tiny spots of iridescence. Under the starry night sky, with light from the city glowing along the shore, she felt like she was moving through one of those caves.

She swam and swam and yet felt as though she was getting nowhere. Progress seemed achingly slow. Her weary body wasn't up for this. Did she really think she could out-manoeuvre them? Her rake thin, ravaged body take on their muscled determination? Her dress was a millstone around her. She managed to approach the ships moored at the quay, the temptation arising to somehow climb on board and sail away to somewhere unknown.

The inky depth of the water crept into her mind and was starting to unravel her like a ball of string. If she just stopped moving her body, she wondered how long it would take for her to reach the silted bottom. It was so easy to give over to panic. It was right there, a breath away. She held her breath, scared of inviting it in. It could all be over very quickly, the struggle, the messy, seemingly insurmountable problems. Maddalena was right. This was just the beginning. Then what? It could only be a long, perilous journey ahead. Or a short one. Either way, it couldn't end well, could it? The brisk motion of her legs sawing through the water eased. And then stopped. Sinking. Sinking. Mother, she cried silently. She could feel her dress mushroom up around her head in the blackness. It was getting colder, the icy depths pulling her into a watery tomb. How easy it was to slip into it. The lid would be shut, never to be seen of again. Nature reclaiming her.

Except the timing wasn't right. She could feel the chain against her neck. The pendant brush the side of her face. The river was both danger and safety, her mother had said. And needed to be respected. She made a pact between herself and the river. Get me to safety and I promise you'll survive. It seemed childish, but it was enough to get her legs, once again, churning through the water. Her arms slapped like albatross wings. She came to the surface and took a greedy lungful of air. I will not fall apart, she told herself.

She silently swam to where the small skips were moored, lining up as neatly as scales along a lizard's spine. Boots could be heard clomping along the wooden boards. The water was black and smelly. She held onto a pylon, the low tide giving her the headroom under the deck she needed to catch her breath. A man pissed over the edge near her face. The boards creaked as he made his way to the other end of the jetty where men were standing, talking. She hauled herself out of the water, her movements clumsy, desperate. Darkness enshrouding her, she untied the rope and climbed into a skip. Her heart beat wildly each time she dipped the oars into the water. Gently, she took herself into the middle of the river and rowed into the night.

It started off well. She wasn't sure where she was going but every step she took away from Ansgar felt good. The skip had been left on the bank before morning light, where she then headed inland to find a place to rest. Cold and exhausted, she felt around in the dark for a thick bush and huddled under it for the remaining hours of the night. Sleep was a long time coming. She couldn't get warm. Couldn't calm the incessant shivering that coursed through her body. Eventually she drifted off from sheer weariness, her bed of dirt not much different from what she had slept on the previous week in the cell.

A tentative plan started to form in her mind. If she could cross the border into Rone, she would be alright. Helena's family lived in the Tilwara Valley. They would help her. The thought gave her a jolt. She tried to recall the map. Tried to think about the villages located near the fork in the river. Where on the landscape the River Kota snaked into Rone.

For the next two days, Aaliya remained away from the riverbank and walked inland where the scrub was thick. Sometimes she wandered a bit too close to the path, before scampering back into the vegetation seeking concealment. Her dress snagged and ripped on the wiry bushes, her legs and arms became a crosspatch of bloody scrapes. She ran her hand through her hair and felt a nest of matted knots. She could only imagine how wild she looked. If only she had a few more possessions. Some decent boots, a flint to light a fire, a warm cloak, string and hook for catching fish. With a few more possessions she could keep doing this. Hell, she could possibly even make it to Lagos.

Small goals were set. "Just get to that bend in the river" or "just walk until that dragon shaped cloud moves out of sight" were formed in her mind to propel herself forward. Apart from her recent trip with Olle, she had never ventured so far away from the capital. Even in her exhaustion there were moments when she felt filled with exaltation. She was alive! She was walking amongst magnificence! Water and light, space and energy was all around. It was like she was seeing it all for the first time. The sky looked a more brilliant blue than she had ever noticed before. The wildflowers seemed to assault her sight with their blooming shades of purple and yellow and red. And birds seemed to be everywhere. Small little wagtails, and large, soaring swifts. Even the ochre dirt beneath her feet had an energising quality.

Time inched forward. By the forth day, Aaliya's feet felt like lead weights. Every step was a gargantuan effort. She felt rattled and depleted, lack of cover during the cold nights imbibing her body with a constant raw ache. Her skin felt as parched as old leather, her lips cracked and fissured. And the hunger that coursed through her body was as wide and gaping as a canyon. Berries and nuts had been found along the walk, but it never felt like enough. She looked longingly at the rabbits and birds she came across, her mind filling with thoughts of how to rig up some sort of trap using her knife and the materials available to her. But in the end, it wasn't worth pursuing. She couldn't cook the game even if she managed to catch one.

Aaliya wanted a fire more than anything, more than boots, more than a cloak. If she could finish each day with a fire, she thought she could get through anything. It would be like having a companion with her, wrapping her in warmth and light and absorbing her burdens. Without fire she felt as though she was little more than a stray animal wandering the earth.

On her second night she had come across a group of men sitting around a fire. From a distance she watched them eat, envied their warmth as they huddled around the flames. For a brief moment, she felt defeated, even took a few cursory steps in their direction. Maybe they could help her? The king's henchmen surely weren't the only people who roamed these parts? The orange glow seemed to be luring her like a starving dog drawn to bait. But with the little cognizance she had, she knew it was a trap. It had been too soon since she had escaped. She stopped moving forwards and kept perfectly still. Her awareness drawn to her bare feet. She dug her toes into the dirt looking for a better hold. If she went to them now, she would be back in the cell within hours. Although the uncertainty of her path was formidable, she at least didn't have four damp walls enclosing her in.

And then there were the battles in her mind. What had started out as a sense of liberty, a world of possibilities, had in a short amount of time crashed into a miserable pit of despair. She laughed at her earlier notions that this was some sort of mystical experience. It was hard, and it hurt. And a sadness crept into her bones like liquid seeping into tissue. The grief that had been there for so long started rising to the fore after being squashed down into a neat, dark place. Without her mother and with Justen also gone, she felt small. She was sure she was almost invisible, just a particle floating through air. She didn't feel anchored. No person to reach out to and touch, no shelter to lie under. What she would give for a friendly face. Even an unfriendly one. She almost wanted to be found just to have the interaction, come what may.

She became lax, walked away from the trees, out in the open. Sure that no one could possibly see her anyway. She looked down at the back of her hand just to make sure she was real, that this moment was really happening.

There was a moment when she stopped, her eyes filled up with liquid making it hard to see. She rested her face in her hands and cried. Cried for her mother, cried for Justen, the mess she was in, what had been done and could not be un-done. Dropping heavily to her knees, she let herself be overcome with the weight of her grief and howled on the ground. They can come and find me, she thought. She was stuck, unable to move forward yet unable to go back to anything.

On the sixth night, the moon rose bright and luminous. Every night her eyes searched for the moon. She imagined a face up there, looking down at her, guiding her like an old friend. The hunger inside her was starting to feel deadly. Her dress was almost reduced to bare threads, the soles of her feet looked like a grim canvas of blood and grime.

As she braced herself for another night in the cold, she saw the faintest dot of orange light through the darkness. She thought it must be a star, but realized it was too low on the horizon. She stared at it until it went out of focus and became a blurry fuzz of light. Aaliya blinked hard and squinted, trying to focus again. It was still there.

This time, she physically didn't have the power to resist. She had to hope that this was the light she was meant to see, the light she was meant to walk towards.

The boat was anchored in the middle of the river. Aaliya let out a feeble yelp and then tried again. Movement could be seen on deck and then the sound of oars slapping the water. Aaliya stood rigid, waiting. The lamp on the skip bobbed and swayed with the rhythm. A man leapt from the small boat as it neared the shore. The whites of his eyes glowed in the darkness. Aaliya removed the necklace and held it out. "Take this," Aaliya said, enclosing the man's fingers around the pendant, knowing it was all she needed to say.

32

The Smell of Old Life

The Quadsun Bank was a new building on Floran Road. One year ago, it had replaced a small theatre that had stood at the site for eighty years. The White Orchid Concert Hall, whilst not the most elaborate theatre in the capital when it was standing, had held Ansgar's most scurrilous and risky productions. Music and dance would transgress into circus and comedy. Men would dress as women, women as men. Clothes would be removed, flesh exposed. Royal families across the realm would be parodied until the audience laughed and squirmed. Love and sex, politics and power. The stories were of everyday life rendered vivid and extraordinary.

At the entrance to the bank, Maddalena noticed the acrid scent of ink and heavy parchment. The building of two storeys featured neatly cut white limestone that shone like child's teeth in the afternoon sun. She figured she would be one of the last customers for the day and told herself to make a move. The longer she stood there, the higher the chances she would be recognized. The two windows either side of the heavy oak door were framed with rods of iron, a heavily armoured guard stood next to the door. Maddalena had a vague memory of this part of Floran Road having a decadent quality to it when the theatre was still standing. It now represented an atmosphere of placid restraint.

It had been five months, three weeks and two days since Aaliya's escape. Maddalena had barely seen her father, let alone have a conversation with him, during the time that had passed. He was a whirlwind of turmoil. She was sure that under normal circumstances Thormund would have lined up another suitor for her by now. His daily routine took on a monastical quality. Early mornings were spent in the study with the door closed. Fin would deliver a plate of warm cinnamon bread and gooseberries each morning after an hour had passed. On more than one occasion, the sound of items crashing to the ground could be heard.

Maddalena approached Fin one day and took her father's breakfast to him. "No," he said, as soon as she entered the room. "I'm not going to talk about this. I'm going to deal with this my way." Morning sessions in the study, where Maddalena suspected her father did little more than ruminate, would be followed by errands, council sessions, meetings with the king, and of course, running the bank. The few times Thormund was willing to talk, he talked in big, voluminous language about the bank, about money, about the next chapter in the Reiner story. He never once mentioned Aaliya or the loss of his much admired business partner. Time was always ticking. No looking back.

At times, Maddalena noticed her father walk with a winced expression on his face. He would hastily return his appearance to one of blank neutrality when he became aware of his body's reaction. But there was a time when she could see that the pain he was feeling was deep and excruciating. "Would you just stop pretending everything is fine," she screamed at him when he dismissed, yet again, her attempts to intervene and help him. Maddalena wanted to engage him in an explosive argument, something to strip paint off the walls. "Let's get this sorted out," she insisted. But he firmly and composedly refused. Ambulating away with the steadiness of a teaspoon resting on a piece of string. Feeling. That's what this is about, she concluded. He just doesn't want to feel anymore.

Rumours flowed like blood from a wound about her sister, which didn't help at all. She drowned. She ran off with a farm boy. She was killed by the huntsmen who set out to find her. And one of the more sensational whispers was that she was actually a phoenix and had burst into flames, her ashes scattering in the wind until finally finding a home beside her mother.

Olle had been questioned again and again by the king's men. Each week, Maddalena turned up at the workshop to see a man bruised and beaten and bloodied raw. But somehow determined to maintain his practice even if all he could manage were simple tasks. Each week she turned up and pleaded for him to tell her what he knew, if he knew anything. And each week he turned her away. Sometimes she would refuse to go. He simply worked around her.

One day, after visiting the workshop every week for four months, she entered the workshop to find it completely empty. Her eyes scanned the earthy, wooden space with a sense of bewilderment. Every tool, every stud, every scrap of leather. Gone. The greasy workbenches were bare. The hooks jutting out from the walls, unoccupied. She wandered through the empty space, running her hand along surfaces in the hope of finding a clue. It was the middle of the day and light filled the rooms. She arrived at the backroom and looked around the walls. Nothing. The stone was timeworn and smelled of old life. She walked across the floorboards to the far end of the room and leaned against the wall. How does a man just disappear? The same way her sister disappeared, she told herself. With help. Although she had suspected it for some time, she knew now, with complete certainty, that Olle knew where Aaliya was. Now she had to find two people.

Maddalena began crossing the room when she felt something raised underfoot. She reached down and felt a small iron ring. She pulled at the ring, and to her surprise, several boards lifted. A square hole in the floor revealed itself. It had clue written all over it. But to what piece of the puzzle she was not sure. She positioned herself on the steps and started walking down. When she got to the bottom she looked around. Come on, Olle. Give me something. The minimal natural light filtering in from above revealed shelves against every wall. But every one of them was bare. She got down low and looked underneath, she raised herself up onto her toes to see higher. Nothing. What was the space used for? she wondered. Additional storage? What had to be kept out of sight?

Maddalena left the workshop jaded, spent. For the next week she thought about where Olle could have gone. Somewhere. Anywhere. The whole damn realm was his home. Someone must know. But who would tell her?

One night while staring into blackness as she lay on her bed, she thought of someone that might be willing to talk.

In the morning, she leapt out of bed and braced herself for the cold. The beginnings of winter had taken hold. The peaks to the north of the capital now stood white and bejewelled. Icy winds blew southward, forcing the inhabitants of Ansgar to clutch their cups of warm milk even tighter. Fires were lit everywhere coating the sky with dense smoke that hovered in the valley and reddened the weak sun. She saddled up her horse and made her way to Qlots Creek.

When she arrived at the tannery, the piercing smell of shit and offal was instantly familiar to her. Salomon Ezcaroz was standing out the front of the red brick shed as if no time at all had passed since her last visit.

She said unwaveringly as she neared him, "You've got to tell me where Olle is. He knows the whereabouts of my sister. I'm not leaving here until you do."

He didn't flinch. He didn't act remotely surprised. His big heavy jaw dropped a little so as to take in air, then he said, "I've been expecting you. Olle said you would come. His location is known to me, and he has given me permission to tell you. If you utter his whereabouts to another soul you will be killed. If you are careless and allow yourself to be followed, you will be killed. Do not think for a moment these are just threats. Do I make myself clear?"

And so she found out. She knew now where to find Olle, and in time, she would also find Aaliya. It was what she had been working towards for months. And yet, suddenly the weight of the knowledge felt leaden and cumbersome. She had to do this on her own, yet she hated doing anything on her own. Solitude was no companion of hers.

For the next week she beat the walls in frustration. She liked her life here. Things could be good, very good. She could be somebody in this life. As soon as she left to find Aaliya, she would become a nobody, an invisible drifter. For the love of the Gods, she'd be poor! Moneyless! Panic gripped her and wound around her like a tourniquet. She ran into the arms of Joshva and Santo with an insatiable need to be overwhelmed by physical power. To feel only heat and wildness and brutality until she could take it no more. The storms that raged across the landscape were no match for the roaring upheaval in her heart. She hurt and let herself be hurt. Biting. Hitting. Whipping. She clung to their flesh fearing that the minute she let go she would be erased. At the very least, she would be left a mere ordinary creature.

Then something departed. Or maybe it was that something entered. But the change she felt when she woke up one day to see a thick blanket of snow on the ground, was one of acceptance. And readiness.

The key to her father's study had been kept in a small wooden box at the back of the drawer of her dressing table. Thormund had left the house over an hour earlier. Maddalena had sent away Nella and Fin to run errands, though she knew in all probability they would only be gone for forty minutes at the most.

Even though she knew she was alone in the house, she unlocked the door to Thormund's study gingerly like a guilty trespasser. So many times she had stood on the threshold waiting for her father to invite her in. Pleading, silently, to be let in. And now she could just walk in. It should have been easier, but it felt like scaling a smooth wall. She didn't know if it was the permission she longed for or just sheer presence. Some sort of acknowledgement, even if it was jagged and bristled. Uneasily, she stepped through the doorway. The curtains were drawn, the room was sombre and silent. The fire was low in the hearth, embers fading and then re-glowing as bursts of air whistled down the chimney. The bottom of the sideboard was cracked and dented as though something had been thrown against it with force. The chamber still carried the smells of cedar and leather, but now there was something new. The hot scent of corked fury.

She placed the leather satchel she had been carrying on the desk, pulled out a piece of parchment and dipped the tip of the quill in the black ink.

She began to write:

To whom it may concern,
I, Thormund Reiner, Merchant First Class of Reiner Limited and Director of Redshade, authorize for my brother, Torben Reiner, to lawfully exchange ten thousand Traegos notes for gold ingot. This is a once only transaction to occur at Quadsun Bank in the Year of the Wolverine, Month of Loryana, on the day of sixteenth Syrea.

Maddalena scrawled her father's signature, blew on the ink, and then neatly folded the letter. She lit the wick of the sealing wax and let the drops of hot liquid fall onto the parchment. Thormund's seal was carefully pressed into the soft pool of ruby red wax and then lifted with a steady hand.

There was a day during the summer five months earlier when Thormund had invited her into his study. He had failed to secure the cabinet where the money was kept, prior to allowing her in. Was this just an oversight? Surely her father didn't make mistakes like that. Could it have been a deliberate act? Did he actually want her to know how to access his money, perhaps in case something happened to him? She could only guess at the inner workings of her father as she opened up several books on the shelf in an attempt to find the one with the middle of the pages cut out and removed to form a little coffin. Eventually she opened the right one. She lifted the green cloth cover to see a key sitting like a jewel in its box.

The key slipped into the keyhole of the heavy cedar cabinet, and it then clicked open. The money was lined up neatly on the shelf. Paper money. Who would have thought paper could have the same value as gold. Genius, Viggo. She wondered if it would last without its founder at the helm, or if the scheme would all fold and crash into one enormous pile of dung. Maddalena didn't plan to be around to find out. She grabbed ten of the bulky bricks of money and threw them into her satchel. A couple of piles remained. She locked up the cupboard and placed the key back in the book.

Before leaving, she pulled out another piece of parchment and scrawled the message:

> *Dear father,*
> *I've gone to find Aaliya. I need to know she's safe.*
> *Take care. We'll both return to you one day.*
> *Love always.*
> *Maddalena*

She locked the door behind her as she left. Dashing to Thormund's room, she made her way to his wardrobe and hurriedly started going through his clothing. She passed over most of his jackets. Too formal, too recognizable, too statesmanlike. Eventually, she found a jacket she hadn't seen her father wear in a long time. A brown leather riding jacket with cross stitching running down the front. Nothing too remarkable, plain but dignified enough. She grabbed a shirt and navy woollen pants and threw them over the top of the jacket resting on her arm.

Back in her room, she threw the items she was carrying onto her bed, walked to her dressing table and took out the scissors. Holding them near the top of her head, she opened the blades and then closed them over a thick handful of hair. She had long fantasized about being a man. How would it feel to be the penetrator? How would it feel to have more physical power? What that would do to one's head? She wondered if she would be any different as a man. Would she react the same way? Would she be motivated by the same things? Would she solve problems the same way? Would she launch out into the unknown with no safety net to find an only sister?

She hacked a little more aggressively at her hair. She knew she could act like a man. She had looked into the eyes of men to know enough about their needs and desires and motivations. If she spoke with her eyes, she would get by today. It would be a performance, her as the actor, the staff in the Quadsun Bank the audience. She'll give them a show, a small piece of her extraordinary life before she disappears and they are forced to return to their regular existences.

The hair piled up at her feet. She began to laugh.

33

A House in the Woods

The morning was silent. The wind of the previous five days and nights had finally moved south letting the mist roll in and smother every tree in the woods. The trunks appeared dark and moist, the first green shoots appearing like jewels on the outermost branches.

Everyday, Aaliya opened the door of the cottage to see that more life had grown during the night; and everyday, ravens cawed and scattered to flight at the sound of the creaking door. She placed the heavy iron pot on the table by the front door and left the threshold. As the damp pressed through her wool dress, she walked amongst the pines, over fallen logs ripe with lichen and moss. Her brown leather boots had been hastily cobbled together by the shoesmith in the village and were of such thin material she wondered how they had got through winter. She wrapped the shawl tighter around her shoulders, her long dress gathering moisture at the hem. On her head she wore a black wool hat, a spectacular pheasant's feather attached to the side. Her long hair beneath it, limply gathered into a hazardous bun.

She circled around the trap when she found it, depressing the bracken with her weight. She squatted down and fiddled with the metal lever, forcing it open. The rabbit's pelt was an attractive fawn colour. She picked up the limp body and walked back to the house. The ravens cawed noisily and swooped in her wake, hoping to find something left behind.

The rabbit was placed on the table, her hand reaching down her back to retrieve the knife. It was market day today. It was a regular part of her week that she always looked forward to. Once she got over her nerves about being seen, that was. But the company, it was tonic. The sight of merry people and banners flapping, the sheer delight of seeing the colour and shape of different kinds of food. And the smells. Spicy bean soups bubbling over huge fire pits, burning hemlock, the whiff of contented but unwashed bodies.

She was happy with the tack she had completed during the week, ready for selling. She still missed the big projects. The challenge of making a saddle from scratch, the journey from start to finish. But she didn't have the headspace anymore. Didn't have any space, for that matter.

Her one room cottage was a basic affair. The four mud brick walls were little higher than her own outstretched body. The roof a flattened cone of straw and bracken and mud. From a distance, it looked little more than an oversized toadstool. Inside was meagre and as draughty as a watchtower. Webs covering the beams overhead constantly shook as air whistled through the one-room space. The air smelled perennially of wood smoke, leather and herbs. The iron stove, not much bigger than a cushion, was nestled into the corner of the room. Her bed occupied another corner; a makeshift thing rigged up out of straw bales held together with strips of linen. Books sat in a pile beside her bed. Her greatest luxury was her table. A vast ancient slab of oak that seemed to engulf most of the narrow space. It sat under the window near the door, but rarely saw light so permanently swathed in leather and tools was its surface.

Aaliya had started new collections. Rabbit feet and bird feathers, pinecones and pebbles all competed for space on the few surfaces she had in the room. A few earthenware cups and bowls, spoons, a knife, jars of legumes and grains lined the narrow shelf beside the iron stove. Drying herbs hung like broom heads from the ceiling.

Last night she had gathered the bridles and reins together and placed them in her satchel, ready for leaving early. She used to think all the items she made had a soul, had a personality all of their own. Now, there was little attachment. She made just to get the money she needed to cover materials and buy food.

Aaliya put on the greasy white apron hanging near the door, inserted the knife into the animal and split it from neck to tail. Her hand reached in and pulled at the gizzards, helping them to tumble onto the table, before scraping them into a bucket. She worked the knife under the skin, unsheathing it methodically until the poor critter was all sinew and big eyes. Aaliya cut into the flesh and removed the meat, chucking it into the pot with the awaiting herbs, onion and water. She wiped her hands on the apron and smoothed clean her knife before placing it back.

The fire inside was low but steady. Another hefty log was thrown into the belly of the stove and the pot placed on top. Her fingers scooped up some strands of hair that had fallen around her face. She kept feeling around her mouth, over her jutting cheekbones and across her eyes. Occasionally, she'd catch her reflection in the window of a night with the lamp burning beside her. She knew she was getting ragged, old beyond her years. Olle had offered more, so much more than this little mud brick dwelling in the woods. He had ways and means that astounded her. But she had insisted. Nothing fancy. Just enough to get some work done. And complete solitude. The offer of a horse, though, was not an easy one to turn down. It gave her that bit of company, that connection with the world when the loneliness became too much to bear. She sensed he longed for her forgiveness. Or maybe it was just that by keeping her happy she was less likely to tell. One day she'd catch up with him and let him know that she was proud of him and that he had a loyal friend in her, no matter what. But just not now.

Aaliya grabbed the satchel and went down the side of the cottage where a horse with a shiny chestnut coat stood behind a stone wall. "Good morning, Mellie," she said, rubbing its flank. The horse blinked at her, it eyes large wet black discs. Steam shot from the horse's nostrils. "You're looking forward to it too, aren't you girl?"

She hauled her body up onto the back of the horse, the heels of her boots resting against the horse's barrelled side. She took up the reins and put the horse forward, nudging it past the house and through the woods.

Aaliya rode back through the woods late in the afternoon happy with the quantity of tack she had sold throughout the day. The thin line of smoke rising above the treetops was a comforting sight. She thought of kicking off her boots, devouring her rabbit stew, peeling open a book, perhaps even a satisfying but wretched hand job. The ride back to the cottage after the day at the market was her most treasured part of the week. A slow journey that cleared the head and nurtured the body. She relished the feel of the horse's muscles underneath her backside, the rhythmic shifting and alternating. It sometimes lulled her into such a trance she would come close to falling off.

Drizzle, gossamer and weightless, floated down through the trees and coated the horse with a light sheen. She heard familiar sounds: the chorus of skylarks and warblers, a sudden rumble in the ground litter, water washing over rocks somewhere in the distance.

The first glimpse of the cottage as she came around the bend was no different today than any other. Initial relief then the creeping feeling of the spirit sinking a little. Here I am again, she thought. She spent so many waking hours thinking that it was all a bit beyond her. That maybe returning to Ansgar, to her family, was the best course of action regardless of the consequences. At what point do you know what to do?

She started down the side of the cottage, smiling at the waft of rabbit stew. The sound of grinding, crunching. The head of a horse, a magnificent inky creature, raised up from behind the stone wall enclosure. Aaliya pulled the reins and silently slid off. Wide-eyed now, she moved furtively back towards the front of the cottage, the knife out in front guiding each step. She wanted to get a glimpse through the window, but knew she would be seen. Probably already had.

"Get out of my house. Now!" she bellowed. "I will kill you if you don't get out. I swear to the Gods I will."

She waited. Nothing. And then the sound of a chair scraping heavily over the wooden boards. Aaliya watched intensely as the door handle was slowly turned. She moved within arms reach of the door and held the knife near her face. Her arm rigid, her knuckles white and strained. Blood rising to her temples.

The person stood at the threshold of the open door. "Aaliya, it's me." Maddalena stepped into view and looked at her sister, wondering, hoping, second-guessing what she was thinking and feeling.

Aaliya wailed a strange animal sound. Her arm went slack, her jaw loosened, and she suddenly felt tired, like she had been swimming upstream for years and could only now float with the current. Her muscles weakened, her legs started to give way. She gripped the table, steadying herself and placed the knife on top. And then raised her arms and stepped forward.

Maddalena fell into Aaliya's offered embrace, and held her close. "It's okay. Everything is going to be fine."

34

The Departed

"If you didn't speak, I would have killed you," said Aaliya.

"I worked that out."

"You look so different. Your hair, your clothes."

"Surely I don't look totally like a man."

"No. Just enough to cause confusion." Aaliya slurped noisily on the spoonful of stew. The warmth of it spread all the way to her fingertips and toes.

The fire in the stove seemed to bring a summer's night into the one room space. An orange glow flickered around the walls, shards of glimmering light caught on the shiny buckles and fittings strewn across the table. The single rickety chair stood empty and forlorn. They both sat on the straw bale bed leaning against the wall. Their warm bowls of food nursed in their hands like precious cargo.

"You have my bed tonight," Aaliya suggested.

Maddalena looked down at it. "It's hardly the better offer."

"Take it or leave it. Up to you."

"You know, I wasn't expecting much. But this is… rudimentary, to say the least."

"It's serving a purpose."

"And what's the purpose? Self-punishment?"

"Let's call it self-understanding."

"Does that involve self-forgiveness?"

Aaliya paused. "Maybe one day." She slowly drank another mouthful, then added, "I just wanted him to go away. Made him go away. It's almost funny when you think about the things you want sometimes. It's brought me no relief, no joy whatsoever. But it just never goes away. That need to do something about it. And then when you do something about it, all you want is for things to be back the way they were."

"I didn't get to you in time. Olle didn't either."

"Probably best. You two are in enough trouble for me as it is."

"What's done is done. Can't turn back time."

"No."

"I don't know. I probably would have done the same."

"It doesn't warrant thinking about."

"Do you think?" inquired Maddalena.

"It's not until you're in those moments, forced to make a choice. Everything else is possibly maybes."

"Yeah, well, don't be too hard on yourself. You did what you had to do."

"Maddalena, I killed a man."

"I can see that on a scale of one to ten you're pushing ten in terms of bad things to do. But maybe, just maybe, you've got to go through the bad to realize the possibilities of good."

"Well, that sounds simple," Aaliya remarked.

"No," countered Maddalena, "never simple. Really fucking hard. But this is not your end point, Aaliya. This is your beginning. It's mine too. We just have to redeem ourselves. No one else is going to do it for us."

Aaliya lowered her head and spoke softly, "Father…I can't go back to him. He wasn't there for me when I needed him."

"You're doing it again! This…judgment thing. Yes, he's an intense bastard. Big expectations. Wasn't there for you in a big way. You want to see the bad in him. The man I saw before leaving to find you hurt himself so much more than he ever hurt you. But he loves you. It's just one of those fucked up situations where he feels he can't show it. You're not all that different, I'd like to add."

"Is he alright?"

"Quite simply, no. But you know what he's like. Just doesn't want to let on."

"I think about him all the time. I think about mother. Oh Gods…" Aaliya said, wiping the moisture spilling from her eyes. "What's going to happen? Are they still looking for me? I want to go home."

"Home might not be the best place for you right now."

Aaliya sobbed. She brought her knees close to her chest and rested a hand on her forehead. Maddalena placed her bowl on the floor and took hold of Aaliya's and set it down. She wrapped her arm around Aaliya's back and pulled her close. Aaliya breathed in Maddalena's scent: patchouli and citrus. Trust Maddalena to keep smelling wonderful after a long journey.

"The timing might not be great," Maddalena suggested, "but I'm going to say it. You're not safe here."

Aaliya wiped her eyes. "Were you followed?" she asked shakily.

"I don't believe I was."

"Olle won't tell."

"No, he won't. But they won't stop looking."

"Is this why you came here? To warn me?"

"Not exactly."

"Why then?"

"To be with you. There's no going back for me. Not yet, anyway."

Aaliya let Maddalena's words sink in. "You've got to go back. A world awaits you back there. A big world, a secure world, a good world."

Maddalena shook her head. "No. Security's a myth. Good is a questionable thing to strive for. And big? It's not big back there. It's small. Out there," she nodded her head in the direction of the door, "is big. It's wide and uncertain. It's big and it's beautiful. It's our new home."

"That's not you talking."

"Hell it isn't. I've been planning my whole life. Thought I had it all worked out. By doing 'A' I'll get to 'B'. Then when I get to 'B', 'C' will happen. And so on and so on. But it's all just a big joke. Because you can never know what leads to what. Who's to say that I won't get there anyway—wherever there is—by doing 'X', then 'J', then 'F'? Maybe the wrong path is the right one, after all? You showed me that it can be done. That you can start again. Back in Ansgar, people only acted like I meant something to them. Not everyone, of course. But it did often feel like I was fulfilling a purpose that wasn't my own."

"So…we'll just…go? Is that the idea?"

"Yes."

"Just go?" Aaliya asked incredulously.

"Yes. We can't stay here."

"Okay."

"Besides, I don't do the hand job stuff in a big way."

"Nothing wrong with self love."

"Not saying there's anything wrong. Just like a nice regular serving of meat."

"Classy, Maddalena."

Maddalena laughed with shameless delight. "Little class left in my life, sis."

"It's good, don't you think?"

"Yeah. It's pretty good actually."

"Do you think it will stay good?"

"Not likely."

They both laughed.

"We've no gold," Aaliya added.

"Oh, we've got gold. And you clearly have means. I enquired in the village before coming out here. Yes, they told me, we know of a lady who makes and sells beautiful leather goods."

"People love to talk."

"See what I mean. You'll never be safe here."

"I knew I wasn't getting safety out here. I just couldn't deal with anything else."

"Not on your own anyway."

"Yeah, not on my own."

"Neither can I."

Silence passed between them, a sweet filament of time that was assuring, indelible. All that mattered was the feeling of warm blood pumping beneath the skin's surface as they held each other's hands. The silence stretched into long, languid minutes but remained a pleasant place to wander.

"I love you, Maddalena. Love you so much," Aaliya murmured squeezing her sister's hand. How violently, how completely she adored this fearless woman beside her. The way she lived in the world with seemingly hedonistic disregard for its rules, yet understanding them better than anyone she knew.

"I love you too."

It was the coolest morning since the commencement of spring. The mountains in the distance stood spectral and wraithlike. Low mist hung over the landscape like a damp blanket. Dawn was barely breaking, just a blush of light splashing across the sky. A promise of something to come. A sense that anything was possible. The quiet was so complete, the only sound the consolatory clopping of hooves on the packed surface. The two horses snorted and whinnied, almost in unison. As if sharing their own dialogue about the journey ahead.

Aaliya adjusted herself in the saddle and looked at the dark, silent figure riding beside her. She felt a tremendous restlessness at what lay ahead. And she sensed it in Maddalena too. She could almost smell it in the bracing, soupy air. They had nothing left to constrain them, no gravitational centre keeping them to a place. It was an incredible freedom that was as fearsome as it was liberating. The road ahead would be wide, and in turn would narrow to become little more than a precarious strip to follow. It was an unfathomable, complex feeling and Aaliya wondered if it would lessen as they went deeper into their journey. She suspected it would. That they would reach a point of acceptance. An understanding that things may or may not work out. And that was good enough.

As for Justen, they still hadn't talked about him, not in an emotional sense anyway. That day would come, of that Aaliya was sure. The past follows you everywhere. He had left an indelible imprint on both of their lives. Although it was three seasons ago, for ten short days his presence was large and emboldening, and the course of events surrounding his death still seemed irrational, maddening. Riding in the pale morning light, Aaliya knew that the unopened box that was Justen would need to be gently eased open at some stage. It was something that needed to be worked through. An open wound that needed to be healed and closed.

Aaliya wished her mother could see her now, riding beside Maddalena, on the path to nowhere in particular. But she somehow knew her mother was watching. She could always hear her coming before she could see her. The long black wings slapping the air as she soared overhead. A flick of her eyes towards the sky told her that Helena was never far away. She might dip out of view for days, even weeks, but then reveal herself again like a shell uncovered at low tide.

Sometimes Aaliya imagined herself up there too, flying above the world and looking down on it as an observer. How small everything would look! How utterly incongruous all problems would seem!

She still thought of her mother everyday. Sentences still filled her mind of things she wanted to say, but they weren't fully formed anymore. Just fragmented, partial ephemera. A silent conversation across time. Thoughts of her flitted around like a tuft of dandelion on the breeze. Difficult to capture. Beautiful and elusive. Beholden. Departed.

Acknowledgements

Warm and grateful thanks to the following people:

To Kellie Lawler and Adrian Potter for reading the manuscript during the early stages and providing simply incredible advice and encouragement; Tony Pitman for nurturing this lady through the ups and downs of writing; and Kylie Mason for truly inspirational editing.